THE POETIC AMBASSADOR

a ZeitGeist saga

*To Heather,
Someone who
likes to ride
ferris wheels will
surely follow
the ups +
downs of this plot!
Enjoy!*

Roger Wayne Eberle

outskirts
press

The Poetic Ambassador
a ZeitGeist saga
All Rights Reserved.
Copyright © 2020 Roger Wayne Eberle
v5.0

This is a work of fiction. Names, characters, businesses, places, events, locales, and incidents are either the products of the author's imagination or used in a fictitious manner. Any resemblance to actual persons, living or dead, or actual events is purely coincidental.

The opinions expressed in this manuscript are solely the opinions of the author and do not represent the opinions or thoughts of the publisher. The author has represented and warranted full ownership and/or legal right to publish all the materials in this book.

This book may not be reproduced, transmitted, or stored in whole or in part by any means, including graphic, electronic, or mechanical without the express written consent of the publisher except in the case of brief quotations embodied in critical articles and reviews.

Outskirts Press, Inc.
http://www.outskirtspress.com

Paperback ISBN: 978-1-9772-2514-6
Hardback ISBN: 978-1-9772-2543-6

Library of Congress Control Number: 2020904651

Cover Photo © 2020 www.gettyimages.com.. All rights reserved - used with permission.

Outskirts Press and the "OP" logo are trademarks belonging to Outskirts Press, Inc.

PRINTED IN THE UNITED STATES OF AMERICA

DEDICATION

To my helpful siblings Blain, Marianne, John, and Mark—each of them stable and understanding enough to keep any old disconnected live wire like myself grounded; to my always energetic and now long-gone but never forgotten father, Christian, who did much more than clothe and feed us all while we were growing up and to whom, for his indefatigable strength, we will always be grateful; to my loving and warm-hearted mother, Nathalia, who taught us all the fine art of compromise, and much more; to my deeply devoted Aunt Linda, who never gives up in the face of often daunting odds; to my dearly departed grandparents, John and Anne Eberle, and Lester and Mary Lokken, whose labours extended well beyond the breaking of the ground and the sowing and harvesting of the crops and who always proved that pioneering family life can yield untold benefits that transcend the limits of time itself. Without the fine collective lines of family and friends our individual roots cannot go down as deep or drink as fully of the nurturing waters of life. Finally, and most importantly, I dedicate this book with inexpressible love and earnest gratitude to my wise and faithful friend, my wife Helen, without whose good counsel and sound, clear-eyed support these characters might not have survived to thrive in all the various phases of this many-pathed trek up the mountain to its fortress, a journey upon which you now embark. The fortress that awaits your perusal at the top of the mountain affords an excellent view, and it is this view, and the paths leading up to it, that I now dedicate to my lovely Helen.

ACKNOWLEDGEMENTS

No mountaintop fortress like the one you now hold in your hands could be carefully constructed without numerous trail breakers who paved the way for publication and the journey of readership upon which you now embark. Gratitude and appreciation for deserving individuals and groups, without whose support and feedback for this author's writing labour and his philosophical growth this manuscript would have suffered greatly, lead me to conclude that I am indebted to, influenced by, and have undoubtedly benefited from the long-sufferance, teachings, recommendations, jokes, advice, and ideas expressed either directly or indirectly through interactions with the following friends, institutions and agencies: Enver Creek Staff and Administration; The Langley Writers' Guild; The Ram's Head Writers' Group, led by Lisa Hatton; Stephanie Candelaria; Lisa Penz; Wayne and Liz Bartlett; Joy and James Lee; George and Jeanetta Zorn; John Jane; Ed Farolan; Kevin Star; Ann Coleman; Alistair Watt; Andrew Yarmie; Kieran Egan; Gillian Judson; Natalia Gajdamashko; the 2009-2011 Cohort of our SFU Imaginative Education Master's Degree Program (which graduated the year after this present novel was set); Bruce Hyslop; Rick Parkyn; David Strugnell; Matthew Price; Tim McCarthy; Phil and Joan Trudeau; Monty and Maureen de Montezuma; Ralph and Rachel Kivi; Jaques and Janet Cloutier; Glen and Diane Halvorsen; Herb and Nancy Thiessen; Anne Aram; Yoko Ueda; Norm Daniel; James Redekop; Russell Kerr; Carol Mammel; Stephen Fraser; Jerry and Debbie Renault; Ross and Sandy Lowndes; Kevin Wainwright; Jerry and "Pudgy" Deol; Paul Gill; Rob Lampard; Lloyd Anderson; Mike Jeanes; Chris Weddell; Denis Poelzer; Mahinder Singh Ollek;

Lori Inouye; Elizabeth Luke; Darren Reynolds; Marvin and Melody Farr; Robert Hepburn; Norman and Linda Rich; Mauva Jo Powell; Stewart Mackenzie; and Arnold Toutant.

As I mentioned, this book—and my very life itself for that matter—would not be the same were it not for the rich contributions made by the above-mentioned people and the invaluable institutions with which they have been associated at one point or another over the past fifty or more some odd years I've been muddling through this wearisome world. More of that to come in the sequel to this novel. But for now, suffice to say I am much obliged to you all, and I wish to now thank you again. Apologies to anyone who feels you have been left out of this ponderous list. If after you read the novel, you feel you deserve to be acknowledged in the sequel, just let me know and I'll comb my memory banks to determine who among you I may have omitted most merits inclusion. In the meantime, please accept my sincere and humble thanks just the same anyhow.

Roger Wayne Eberle | February, 2020

CONTENTS

PART ONE: FROM SHORTLIST TO CELBRATION – September 15 – October 1, 2010

Chapter One: Unorthodox Interview – A Strategy.......................... 1

Chapter Two: Prelude to the Portfolio 14

Chapter Three: Entrapment.......................... 19

Chapter Four: the Front.......................... 28

Chapter Five: Getting to Know your Adversary 35

Chapter Six: Anticipating the Afterglow 43

Chapter Seven: So Many Courses, So Little Time 54

Chapter Eight: Afterglow Aftermath 68

Chapter Nine: On and Off Course 76

PART TWO: EXECUTIVE DECISIONS – September 30, 2010

Chapter Ten: Formative Considerations 92

Chapter Eleven: Objectivity on the Wane 98

Chapter Twelve: Who Votes for Otto? 104

Chapter Thirteen: Diamonds and Duration 108

PART THREE: LIAISONS – October 8 – 15, 2010

Chapter Fourteen: Heavy Petting and Firm Incursions 113

Chapter Fifteen: Tequila Shots and Moby Dick 124

Chapter Sixteen: Like Falling off a Log – Summer 1979.......................... 136

Chapter Seventeen: Velociraptors have the Moves.......................... 139

Chapter Eighteen: Just Who is this Cervantes? - Summer 1983 141

Chapter Nineteen: Paternity — Summer of 1960 146

Chapter Twenty: Eternity and Time – 2001.......................... 156

Chapter Twenty-One: Thread of Separation 161
Chapter Twenty-Two: Mr. Reliable 166
Chapter Twenty-Three: Cynthia's Smile.................................... 170
Chapter Twenty-Four: Gladiolas for a Gladiator 174
Chapter Twenty-Five: How to Solve a Riddle Named Stacey...... 177
Chapter Twenty-Six: Game of Knowledge 182
Chapter Twenty-Seven: Off the Balcony.................................... 185
Chapter Twenty-Eight: A Matter of Perspective 190
Chapter Twenty-Nine: the Original Architecture Tour............... 194
Chapter Thirty: The Rapier's Thrust.. 198
Chapter Thirty-One: Mrs. Reliable and The Heartaches............ 202
Chapter Thirty-Two: Confession 207
Chapter Thirty-Three: Who is Playing Whom? 220

PART FOUR: THE GALA AND BEYOND –
October 31 – November 5, 2010

Chapter Thirty-Four: ZG Halloween Gala 229
Chapter Thirty-Five: ZG Halloween Gala II 244
Chapter Thirty-Six: Clearly a Day for a Change 275
Chapter Thirty-Seven: A Million Reasons 283
Chapter Thirty-Eight: The Burning Bridge................................. 290
Chapter Thirty-Nine: Who is the best Droid? 293
Chapter Forty: Owls of Understanding...................................... 304
Chapter Forty-One: Pillow Talk - January, 2011....................... 308

One

UNORTHODOX INTERVIEW – A STRATEGY

After first carefully crafting a calligraphic 'M' instead of lazily scrawling his playful trademark affirmative response to the sex query, Zack Speller set about proving just what a veteran of forms he truly was. In just under ten minutes he hastily transferred the terse and tasteful version of his personal bio from an account in his overdrawn memory banks onto the ZeitGeist (ZG) application. Guided by what was for him an uncustomary nagging sense of the need for discretion, he also refrained from including his two-year stint at Rank Enterprises in the Past Experience section. Something his Uncle Roger had said about ZG stuck with him: "Remember they have an impeccable sense of moral and ethical propriety." The cautionary lead buried in this little admonition caused him to pull Rank from the equation. Little good could come of avowing an association with British Columbia's most notoriously compromised publishing company. Selective amnesia had always proven to be a useful trait for Zack, and he felt certain it would prove so today. With a swift and gallant flourish, he signed the form.

In one smooth athletic motion he rose to his feet. Then he ran his hands through his shoulder-length dark brown hair, threw back his broad shoulders, thrust out his chest, and deftly approached the large heavily polished mahogany desk behind which sat a receptionist who was every bit as shapely and attractive as her ebony eyes were expressive. She immediately dispelled any illusion he may have had about her either paying any attention at all to his preening, or being poised and ready to accept his completed application, by half-turning towards him and raising her fingers to her lively lips, indicating that he must wait while she completed a pressing phone call. She then promptly turned her back once again on the tall, young applicant. Tearing his eyes away from the point where her curly auburn locks gathered in ringlets around her athletic shoulders just before cascading down her back in luxuriant profusion so as to completely defeat the purpose of the backless dress she wore, Zack gazed out through the enormous plate glass window that fronted the office at the vista of greenery festooning a colossal fountain in the centre of a low rock wall. Just as he found himself lost in reverie upon this scenic picture, his musing was broken by the musical cadences of the well-tanned receptionist pulling him back to the task at hand with one disarmingly simple question: "Is there anything you feel you need to add to this application, Mr. Speller?"

"What's that? Oh. It adds up just fine as it is, I believe." Zack's affable offbeat humour invariably worked to his benefit. Or so it had always seemed, before today. Before Pamela. "Thanks anyway," he added with an air of genuine appreciation that masked his mildly growing sense of a need for a tone somewhat more like guarded civility. He straightened himself to his full six foot stature, and cleared his throat expectantly. Exactly what type of training did this bodybuilder of a receptionist have, anyway? She seemed to be acting like this was an interview.

"I notice that you've listed guitar as a hobby," she continued batting her heavily lashed eyes at him after pausing only slightly—in what Zack mistook for an innocent flirtation—then pursuing what appeared to be an innocuous, tangentially-related inquiry. "Is that lead or rhythm?"

Shifting his stance, he spread his strong legs widely, and then bent at the hips and leaned forward to gaze directly into his inquisitor's dark eyes. Zack smiled broadly, revealing two even rows of sparkling white teeth and then, noticing her name tag, he took

The Poetic Ambassador

a chance. He struck out toward uncharted territory on what he hoped might soon be more familiar ground. But he immediately found himself in terrain that, like quicksand, grew considerably less familiar and far less secure than he had previously imagined he might find here at Zeitgeist. She held his gaze. Still he forged ahead. "Well, to be honest Pamela, I only dabble in guitar. For me, picking up the axe is like chopping wood—I tire quickly after a chord or two." He paused a second, then added his own coyly flirtatious rejoinder. "Do you... play?" Turnabout was fair, or so he supposed, embarrassingly aware that his attempt at a punch line pun seemed to have fallen flatter than an unlucky parachutist whose rip cord malfunctioned, leaving only the dread of impending impact.

"Ahem," intoned the receptionist, whose real name was not Pamela at all. "I am sure *I* am not the subject of this interview, Mr. Speller. Now. If you will please be kind enough to answer all further questions directly, we shall get along admirably." With this, she gave him a most concentrated look and then resumed her careful survey of his application in a manner as deliberate as it was deft. Zack pried his flattened body off of the ground. Freefalling was great. Landing was a bitch. Actually, he deposited his derriere in the leather chair over near the aspidistra in front of the large window. This particular landing was a bit softer than the metaphorical one he had just 'experienced'.

Glancing around the vast vestibule, Speller began to take stock of his surroundings. Prior to what was fast becoming a crash course in diplomacy buttressed by recommended protocols for tempering enthusiasm and harnessing humour, his attention had been concentrated on his application form and the receptionist he presumed to be Pamela. Now he noticed that aside from the one elevator door from which he had emerged into this room, there were no other visible office doors. The stark austerity of this architectural feature coupled with the sudden onslaught of questions from Pamela—ostensibly the receptionist—put him off just ever so slightly. Also, he knew he'd blundered by sitting down. His rear end sank way down in the seat, while his knees rose up. The chair had embarrassingly swallowed both his body and most of his remaining pride.

Odd business this. He had supposed this receptionist was merely some show-stopper of a steno with an eye for detail, perhaps an amateur Impressionist at her easel, equally adept at her shadings and angles. But now it seemed clear that she was conducting an impromptu interview for the position. He imagined her in a rather different position. Never mind that! Back to the business at hand. He hadn't expected an interview so soon, and yet here he was—the subject sitting for his portrait—warts, blemishes, and all. Sitting in that chair made him feel awkward, and getting up again would probably be even more embarrassing.

Pamela started again.

"You cite *claustrophobia* twice. First as a medical condition, and then as a strength." At this point, the receptionist casually got up out of her chair, and strolled out from behind her desk, swiftly removing at least one barrier by sitting down on it in a manner Zack felt could only be described as *coquettish*. Now there were only a few feet between them. If her movements seemed designed to crowd and thereby unnerve him ever-so-slightly, she succeeded admirably. Crossing her legs and letting the cut of her bright red dress slide up to reveal just enough of her shapely calves to make most healthy heterosexual males think twice (once for each leg), she continued. "Can you elaborate upon this apparent paradox?"

Somewhat surprised by this unorthodox interview approach, Zack imposed a wee bit more space between them by sliding his chair slightly away from the desk. He then looked directly into Pamela's dark eyes and gave his most philosophical reply: "By facing and attempting to overcome my fear of enclosed spaces, I have come to value the fact that the more confined the space, the greater the opportunity there is for personal growth, thereby turning my weakness into my strength. An attitude which often helps me extract myself from any tight spots I get myself into throughout life's convoluted matrix."

Pamela glanced over at the elevator door for an instant, then took her blue-framed low-profile Gucci's off and leaned in towards him, turning the full force of her intense gaze upon Zack. "The ride up," she smiled, her voice pitched in a tone of demure irony, "must have been quite an opportunity for you. Matrix or no matrix."

For a second, it looked for all the world to Zack like he was about to suffer yet another loss to a feminist in a what was beginning to look a lot like a zero-sum game. But then he pivoted and parried. He rose as gracefully as he could from the chair and said, "There's nothing like rising to a challenge." Then he smiled back with a candor that was as simple as it appeared to be innocuous. "And I always pepper both my prose and my poetry with as many meanings as the occasion warrants. And I'll take the red pill."

Pamela sized him up with crisp detachment. She put her glasses on, slipping the blue feet casually over her ears, letting his words linger in the air for a few seconds, and then went on in a voice that spilled forth her own special brand of chilled liquid honey. "Mr. Speller, I'm not sure how I'm meant to take that. Demand expectations vary from situation to situation as is the case with various poetic genre. But I do notice here that your contemporary poetry is couched in traditional forms. Should you be short-listed for this writing position, you would be expected to turn over all your poetry—even unpublished poems—to our professional editors. You are prepared to do so?"

Zack turned his back on his interlocutor to gaze out the window again. "I'd have to see their editorial license before I do that," Zack quipped, completely forgetting the previous parachute fiasco, and grinning as he met her smoothness with his most affable chuckle, managing somehow to make himself sound like a schoolboy trying to impress his first date.

She abruptly quelled his witty froth with a placid, "I'll take that as a 'No'."

Zack folded easily under pressure. Turning back to her quickly, while he secretly wondered whether his yellow Tommy Hilfiger shirt had been the best choice for him today, he decided that the shirt had only been the first of his blunders. Running over her rush to negation, with blustery overkill, like a panicked driver who intentionally plows someone down just because he thought she'd misrepresented herself as a dangerous pedestrian, he protested, "Look Pamela, or whatever your name really is, I want to be clear. I am so keen on writing for ZG that I'd probably agree to sign away the movie rights to my bestselling novel if it gets me into the running for the ambassadorship."

After letting an awkward moment of embarrassment sink in from what may well have been an overly desperate gambit on Zack's part, the ZG employee cleared her throat and proceeded with the interview. "Perhaps we'd best move on to character references," ventured Pamela in a tone that was far less tentative than the tersely-worded suggestion implied.

"*That* would be a truly moving direction," chirped Zack, attempting in his punishing yet oblivious manner to deflect scrutiny once again with comic misdirection. Yet another flight of fancy, yet another malfunctioning rip cord. This was déjà vu all over again. He glanced back at the leather chair.

Pamela eyed him with a barely-concealed incredulous disdain as she prolonged the ensuing pause—so pregnant it practically delivered quintuplets—with the added emphasis of a look so witheringly severe it dropped the temperature in the room by a few degrees (in addition to the third degree she was already giving her subject). Was he really going to sit still for her Impressionism? Or would he be better off in the Abstract? At least he had worn his lucky brown loafers.

Electing—like a preppy at a prom—to fight cool with cooler, Zack drew out his own unique brand of tenuous logic from his vast repertoire of responses and teased Pamela with it. "None of my references will vouch for my sanity. You'll have to take my word for it. I'm so insanely ethical that were I a custodian, I would surely put the 'sane' in *sanitary engineering*." Where was that 'badabump' drum riff when you needed it?

"That," Pamela mused, missing not one beat, "would appear to be one incredibly *immaculate conception* now, would it not, Mr. Speller? My, but you do love your paradoxes, don't you?"

"My poetry, now that—even at its basest level—is *truly* divine."

"As I was saying, your references—"

"Actually, they're more allusions than references."

Pamela paused, glancing down at his application: "Yes, here it is. Under references, you write, 'Who is it that can tell me who I am?'

"'Lear's Shadow, quoth the Fool,'" Zack quoted, clasping his ample chin in his right hand and stroking an imaginary beard.

"Nevertheless, my *dear* Mr. Speller," Pamela interjected, managing simultaneously to convey both boredom and infinite patience, "ZG requires something more, shall we say, substantial."

"If I could just bring an echoing prefix to bear on the prefix of that last word—" But again Zack found the razor sharp wit of his questioner bringing him up short with a laconic prolixity he ought to have found unsettling. It was *Groundhog Day* all over again: a variety of responses, but all with the same galling attitude. This time he landed so hard, the earth swallowed him and his useless parachute up entirely, and he imagined he could *feel* what he knew must surely *be* Pamela's scornful contempt for his cavil.

"Such extempore temporizing would invariably render the results sub-substandard," opined the auburn-haired beauty.

Not used to having his hand forced so adroitly, Zack reluctantly acquiesced. "Actually, there is a significant substratum of substantial editors upon whom I regularly rely to affirm my character on any given day. Their names and particulars are available upon request."

"We will," Pamela iterated forcibly, "require each and every one of those names."

Zack paused for a second and then reluctantly and tersely—as if detained by a parole officer who had browbeaten him until he was forced to reveal all of his accomplices—trotted out his shortlist of editorial references: "Aiden Bodega, Christian Quarterson, Miguel Roy, and Paula Cromer; not to mention, Frank Jimmy Cooper."

"All of these editors work for one magazine, do they not? *The Trope*." Pamela shifted her Gucci's so as to rest the bridge on the tip of her perfectly aquiline nose, gazing intently at Zack over the aquamarine rims as she spoke, practically spitting out the title of the magazine.

"That's right!" said Zack, masking his growing diffidence with an energetic nonchalance.

"Actually, it's a whole lot *left* of right," rejoined Pamela, replacing her glasses back to their customary resting position and brushing away the dust from a thin veneer of disdain with her own special brand of bristling innuendo.

"The views of the writer do not necessarily reflect the views of the publisher, and vice versa," disclaimed Zack, still certain that he had enough skin in the game to warrant his seeking a way out of this uncomfortable guilt by association.

Segueing away from this tension like a smooth politician covers up scandal with genial misdirection, the nimble young receptionist said adroitly, "Legalese you seem to know. My next question relates to computers."

Grasping at a familiar aphorism in an almost futile attempt to gain a conversational foothold on a vetting climb that seemed increasingly full of hazard, Zack determined he would not be outdone: "To err is human, to really screw things up takes a computer."

Pamela paused again in what was becoming a fast-paced interview, this time for dramatic effect. Her reply seemed intended to be flippant, "*So.* You're an android are you?"

"Saluting his interlocutor in mock deference, Zack tossed off his own personal credo with relish, garnished with a sprig of defensiveness: "A hacker who lacks what it takes to write more than mere code is just a hack, Ma'am. Literature is more than mere code. I write literature."

"If it were only that easy, Mr. Speller. If it were only that easy. And now, finally, a personal question: How many significant others are there in your life?"

Pamela's dark oceanic eyes threatened to drown him for a moment. Just as he pondered whether to swim for the safety of the 'out of bounds' buoy or dive deeper towards the 'off limits' trench she seemed to be inviting him to explore, he heard himself say,

"How many do you need?"

Her reply came out caustic, in three measured staccato bursts: "None," nailed itself to his forehead; "will" drove that spike home; and "do" lingered in the air to spread itself over his consciousness like a fine mist—maybe because Pamela pronounced the 'do' like 'dew' and drew out the final syllable so as to accentuate the pucker it made with her satin lipstick. Whatever the reason for her dramatics, Zack was prepared to consider both senses of her terse trifecta of 'pith and vinegar' as a personal challenge to his masculinity. They locked eyes for a moment. Then, fully conscious of the impact she'd just made on her interviewee, the woman who wore the 'Pamela' nametag suddenly turned on her heel, repositioned herself at her desk and promptly fed Zack's application into the shredder.

Infuriated, but still hoping the mask of the 'great pretender' had not slipped, Zack shot back with barely faked cordiality not quite able to conceal his sarcasm: "You're funnier than an unrecoverable disk error!" He started for the elevator, but stopped midway, did an about turn, and faced the music once more. "Don't *I* get to ask any questions?" he inquired intently. No more abstractions, or false impressions. The time had come for realism, and it better be quick, before the paint had dried.

Pamela seemed to adjust her smile to fit her face. In Zack's mind, it had nearly slid off, and she was reaffixing it graciously, like losing and then refastening a favourite piece of jewelry. She leaned back in her chair, and crossed her long legs again. Then she straightened her crisply aligned posture until it resembled something as close to an impossibly rigid fixed integer as her curvaceous form would allow. Finally she replied, in tones as painstakingly composed as the apogee of an overture; and as clipped as they were condescending, "How might I be of assistance?"

Zack smiled evenly as he found himself concluding once again for at least the sixth or seventh time since arriving at ZG that there was definitely more to this Pamela than her ravishing outward appearance suggested (as if that was not enough). Then he flashed her his pearly whites once again, and waded into the deep end.

"First of all, what kind of a company conducts its interviews in such a random manner, and with so cavalier a tone? Next, what kind of an interview do short-listed candidates get? Third, how soon will I know whether I have been short-listed? Finally, who are you, really?"

The receptionist who went by the name of Pamela—famous among ZG employees for her artful spontaneity and pseudo-scientific wit—drew herself up into an ever more proprietary pose and held forth with all the succinctness and alacrity her pride and dignity—not to mention her audacious sense of corporate irony—would permit. "My dear Mr. Speller, each ZG interview is subject to the most meticulous oversight. All questions have been carefully considered (including the spontaneous ones), and final selections are made only from those whose work meets probative standards of quality and whose character proves to be as propitiously full of circumspection as it is wholly without salaciousness. All questions and comments are conscientiously delivered. Judging from many of your more flippant responses, I can only conclude that this cavalier tone of which you speak is a subtle manifestation of one of the most insidious forms of what Freudian psychologists characterize as a projection of the defensive mechanisms of the individual psyche onto the subconscious mind of the subject, which the aforementioned psyche must face and with which he must come to terms. And that may also go a good way towards accounting for whatever random-sequential meanderings may have occurred during the course of the interview, and here again I am speaking in large part about *your* contribution. My true identity..." Here the receptionist paused as if to heighten the dramatic effect. "*That* will remain undisclosed for the present time. As far as the short-list goes, it will be comprised of only three people selected from among close to a hundred prospective applicants. These three candidates will be given a 'final interview' consisting of a Portfolio of Poetry to be completed within a predetermined time period. Should you find yourself fortunate enough to *rank* within that percentile, you will be contacted within a fortnight. That concludes our interview. Good day and good fortune to you, sir." This last obligatory farewell gesture was delivered with a cursory dismissive motion that vaguely resembled a sophisticated blend of royal wave and involuntary seated curtsey. Within moments after this exchange, Pamela turned perfunctorily towards her well-lit-up switchboard and began to engage herself in a series of animated electronic conversations, presumably with other prospective ambassadors.

Zack entered the elevator flushed. He wondered exactly what these defence mechanisms were with which he must come to terms. But he did not spend too much time worrying about it, because his ears were ringing and the room seemed to be humming. Wait a minute, he thought. It's an elevator. They're supposed to hum. Inescapable among the flood of anxieties that leapt upon his impressionable mind during his descent from the interview was that they must know about his stint with Rank Enterprises. Why else would that prissy chameleon who passes herself off as a Pamela so deliberately stress the word "rank" when she answered his question about the short-list? How would it look that he had purposefully left off mentioning his two-year stint as regular contributor to *Outranked Magazine*? Being associated with *Rank*—as prestigious a house as it was profligate—could well be the kiss of death with a publishing conglomerate such as ZG. He was correct not to have included them. Yes, he'd done the right thing by slanting his application and his interview with an air of insouciance in just this manner. Besides, he'd worn his lucky brown loafers with his even luckier green leather Chino cargo pants. Good for them if they had done their homework and found out about *Outranked Magazine*. He'd not worry. They'd be fools to pass him over. His friends all said he'd make poet laureate by age 40, and he still had a few years to go.

Had he given them too much zaniness? No. The adage about too much of a good thing would hold true as always. He'd struck just the right balance, to be sure. From the Bard to anonymous Luddite banter out of the Farmer's Almanac. An eclectic blend. A hint of enigmatic pathos and a smidgeon of clever coyness for good measure. Rip cord be damned, he'd freefall forever! He was surely right not to have counter-balanced that with a weighty publisher's house pedigree. Leave them wanting more and let them know where they can get it when they come asking. Besides, he thought, my poetry speaks for itself. I raised it right. It can stand on its own two feet.

Clever one that Pamela, though. Never expected that psycho-babble at all. Especially after the snide quasi-religious witticism at my expense she lobbed into the wake of my feckless janitorial joke. Immaculately conceived, that one! Goes to show you she was not the type of Pam to "map out" in a single sitting. Unless of course, you're the poetic equivalent of Salvador Dali and Time itself goes limp in your presence, hanging on every word that branches toward a new inquiry—or at least on a "canvass" that merits further inspection. Come to think of it, this so-called Pamela's entire interview strategy seemed to be a little surreal, a little soft to watch. A purposeful toying with perspectives of distance and focus wilfully designed to achieve a desired effect—the seizing of an opportunity. He could just see the neon headlines crawling along on a scroll under a head and shoulders shot of him digressing about putting the 'sane' in sanitary engineering: 'Fashion plate flaunts herself to taunt and jibe would-be-writer. Teases out the *chimp* within.' Oh, there were surely hidden cameras in that vestibule recording the entire interview. Why else would she so provocatively shred my application if not to gauge my reaction?

But Zack was, as usual, more concerned with related words than with would-be video-recordings, and he could not help noticing the possibility of a triumphant vowel shift. What a difference a letter makes, he thought, substituting an "a" for the "i" from the "chimp" within, and then sizing up the difference: This *champ* is made to measure. As he walked away from the ZG office, Zack pondered over whether or not it might just be the *chump* that keeps waiting at the starting gate who's really the monkey in a cage. This could be a long fortnight. He'd far rather take a leisurely stroll along the Champs-Elysees than *chomp* at the bit for ZG, but right now both prospects seemed equally foreign, and he'd about played out all his lines, mixed all his metaphors in the sequence. Wait, he thought, there was always the prospect of a champagne celebration to come. Then again, it would do him no good to get ahead of himself, especially when skydiving. The ground can be quite hard, regardless of how far off the figure appears to be. It's all a matter of perspective. And, thought Zack, as he walked past the fountain in front of ZG, if you've got the right perspective, no matter how hard the ground is, all that matters is who is doing the figuring.

Two

PRELUDE TO THE PORTFOLIO

A light rain drizzled down, misting in myriad voluble streams out of a soot streaked sky, as fireplaces about the city of Vancouver coughed and belched black smoke into the sullen night, smudging the urban landscape like an artist daubs darkening hues of grey onto an ever blackening backdrop to create and simultaneously destroy a bleak image, deconstructing it to construct an altogether different impression. Trudging pluckily through this melancholy melange—step by stodgy clomping, splashing step—Cynthia Davison pursued more pressing concerns than the terrible weather. Puddles kicked up descending showers, making themselves appear like the scattered stricken silver surfaces of agitating Jacuzzis regurgitating explosive drops, sending them up again to meet their rainy day relatives somewhere between earth and sky. A moaning wind mourned and gusted about the wet glistening streets, but Cynthia's imaginative mind settled on antithetical polarities: the wet weather, sidewalks and streets ultimately resolved themselves into burning sun-swept desert dunes. She gingerly caressed her winsome way across those shifting sands of intimacy which only the hidden intricacies of her baroque Victorian prose poetry self-talk— embellished with the wrought iron detailing of a thoroughly modern romance as intense as it was forbidden—could ever hope to hide in plain sight. No one but her lover could make his poetry more exquisitely labyrinthine. No one could flutter her pulse with a touch so soft and cunning, and yet so canny and sure. And no one but herself, she concluded, could put an end to it for good. Regardless of how much they had together, and how torridly raw their relationship had become, it must now end—and forever. No one could know of their shared secret bed of crimson joy. She smiled as the rain camouflaged her tears. How his sparkling wit still burned her psyche; how his generous touch still scorched her skin. He held "all the promise of accrued interest, with none of the guilt associated with a bounced cheque." Or so he had said (checking her cheeky bounce behind the bustle in her hedgerow). As the rains picked up, Cynthia's parched mirage—and all its uncanny desert heat—gradually submerged itself, until only its meagre reflection shone from the reaches of her fervid imagination. And from the depths of the bleak tarn the rain had imposed upon the concrete foot the ZG tower had once long ago settled down upon the street, she found herself filled with a kind of awe. It was not just this imposing structure before which she now stood—her reversed image laid out in the tarn behind her, reflected by the eerie backlit glow of a yellowing streetlight, as the city traffic rushed by to liaisons, the nature of which were as unknown to her as the one waiting for her somewhere among the rising rows of plate glass office windows that seemed to stretch reflectively beyond the dark and angry rain-clouds—but also all the unknown future this structure represented.

It had been weeks since she'd answered the ad that practically shouted submission (a word whose conceptual meanings were surpassed only by those of its antithesis for the thrill factor in *her* mind). That impossibly seductive 'ZG Offers the World' ad. All she had needed was an interview. And now she had been shortlisted. Questions fled her mind and swirled around her shapely petite body like stripes on a curvy candy-cane, but from what she'd heard it was impossible to imagine that the answers were going to be anywhere near as simple as the sweet image of that Christmassy confection she'd just conjured up. Still, the receptionist had almost sounded friendly. If she was lucky, then that woman Pamela who had conducted her interview might be working. Cynthia knew that they had hit it off right from the moment she had been asked who was her favourite poet, and she'd told her of Carol Ann Duffy, reciting Ms. Duffy's best short poem "Talent." Pamela had smiled and given her a most amusingly affable salute: the dancing fingertips prancing upon a palm salute—the soluble sound of one palm being tap-danced upon by the fluttering fingers of the other hand. Then in a surprising turn of events, Pamela had asked Cynthia about whether she liked the way that this particular poem gave the reader so much choice in its outcome. Cynthia had smiled, knowingly; then after a pause, she'd given her most succinct interpretation of the three key elements of this highly resonant poem, one of which was the word applause. Now, as she looked up at the ZG building again, she began to think of what kind of word applause for ZG she would use with Ms. Nolan in order to make just the right impression.

Hoping the tarn wouldn't swallow her optimism all House-of-Usher-like, she found herself taking a deep breath as she swept through the revolving doors. Entering with an unaccustomed buoyancy, and practically pushed along by a sudden gust of wind, Cynthia veered about in the tiny enclosure with just the slightest sense of vertigo—she'd missed the entrance and had to revolve once more. Still, she wondered, as she stood on the ground floor looking out at the street through the immense plate glass windows, what kinds of mysterious baggage lay, like the bottom half of an iceberg, submerged below the tarn outside (or at least in its reflection) which seemed like it should stand for something... instead of being such a layabout. A little less imagination, she told herself. ZG lay straight ahead. Or at least, what she could see of it. Meanwhile, all her own romantic sacrifices and even her pride of ownership—at having owned her own mistake—she left behind, beneath the tarn outside. Damn it anyhow! If he was a mistake, he was *her* favourite mistake (but that was nothing to crow about).

Cynthia's wavering notwithstanding, ZG Publishing was in fact no stranger to romantic sacrifice, either (there had been more than a few men and women over the years who had forsaken all others for ZG—and even more who'd been swallowed up by the tarn, never even making it *into* the building), and although ZG held stringently to its practice of keeping such things behind closed doors, (many happy interns benefitted from this policy) it did desire that as many people as possible know that it had recently distinguished itself as one of the most enterprising and innovative among the dozen or so fledgling publishing houses at the forefront of the industry (all since Jonathan Holland founded ZG in 1966). By the early Twenty-First Century it had arrived—due largely to the evolution of a board of executive directors that had proven itself as both a prescient arbiter of public taste and a bearer of standards that put a contemporary spin on traditional poetry—at that enviable threshold of ranking uppermost among publishing peers in the area of poetry. It was in the years that ensued in the wake of this long-awaited public affirmation of literary excellence (finally firmly established with their 2009 publication of the Anthology of *Twenty-First Century ZG Poetry*), that ZG, seeking perhaps to augment their past achievements and sustain their contribution with an eye towards achieving a lasting legacy, initiated an extensive search for their first Poetic Ambassador. They sought someone who would herald an exciting new era in poetry. But above all, they looked for someone with the freshness of perspective that 'might' could not withstand and even 'the Right' could not completely subsume—despite their customary condescension. Additionally, they wanted someone whose ethos and aristos embodied the zeitgeist of a new era.

Prospective applicants were carefully selected dating back from the summer of 2010, and soon after the interview process concluded in late September, the search was discerningly and painstakingly narrowed to three individuals. Each shortlisted candidate was to receive the same portfolio assignment, particulars of which are now being hammered out in the executive boardroom even as you, my perspicacious reader are considering our young Cynthia, who has been pursuing *her* arid reflections around the revolving entrance. Consequently, the prestigious title and lucrative job of ZG Poetic Ambassador will be given to the man or woman who prepares the best portfolio. But what will that portfolio assignment look like?

Determining this critical path might be a complicated process, as fraught with unexpected conflicts as it is filled with surprising alliances, many of which are being forged by the ZG board of executive directors on this very rainy last night in September, 2010. And others of which, Cynthia Davison has already begun to put in motion as a part of her grand plan—a plan you are by now beginning to guess at, since she is the type who likes to keep people guessing.

Cynthia went in to the office—to quote one of her favourite strumming duo's quests for a glimpse *Closer to Fine*—"seeking clarity." But she was not expecting Southern hospitality freshly arrived from an exhausting executive board meeting that had gone on much longer than had been expected. Cynthia hardly knew which metaphor to mix or what not to anthropomorphize when sizing up her belletristic lady of the boardroom with the soft-spoken Southern charm, who had sounded so provocative on her answering machine informing her that she had been short-listed. Had she been an eidetic steno at that board meeting, Cynthia would surely have been in the market to forge a few more alliances than the ones you, daring reader, have already sussed out. But as she pushed the button for the thirty-first floor, she began to muse upon the connection she had already made with the enigmatic Misty, as the receptionist who sometimes went by the name of Pamela soon asked Cynthia to call her.

Three

ENTRAPMENT

Entrapment never felt quite so delicious. If Felicity Traviss—who was known as Misty to her close confidantes and associates and Pamela to those applicants she interviewed for the position of Poetic Ambassador—held tight to her publishing house principles, it was because in them she recognized the coarse trusses and supple bonds of faith in that publishing house seal of approval; in them she cherished a mutually satisfying relationship with the responsiveness of the printed word; and in them she perceived what was ultimately a trial and error approach to liberation and education, respectively: Freedom came through trials, and a close examination of one's mistakes led one to learn greater self-awareness. Most publishers would never have chosen to entrust just one person with so significant a task as short-listing applicants for the prestigious post of poetic ambassador. For that matter, ZG was the only House to have created such a lucrative and potentially influential position. And as far as the entrapment went, Misty was, after all, a most willing participant in the proceedings, because thanks to her cleverly negotiated contract the entrapment invariably cut both ways.

Actually, her relationship with ZG was far more paternal than anything else. ZG was the only father figure she could accept—conditionally, of course. That suited Misty just fine, because she had never known her real father and had never enjoyed a very good rapport with any of her stepfathers, either. Hence her feelings of being entrapped were really much more concerned with the subconscious Freudian defense mechanism known as projection than anything else one may have imagined. Her mother had been a stripper who had always wanted a daughter, so she was used to dressing Felicity in provocative, tight-fitting clothing. Not that Felicity minded the occasional constriction of a closely cinched corset either—it went without saying that waiting to exhale was all that much more satisfying, not to mention suspenseful, under uncertain circumstances.

Suspension—whether of disbelief or of any other temporarily enjoyable skepticism—kept one on the edge of wherever one's derriere happened to descend, and often gave rise to the most illustrious, and even belletristic, adventures. These thoughts—and many more the censors would surely redact—all crossed Misty's mind as she sat with pensive pleasure in the same position where Stephanie Nolan usually enacted her role as receptionist for the CEO, Rudy Sorensen. It appeared the board meeting had gone overlong, and Cynthia Davison was due any moment for her meeting with Ms. Nolan. The word applause was written all over that one, thought Misty. Of all the prospective candidates she had interviewed, Cynthia had emerged as singularly qualified. Not only was her poetry published widely throughout writing periodicals and scholarly journals, but she also found the time to write *about* writing for popular magazines like *Writer's Digest* and *Writer's Journal*.

As stultifying as some of these more proscriptive periodicals might prove to be for aspiring writers, it was equally true that the ZG emphasis on both form and function was also analogous to the aforementioned 'corsets'—and when the rhythms of one's verse are constrained for a period of time, the space for one's thought can often expand significantly, thereby affirming the adage that less is more. In that respect, Misty would no doubt have found it amusing to have heard the heated debate going on at this very moment in the executive boardroom. It seems the only real consensus most people ever reach over this contentious issue is that the truth may very well be that less is invariably more than enough, if the writing does not pass muster.

Misty was suddenly reminded of Cynthia's having mentioned during the interview that Carol Ann Duffy's *"Talent"* uses subtle signals to communicate much more than merely a difference between concepts and the language we use to convey them. This significance, she had said, could perhaps be best discerned by considering each use of the word 'word' in the poem as the first part of a compound construction, a fact which resolves the ironic subtext of literalism inherent in the text into a series of neat and allusive abstractions. Structurally speaking, Cynthia had said—elaborating upon her original thought with what Misty had quickly discerned was her unique charismatic flair for the dramatic—this semantic strategy resolves itself into three compound words or word compounds (depending upon the reader's perspective). Then she had emphasized that the real turning point in the poem comes with the presence of its only question.

This question triggers a reader response which renders the poem much more complex, finally affirming that it is ultimately the reader's freedom of choice that determines how they will interact with the text, as well as how the ending will be written for Duffy's main character—the tightrope walker. His success at crossing his particular high wire is not guaranteed, despite how likely or unlikely such an ending might appear on the surface. Ambivalence or uncertainty is just as valid a response as affirmation or negation; and an ironic reading may be indicated as well. It all hinges upon the reader's response to the poem's central question about whether the reader wants the tightrope walker to fall. Misty had, of course, already known all about Ms. Duffy's poem having read it years before, and she had previously come to appreciate some of its semiotic implications. But Cynthia had taken the making of its meaning to new levels for her, and she had been impressed by this prospective candidate's acumen and ingenuity.

During her interview with Cynthia, Misty had begun to make the meaningful leap of logic onto the word tightrope of Cynthia's own mind, crossing over to her point-of-view with ease. Cynthia had articulated how she imagined all the laudatory praise, professional accolades and other word applause from various media that might yet await her high wire ventures in wordplay with no word net. "Vying for the title of poetic ambassador was as risky as it was rewarding, for several reasons," she had said in response to Misty's probative question as to why she was interested in this particular competition.

Cynthia said that although "the ZG brand had a very limited but relatively popular appeal, it rested largely among readers who shared a passion for excellent poetry based upon contemporary themes dressed in traditional forms." Also acutely aware of this selective target audience, Misty's careful shortlisting of Mr. Speller and Mr. Upton was based upon how they had made their impact on literary society felt most readily through their own popular appeal, their imaginative re-envisioning of traditional forms and their distinctively engaging style. However, Ms. Davison's poetry was as equally original as it was intellectually provocative, as conceptually challenging as it was figuratively definitive, and as refreshingly approachable as it was sophisticated. Her work had the potential to broaden the base of ZG's audience, while at the same time increasing the likelihood that ZG would retain their core readership.

None of the other women Misty had interviewed fared as well as Cynthia or the two aforementioned men with respect to Pamela's own uniquely-delivered and scrupulously-analyzed word test. She soon found that her own interest in Cynthia's contribution grew in direct proportion to each prospective candidate's comparatively less significant word compound potential (or their textual power, to borrow a titular phrase from the great semiotician Robert Scholes). At any rate, Misty's process was such that before long it finally became obvious which wordsmiths could best be trusted to cross the word tightrope with no word net in order to elicit the greatest potential word applause. Casual readers might mistake this mutually agreeable semantic connection for partisanship or an overly impressionable nature on the part of Misty, but when an applicant appeals so successfully to an interviewer's own well-cultivated sense of poetic excellence by reciting a poem as influential as Ms. Duffy's "*Talent*" word for word, and then explicating its most complex aspects in forceful, simple, even elegant language, there is only one thing for the interviewer to do—short-list her without partiality. Besides, she was the only woman amid the field of female applicants who merited selection, so she was the *only* woman selected.

Breaking down barriers in the canonization process meant giving more women like Cynthia Davison opportunities to push through the pain to shatter the glass ceiling of institutionalized sexism, and deliver an historic drop kick to that badly stained glass ceiling, which had for years rested high atop the elite world of poetry publication. At least that is the gist of the mixed metaphor Rudy Sorensen used when he had briefed Misty on inclusive interview strategies. ZG has strict sexism policies, however, and they favour ameliorating gender injustices and inequities. If there had been a worthy transgender applicant who managed to pass the vetting process, such a selection would have gone further to mitigating the potential for gender imbalance created by the choice to short-list two males out of the three prospective candidates for the position. But there was not.

Misty paused here in her reverie to reflect upon her own successful gender reassignment. Her own sex change was just a decade past now, though the process had first begun forty years earlier when her mother started dressing her in tight skirts and blouses at age five. Now Misty decided that—given the current climate of relative acceptance, tolerance and mutual respect—she probably would have applied to become the poetic ambassador had she not already been employed by ZG in her present capacity. She had intimated as much to Rudy during their preliminary sessions, and he had said that she would undoubtedly have made an excellent poetic ambassador; he then went on to assure her that she was even more invaluable to them for all of that, because it made her even better at interviewing prospective applicants. However, trends being what they are, she thought, it's only a matter of time before ZG selects a transgender applicant, and who knows what kind of an influence our first such ambassador might have on androgynous young men and women intent upon exploring their sexuality through non-traditional forms, while exercising their literary licence in a traditional House.

Cynthia burst through the glass doors just then.

"First the doors, next the ceiling, Cynthia." Misty flipped her auburn curls away from her attractive face and rose to her feet. She smoothed out her form-fitting bright yellow dress, and welcomed her young prospect to ZG, extending her hand for a warm shake.

"That's some tarn you've got out there," Cynthia offered, reaching out to take the proffered hand in cordial camaraderie, then pulling the tall, athletic woman in close for a celebratory squeeze. "Thank you for selecting me!" She was happy to see a kindred spirit and a warm, friendly face atop this intimidating tower of glass. "Are you riding out the storm up here alone?"

"Reinforcements will arrive at any moment," Misty replied, resuming her seat behind the desk and waving the hopeful prospective poetic ambassador towards a comfortable leather chair where Ms. Davison might relax while she awaited the by-now-late Ms. Nolan. "You mentioned something about a tarn?"

"Yes. Whenever a puddle has the audacity to envelop the building it surrounds, it assumes tarn-like tendencies."

"I have seen this tarn. But I am sure the building is still secure, not yet fully enveloped. On the other hand, it could be that the sidewalk has developed a concave surface. And when concrete is depressed... it might need psychological help from one of its peers. I speak purely in abstractions. After all," Misty continued, in tones as earnest as the humour was dry, "one good tarn deserves another."

"Don't expect me to re-tarn if you are going to punish me with bad puns," Cynthia replied, laughing easily at the silly turn the conversation had taken. "But don't you mean to say concrete poetry? Now that could easily get very depressing. The only solution is to have it tarn up dead, and as all good hits end up—encased in concrete."

"Stop!" Misty's gentle but robust laugh carried throughout the room. Then as quickly as her jocularity passed away, her look of restrained severity resumed its rightful place (if only to mock its conviviality), and rose phoenix-like on its still-glowing pyre. "That's probably what I meant. You see, we were having a concrete poem convention here in the building just this past weekend. And I'm convinced the proceedings *ushered* in this tarn problem of which you speak." Here she paused for effect and continued with a conspiratorial whisper. "There may have been one or two Rodericks and perhaps even a Madeline in attendance. I'm honestly concerned that it might *tarnish* the ZG brand." The solemn tower of rectitude who sat demurely before Cynthia evinced a formidable confidentiality, and an even stricter probity of spirit. One that probably would have sobered even the severest judge.

Consequently, Cynthia really did not know whether or not to laugh at first. But then Misty slowly and quite deliberately ran her strong fingers through her curly dark reddish brown hair which hung well past her shapely bare shoulders, almost halfway down her back. Then she tapped her strong aquiline nose for detail. When she brushed her hair, Cynthia took it as a sign of relief. But the nose for detail was what finally gave it away. She knew instantly she could laugh at the ridiculous whopper of a lame joke, and she giggled a little (hoping it might sound uncontrolled).

Decidedly amused, and more than a little impressed... with Misty's luxuriant mane, (she had had her hair in a large bun on the top of her head during *their* interview) Cynthia felt it was time to affirm her allegiance to ZG. "Well I, for one, would not wish to tarnish the ZG brand," she said in a tone she chose carefully, to come off sounding much more grave and circumspect than a mere ingratiating endorsement of puns or ZG for that matter. It was evident to her that Pamela was an expert at misdirection—at least when it came to evincing a sober-minded demeanor while delivering a tongue-in-cheek speech—but she was not yet quite sure how to take her. Then Cynthia launched a light-hearted protest, in terms that were cautiously orchestrated to be both endearing and entreating. "Geeze

Louise, Pamela, won't you be serious once in a while!"

"Listen, child." Misty stood and came around to sit on the front of the desk, crossing her legs to showcase her well-tanned and shapely calves (the slightest of tells that alert readers might recognize). She folded her arms, but adopted a conciliatory tone, as if she were about to lecture a wayward orphan. "I'm always serious! My laugh is serious. My car is serious. Even my girlfriend is serious. She better be. Because I'm as serious as a stroke—a butterfly stroke—the length of the entire pool—the gene pool. Now don't take me the wrong way again or I might crack myself up from being so serious or give myself a hernia from mixing metaphors.

And remember—it's all a matter of tone. Set the right tone immediately, and then nobody will mix up the message you're sending no matter how much of a metaphorical mash-up you may choose for the music you want them to face. Match your tone to the emotion you want your reader to experience." Here Misty paused dramatically, and then went on more slowly. "Oh, and Pamela is only my stage name (Ms. Nolan calls it my strange name—my 'make-strange' name). The interview is long over. This is real life now. So you can call me Misty when it's just us, otherwise it is Ms. Traviss. And remember, Ms. Nolan will be giving you your rivals' phone numbers soon, so you never got them from me, now, did you child?" Misty stood up, interlaced her fingers, stretched her hands towards the ceiling, moved back behind the desk, and slid her body like liquid honey back into her comfortable seat.

Cynthia smiled broadly at her candor, marvelled at her languid intonation, and stood herself, as much for a better view as for a change of position, because truth be told, she was a bit awe-struck at how well Misty's form fitted itself so well to every function. If only my poetry could match that poetry, she thought. Then I'd never worry about intonation.

"This would be Ms. Nolan now," Misty said glancing through the glass window down the long hall that extended to where the boardroom was situated well within sight of the reception room in which they had been sitting. Smiling through her perfect sparkling white teeth, she spoke again in a hushed conspiratorial whisper, leaving Cynthia (who now had no doubts about her complete earnestness) with her first daunting impression of Rudy Sorensen's private secretary. "You can always tell Stephanie by the way she walks, same way she talks—softly but with stealth—and you'd best be careful, child, because behind the mixed message of her comfortable southern deportment and breezy civility there beats the clockwork heart of a calculating bureaucrat."

Then, she got up, thanked Cynthia for the enjoyable conversation, reminded her to make sure her tone flouted her readers expectations (or at the very least ignited their passions), implied but did not say that she must be going now, and left the office worse for her not being there—meaning that those left behind still felt her presence even in her absence. Such was the favourable impression Ms. Felicity Traviss made upon the people with whom she became involved, especially if she liked them. They invariably talked about what a vivacious personality she had, how charming her demeanor was, or how elegantly she moved. Few would have ventured to guess that she had not always been a woman of means, depth and grace—or not even a woman at all—although Misty herself would have crisply corrected this misinterpretation by affirming that she had most certainly always been of the feminine persuasion.

None of this would have phased Ms. Stephanie Nolan. She was a died-in-the-wool traditionalist, the most cosmopolitan of modernists, and an erstwhile denizen of Southern climes and genteel hospitality—specifically South Carolina, with its country-club pedigree and its colonial heritage. Although her surname originally descended from the Gaelic word for 'shout,' this information might have been construed as ironic and misleading, because Stephanie's voice seldom rose above a soft, richly accented whisper and never above a stage whisper. At the same time, those placid, even tones could convey an idea with as much force as even the most ardent and voluble prima donna in the room. Something Cynthia was about to find out.

Four

THE FRONT

Taking her cue from Ms. Traviss, as if a torch had been indirectly passed, Ms. Nolan assumed her place and the role it entailed with an air of ownership borne as much out of habit and experience as it was of disciplined devotion to rich detail. She set her red satchel down carefully, leaning it against the large blue pot that housed the healthy fern behind the desk. Her lifelong labours stemmed from her love for literature. Just as Felicity Traviss clearly and comfortably wore her responsibilities as a ZG gatekeeper with dignity and professional detachment, (her surname, Traviss, actually came from the Old French for toll-keeper) Stephanie Nolan was likewise, even more at home in her official position of Communications Coordinator.

Now she turned her considerable charm upon Cynthia, opening the meeting with a direct question accompanied by her customarily disarming smile. "I hope you haven't travelled far in this inclement weather to join us here tonight?"

Cynthia immediately reverted to her comfort zone—all posture and perspicacity—to allay the small amount of anxiety which had just recently made itself felt—as if an ever-so-slight hit of adrenaline had been injected into her heart—heightened, of course, in the wake of Misty's wee bit of a warning. Playing from her strength, she opened with a poetic gambit designed, hopefully, to ensure that she made a favourable first impression upon this woman. Nor did she fail to discern that Ms. Nolan subsumed ZG into their dialogue right from the get-go, using 'join us here' instead of 'join me'. She noticed this, and the self-effacing dynamic it entailed, almost at once, making subtle adjustments of her own in the bargain.

Leaning in for added emphasis, she strove to hit just the right earnest tone to accentuate her theme of unity in the face of adversity: "There is in the distance between us no space that light and good will cannot erase. But since the night's storms are surely only a front we face, it matters less than keeping our common ends in sight."

After the barest of hesitations, Ms. Nolan spoke with deft and cool precision, and her query was compounded as much of mock disdain for pretense as it was of formality and the irony of literal-mindedness. "Even though the front may obscure those ends? I speak of the weather, of course." She folded her hands and her azure eyes probed intently over a mirthless smile into Cynthia's rich green eyes. Although Ms. Nolan's smile seemed on the surface to radiate some warmth, in reality it did not quite convincingly generate the heat of even a stone; which was the exact verisimilitude of her general demeanor and deadpan expression.

Ignoring, or rather glossing over, the implicit irony that lurked like levels of subtext behind Ms. Nolan's ostensibly innocuous question and her considerably less expressive facial features, Cynthia offered her a vista of serene composure and cordial civility in her own efficacious smile, remembering what Misty had said about Ms. Nolan being a bureaucrat at heart. Then, she corrected her course, adopted an even more officious veneer, and ventured towards the business at hand: "Weather or no weather, the means to our mutual ends depend entirely upon whatever forms and subordinate details ZG stipulates for our portfolio. Have all these details been determined? If so, may I enquire about deadlines, any related stipulations and the exact nature of the formal requirements?" It was not her nature to offload all these inquiries in quite so direct a manner, but she found herself still thinking of what Ms. Traviss had said—not only about Ms. Nolan, but also about tone and audience.

Cynthia had quite rightly decided her interlocutor was probably tired after a lengthy board meeting. The hour was getting late. Best to take a straightforward, professional approach and leave time for the *rest* later, in both senses of that word.

Apparently, Ms. Nolan concurred. Nor was she above condescending to the young lady to whom she had displayed such patience and broad civility—both of which she was renowned for trotting out at a moment's notice. She arched her back ever so slightly, and with deliberate poise, swiveled in her chair to turn away from Cynthia—a gesture which could easily have been misinterpreted for brusque detachment by someone less secure, but was in fact merely practical maneuvering. Bending to retrieve the red briefcase from where it lay adorning the foot of the effusive fern, she opened it and withdrew a rather large packet of papers. Thumbing through the sheaf silently, she carefully made her selection, sliding it out with aplomb to place it on the desk well within Cynthia's eager view. "The executive has laboured, now we must deliver. Mr. Sorensen has asked that the portfolio assignment be ready for pickup at our Burnaby office by noon tomorrow. I plan to draft a good copy of these specifications in the morning. After that, they will go out by courier to Burnaby for pickup. I see no reason why you should not be allowed to peruse the results of our exhaustive deliberations right now though, since you managed to brave the weather with such a stout-hearted front."

"Wait." Cynthia was now sure she heard the subtext behind the front that Ms. Nolan was obviously putting up, and couldn't let it go by. "You do still mean the weather front, don't you?"

Ms. Nolan barely disguised her Southern discomfort at being called out in so unsubtle a manner. "Why whatever else could I possibly mean, child? Of course I was wondering about whether... whether or not you're ever going to drop that inauspicious form of ingratiating *yourself* to *our* vested interest in *your* success."

Cynthia sat stock-still.

Ms. Nolan proceeded in her calm, quiet, even-handed way. "You may wish to listen to what people are *not* saying behind the words they bend towards your ear, rather than painting them into a self-portrait from what you presume they might want you to hear."

Cynthia moved not one inch.

"This contest is yours to lose. Your chosen path will walk you, or you can walk your chosen path. There are more than a few here at ZG—and by that I mean executive and editorial staff alike—who think that a little more estrogen would go a long way towards restoring balance, poise and feminine perspicacity to our public profile. Judging by your initial success, and in spite of my own first impressions, I'd say your chances of beating out the competition are probably pretty good—if you don't defeat yourself in the process of vying for victory—and you can take that any way you like."

Cynthia leaned forward slightly, then spoke; hesitantly at first, and gradually more definitively, letting her words meander in a seemingly haphazard manner. They left her lips as if they were leaves. Leaves of the autumn ash tree, carrying seeds that spiralled downwards, landing at last with a barely discernible thud whose hope only the ground grown gravid would hear. "From throes of fitful sleep, one may awake to many truths, and see in pictures meanings deep, or only fronts resisting proofs. A lighthouse beacon beckons clear, though storms arise obscuring beams. Harbingers call from far and near, to be understood is the stuff of dreams."

Ms. Nolan now turned her statuesque features towards the glass, reflecting upon their reflections. Finally, after a moment's silence, she sighed. Her eyes were moist, and she smiled. A genuine smile, candid and warm. "Do you write all your poetry off the top of your head like that?" she asked softly.

"It depends upon many things. But mostly, upon how inspired I am." Then somewhat coyly (a habit hard to break for Cynthia), she ventured her last ingratiating query of the night. "Maybe if I were to come in and talk with you a little more often, my inspiration would not run dry. What do you think?"

Ms. Nolan seemed to ignore this, but her response glanced at it obscurely, and then she continued in a business-like manner. "I don't think you need anything more than to talk with poets. I'm sending out the names, email addresses and phone numbers of each of your two competitors tomorrow with the portfolio package. All three of you will receive the corresponding contact information. Whether or not you get in touch with them is entirely up to you, but our experience here at ZG involves the philosophy that knowing one's adversary enhances the competition in healthy ways, and one's true mettle can always be tested and augmented through the crucible of an amicable rivalry. It has truly been a pleasure meeting you, Cynthia. I look forward to reading your forthcoming portfolio. Do take advantage of the contact information I'm including with this assignment. And should any further questions arise about our competition, don't hesitate to contact me." At this point Ms. Nolan stood. "But above all, don't let the façade of a stormy front inhibit the poet within you from revealing her true persona."

Cynthia seemed almost to blush, and then she could not help but smile... at what she took for so disarmingly naïve an outlook. "Thank you. I hope that my poetry will be the true revelation," was all she managed—or wished to appear to manage—with the kind of equivocal terseness she felt sure would pass for humble gratitude, knowing all the while that Ms. Nolan would likely figure out fairly quickly that what Cynthia was negating with her comment may just as easily have been the first of the three Polonius-like pieces of advice she had been offered. Thereby seemingly affirming her tacit intention to ignore both of the other two as well. But here she was again with her super-subtle wit, spurning the wisdom of her elders.

Musing over her encounter, she pondered what dear old nubile Nolan would think if she knew her young ingénue was already sleeping with both of the enemies. Her battle was going to be waged on both fronts, and the only thing amicable about their rivalry would be her friendly fire. Forgetting for the moment Ms. Nolan's flourishes of erstwhile interest in her prospects, Cynthia cursed her silently for the meddlesome manner with which her surreptitiously supercilious demeanor had dominated their dialogue, distracting her from finding out anything of substance about the portfolio, except when the deadline was.

She was splashing childishly through the tarn again before she realized she would have to wait until high noon tomorrow to discover exactly what kind of a challenge she was facing—but of course she would be prepared for any eventuality, and she was sure there would be plenty of time to implement her schismatic designs towards both of her adversaries. The sky was still overcast, and her pensive mood suddenly seemed to be as black as the tarn. She hailed a cab and began to compose her thoughts. Outside, the front seemed to be lifting, but other fronts would soon descend. Some would hold heartaches. Some could even presage honour and distinction. And one day soon, she thought to herself, Ms. Carol Ann Duffy's abstraction of a 'word applause' may also be written all over me! Then, my poetry will yet again yield new worlds of great net gain. All at once, acting on a sudden impulse, she waved the cab away. Something had caught her eye.

The green neon sign flashing the words 'Internet Café' above the dark wet street down on the secluded corner had caught her eye. Sleep would keep. She was too stoked not to waste her energy, so she headed towards it, formulating an outline of what would be the first among many emails for the 'mutual benefit' of the other two short-listed candidates, each of whom she intended to fly like a kite until the high winds of lovelorn betrayal brought an end to their respective meanderings. Although she did know how to get hold of them (in more ways than one), she decided not to send the messages tonight—both of which were directly related to the ZG competition—for the sake of appearances.

As of yet, she was the only one with the knowledge that the shortlist had been made or who was on it (thanks to Misty, an unexpected ally, it seemed). So technically, logistically nobody could know the contact information (though Misty had just a few weeks earlier—prior to the official announcement naming the successful candidates—found it amusingly Machiavellian to clandestinely send it to Cynthia in her own personal hand-crafted 'literary' postcard). For this reason, Cynthia decided that sending the emails prematurely might give rise to the type of inauspicious suspicions which could conceivably undermine what Dylan Thomas, were he alive and cheering her on over a pint, might have called her 'craft and sullen art'.

Cynthia would never have pretended to invoke the great Welsh poet, though she thought she might welcome such an endorsement, just as it inadvertently crossed her mind. Or would she? Sure she would—after all, they would have agreed about not going gentle into that good night and a whole lot more by way of her own tactics besides. All the same, she was content for the moment to continue to strategize. No plot is complete, she thought, without a hint of conflict, and this one was sure to be broad enough to guarantee that both Zack and Trevor would soon be embroiled in a controversial struggle that may, with luck—and a healthy amount of her own personal 'spin'—constrain and simultaneously stymie their quest for the position of poetic ambassador, while propelling her forward with impunity.

Hew a post or two, for tonight, and tomorrow the pièce de résistance—deconstruct their textual foundations. For a moment the robust vessel of her mental machinations ran aground on the sandy shoal of an old adage—"the best defense is a good offense." Hers—whether 'o' or 'd' fences—were sure to be barbed and wiry, like her wit.

It looked like a good place to get off. And there was the neon lighthouse beckoning her. Under the green light was a red door. She stepped inside a golden room, crossed to a kiosk, paid for a terminal, and found herself a quiet spot amid the scattered clusters of customers who sat hunched over their monitors, clattering keyboards in an aura burnished by avid concentration and copious quantities of craft beer. She settled in for a few hours of the constructive game she liked to call 'follow the blinking cursor' and caught the waiter's attention. Outside, the storm was revving up again, buoyed by a fresh front, just as if a ton or two of tuff muscle cars had decided to race across the corridors of the sky. But as Cynthia quaffed her ale and pondered her plans, there were storms of another kind brewing—like Starship's signature song—in her eyes.

Five

GETTING TO KNOW YOUR ADVERSARY

From the second he picked up his phone on that rainy October morning, Trevor knew his life was about to change. The phone call was his chrysalis. His natural prescience notwithstanding, there was something momentous about the imperative tone of the female voice at the other end of the line. And there was also something unexpectedly revealing in her purposeful pitch. Not to mention that the telephone line itself had seemed heavily charged with significance: an electronic hue of importance, an aura of amplification. Or maybe it was just the static—it really was a bad connection. What exactly was it that the richly cadenced woman's voice on the phone had said? Details were a blur. Worse than a moonless night fog, than a polar bear being swallowed by avalanche in a hailstorm. Words scattered to the dull dewy daylight, like autumn leaves falling, blown by the wind to land willy-nilly. Only a smattering of what had been said penetrated his concrete pony wall of reserve. Still, it left him with a mildly pervasive sense of euphoria. That quickly passed, replaced as suddenly by an optimism as well-guarded as the true reasons for a cabinet shuffle hidden in one of his carefully-scripted political speeches. Was he over-reacting? He could only recollect these few words: 'ZeitGeist,' 'shortlisted,' and something about three or four nights? No, it was three fortnights, and he must come down to the office this very afternoon to pick up *the Poetry Portfolio Assignment.* It all seemed so enigmatic. As electrically enigmatic as Tesla himself! Time and space contracted, disorienting him.

Suddenly, he was in the ZG elevator, rising to plateau. He scarcely knew how he'd gotten here. Felt like he'd been beamed over from the deck of the Enterprise. Yet here he was. Waiting for the elevator to stop. He hoped he'd dressed appropriately. Right. Crushed grey velvet gingham button down collar dress shirt untucked over his black Calvin Klein modern fit performance dress pants; and his black Doc Martens. He glanced at his Armani and noted the time. It was half past noon; would the office be closed for lunch? Then he looked down at his keys, as if to remind himself that he'd actually driven from upper Lonsdale to the ZG office on Burnaby Mountain. He tried to picture something definite that would bring to mind the route he'd travelled, but all he could fasten upon was his neighbour's old dog barking half-heartedly from the walkway at the side of their house. More like the faint echo of a bark, really. They should put that mutt out of his misery, Trevor thought. But dim as the memory of that feeble old Beagle's bark was, not even the barest vestige remained of buildings? Bridges? Pedestrians? Nothing from what must have been an automatic piloting of his Hummer from home to here. His mind had understandably been fixated on the exciting news of his acceptance, and he was practically certain he had held his breath all the way. He had to be dreaming that he'd been shortlisted, or was he... dead? He certainly did not seem to be breathing now. The elevator stopped, and he almost passed out. I'm not dead and I'm not dreaming either, he said to himself. The door opened, and he exhaled.

Now, directly in front of him, was the same auburn-haired beauty who had interviewed him. She wore that baby blue mini dress like a sheath! And her mien was as regal as her mane. He had spoken with her less than a couple of weeks earlier. He recounted their conversation, and how he had been caught off guard by her unexpectedly casual tone, combined with her eccentric questions and offbeat manner. He wracked his brain trying to remember her name: Patricia? Amelia? No, Pamela! That was it. Now she was smiling cordially, welcoming him. And was it his imagination or was she even more casually composed than she'd been before? She seemed intent upon setting him at ease. He hesitated and then said, "Nice to see you again Pamela."

"Mr. Upton," the shapely receptionist said warmly as she handed him a brown manila envelope. "Pamela was merely my "stage" name, to be used for that... uh, stage of the proceedings. You can call me Ms. Traviss now. I wish to congratulate you on behalf of the Board of Directors for ZG. You have been shortlisted." Her smile was warm and inviting, an inviting bridge leading to who knew where. "You are one of three prospective candidates for the position of ZG Poetic Ambassador. Please accept this envelope. In it are the requirements of your final "interview". It takes the form of a poetry portfolio. Submit the assignment to Ms. Stephanie Nolan at our downtown office by Monday, November 15 if you wish to be considered for this position. Don't hesitate to contact either Ms. Nolan or myself should you have any further questions. All the particulars, in addition to the necessary information concerning your competitors, are included in the package. Good day and good luck." This particular bridge, it seemed, was like a bailey—short and to the point. Suddenly he was on the other side, still thinking of the scenery.

As Trevor turned back towards the elevator, his step was light and his heart was lighter still. It followed imaginary golden butterflies, fluttering in diamond-shaped clusters upwards, ever upwards towards the grey clouds that suddenly did not seem nearly as grey as they had before he entered the ZG office. Not that he really remembered the weather, or whether time had stood still as it seemed to have until now. He glanced at his watch, and remembered suddenly that he was officially 'on the clock' as of Monday. How nice to lose oneself in the butterfly logic of poetry. The logic of golden butterflies, fluttering haphazardly between the earth and those puffy white clouds whose meanderings they mirror (albeit in a manner more artfully fused with manic liquidity, he thought, noting a few fledgling drops of rain streaking the elevator window).

As the smooth glass elevator ride ended, with his feet firmly planted on the solid ground of earth, Trevor wondered just how long it might be until he found himself on a far less tranquil ride. Live with the joy, he told himself—live in the moment.

Outside, he sauntered over to the short, round rock wall that skirted an exceptionally large and active, circular fountain whose individual jets gushed out to within a couple of yards from the circumference of said wall. He threw a penny in the fountain for luck. *Copper for caprice meets a flood of foam for passion.* And so thinking, Trevor was about to set off, when, out of the corner of his eye, he noticed an intense-looking young man around to one side. Tall and slender, with an athletic build and long wavy brown hair that hung in wispy thickets about his ears and down towards his shoulders, this strange young man pierced him with what he could only characterize as a hypnotic stare. Trevor wasn't sure, but he felt almost certain he had seen the man tuck away a manila envelope similar to the one he himself was now holding. Had he seen him furtively stuffing it into a pocket inside his lengthy overcoat? Yes, he had! Suddenly the stranger strode towards him, holding out one of his large hands, and assailing him at once with a gregarious salutation. Trevor was taken aback.

"Hello there, friend." he said confidently. "My name is Zack Speller."

"Hi," Trevor said, somewhat hesitantly. "Do I know you?"

"I'm doing some business with ZG." The stranger replied, smiling with what seemed a genuine friendliness.

"Of course. A little writing?" Trevor speculated, putting on a puzzled expression.

"Well," Zack paused and then cocked his head off to the side. "You see," he continued with a faraway look in his eyes, "it's a sense of longing. I'm creating a sense of longing... for ZG." At this point he paused again, gestured towards the fountain, and smiled a knowing but not at all disarming smile.

Trevor felt a twinge of uneasiness as he glanced over at the gushing water. Who was this Speller fellow anyways? He began to wonder whether he had anything to do with the assignment. Was *he* another one who was longing to be the poetic ambassador? Or did he work as some kind of public relations guy for the publishing house?

Zack for his part was relishing his advantage and playing his opponent like some small salmon he had just hooked. Pushing this fellow—who had obviously not yet glanced at the contents of his envelope—into an awkward corner was part of his offensive strategy. All that remained was to see how long it would take to get him to say his name (though Zack had already perused the package which held all this pertinent information). Nevertheless, he pressed him purposefully, endeavouring to mask his driving ambitious bent, with a casual air.

"You're working for ZG, too, aren't you?" He asked innocently, letting out a little line.

"Well, I... um..." Trevor hesitated again, unsure of what he ought to say, but aware that he didn't trust this fellow enough to divulge his recent news.

"You're a writer, aren't you? I've seen your face before." Zack pushed further, working on the young man's vanity.

"Well, yes. I'm Upton, Trevor Upton." His customary, if amusing, use of Ian Fleming's trademark syntax for Britain's most well-known super-spy's introduction conveyed a good deal more than the fact that Trevor was a sometime fan of 007, and the point was not lost on Zack who read text, even in conversation, far better than he read faces. He reeled in his catch with precision.

"Of course! You are 'the' Trevor Upton. You are *the working man's poet*, aren't you?"

"Philistine critics! I like to think I've outgrown that ironic moniker." Trevor's best poker face included his bluff of affronted audacity at betrayal (real or imagined). If he was at cards, such a bluff was invariably directed towards Mistress Hazard herself (along with her harpies, Chance, Luck and Fate), but at this moment he turned his spleen towards those particular arbiters of public taste who had been less than glowing in their estimation of his literary contribution. And he had in fact spent a good deal of private time seemingly overwrought at the fact that he must bear the brunt of their sarcastic nicknames and generally poor judgement. But he sensed to his advantage that the young man in front of him now seemed intent upon conflating the subtle differences between bluster, bluff and bravado.

Zack egged him on with a rejoinder that was laced as much with provocation and sardonic condescension as it was short and to the point. "Of course you do. And so you should! Critics are a loutish lot." Then he smiled blandly, immeasurably content that his nettling barb had—at least ostensibly—done its work. Unfortunately Zack was practically oblivious as to any possible ulterior motives his latest pawn might be considering from behind his wilfully misleading mask, worn well for his favorite cause—self-promotion by any means, preferably forceful and indirect.

"See here, Speller," Trevor sputtered ahead disingenuously in the wake of his pretentious jettisoned debris; and anxious to make himself seem as if he were totally taken aback by Zack's rude manner, he settled upon his own gambit, which involved an over-reaction designed to feign an insecure need to vindicate himself. "I don't know what your business is with ZG, but I plan on becoming their next poetic ambassador, and that's no pedestrian honour, I can tell you."

"No sir," Zack countered with mock deference, more certain of his adversary now, or so he thought, than before, but forced on the spur of the moment to let this fish run, at least until his energy was spent. "You'll want to walk warily towards that distinction," he laughed. At this point Zack paused and looked around clandestinely before continuing in a hushed conspiratorial whisper. "I imagine it will take your utmost stealth Upton, Trevor Upton!" Then, just in case this wasn't infuriating enough, he added the punch line with a loud guffaw: "...and more than your typical odd assortment of specialized weapons!" Zack's loud laughter could be heard well over the white noise of the rushing water in the fountain. He was reeling his fish in again.

The Poetic Ambassador

"Hold on now, you Cretan," Trevor countered, spitting out his carefully-chosen adjective with a plosive force that made him appear almost to lose himself in vitriol; and then, just as a glimmer of recognition flickered across his mind, he composed his retort: "Wait just one minute. " Trevor suddenly knew who Zack was. "I know you. You're that jingle writer aren't you? Zackary Speller the story teller?" He threw the words out at him with a kind of childish sing-song glee. And once again, the salmon was free!

"Stellar!" Zack shouted, slapping Trevor forcefully on the back. "Just stellar!" Zack was of the opinion that if you think you might have met your match, strike it at once and then you'll see it burn out like a matchstick. He fervidly imagined Trevor's creative flame slowly extinguishing, as his own blazed on and on, before turning into an untamed bonfire of rare vitality. He punched Trevor in the shoulder jovially, and regaled him loudly. "Hale fellow well met, we've not begun yet!"

Understanding braced Trevor as if he'd suddenly had his face splashed with the fountain's frothy water. And then as an awareness of the pattern of moves his adversary had been making hit him, he let him see this realization spill slowly over his face like molasses slides down a frozen ice cream slope—sweetening the exchange by degrees. Gradually, but steadily, he allowed his eyes to brighten. His mettle was being tested by this iron on iron exchange. His countenance composed itself along the settled contours of competitive determination. Rain had begun to spit steadily down upon them now, but Upton became animated. He taunted Speller, seeming to read his mind, and impaled him with a quick decasyllabic retort: "Pale fellow, you've met your match! You're all wet!"

"Hah! Touché. Let the games begin, may the best man win!" Zack threw back another effortless 10-syllable response of his own, buttressed by internal rhyme. True, his catch had taken the bait— hook, line, and sinker—but, by replying in kind, as he cocked his head, laughed raucously and stuck out his hand in an open and honest gesture of friendly rivalry, Speller seemed to be implying the game would be played fairly. Upton's work as a speech writer had inured him to duplicity; however, he was now determined to reserve judgement. Both men felt the other had gotten the worst of the exchange. Like two professional boxers who are each convinced he should have been declared the victor after fighting all twelve rounds to a draw, both men guarded their sense of superiority with a fearsome pride, a source of weakness and strength they shared. A badge of honour some are drawn to more than others. And a characteristic that can sometimes, but not always, be riskily defining.

Six

ANTICIPATING THE AFTERGLOW

Trevor glared at Zack for a few seconds, then he spun on his heel disgustedly and started away, peeved that he had let this 'little' man goad him into so pedestrian an encounter. Behind him he heard what he imagined to be Zack's banal jibes exuding their sharp sentiment in the autumn mist, and vying for airtime with the raindrops that dampened and muted their plosive force. "Upton… something… something… no rite of passage writ?" He couldn't quite make it out. No matter. Petty man. Must not let him ruin the splendour of the day.

There were still those Golden Butterflies to chase. He had dreams to pursue. ZG had chosen *him.* But it appeared that they had also chosen Zachary Speller to be his nemesis. Who else had they chosen? He had a sense that he knew who the third competitor might be. What if it were? She'd be the one to beat. No matter now. Lost in his rare and radiant reflections—only slightly less so than they had been before—Trevor Upton headed for his Hummer and made his way homeward. But not before he'd torn open that manila envelope and confirmed his suspicions about Cynthia Davison having also been selected. Her name and contact information was included, along with Zachary Speller's.

Apparently ZG expected them to interact; something about honing one another's skills. Speller had obviously known this already, and had begun to try to manipulate him. His opening gambit had caught Trevor slightly off guard, but that was neither here nor there. If there was one thing ambassadors were good at, it was diplomacy—especially in the fine and not so fine art of war. Trevor quickly realized he had been pitted against two worthy adversaries in a pitched battle of poetry that only one person could win. Words were their weapons and psychological warfare could wreak havoc amid the quest to create a portfolio worthy of an ambassador. Trevor knew one thing for sure—his lifelong battle alongside his sister Katherine (who had been diagnosed as having Multiple Sclerosis in her teens) had made him a master of mediation, a diamond of détente. Apart from helping his sister in this way, the last few years mediating for her and advocating on her behalf would finally yield some benefits with respect to his own endeavors. He would use the skills gained in his work on behalf of Kate to help him triumph in this poetic skirmish. And he would take no prisoners.

Tonight he would begin a schematic outline of his portfolio. But now it was time to celebrate. He pulled up Miranda Sung's number on his speed dial, and called her first, because he knew she would be able to secure a last-minute reservation at the restaurant. What good were ex-girlfriend's if you could not use their connections (good thing the split had been amicable). He also made sure to ask her to bring along her twin sister Celeste for their celebration at the *Afterglow*. Next came Monique Sloan and Heidi Egan. Then Paul Schulz, Kern Jacks, and finally Eddie Patterson. They were all excited for him and—happily for him—they were all free to celebrate together on such short notice (English majors are not always in high demand, as it turns out). Two of these five colleagues—Heidi and Eddie—had also applied to ZG for the ambassador position, so needless to say their enthusiasm for his news was tempered somewhat by their own disappointment at not having been shortlisted.

Still, they were all good friends so he could easily resist the temptation to gloat. Since most had remained starving students doing freelance writing work where they could and augmenting their incomes with menial work when they couldn't avoid it, they wouldn't pass up a free meal (Trevor had insisted that he was paying). Somehow along the way, he unconsciously left off phoning his current girlfriend until he'd confirmed all the others, and then, as if on impulse, he punched in her number. Busy. She would have heard by now. She had probably been trying to get through to him. How many in their party would be the question. Something John Lennon had once said about the number 9 stuck with him, but he also decided the night would not be quite as perfect without at least an effort to include his newfound nemesis, Zack Speller; and with Cynthia and Zack, that would make 10 guests for his ten-course extravaganza at the *Afterglow*. It was shaping up to be a busy night. He tried Cynthia again. Still busy.

Yes, let the games begin, he thought serenely, and poured himself a Martini. He was about to pick up the phone to ring Cynthia's number for the third time, when he got a call back from Schultzie who was, as it turned out, unable to make it due to the sudden unexpected arrival of his favourite uncle Karl, visiting Paul for only one night. It had just turned three in the afternoon, when he finally succeeded in getting a call through to Cynthia. Maybe she had someone else in mind to round the party out to ten. She picked up on the sixth ring. "Thea, darling, I'm so happy for you."

Cynthia was dripping wet, and the oversize beach towel she'd grabbed upon hastily exiting the shower seemed less interested in grip than slip, leaving her coolly over-exposed, and she stood like the Venus on the half shell, dripping after a downpour. As of this moment, she was not favourably disposed to the idea of being wined and dined in so "intimate" a manner as Trevor suggested. She told him as much, slightly peeved—both that he was not suggesting a quiet dinner, just the two of them alone, as at not having left the phone off the hook. But her reluctance translated in Trevor's mind into a need for some poetic persuasion.

"Just a few friends to help ease our transition—buffers for the bumpy road we're on, moving from lovers to fighters," he coaxed.

She replied with casual indifference to his first foray into the woods of her tepid responsiveness, making a more emphatic secondary encounter necessary. It is impossible to say whether his switch to Elizabethan "frankness" softened her more than his overweening expectation.

"Madam Ambassador, my Hummer sulks in the shade of your approval." His British accent was as impeccable as dust is wet, but Cynthia always humoured him by returning in a kind of kind: She put some Cockney into her Shakespeare.

"The robes you dress me in are borrowed, m'lord. Wait'st thou no longer?"

"As long as it takes m'lady, twixt now and the time of our feast."

"No need your steed to sulk and stamp
Your fickle friends will soon away.
But I am cold and I am damp.
I must dry 'ere I may play."

By now Cynthia had begun to drip dry, and just as those rivulets of moisture slowly disappeared, so too went her melancholy mood, replaced by a more sanguine demeanor. Affirming her acceptance, she had prepared herself to hang up on her "beau du jour" (who had for a few weeks now become rather routine faire for her), and retrieve her fallen towel to apply it to her straight shoulder-length blonde hair. Meanwhile, Trevor chattered on, and she found herself smiling in amusement at his efforts to assuage her cool temper with his throwaway throwback poetry.

She reflected as she composed her lines off the cuff that his friends would probably ease comfortably into their relegated roles at the dinner party. Still, how long could one endure sycophancy without seeing through it and finally pushing it away—like a plate of overcooked turkey without the stuffing—to let it stand alone, dry as a disgusting gizzard. Something was really off, she thought, repulsed by her imagery. A night out would do her good. And why not have a celebration. It wasn't every day you found out you were selected to possibly become an ambassador—even if it was only a poetic ambassador. A small niggling whisper (almost a simulacrum of humility) somewhere in her subconscious mind prompted and perpetuated this tendency to discount any distinction she had not yet acquired. As if she were Caesar, feigning a shyness to accept the crown from his fellow Romans on Lupercalia day.

A verse from Keats (perhaps the only Romantic for whom she did not altogether have an acute aversion) had suddenly reminded her of her sister Anika (it was one of their mutual favourites) and she determined there would be no better way to balance the tedium of tawdry talk than by having her own vivacious twin along for the ride. So, buoyed by the mascot to negative capability—the nightingale—she hit upon the ideal way to tease Trevor with what she thought would be her parting shot, "Already with thee! Tender is the night to come. Pick me up by six. Now say adieu, lest I succumb... to tedium."

Trevor had smiled so broadly she could almost hear his grin over the phone. Then he had a surprising thought (at least Cynthia found it surprising). "Listen, dove, why don't you give Zachary Speller a call and invite him along as well. It might be better coming from you than if it were me asking him along. We met earlier today and I'm not altogether convinced that we left each other on the best of terms. What do you think?"

Now it was Cynthia's turn to smile. After a short pause, she continued. "I think your convoluted syntax is confusing you more than you know. And I also think that you two old boys will have to learn to play well together."

Trevor had of a certainty rolled his eyes. Cynthia could see him masking his incredulity. "We two *old boys* are just getting to know each other. You might even have an advantage in that regard, darling. Seeing as how you'd have considerably less to prove... in a pissing contest! And as for my syntax—"

"Well la, di, da!" she interrupted. "If that's all there is to this little contest, I am definitely not impressed. Nor am I convinced that either of you will measure up, if it comes to that, since I am sure I've far less to prove with respect to my poetry than either of you. So there!" She hurried on though, before he had the chance to take offense at her umbrage and interrupt her flow of thought. "Now leave me to ring up Sir Speller, because I need to go get dressed.

Oh, and you'll have to chaperone Anika through the evening, because I've a feeling she'd like to make an appearance at this soiree." Cynthia finally put the phone down and paused before the mirror to explore her petite but curvaceous body admiringly. Deciding that her fine form was virtually unblemished, she dried the hard-to-reach bits and banished her misgivings about Trevor far away until they were 'buried deep in the next valley glades.' "If only he were a good sot, she said smiling her most precocious smile at herself as if she'd just had a sudden whimsical need to preview her dimples, "but he's not, and there's the rub-a-dub-dub."

A rich baritone voice spoke up from behind her.

"Who was that on the phone?"

"Nobody important."

"Not a good sot?"

"Dry as a martini. Shaken, but not stirred."

"Oh, you mean Upton? If not a sot, at least besotted."

This was met with a long stare. "Oh you're good." Cynthia turned from where she'd been gazing in the mirror at Zack's reflection. He had come up to stand behind her.

"He's good too. I'd hazard that much," said Zack just putting his bathrobe on after having finished his shower while Cynthia had answered the telephone. "He's just not a sot, and there's the real rub. Speaking of which, didn't you want a back rub this afternoon? You know I was a masseuse in one of my many past lives."

"No time for that, I'm afraid," said Cynthia, "We've got reservations at seven o'clock, but I have something else you could turn your considerable... attention, towards."

"I can be very attentive," he replied as Cynthia pushed him towards the bedroom.

"You've a proven record. Ten minutes is all we have. So get ready to put the 'ten' in 'attention' because Trevor will be here just before six. If you're still busily dressing at that time, all our attention will be reduced to plain old unsatisfying... tension."

"We'll need another shower," he added. By now his strong arms were holding her lithesome body in a firm but sensuous embrace.

He quickly cast aside her towel, tracing her curves softly with the back of his hand. Soon his nimble fingers were digging into her thighs in a deep massage that enlivened her while also stimulating her desire. She felt the warmth and vigour of his fingers, and sensed his masseuse comment had been on the mark. Meanwhile his full ardent lips and penetrating tongue had begun to prove that spoken eloquence was not their only virtue.

She kept her hands busy as well, because she agreed with the Beatle's white album philosophy that happiness is a warm gun. The two of them really had nowhere else to go, but up... and down. So they spent the next ten minutes of passion triggering a celebratory feast of the flesh that—at least for these two poetic ambassador hopefuls—would prove much more memorable than even the most lavish ten-course meal at the most opulent of restaurants. Still, they both agreed—after first getting to it, then putting a fine finish on it—that there was something to be said for basking in the afterglow. Though neither of them were thinking of the restaurant at the time, either.

Still later, they both agreed that an equally celebratory, albeit entirely different feast—a feast of friends may be a reasonably good way to sate one's appetite, grown so large through such avid attention... to detail.

"The *Afterglow* at 7 it is then," Zack whispered at last as he stood in the hall outside her apartment, peeking through her door, held slightly ajar—purely for discrete conversational purposes. It was just half past four.

"I'll be the one with the pleasant tingle in my summer place. Don't be late again or I might not let you in." Cynthia closed the door a smidgeon more, as if to deceive him into thinking she was speaking literally. Nevertheless, he seemed to sense she was not talking about a cabin in cottage country. Nor was he particularly worried about not being able to get her heart out from behind what the cerebral Beatle called "that locked door."

"You have the best lines, Davey," he whispered. "Now remember, don't make strange."

"Have we met? I could swear I've seen you somewhere before. What's your sign?"

"I think not—unless I lose myself in it."

"Such an attention span, so self-referential. But what a valuable loss... "it" sometimes proves 'to be.'"

"Other times it proves 'not to be'—and that is the noble, if tragic question."

"Oh go home. You're nothing to me. Nothing but a member of the fallen aristocracy... now that's a thought to lose oneself in, isn't it?

And with a withering look Cynthia could read all too well, Zack spun about on his heel and left. His timeline was tight, and Trevor was due to pick up Cynthia in a couple of hours. Time prevented him from going all the way to West Vancouver (although it had not prevented him from going all the way with Cynthia—twice, he thought fondly). He would have to change for dinner in his downtown loft.

Back in her apartment, she crafted a terse but timely text to Anika. *Time for you to meet the two men I've talked to you about. The Afterglow. Tonight. 7pm. Reservations under the Upton party. I'm dressed to kill. Don't be outdone. And... please prepare a congratulatory toast.*

That done, Cynthia waited for the reply and turned her attention to her décolletage... then to dressing so as to best accentuate it. She found that the golden punch of her little Chanel Coco Crush earrings set off her flushed complexion quite nicely. They also provided a fine contrast with her form-fitting off the shoulder Versace black leather dress and her inexpensive, but stylish Bakers gold yellow pumps. She paused but for a moment to retrieve her most eye-catching purse—a Tory Burch envelope clutch in pebbled patent leather. By the time she put the final touches on her look, it was a quarter of six. Just enough time for perfume and a poem. She spritzed a cloud of Angel and sashayed through the air of perfume. Her iconic waif-like image gazed back at her from the mirror.

Taking out her compact cassette, she pushed record and went to work on her portfolio. "Two long roads to the town took ten days to go down. Both held views one would choose to enjoy and peruse. *Note to self: Alexandrines may be best when centered with a chiasmus, but avoid sing-song rhythms by keeping the monosyllables down to a minimum and avoiding unnecessary internal rhyme..."*

Then she listened to the opening two Alexandrines she'd written, and began a small revision that she added at the end of her personal addendum.

"This three fortnights' intent, twice told through different hearts, raised our girl's discernment, to satisfy her arts. But sober second thought, the child of borrowed time, swore never to be caught, entangled by her vine, or be heartbroken in a plot buried within the spine. Deeper thoughts than their sharp minds, shine like stars in her night, seduction's children tend to lose their sense of fight. In their ways and their cares—waters to be troubled—one sees loads one must bear, cards who must be shuffled. Turning and returning to old familiar ways, their hearts within them burning, they must forsake their plays. Ill-equipped to give up one become so dear to them, their mettle they'll mistake and their lanterns they'll not trim. This girl's not to love bent, nor will she e'er be tamed. This moonlit night's intent? That desire be inflamed."

Cynthia was halfway through listening over her practice session—a mere rough sketch outlining her ambition—when she heard the doorbell. She quickly checked the time, and was surprised to see it had edged towards a quarter after six. She popped her wallet, her compact, some cash and her cassette into her clutch and walked over to the door, knocking her knuckles against it with two precise raps.

"Who's there?" came the quick retort as Trevor's voice sounded on the other side of the door.

Cynthia countered the banal straight man's line with one curt pronoun: "She."

"She who?"

Opening the door to reveal his present, she emerged as Trevor backed away to make space for her, whistling sharply at her stunning entrance of an exit. With a measured quickness borne out of studied and steady alacrity, Cynthia sarcastically replied to the role he'd been relegated to (raising a simpleton's question) at the same time as she locked the door behind her. "She who loves knock-knock jokes just about as much as she loves to be kept waiting—but not as much as she loves to be obeyed."

Dimly aware that he'd just doubled down on what he misperceived to be a self-dug hole, Trevor thought he should probably just say nothing now, which he thought worked rather well as a silent 'oh wow' reaction to her knockout of an ensemble, but which actually further entrenched his role in their relationship as a submissive. "If I'd known you were going to dress like that, I'd have put the Hummer into four-wheel-drive and driven over all the other vehicles ahead of me in the traffic jam in my hurry to get here on time."

"Move along big fellow, there's nothing to see here."

"That flimsy argument sure won't hold under a cross."

"In the immortal words of Jim Croce then, 'I can't hang upon the lover's cross for you.'"

"Pretzel logic," he replied.

"A good title for Becker and Fagen," she countered. Then she and Trevor left the building before anybody mistook them as having been beamed in from the Seventies.

Trevor's loud red beast was at the curb, and since they were already going late for their reservation at the *Afterglow,* he set about proving to Cynthia that the only further delay in their plans would be gratification.

Anika Cervantes and Zack Speller were already there, waiting at the table with the others, when Trevor and Cynthia arrived. To most of the less than discerning guests, and even to the gracious host, the sometime oblivious Trevor Upton himself, Mr. Zachary Speller was meeting Ms. Cynthia Davison for the very first time. Her sister did her level best not to disabuse anyone of this assumption. She was the only real ingénue in the group, for aside from the deviltries Cynthia had set loose upon her concerning the two competitors against whom she was vying for the distinction of poetic ambassador, Anika herself had no personal experience with either man, or with any of the others at the table, all of whom she could only assume were close friends of Trevor (Cynthia had actually texted her as much). A lively conversation was in progress, and so far everyone was playing at nice.

The evening would prove to as interesting as it was incipient. It was as if a group of temperamental artists had assembled to appraise and laud a new triptych, whose form, content and texture were to be incorporated as the basis for an upcoming feature film. Yet all were acutely aware that this particular living, breathing triptych could not remain intact; and in fact, only one of the three panels would survive to receive international acclaim. Of course, it would not take a very bright fly on the wall of that gathering to figure out that the only pictures these people painted were with words—a commodity that film-makers consider to be of relatively little value except to writers, publishers and public relations brokers. As the hour edged towards 7pm and the chatter around the table grew louder, Anika paid close attention to all of the conversations around her at once, a skill she was grateful that her training as a teacher had fine-honed. It became evident from what she heard that there were some among the guests with definite agendas, both concerning one another and the human 'triptych' ZG had created by having short-listed the three contenders being celebrated tonight. Outside, dark clouds had begun to gather, brood, and threaten rain; but there in the Afterglow, at the best window table with the killer view that overlooked Vancouver's night lights and the mountains of the North Shore off in the distance, all was froth and frivolity. For the moment.

Seven

SO MANY COURSES, SO LITTLE TIME

Like Ricky Nelson's now-famous garden party, each of the guests who arrived at the Afterglow on that stormy evening to kick off October, and officially congratulate the three talented ZG conscripts, was out to please or tease somebody. The 21st Winter Olympics held earlier that year in Vancouver were a distant memory, but only one contender would emerge from this competition and take the ZG Ambassador's podium. The truth about who wished to please or taunt and torment who at this table—if this truth was made clear at all—would only emerge by degrees (nor does the mere fact of possessing a degree guarantee one would recognize any truth at all, even if it did deign to divulge its secrets at a dinner party). Cynthia arrived fashionably late and dressed like a diva with the host, and Trevor himself was eager to enact his role as chaperone for her equally chic sister. Anika—always out to surpass Cynthia's considerable charms but reluctant to be overtly seen doing so—wore a stunning half-sleeve lace maxi-dress, cut discretely as far up the front as propriety allowed (for those rare occasions when on a whim she might wish to reveal her strong, shapely, well-tanned quads). The dress included various tones of forest green (and—through envy of her selection—the other women in the restaurant all turned that colour, although their dresses were as varied and distinctively enamouring as the ease with which a Tiffany twisted mind moves from one topic to another—in Speller's view of those dresses anyway). Zack was on point. He quickly complimented Anika on how well her crystal rhinestone earrings complemented what he called her "tiger dress".

"Why, Mr. Speller," Anika smiled casually, looking up admiringly at him. "I'll have to give you the benefit of the doubtful compliment, since I cannot begin to guess your reference. I mean, aside from the fact that it somehow relates to my attire, of course."

"But surely as an English teacher you must know Blake? (for she'd confided her profession to him during their short conversation, immediately upon her arrival, after he'd recognized her by how strikingly identical she and her sister's petite but statuesque looks really were—you could scarcely tell them apart!)

She paused, momentarily lost in thought, while appearing on the surface as placid and meek as the subject of the companion piece *to* Blake's Tiger poem (something that came naturally to her). But Trevor noticed she had flushed at Zack's incredulous tone and he broke in at once, overly conscious of his role as chaperone— and still distrustful of Speller's virtue—to ask Anika if she'd met the other "fearful symmetry" at the table. He proceeded to introduce her to Miranda and Celeste Sung, but not before he swung his verbal axe to curtail what he perceived as a rather feeble foray initiated by his 'hale fellow well met' competitor (thereby giving Zack a testy token of his intent, and suggesting by the way that he'd be happy to do more than wrangle with words should Speller decide to put him to the test): "If you mistake the forests of the night for the trees of conquest, then it's a sure sign that you're not out of the woods yet... and you might not even be burning that brightly, either, Speller."

Swinging around from where Zack had seated himself on Cynthia's left, he took out the seat immediately to her right, and offered it to Anika. She declined, whereupon he took it himself. Anika then sat down beside him, just to his right, in the space between Upton and Celeste Sung. Trevor and Anika became engaged in an animated conversation about art and the appetizers that had recently appeared on the table in front of them, the latter proving to be an all-consuming passion of Anika's. Composing herself while reluctantly turning the conversation from pastries towards Pulitzer prize-winning poets, Anika secretly held fast to her first impressions, forging unforeseen alliances within the furnace that was her brain. Meanwhile, over to her right, more than mildly amused at what she had overheard of the peevish exchange that had just gone on between the two men, Celeste toyed with a delicately battered shrimp. Noticing a momentary lull in the exchange between Anika and their principled host, she made an impromptu decision and leaned in towards Anika, whispering conspiratorially behind her hand.

"What do you bet that one is a member of the Well Hung Dynasty?" She nodded in the general direction of Trevor Upton, but she could just as easily have been indicating Zack Speller, since he was located in the same vicinity of her nod.

First there had been the remark Speller had made, implying she had not recognized his oblique allusion to Blake. Naturally, she had. Nevertheless, she had elected to redden slightly rather than evince any awareness of his reference. Modesty prevailed. This choice was made decidedly, stemming more from her shy awareness of his attention, and from her desire to appear less acute than her sister, than from any false embarrassment over shortcomings of her own. Now after this crude comment as to Upton's or Speller's possible prowess coming from Celeste Sung, she was nearly as crimson as the table cloth. Was Ms. Sung playing a guessing game, trying to tease out her thoughts? Such questions invariably left Anika puzzled.

Anika smiled at Celeste, hoping Trevor would rescue her again. But she could see out of the corner of her left eye that he was having a dirty little dialogue of his own with her sister. At least she assumed it was smutty, since she'd overheard a few phrases, and the words 'clandestine' and 'lover' stood out prominently among them. No rescue seemed imminent, so she'd have to soldier on. Celeste was pillaging the shrimp again, looking expectantly at her. Anika smiled, and began to absently play with her earrings. She too held her up her hand as a shield, and in hushed tones nobody would hear, she offered Celeste a ball-breaking bon mot to bond over. "Neither of them probably has the stones that can even come close to comparing with *these* rhinestones," she whispered with porcelain precision.

Celeste's musical laughter percolated pleasingly, more refreshing to her hearers than freshly ground and brewed coffee might have been to their taste buds (if they hadn't still been sipping wine). Anika merely looked on with her cryptic half-smile, as clear as an insoluble puzzle, while her companion's fettle frothed away with more bubbly than an overflowing glass of champagne. Most of the others had looked up from enjoying their appetizers and conversation to see who had played the latest trick on whom. Trevor, Cynthia and Zack alone seemed not to have noticed. They remained completely engrossed in their own repartee. Finally, after a few meaningful inquisitive looks, Celeste made it clear by a shrug of her shoulders and a scrunch of her face—which wore this mask of mock bewilderment so well she seemed almost to have been born with it—that there was nothing else for them to do but to dismiss her as slightly deranged, or at the very least quirky. And now it was Anika's turn to giggle... a tiny bit—at having put Celeste into this awkward position.

Here she was once again, Anika thought self-reflectively, winnowing the field of competitors for the object of her sister's affection. Cynthia could thank her later. As Eddie, who had seated himself just the other side of Celeste, diverted her attention with some brilliant (or so he thought) insights on the latest reader-response theories, and on his own lamentable failure to make the shortlist, Anika glanced over to where Zack now sat commiserating with Heidi (at his immediate left) over *her* not having been shortlisted. Anika overheard him urging her to confide in Cynthia, who happened to be occupied at that exact moment, suggesting Trevor might encourage Eddie about what not being shortlisted had saved him from having to do. There was a momentary lull in the other talk around the table as this discussion turned portentously towards the impending portfolio.

Anika decided it was time for a diversion, and just at that moment the Dom Pérignon arrived at the table. She promptly stood and made peremptory preparations with her customary poise. The appetizer trays had just been cleared away, so she had one less distraction, and she used her spoon to tinkle the crystal glass in front of her, thereby signaling her intention to address the entire table. All eyes turned her way. She cleared her throat, took a second or two to compose herself once again, and began in tones reflective of the utmost delicacy and decorum to prepare the table in the presence of her 'anime'—a term she frequently, if discretely, used to refer to any group assembled to listen to her speak (for Anika bolstered her public speaking persona by imagining her audience was comprised exclusively of stolid but harmless characters from some Sailor Moon type of Japanimation). Cynthia had asked her to be rather deliberate about her own experiences with ZG and give as generic an overview of their competition as she could. Anika felt confident her speech would please and pique her sister. The sisters had inherited a sibling rivalry from their mother that was both epic and—fortunately for their friendship amusing to each of them— perhaps more so to Cynthia, truth be told (however, tonight was not about the legacy of their mother Melanie and *her* twin sister, their Aunt Jill). The English teacher in her came to the fore, and Anika began to speak.

"If you will each pour a glass of champagne we'll begin the toasts." Anika waited until each glass had been filled, then she spoke again. "There has been some talk among us, especially by those honoured enough to have taken part in the ZG interview process, about the extent to which a kind of publish or perish mentality is primarily influential when ZG considers shortlisting its applicants. There is really no other way to characterize such an emphasis than to state unequivocally that it is a quasi-militaristic ethos, no different from the typical flight or fight response. Strategies like this devolve into a survival of the fittest ideology. Such manipulation is anathema to me, and I had to discover for myself whether or

The Poetic Ambassador

not it is was the overarching principle behind this competition. So when I first became aware that my sister was in contention for this prestigious award, I took the earliest opportunity to find out whether or not this ideology was the sole basis for inclusion. I contacted ZG in late September, and they referred me to Ms. Felicity Traviss. She at once assured me not only that she was exclusively responsible for conducting the interviews and ultimately determining who would make it onto the shortlist, but also that her criteria was based as much on personality, intellectual aptitude and general well-roundedness as it was on the quality, creative depth and traditional excellence of the poetry considered as compatible with ZG standards. I understand that there are others here tonight who also applied alongside these three successful candidates whom we now celebrate. Please accept my assurance that you are in a very select group, despite not having been chosen. I'd also like to offer my affirmation that the standards are indeed high and so competitive as to practically preclude the type of exclusivity and parochial preferences common within most publishing circles. Please join with me in raising a toast to all the poets here, and particularly to these three nominees who are competing for the enviable title of ZG Poetic Ambassador!" At this point, she raised her glass, held it outstretched toward the center of the table, and concluded with a terse salute, "May the best man or woman emerge victorious." Each of her sailor moon clones followed suit, and they all drank a solemn toast to the triumphant trio.

The second course had not yet arrived, and Miranda Sung felt like having a little fun at Trevor's expense. Every bit as minxy (but not nearly so promiscuous) as her sister Celeste, Miranda eased her tall, lanky body out of her chair, casually flipped aside her majestic black mane, and smiled knowingly at Kern Jacks, who was seated just to her left. Then she adopted a whimsical attitude to modulate her husky stage whisper, while raising her voice to a level just loud enough so that everyone had to strain to hear, and thereby upping the ante on artful elegance. Turning the tables on Anika's solemn tone, and moving the momentum mirthfully from toast to roast,

Miranda spilled a little froth into everyone's ears. "Kern knows Trevor never met a women he couldn't handle—as long as he has his trusty oven mitts! Do dish, Trevor, darling. How many kooks are in your kitchen now? Don't worry girls, he's probably got that timer already set, along with the temperature. Just don't open that oven door too many times, Trevor, because it may well be that, like your poetry, the pastry may well fall short of expectations." Before she resumed her seat, Miranda raised a glass and once again flashed her incomparable smile as if in accompaniment to her teasingly conceived send-off finale: "Diplomatic derring-do, like a line of pure haiku, is all I wish for one of you. But since ambassadors three there simply cannot be, subtracting two men leaves she... who must be obeyed, of course. Listen up, boys!"

Looking every bit as amused as everyone else was by this culinary cut up, Cynthia raised a glass to clink with Trevor who was busy making a show of enjoying his ex's flamboyant send-up. Zack barely concealed a scowl that crossed his face as a summer storm glowers across the sky and is gone. He raised his glass along with everyone else, his smile reasserting itself with the warmth of the sun breaking temporarily through scattering thunderclouds to resume command of a momentarily dismal day. Cynthia was already sipping her champagne. On the surface, demure and distracted. Inwardly, she despised Miranda for her evident history with Trevor. She glanced over at their host. He was flashing his pearly whites across at Miranda like a painted billboard advertising pleasure on the beach in a bathing suit, while shark fins cut the surf with fine precision in the background. Miranda knew her nettling barb had done its work. Upton never smiled at a tease unless he was piqued. He had just clinked Anika's glass, and he raised his glass towards Miranda. She suspected that he was already formulating a witty come-back to her playful jibes.

Trevor did not disappoint. He got to his feet, hurriedly apologizing for the interruption, and assuring the group that he was happy to hear any other roasts that might arise should the spirit seize them. He went on to intimate that he would merely like the chance to respond to each one as it was shared. Then he spoke across the table directly to Miranda.

"Miranda Sung has got me dead to rights," he said, pausing to flash his own gravid grin. "But kitsch is best served raw like tartar steak." The oohs began, a kind of low background bass. And Monique and Heidi chimed in with a few good-natured sibilant hisses. Miranda returned Trevor's smile with her own, but it seemed hers had more bite. "Can't you feel the hot air as it ignites?" he continued. Jovial laughter spilled out freely now, and Miranda joined in with the rest, although her own laughter masked a closely guarded jealousy, for she had begun, in her own audacious way, to hate Cynthia for having come between her and Upton. Trevor went on, glancing over at the rival he had only just met this afternoon. "Zack and I are worried." He paused to emphasize the irony, and then continued his rhymed decasyllabic rebuttal, "Look at us shake."

Speller had enjoyed this little show and he found Trevor's versifying vitriol amusingly infantile. It was clear to him from the various reactions they had elicited that most of Trevor's friends were not only pleased he had attained this enviable distinction, they actually thought he had a chance. Especially Miranda, who he now felt must be harbouring some type of a crush. Heidi's hisses had been loudest for him, as she sat immediately to his left, and he wondered whether she might be openly hostile at not having been short-listed. There was no telling what covert malice might hide serpent-like under a warm smile. He decided he'd give them all a wide berth, but not before he'd fire an opening salvo of his own, just a moderate taste of his poetic agility. Passing up a chance like this was not in his nature. He tinkled his glass, and rose to his feet.

The table had quieted. Just then Miranda interrupted him before he could speak. She apologized, and said, "Excuse me, but you'd better do the math, gentlemen. Three's a crowd, and though a tie for second place is allowed, second won't do, so you boys are through!" The biggest laughter this time came from Monique Sloan and Heidi Egan. Celeste gazed intently at her sister. She was surprised at how scathing her patter was becoming, because Miranda had confided in her during the drive over tonight that she'd be glad to see Trevor win this competition. She wondered why her twin sister seemed to be goading him so publically. It was not like her to draw attention to herself.

Speller was still standing. He had decided that Miranda Sung might be jealous of Cynthia. That seemed to be the only way to account for what was rapidly becoming rather boorish behaviour. She was probably trying to set her up on a pedestal so that her former beau could triumph by toppling her should she become overconfident. Best ply another route. He quickly revised what he had intended to say, and began with his customary zeal. "We're right on course, desserts been baked. Don't force feed us, our thirst is slaked. We've all a shot at that brass ring, but it's not over till one of us sings. The fat lady's not ready just yet. This meal's not done, and we've just met." Here Zack paused, and looked directly at Miranda. Then he concluded with the following couplet: "Smiles, like wiles may love extort. Some must plead in lover's court."

Miranda Sung's broad smile beamed back at Zack. She held his gaze as she raised her glass. Celeste never took her eyes off her sister. Likewise, Anika riveted her eyes on Cynthia, who was meanwhile watching Speller intently. The rest of the table had all listened carefully and now they joined Zack in his toast. He simply smiled, and finished with a flourish. "To a feast of friends. May your laughter never end, but if the sun won't shine tomorrow, and the weather never mends, the rains will drown our sorrow. Here's a health to one more happy time, and an end to one more strangled rhyme. Cheers!" Everyone drank their glasses dry. Within a minute or so the second course—deep fried stuffed Hokkaido crab legs with a mixture of shrimp meat—was on the table, and everyone dug in ravenously.

Trevor was feeling especially stoked, and he was eager to give Speller his due. Cynthia pulled at his sleeve, just as he was about to rise to his feet again. She leaned in and whispered, "The art of the meal is knowing when not to steal... the show will onward go whether you abstain or fly solo." Heidi Egan was lifting a fork. Kern

Jacks was dropping a name. Eddie Paterson dabbed at his mouth. Celeste wondered why she came. The narrator teased them all out of thought, rudely intruding upon the feast. Anika sat stock still, watching her sister soothe the savage beast.

Miranda Sung took great pleasure in watching others enjoy their food, while turning to Kern with a mouthful herself, trying hard not to be rude. The waiter filled up their glass with water, and Anika leaned in to talk to Trevor. She made small talk, she asked of his tastes, of the books that he'd read, of the bulls that he'd faced. Bulls that he'd faced? Why surely that's forced. Upton's no matador, the rhythms off course. Anika's smile veils the wool she will pull over his eyes, as she ponders the lull in a dialogue that panders to wherefores and whys. Trevor's impressed that she's shooting the bull. Just like her twin, she is dyed in the wool. Outside the storm clouds' lowering rain portend something sinister like struggle and pain. Meanwhile, Zack chats up Heidi whose strength is going the distance no matter the length. Monique pours more bubbly, and washes down crab, but Kern prefers Chablis, and continues to blab on his latest conquest—the mid-term test. She wishes that he would just give it a rest. Still sits Celeste, bored by all that's predictably lame, and hoping the third course is some new type of game. Cynthia smiles as she sits by herself, alone in the crowd (are you sure that's allowed? Clichéd paradox; it sounds like a country church where everyone sits outside in the stands, listening to birds in a field full of birch, while Cinderella makes other plans). Alone in the crowd, a well-thumbed text on a shelf, concealing between the covers what she's never publicly avowed, that game is garnered by stealth and by wiles and with words that mint pelf. Poetic pelf, pliant, not bowed; high- or low-browed; the type that pleases a clever kind of crowd who look with disdain at those lesser than; at the patently vain who work for The Man. Cynthia looks at her sister, wondering who here most interests her; and sure she is complicit; happily so; aware that few can resist her.

Heidi gives Mira an earful of fun, and Zack livens their lives with a joke about dogs that can talk with candid precision. The poodles, he says are most finely attuned as to making the most of their vision. It stems from their breeding, he says with a smile. But don't take my word, it's all in their name. They have such elegance and ample style, and just like the Beatles, they hale from Liverpoodle, hence cometh their fame. Mira balks at the balmy banter, and reminds him to tell about their vision? Whereupon Zack regrets the encounter, and promptly plans an evasion. He quips that their sight is both tawdry and trite, and prays to the god of omission that his sins be forgot, or some such rot, and then spins a yarn on Confucius. Rescuing him from his estrogen horse faux pas by spilling her water in the general vicinity... of his groin, Cynthia is amused at his je ne sais quoi in the face of rich calamity... then he asks her to explain. She wonders if he's ready for another course, and he quite naturally affirms it's true. Noticing that he shows no remorse (for his senseless banter), she contemplates his soggy assets, too (and passes the decanter). Trevor makes a snide remark about the tardy waiter, whether or not there will be shark, and who has tasted alligator. As if he had a direct line to the tense kitchen or the cool cook, *all* the courses and the chilled wine come out at once, and judging by the look, presentation is perfection, and they taste in fact so fine that all the men had an occasion to eat and all the women submitted to their appetites, admitting that defeat was spectacular at the hands of so exquisite a chef. So it was, that after a glowing retribution, even Trevor conceded that it was indeed spectacular, and everyone begins to dine. Lively table talk ensued, and Anika alone became so engrossed with her meal, that she did not want to intrude... (Truth be told, Celeste held grudges, real or imagined, so she had turned to Eddie, and Trevor was otherwise occupied with Cynthia, leaving Anika alone with her feast!)

There were sautéed prawns with snow peas, followed by braised deluxe swallow nest with crab meat soup. Next came the main course, a Peking duck. Following the duck, came braised whole Abalone served over bok choy, braised in oyster sauce, along with sea cucumber and greens. There was steamed fresh whole fish, topped with scallions and ginger and flavored with soy sauce.

The Poetic Ambassador

Fit for royalty, along came the baked Lobsters with ginger, garlic, and green onion. As an appetizing aside, there was fried sticky rice with diced Chinese sausage. Also, for dessert there were Double Happiness cookies and Red Bean soup, thick and sweet with tapioca pearls.

Soon they were all enjoying their sumptuous meal, and the conversation quieted. Anika noticed she was not alone in having discovered that the lag time between the third course and the remaining courses—which all arrived at once—had left her with a sizeable appetite. She was, it must be said, ravenous. A good twenty minutes of uninterrupted eating passed before she realized she could not eat anything else. She looked up to see that the others had all pushed their plates away by now, and were scrutinizing her with an almost incredible interest, as if she were a hitherto unseen specimen being studied carefully under a microscope for signs of intelligence—or gorging techniques. How long had she been eating obliviously in front of them all? Cynthia was smiling cryptically at her. Did she have food on her face? She reached for her napkin and daubed at her cheeks. They were all laughing now. This was horrible. Surely she was dreaming. She pinched herself, and that was when she realized she was the victim of a cruel hoax. What an insolent narrator! Why had she wrecked their wonderful banquet by trotting out her doggerel to crap all over our evening with her paltry poetic excursion into inanity? Why was she now busily ruining the remains of the day? Who was this boor anyways? Who, indeed?

Anika's smile peeked shyly in the general direction of the table. As graciously as possible under the circumstances, she excused herself, pushed her seat away and stood up. It was just after 9:30, and the night was a lot younger than her timeless resolve to be quit of what had by now become a terribly tiresome scene. Once it became evident she was intent upon leaving, Cynthia walked her to the door, accompanying her into the covered breezeway just outside, and trying to get her to stay, to get to know Trevor a little more. She reminded her sister of how endorsing he had been, how protective and how gentlemanly. She also thanked Anika for having made such a pointed speech, and for having set so appropriate a tone for the evening with her toast. Cynthia went on to say that it had been a pity that petty Sung woman had sidetracked them with her taunts. They then exchanged some more private thoughts on Trevor and Zack, a good hearty laugh or two at Celeste's expense, and a promise to see each other soon. Finally, Cynthia urged her to take a ride home with Trevor. But she declined, suggesting that there would be plenty of time for her to get to know him later. She opted instead for a cab. Within a short while, she had left Cynthia to her new friends, most of whom were now readying to leave as well.

With a formal cordiality that was as businesslike as it was brusque, Zack offered to drive Cynthia home, and she acquiesced, telling Trevor they'd want an early start on the portfolio anyway. Agreeable in the wake of what he felt had been a largely success- ful evening, but still somewhat peeved that he had not been able to make a proper farewell to Anika, Trevor remained behind to bid adieu to his guests. He prepared to give Miranda a special send- off, and paid the bill. Zack had tried to get him to split it with him, but he had insisted, rather good-naturedly, on paying all of it him- self, suggesting that you could never out-give an Upton. Besides, he wanted to show how glad he was for the opportunity to share with his friends and colleagues how happy he was that they could join him in this celebration of their good fortune at having been short-listed for the ambassadorship. Soon he joined his guests in the breezeway.

Miranda was the first to thank him. She clasped his hand and drew herself into a close hug, taking a moment to whisper in his ear that she secretly hoped he would become the ZG Poetic Ambassador. Trevor returned her warm embrace and thanked her cordially for what he sincerely believed was her unselfish wishes for his success. The others took their turns and at last Heidi's petite form stood before him. She proffered her hand and smiled ingra- tiatingly as she said in deliberate tones that seemed to suggest he was already poetic ambassador that she could not have wished it to happen to a better man. The evening soon ended, with nothing much portended (unless you consider what happened to poor Anika or the unfortunate narrator, who is really far less of a hard-hearted doggerel bitch than she is framed to be—"Adieu! the fancy cannot cheat so well as she is fam'd to do").

Eight

AFTERGLOW AFTERMATH

Thunder rolled down the highway of the sky, triggered by the lightning, which spilled its bright yellow fire over a horizon awash with it. This vivid display hovered for mere seconds above the austere sliver of a fuchsia sunset in the evening sky. Trevor and his guests had enjoyed a panoramic perspective of the impending maelstrom from their glittering table behind the floor-to-ceiling plate glass windows of the *Afterglow*, though truth be told, they had scarcely noticed it because the events of the evening had held them rapt.

Now three hours later, the rains poured down as if in a deluge designed to drown Trevor's fancy dreams. No dream. It was a deluge. It was a good thing he had no faith in the Pathetic Fallacy (or maybe he should have had just a little). A potent lightning storm is always just that he maintained; never really an omen of disaster or the heavenly shows from literature of regal earthly conflicts wrought by spiritual forces from ethereal realms. Well, almost never.

Hastening his steps, as he walked away from the restaurant, he headed towards his Hummer in the parking garage. An instant later, he was wrapped up in leather, with cozy thoughts of rare verse. As he drove effortlessly through the heavy rain, and around the light traffic, and his inner speech slipped the surly bonds of earth to traverse the unknown universe, he gradually lost sight of his immediate surroundings just as he had done earlier that day while proceeding to ZG Burnaby until he put the truck in reverse and backed up. And over the neighbour's dog who had curled up and fallen asleep in the middle of his driveway. Trevor felt the bump, but it was not until after he had slid his Hummer into his double-wide garage and was just about to hit the door button, that he finally took notice of the now-dead animal.

His neighbours had always been friendly and inviting, but they had never been too careful about their pet, an aging Beagle who had frequently wandered about Trevor's yard a little too much to suit him. Far too much for its own good, or at least that was what Trevor had always thought. And now look what had happened. How was he going to explain not having seen the dog lying there?

God alone knows (and as with doctrines like predestination or the divine right of kings, he seems sworn to secrecy) how many times the Uppal's had invited him over for dinner. Far too many times to count. He had not intended to, but he supposed he had gained a bit of a reputation as being snobbish. He had declined every single invitation, almost always with the same excuse. He was in the middle of a huge writing project, and it consumed all of his time and attention. Now, standing at the neighbour's front door, drenched with the heavy rain, with their dead dog in his arms, Trevor fully expected them to take out all of their heretofore invisible and self-contained fury on him (he had previously heard but not seen the results of several loud albeit muted yelling bouts coming from within the walls of the house). Now surely Paul Uppal would lambast him for his dereliction. But his neighbours were always friendly. Maybe they would understand. Blame it on the storm. What an ignoble ending to an otherwise amazing day.

The evening had been splendid. Cynthia was ebullient. His friends had offered congratulations all around for their great opportunity, reminding him what an outstanding achievement he had made by securing the chance to become ZG Poetic Ambassador. Even Speller fit in so well, except for that incident over Blake between him and Anika. And even Miranda had come round to intimate that she still had feelings for him and wanted him to win. But most surprising of all, Zack had actually turned out to be a reasonably good fellow, offering to give Cynthia a ride home, and even offering to pay part of the bill. They had been able to get past all those previous unpleasant feelings arising from their conversation at the fountain in front of ZG.

Where were those neighbours? The dog was getting heavy. Maybe he should just leave him on their doorstep. They did not seem to be home. The evening was turning out for the worst. He was soaked. Unlike Professor Belton, this was one old dog he wished he had never met.

Zack had actually seemed genuinely glad to have been invited, and was really quite an affable guest. Cynthia and he hadn't seemed to have hit it off all that well, but unexpectedly she had accepted his offer of a lift anyway. If she could put herself out like that, he would definitely try to give Zack another opportunity to prove himself a good sport. But this old dog here was out of second chances. He rang the doorbell one more time. There seemed to be some activity. He thought he heard noises. Not since he'd let the parakeet out of its cage on his twelfth birthday had he felt so nervous. Mom had refused to speak with him for a week then, even after the bird had flown back into the house a day later. But now the Uppal's dog was dead, and his day of reckoning had come. Or had it? The dog had been old, exceedingly old—maybe even sick and old. He had been quite sick lately. Maybe he had died of natural causes and wound up in a heap on his driveway. His neighbours were taking too long. Maybe they had been in the shower. Or in bed. What if he had interrupted their lovemaking? This was sure to be an emotional scene.

The way ahead lay before him in verse, no in a hearse, where Paul Uppal in his rage was likely about to send him. No, get a hold on yourself, Trevor. Each reading of a line meant so much more than he could possibly wish to say, stood for so much more than he could possibly want to represent. He might need a lawyer to represent him now. Would his dad take the case? Clearly, it was time to write.

The spirit of the age seemed to be upon him. Or was it? Clearly he'd lost his focus. Paul Uppal, his neighbour, had suddenly answered the door, seen his loyal best friend in Trevor's arms, and now he had him by the throat, and was seemingly bent on wringing the life out of him. Paul's wife Shelley desperately attempted to restrain him. To pull the two of them apart. It was not working.

Shelley shouted at him, pulling away his arms, "Paul, Billie was old and sick. He probably couldn't get up. Listen Paul, let him go!" Meanwhile, the lifeless dog had fallen from Trevor's arms, and he was in danger of tripping over its soggy carcass. Still the rain kept pouring down. As Shelley finally succeeded in tearing Paul's hands away from Trevor's throat, he gasped for air, stumbled over the dog, then over his neighbour's short hedge, and finally onto their lawn where he rolled onto a bed of azaleas. He was already soaking wet from standing in the rain, and his good clothes appeared to be ruined; but now he was fast becoming even more drenched and dirty from rolling around on the wet lawn and their flower beds. Before Paul could dive on top of him, he jumped to his feet and cried out that he was available for dinner and a talk tomorrow night if they wished. He'd gladly pay for a new pet if they wanted. Surely it was time to right... a few wrongs, undo a few mistakes. Paul ordered him off their lawn, a curt command with which he only-too-readily complied. As he hurried home, he heard his irate neighbour yelling that he never wanted to see him near their house again.

Once inside his own house he stripped, threw his clothes in the hamper and headed for a hot shower, well aware that although he could wash the smell of the dog off of himself, he couldn't shake the image of the dead Beagle, whom he had not seen while backing up. An image of the dog, crushed like some abandoned ideal, would nevertheless remain under his wheels and forever imprinted on his brain. He tried to find consolation by reminding himself that Shelley Uppal had said he was old and sick. He probably wandered into his driveway sick to death in the rain; he likely could not have gotten up if he tried; and he may even have died long before Trevor had the rotten luck to have backed up over him. That must have been the way it had happened. He needed to believe this scenario.

Warm in his robe, he returned to his cozy study, where his answering machine sat ready to accept incoming messages. And one such message sat waiting... like a loyal and obedient friend. He tried to tear himself away from that morbid thought, and pulled out his notepad to jot down the particulars of the message which awaited him on the machine.

As he pressed the blinking button and listened to the musical lilt of the Southern accent that had mouthed so puzzling a rhyme as that which his answering machine now played, he couldn't put the Beagle's mangled body out of his mind. I've got to exercise my stop-thought technique, he decided. He had to move beyond the unfortunate incident. There would be time to make amends tomorrow. Surely Paul would relent. Now he must move beyond the whole sordid scene. What a horrid ending to a wonderful evening.

"Stop," he said to himself. And then he hit the rewind button and played the message one more time. Soon he began to get the sense that there would be much more to this portfolio assignment than he could ever have imagined:

> *Freer than Golden Butterflies may be*
> *is the Spirit whose wings have eyes to see.*
> *When Visions dark appear your way to cloud*
> *Art's fine frameless Age calls your fame out loud.*

Trevor replayed the message, scribbling out each line, until he had copied down both rhymed couplets. Although he did not recognize the voice, the verse held a special significance for him. Whoever wrote it had taken his signature image—the golden butterflies—in an unexpected direction, pointing him—or so it would seem—towards his inspiration. Yes, even towards a realization of that elusive ambition for international critical acclaim. But of such hopes he could only dream. So as the night rains beat down upon his window panes, he pursued those dreams while he travailed through his poetic labours. Not unlike a lawyer following a witness's argument with relentless passion, the tenacity of a cross-examiner's

The Poetic Ambassador

eye and avid attention to detail (and a mismatched modifier or two for just the right added touch of realism). He set about it, dressed—for inspiration—only in his togs, his toasty slippers, and his husky Lions sweater.

Sometime after 4am, Trevor was putting the finishing touches on his third sonnet—an elaborate and dark revelation of the tormented psyche inhabited by a key tragic figure from the world of William Shakespeare—when he was again reminded of the cryptic telephone message, and its portentous report of "Art's fine frameless Age." He concluded that if the Acts and Scenes of the theatrical world *frame* a drama for the stage, all but disappearing in the actual performance, then what a poor player the poet must make, should his stanzas divide not, in order to unite every reading, gilding by empathic association. Readers are embellishments to the poem, he thought. And their responses make it so much more than it could have been if it were left in the hands of the poet, who must use as many objective correlatives as is necessary to fully enhance and evoke the emotions and concepts that elicit such responsiveness. This is what he must do to prove his case for the ZG editors. Trevor came by his pretentions so naturally that he seldom recognized them for the condescending claptrap they really were. But he was as overtired as he was overeducated... and he may have just killed his neighbour's dog. So even if he was overcompensating, he often rationalized it away to assuage his guilt, by empathic association.

It almost seems redundant at this juncture to suggest that Trevor had also been influenced to a certain extent by his father's profession. As a crack criminal lawyer who had tried an untold number of cases, Trevor's father William could count his losses on one hand. Nor had he ever failed to smile satirically albeit beneficently at his son Trevor, impressing upon him—with his attorney-shark's teeth glistening below his dark shades in the cooling summer sun—the need to guess whether or not the legal system may best be seen as a parody of justice, an examination of virtue eclipsed by vice and avarice in a world run completely amok. And if the environmentalists were to be believed, the world would also soon be running completely out of breath and oxygen in the bargain. Invariably he would end his little diatribe with some Italian nugget (William liked to trot out his smattering of Italian in a catch phrase or two) such as "it is all ultimately a *dimostrazione per assurdo.*" Trevor's thoughts raced on past this prolix conundrum (and again regretfully over his neighbour's dog) straight into the comforting armature of his mother.

Fortunately for the young Mr. Upton, (especially considering his father's penchant for prolixity) his mother Imogene had a bigger impact upon him than his dad had, although were the truth to be told, both parents had been highly influential (especially upon his choice to take the job his father secured for him as a speechwriter in B.C. for the federal Conservative party). Mama Ginny taught high school English. She lived for syntax and symbolism, myth and metaphor. She liked 70s music. And she wrote traditional poetry. The trials and battles between his parents for his affection were epic, contentious, and ultimately one-sided, but God knows (just try to get it out of him) that father knows best rhetoric could not contend with mother knows better poetic come-backs, and in the final analysis the senior litigator (who was arguably a far more illustrious wordsmith) graciously conceded victory to the senior lecturer (not to the fairer sex as a whole, just to the fair one who lived more by the pen than any old Damocles sword).

This dreadful type of mindless narrative psychic—or was that psychotic—meandering was what came of staying up so late, thought Trevor, as he realized that he was desperately trying to avoid thinking of the poor Beagle and that it was high time that he headed for bed (the fact that both realizations hit him at the same time did not bode well for any attempt at a restful sleep). But he decided he had gotten a good start on his ZG portfolio, so he worked on his final *thought* for the day, writing down this penultimate line:

Corruption gains meaning when you omit the space in justice.

At the end of what had been a very long day, Upton turned out the light, reflecting on the tenuous link to logic that such aphoristic text-based lines like this probably held for his readers, who possibly interpret the space injustice as simply another way of speculating about 'gods behaving badly' (and in ways Marie Phillips never could have dreamed of in her frothy 2007 book of the same name). As his head hit the pillow he very slowly drifted off to sleep, musing wearily on a few of the many ways he could ensure that his poetry would secure a favourable verdict from ZG—and on how his apology would hopefully secure forgiveness from Paul and Shelley Uppal. He decided to leave the issue of 'filling in the gaps in justice' as a sign of corruption for the next day, when a clearer head would hopefully prevail, but as he drifted off, his mind's eye flashed on the horrible image of a dirty rain streaking down through the bright beams of his headlights as they hovered over the limp and lifeless form of his neighbour's dead dog.

After wondering aloud why he had written a sonnet on Macbeth tonight, since the curse of the Scottish play had clearly descended and he too had murdered sleep, he achingly concluded that the day had been a random miscellany of emotions, each successive experience more intense than the one that had come before. And then he thought of Wordsworth's *"The Rainbow"* and the natural piety with which the famous Romantic had wished his days to be bound, each to each. But try as he might, he could not recapture a sense of the overarching joy that poem usually elicited.

It would be some time before he could break the psychic bonds that threatened to engulf his poetic inspiration. When he finally fell into a troubled sleep, it was because he'd managed to sustain a sense of Cynthia, ravishing in her stunner of a leather dress, for at least a little longer than that pathetic picture of Billie the Beagle, the forlorn four-legged companion whom he had torn forever from the Uppal's lives.

So much for the Afterglow.

Nine

ON AND OFF COURSE

I n medieval res. That was where the old dog—as Professor Neil Belton insisted we call him—recommended that all contemporary stories should begin. And that is, he added emphatically, the message. Confusing admonitions like this invariably resolved themselves in some degree of clarity when one of us lowly peonies (as the old dog affectionately called his students) in the Honours MEng. Degree Thesis Summer Session Course of 2001 would offer him a suggestion or he would thrust upon us a point of clarification (academic bullying like his euphemistic malapropism for peons certainly did not endear us to the old dog or his 'new tricks'—as he was wont to call these clarifications). In this case, Roberto, the class misogynist, provided some rudimentary insight into the possibility that the original Latin might be "in medias res" instead of "in medieval res" (score one for the misogynist!). In a reply that was as cryptic as it was cunning, the old dog quipped that his point (which we would, he patronizingly assured us, soon find penetrating our thick skulls) was precisely that the media *is* in fact a medieval concept. Lady Malaprop herself could not have been more perversely obstinate or opaque. Outcries. Didn't the Latin mean "middle"? What a muddled little Latin adage this was proving to be. Then the synapses fired collectively and I knew, as surely as I know that my name by any other rosy ornamental would still smell like 'Trevor,' that the old dog was blending butchered Latin phraseology with an oblique allusion to a much-maligned slogan made famous by the late Marshall McLuhan. I no sooner raised my hand, than he called on me to share my suspicions. After I had dropped the famous media guru's name, Belton went on to say that McLuhan was himself a medium whose message ended when he died in 1980, on the last day of that fitful year. "As lectures go," he said, soldiering on past his fatalistic myopic conclusion with intrepid focus, "this one ranks a medium grade, but since most students like theirs rare, I'll give you the unexpurgated version" (from there it got racier than I'd care to divulge, and in the end it left us all wondering whether the wife of Bath had been unique as an iconoclast or just one woman among many who reflected the medieval spirit of the age and had no qualms about divulging explicit content in mixed company).

How could we have missed the edginess, the probity and the candor of his point? Maybe it was on account of all the interrelated libidinal digressions; but then again, maybe it was only the obliquity. The initial shock wore off once we finished shaking our heads over our failure to see this cleverly revamped Aristotelian strategy for the oblique McLuhanesque Trojan-horse style reference that it was intended to be seen as in the first place. The old dog had slyly gained entrance—he was within the walls of our minds, (was the media really as archaic as a guild?) and now with a mental agility that rivalled a Rushdie on psychotropic drugs, he was insinuating that perhaps it was not even Robert Frost after all, who was the first to poetically derogate 'walls' (although he certainly was the most interested in mending them, wasn't he?). "Centuries earlier, Chaucer reminds us in his Canterbury Tales," the old dog added—his tongue firmly in his cheek—"that pissing on a wall was a serious legal matter" (literate scholars know that the juxtaposition of this crass action merited the death sentence not at all—Chaucer was certainly not implying a causal connection despite how closely related the two concepts seem to be within his text). "Regardless," Belton intoned—passing beyond the Socratic phase of his lecture to further fan the flames of his pale fire—"humankind has perennially found ways to tear walls down, or cleverly found ways to render them inconsequential" (as with what the Greeks did to the Trojans). His peroration proceeded apace and, with its obscure but challenging conclusion, we soon caught a glimpse of the deconstructive difference in the old dog's cagey opening malapropism (not to mention the difference between "whizzing" to pass urine and "wheezing" while passing away from being executed for having gotten caught doing it against a wall). So, where to begin? And what kind of a wall to build? Are these not questions that have plagued the scholars throughout the ages? Such questions arose out of the lecture, like media moguls rise to take their rightful place as bricks in the wall of our collective psyche.

Then we all broke into groups to discuss the class.

Our study group concluded that it had to do with something about how the beginning of a story sets a context for your reader, and that context governs the content as surely as a medieval worldview governs the relationships guarded by the very walls built to establish and maintain those relationships in the first place. The old dog told us we had constructed a summary that was "half-truth, half tautology and half circular logic". When we complained that three halves don't make sense—or even a whole, he said that "if the whole was to be greater than the sum of its parts, sense had to take a back seat to incense, and that if we thought he was just being insensitive, we could take it up with the 'board of nonsense' executives or get a better idea." "Besides," he concluded, with a wave of his ridicule—in which he had previously deposited all of our essays—"not all that is medieval about beginning in the middle is even close to a beginning with a medieval action, ala Eco (or Dante or Chaucer), no matter how one conflates similar sounding terms, other malapropisms or interminable literature." He then assured us that "beginning with the end in sight means one's message must move from a start, beyond the middle ground of the medium, to a conclusion which conveyed the higher ground of the end, because what is a walled fortress high on a mountain for, he said, if not to be reached, renovated, read, and reread."

Elaborating upon the effects that the old dog's new tricks had on me would be premature—not to mention a potentially fatal excursion into the unseemly realm of highbrow didactics—simply because the newer those tricks get, the older they seem (and that is not such a bad thing, either—unlike some old music videos which do little but distract from their accompanying music... but I digress). Besides, I was so much smarter then (I'm dumber than that now... nothing like Byrds in flight!). Everyone has a past and a pedigree, replete with its own unique dark ages, and as a rule our future finds itself most often influenced by those dark ages—subliminally, at least. Although I've been known to swell "progress" with the winds of change (or churlish behaviour), I am generally speaking no exception to what I like to call the "dark ages rule," and if I am not then my last name doesn't really have its origins in the Old English word which came to signify a family who resides in the "Upper Farm". And of course it does. Nor is it exclusively from the name Upton that I derive my perspectives on those around me—however much connotations arising out of my nominal heritage may conspire to convince some that such a patrilineal factor is surely a significant vantage point from where one may discern my predilections towards peers, and others who occupy less meaningful positions within my sphere of influence. Being tall is also a factor. Especially considering the extent to which my viewpoint, as afforded from a height of approximately six foot, two inches must of necessity involve a certain, shall we say, "depth perception"—a personal trait which is heightened all that much more when you reflect upon, for example, my erstwhile involvement with the politics of honours English seminars and my ongoing professional pursuits in the publishing of poetry, not to mention my occasional profession as a political speechwriter.

Born on the 15th of November 1979 in Steveston BC to Ginny and William Upton, I learned at an early age to argue, debate and pontificate mostly from my father, who was an extraordinary lawyer and a card-carrying member of the federal Conservative party. I, myself, joined the Conservative Youth in 1997 at age 18, the same year that the movie *Titanic* was released to considerable public acclaim. My academic career led me into Honours English, and I've been writing and publishing my poetry professionally and my prose politically ever since.

Needless to say, the old dog's new tricks gave me many heuristic tools, most of which I've found increasingly useful while navigating the high seas of life. Digressions into wordplay for its own sake and often at the expense of logical continuity may be a flaw I come by honestly, but I'm not above breaking the flaw once in a while if there is an end in sight, and a means to assist those too blind to see through the walls obstructing relationships designed to inform that sighted end exactly how its peerless poesies may be best understood.

So, through a glass darkly we peer, or so I heard some menial martyr once said. Pressing forward until we pass permeably through the pane to penetrate a vision so fine it may well be a mystery shrouded in the misty moors of time, we admit the ghosts of hearsay about lectures past still ringing like evening vespers in our ears (to even out the cost of admission, all the while admitting nothing less than the thoughts that you, my clever readers, now perceive as having arisen out of this dark matter Trevor chooses to include as previous experience for his poetic 'palimpsest' only just beginning to emerge) have held us rapt or if not spellbound, at least somewhat intrigued. Would you agree that his experience is somewhat more derivative—only in the sense that it reveals a little of the extent to which academics influenced the nature and eccentricities of Trevor's formative stages of life—than say Zack's gamey gambits with Pamela or his rough and ready reference to the Trope? What's that you say? Zack is arguably as derivative? Perhaps, but only in the most mundane sense of that word. Something borrowed makes me blue; why not steal it outright? That is not to say that Trevor derives his style exclusively from the labyrinthine wisdom of learned professors leaning with prolix intensity upon their lecterns. Nor does it suggest that Zack alone puts the "luck" in pluck (or for that matter that I, your nosy narrator, am some type of generic "Prozac" clone—or any other type of an inhibitor designed to counter-act negative emotions). Actually, I am neither completely objective nor completely without ulterior objectives. But if you've begun to take sides, whether it be 'ProTrev,' 'ProZack,' or 'Pro-Thia' or whether you are overly influenced by what our more super-subtle characters like to call pro-professorial, over-prescribed ne'er-do-well narrative proscription, you might want to remember that both narrators and characters often push their own brand of Antihistamines, playfully known as 'Auntyhastwomeanings'—despite the lack of clarity and other equally questionable side effects, (because, as you'll see, our illustrious third lead character Cynthia has an Aunt Jill who is practically addicted to ambiguity—whether tastefully resolved, or left to its own erratic devices).

Nevertheless, you may also wish to remember that such a rush to judgement, while not recommended, probably stems from the textual cells you've already begun to construct—and examine carefully under your literary microscopes—out of your own mental images of these three lead characters, or from the solitary stellar example of narrator interference you are currently enduring (further research into these cells may yet unlock untold dynamic advances for humankind, or more pointedly, for your own understanding of how such advances and these narrative features of our rigorously conned prose are intertwined).

Prepare your portraits as you will. But be forewarned. These poetic heroes may well build themselves to flout (or deconstruct) the portraits you "paint" (or overtures you compose) of or for them during the course of this novel, wherein, as you no doubt have already deduced, you find several narrators (at whose true identities you may guess while—like our characters who know us better than you know yourselves—you hurl insults our way as if perturbed by having to drive slow in the fast lane because of a complex construction zone): Narrators such as myself, a quiet unassuming type who prefers to *give* occasionally as well as *take direction* from headstrong characters—many of whom suggest we narrators are overexposed.

Additionally, you are now fully involved with a novel wherein we narrators are, as has already become evident, likely to arise unexpectedly to pigment or shade our characters' illustrious personalities—or perhaps deface them, depending upon either your point of view, their own estimation, or our poetic licence.

Meanwhile, I've appeared here in somewhat of a snipingly Snape-like "Halloween" mask on this dark and stormy night of the reader's soul, among other reasons, so as to "egg you on" while you pursue your own 'lords and ladies of misrule' inquest. Mindful of your considerable expertise in several fields of study and the many years you have spent sailing upon the wild waves of interpersonal relationships, I wish now to relate that my career as one of the narrators you'll meet within this text is *made* (this ante has at least two meanings and just to sweeten the pot, all are to be taken at an about-face value) here in this prosaic passage not only in order to undeceive you of commonly held misperceptions about your role within the grand illusion that our "fortress" has come to represent, but also to expose a few of the other lively characters who inhabit and animate the textual 'Corpus Delicti' your reading must resuscitate in order to fully examine (did you actually think that your literary electro-microscopes were obsolete artefacts?).

After all, novels are really only dead words until you breathe new life into them through your reading. Don't be afraid to talk back to, or think around these characters. Otherwise you run the risk of letting them, or our narrators (among whom I number only one), impose their own values upon you. Then, when with a final flourish you frame your finished portrait—painted, filmed or reformed—that portrait will have acquired, by this time next year, the composition and attention to detail that comes only from the steady hand and deliberate touch of a seasoned artist whose eye for balancing perspective with just the right emphasis on characterization and meaning assures that the full artistic vision will have been achieved (or the book will be in the fire). Considering the fact that a raging fire already burns throughout the various conflicts, actions, and dialogues of the book, and that the 'eggs' I'm using to 'egg you on' will hatch an interpretive "phoenix" sure to arise from the ashes of its own textual pyre, you may find yourself getting a little lit up about this symbiotic bonfire of the humanities, alongside those who contend in the hopes of becoming an ambassador sometime before we are all form-fittingly attired, fresh from having attended—and, as one would-be ambassador will surely have it, fresh from celebrating—the grand finale, whether it be or seem to be.

So you see, we are seemingly yoked together in this shell game like some eponymous emperor of ice cream in a Wallace Stephens poem. Embarking with one another on a quest in a novel undergoing a shelf-life journey of "clinical" discovery through which there is no return from the end alluded to in the beginning, unless, of course, you advisedly reread, whereupon you might suspect, and rightly so, that the "uptown boy," the merest smattering of whose Honours English lecture kicked off this chapter, opines that since what was once only "discovery" will invariably compound interest to become "self-discovery" over time, and since this compounded term—so reflective of Solon's famous injunction involving the essential introspective exploration of one's own psyche, in addition to the more covert connotations of opening out something that is carefully hidden until the true influence of the adjectival lens so endemic of objective scientific detachment magnifies that yet unseen worth, as yet only hinted at prior to the present ponderous parenthetical pigmentation, comes to connote both the objectivity and disinterested realism brought to bear upon the subject of "individualism," itself a concept wrapped up in the indivisible cloak of "self-discovery," that quest must of necessity be fraught with subjectivity and distortion. However much Upton still opines that it ought to have read "cynical" discovery instead of "clinical," that is clearly beside the point.

That does not mean of course that Wallace Stevens is the ideal reader for this text, since he died in 1955 (a very good year, incidentally), well before most of the lead characters in it (but not all the narrators) were born. But because what these characters don't know—including that puzzling aforementioned injunction, obliquely alluded to above (namely, "know thyself") that most people, attribute to Socrates—might not only hurt them, it could actually make them keelhaul their loyal narrators, it is probably best that you promise not to divulge the denouement (since you've obviously read ahead if only to—unwisely—avoid this interminable chapter, and rest assured that in keeping the bounty under the hatch until you are sure of your final destination, you are doing it for the good of us all). But whatever you do, please don't let the narrators or even any of those ne'er-do-well main characters do all the talking. From what I've heard, you'll have no problem with that since you've no doubt been talking to yourself practically non-stop since you made it to the other side of that dark glass pane (What's that you say? You should know that only my characters are allowed to call me a pain!)

And all for the sake of elaborating upon a single Biblical allusion. St. Paul quite naturally deferred his dream (though some misguided optimists say that he is still living it!), but that does not mean we need follow his lead, knowing as we know we are known. Because time itself must go, and soon enough it will go... limp as a soft watch.

Farther along, you will have made up your minds about our characters strengths and weaknesses and about where you situate yourself in the context of those perspectives, both of which are a significant part of your own journey of self-discovery. Tensile strengths and weaknesses will emerge. And bridges will be built. Some may even end up being burned. Regardless, you may agree with me when I tell you that we have our work cut open for us. Keep those scalpels at a ready, because we're turning and returning back to the scene of the sublime, and now for the ridiculous: our characters would like to interject a question for your honour at this point (you're surely up to speed in your role as magistrate by now!).

The Poetic Ambassador

And yes, they've commissioned me to bring it up before you (but I won't litigate for you).

They're asking for your permission to treat the narrators as hostile. Rather than give them the last word, I'll simply request that, for the moment at least, you reserve judgement. Besides, not all narrators are created equal, though we all firmly believe in the equality of every individual, because nobody is above the flaw (ahem, especially the tragic variety, of course).

What mysteries yet await those of us who take the time to think about the clash of wills and poetic temperaments which are sure to arise when our two young male competitors clash for the elusive title of poetic ambassador, must give us pause. Especially when that stealthy steno we met in the first chapter—who may well have chosen to assume the name Pamela because she wished to portray, at least nominally, an unassailable moral rectitude associated with her namesake, a young servant central to the 1740 epistolary novel by Samuel Richardson named of course, *Pamela*—especially, as I say, when this stunning steno short-lists an unquestionably compelling female candidate for that honour. Yes, this is good reason to pause. Yet, for every Pamela there are surely dozens of Shamelas (with special thanks to Henry Fielding, one of the original judicial British satirists) who conspire and connive with wily cunning, and who will use every means at their disposal to secure their ambitious goals. Is our leading ZG lady a Shamela or a Pamela? Or is she a more unlikely but eminently likeable (she made me say that) contemporary alternative? Or will she break with all conventions to beg off their mores, borrowing only what she can use, or staling them entirely, as it suits her fancy? It remains for you to use your acumen to discover whether you agree with the sagacity of those astute readers who also scale the fortress along with you to peruse the pages of this circuitous text (present succinct chapter excluded of course!) and ascribe the motives—mercenary or altruistic—along with the intentions, ambitions, accidents and alliances of our three rivals.

Admittedly, the goal of becoming a poetic ambassador for the ZG Publishing House is common to them all, however much the means to that end will of course invariably vary (the truism that the only constant is change has some bearing here). And though some say variety is the spice of life, that banal cliché masks to generalize a far deeper truth. A truth our three aspiring ambassadors would do well to remember as they each embark upon this quest. *Variety is a course. It is a course to be consumed (like courses in a ten-course meal); a course to adapt (one must naturally always "chart" one's variety to suit circumstances, both outward—the weather or society, etc.—and inward—one's personality); a course to be followed (map out your journey, even if your journey is a person); and a course (sp?) to circulate or move swiftly—like blood—through one's veins (one need give no apologies for a pun that pithily points up an important truth).* Lest you think that this didactic digression pulls us off course, I have no recourse but to remind you that if you curse me for my cursory recursion, you may recount my recent cant given only as a rite of passage (did you read it only once and not quite get it? You might want to give it another go before you jump to the conclusion that my definition of variety is neither a customary observance nor a common practice—yet).

However, I can't recant without revisiting the course altogether and making a revision, which would probably result in another edition. Doing that would be as plausible in this narrator's eyes as if, say, Belton were to bereave himself of his Fool's cap and bells, and replace the opacity of his linguistic style with the concise, plain-spoken brusqueness of either myself or a trial witness who must, without obfuscation, come straight to the point (because the judge allowed him to be treated as hostile, perhaps). Are we off course or still just taking the scenic route? Have you come to appreciate my characters' appeal that you turn me into a hostile witness? If so, I am glad you find my characters appealing. If not, you may very well be the ideal reader for this text. Either way, you have vindicated my narrative strategy, and I applaud both your stamina and your linguistic expertise.

In addition to the fact that our aspirants—only now testing the limits of their adversarial range—share the same penchant for selecting their own course, the truism that variety inheres per se throughout that course comes to us from an old song by a band of river poets searching naivety (red herring—they're not R.E.M.) who suggest, and I'm paraphrasing here, that there are 'many ways up the mountain though the view from the top is still the same.' Perhaps the most intriguing feature of the paths each of our main characters take is the extent to which they intersect, and the ways that these characters' interactions influence their course, for good or for ill or for better or for worse. But don't go off half-cocked (not just because this is not a gun fight either). "Let me not to the marriage of true minds admit..." anything that may reveal an overly facile conclusion, or otherwise impede the self-actualizing process inherent within the development of these characters, either individually or collectively. And at my back I hear, not Time's winged chariot nor the ladies' last call in Eliot's Game of Chess; though you, patient reader, might wish that I had; but rather the emphatic insistence from our characters that the M-word must not be mentioned again, ever—unless it is within a performative context and for exclusively pecuniary purposes (our presumptively mendicant female lead made me say that as well).

Now if a person gets "hitched" for the money, what might that say about her morality? Should that union fail, what remains to be said about the emotional or psychological costs that accrue over the course of "lessons" about the aforementioned morality that she might learn? And how does a Cervantes come to be a Davison? Putting it in more general terms, one may well ask to what extent is one significantly changed by the position to which one aspires, or does that position carry with it the potential to be significantly changed by the aspirant? Shall we allow these characters to make or mar themselves as they see or fail to see what you as an arbiter of their taste must surely grasp, irrespective of the fact that their vision must of necessity change as their spirit—or the spirit of the age— moves them? If you as a reader plot to discern the true nature of either the characters or the intrusive narrators, you may find that they move you too.

Consider the price of such an admission a moving fee. Of course such an admission would constitute a constative utterance. One can only make such statements after the facts have all been weighed, the pages have all been turned (or burned) and a true or false value has then been determined and assigned. All of which assumes, of course, that our plot stays *on* course, (varied as that course may be) and that you are as true to your probative nature as these characters are to theirs. If so, we must agree that regardless of how heavy the petting gets, romance is heretofore exclusive—which is surely a malapropism for "explosive," a malapropism that someone who likes to take the lead as a character, and who derives her name from the moon goddess (who all lovers of myth know as Cynthia, and who will likely remain shrouded in mystery long after she seems about ready to finish her Frappuccino) somehow managed to have coerced me into blurting out (although you may have your doubts as to her sincerity in regards to how exclusive or explosive that romance might end up being, depending upon your perspective, and I urge you to suspend your disbelief until the moment of truth has arrived). Even if it is a bit of a heavy... hearted ploy. "Bear with me, my heart is in the coffin there with..." my treacherous characters, who not unlike Caesar himself would do practically anything for public acclaim (but don't take my word for it, you can see for yourself). Our main characters insist that hopeless romantics have no place in this fortress.

And they have scaled the walls once already. Now they are busying themselves with outdoing each other in pursuit of the perfect path forward from fortress down to their quayside cottage enclaves, "enfolding sunny spots of greenery" despite how much they each insist upon despising the impossible coloratura of the Romantics. Ah, head... strong and nubile (see there I meant to say "noble" but one character in particular—can you guess which one—likes to play with my... hood) characters like these have plenty of it, "head not hood." And if you give them their head like wild mustangs they'll bolt to be free of the bit. Good that their hearts vie for attention now and again. But they've grown weary of being made a public spectacle (by me, anyways). They'd rather be showing their stuff than being carved up by some 'thanks' giving turnkey who guards his fortress like a jailor lacking convicts, despite his frequent convictions. And do you see where this is going, now? They're out to make me into an unreliable narrator—a slight deviance from the truth which no self-possessed narrator will ever admit he is guilty of engendering, and that is precisely why you can be certain they are luffing us toward that ill wind. Merciful gods! What self-respecting narrator would so mangle and mix his metaphors were it not that the editor allows impudent characters to tease at a word or two here and there, until they've made a mockery of the narrative strategy. Hostile witness indeed! It's time we return to the scene of the perfect crime so that we might know the place for the first time.

Friendly reader, together my sometimes churlish characters and I, one of your more honest forthright narrators (pardon me while I take my tongue out of my cheek), appeal to your sophisticated sensibilities for the gracious gift of your skill, discernment and patience as we traverse what will, I affirm, be an uneasy but eventful and ultimately significant symbiosis. If none of us capitulate, romance itself may even quell resistance to find its way into the fart rest (stop it you bad Speller, you irascible rapscallion you!... surely you can see his impu—oh, you know what I mean) ...'fortress' is, of course, what I meant to say... fortress of solicitude for style, for poetic contentment, for composition, and for frequent, enjoyable, conspicuous public consumption (like good craft beer); but seriously, like Poe's *Masque of the Red Death*, this fortress has several rooms (you may call them chapters) and each provides opportunities to catalyze self-discovery. It is almost time to rejoin the action (still in media res, of course) and as you get ready to swing back into the rhythms of prose our narrators consider as most conducive to an affable and articulate representation of plot, character, context and content, bear in mind how closely to Nietzsche's definition of the Superman each lead character manages to come in the presentation of him- or herself throughout the context of their stories, actions and interactions.

It has been productive sharing our ideological banter with you (I meant to say "bent," but I'm being gonged up on again (You see what they're doing, don't you?). Au reservoir!

Don't flush just yet! (It doesn't take a defective to see that they just won't stop until I bid you all... and I'd bet some pared down prose (I might have some to spare!) you know what they almost inserted there. Even a narrator can go against tripe—unless the die is cast, as they say). They're just dying to have the last lien. And now I'm indebted to them for making us luff (I'm scrambling to keep up here, aren't you? Since when is the word for sneeze a cognate for "adieu" anyway?). Time to tack. Their last perversion of my prose was as inspired as a luffa is green! The wind is up. Let's sail out onto the open sea. That way if you feel a bit at sea, you'll be able to empathize with at least one of our characters who is about to experience his own sea change. He tried to get me to say "cool change" because he likes Little River Band, but I remained intransigent, because we'd already referenced that band earlier on if you picked up on the indirect direction (besides, I met him halfway with regards to the title of this chapter in the first place). I'd say, "Smooth sailing," but I've a feeling there is going to be some rough weather ahead for our would-be ambassadors. On the other side... of every coin is a tale ("told by an idiot, full of sound and fury")... and at this juncture, we'll have to part company with the bloody Thane of Cawdor to conclude that our tale signifies the transformative nature and beauty of indirect direction.

More than this will by now have met your watchful eye, my alert reader, for whom the media has, as of this chapter, become a medieval concept designed to perpetuate a divisive society (those who suspect I'm the old dog should look to their cynical credo of complete objectivity where they will find a tree underneath which lies a detached branch holding a single apple. It may not take a Sherlock to deduce, before too long, who I really am (and by considering this solitary image you should find an aphorism that must ultimately disclose my identity better than let us say Lear's shadow alone could tell the king who he really was, despite being a consummate

Fool!). Surely you will too, my puissant, scholarly patron of the poetic arts. You, too, will be able to reveal who I am. Then, siding with or turning against the characters on trial, you may concur with or reject their attempts to have you treat me as a hostile witness. And now, while I can, before I am once again bedazzled by buffoonery, I might just as well say, "Ciao, mio bello amico!" I am done with this witness!

Ten

FORMATIVE CONSIDERATIONS

Closed boardroom sessions like this are like the pillow talk of intimate lovers in a private embrace, and only active participants are privy to what is done and said. Okay, so it's not really an executive orgy in the boardroom (only somewhat less interesting, perhaps, depending upon your predilections), but you get what I mean (or you will soon savor its double meaning). Another analogy would be like the subtext of a narrator breaking into the action of a novel to pigeon-hole readers with not-too-subtle suggestions about characters and subplots, because this board meeting is designed to formulate the portfolio assignment foundation upon whose basis the work of the successful poetic ambassador will rest. Convention tells us that you better believe our board members would not allow any 'eavesdroppers' or eidetic flies on the wall listening to their embarrassing statements and covert whispers. But if they are to be understood clearly, these minor characters must be granted that lowest common denominator that we all share with the main characters—namely, humanity with all its strengths, weaknesses, pratfalls and pride.

All human distinctions, all forms of fame, infamy, notoriety or respectability (or any lack thereof) arise from customs and conventions. We flout these conventions at our own peril, and that is why, when we find ourselves reading that 'Rudy Sorensen's broad six foot three inch frame cast a long shadow over the boardroom as he strode confidently to the head of the table,' his frame and that size-able shadow are as much a part of the consensus of other board members, as they are a convention (the Quarterback, always tall and athletic, invariably inspires admiration among his followers). Obviously, Rudy knows his height, but his influence—the shadow—is as much a factor of his frame (not merely physical) as it is a feature of what each of the other board members respect or dislike in him; and it is also a feature of their choice to defer to his leadership or run against it. He frames his material carefully. And if the characters have decided what they need from each other—and that is largely a determinant of their individual natures, but also of what the others bring to the table—they are no less compelling for all the ways that you, friendly reader, complete the story of their ulterior motives.

Considering this—as you participate in the upcoming closed board meeting and as you break with or buttress tradition—don't forget to challenge and critically assess the ways that these characters follow or flout customs and conventions as they strive to find the best possible portfolio assignment for all three prospective Poetic Ambassadors. And I need not remind you to impose some approximation of your own standards that most closely aligns with each particular value system held by any given character. Or just enjoy the repartee. Choices arise and fall all around us, and we are all implicated, regardless of whether we fully appreciate the implications.

—◦《◉》◦—

All eight chairs had been filled, and Rudy's was the only vacant space left. He remained standing. He spent a minute or so watching the executive board as they carried on animated conversations. Off to Rudy's right, at the far end of the table, Rod and Norma chatted comfortably about the theatre; meanwhile, closer at hand, Nathan and Anne discussed Nate's favourite poetic genre, cowboy poetry. Immediately to his left, Stephanie looked over the dossier Misty had prepared on the short-listed candidates. Farther around, across the table from where Norma and Rod sat, Maureen filled Donavan's ear with the latest juicy gossip from the Tri-Cities Chamber of Commerce meetings. The only odd one out, old Cassie Ellis sat brooding alone at the far end of the table.

Despite the disparate conversational buzz, there was a heightened air of expectancy in the room, and a temporary hush had greeted Rudy's arrival. It had been a couple of months since the applications for the position of Poetic Ambassador had begun flooding in to ZG Holdings and during the whole of this long period of time, the board had been painstakingly reviewing the interviews for all applications. Now the field had been narrowed to three contenders. The purpose of the present meeting was to discuss the formal requirements and the time limit for the Poetry Portfolio, an assignment that would upon closer examination by the editorial staff, determine which applicant was to become the first ZG Poetic Ambassador.

The brooding dowager widow Cassie Ellis stood, and in her characteristic osteoporotic shuffle, hobbled around the table behind Donavan, Maureen and Stephanie until she came right up and caught Rudy's ear. Speaking in low, confidential tones, she reiterated her displeasure over the choice to shortlist young Zachary Speller.

"The radical views held by Mr. Speller, never mind his chequered past, are not in keeping with the mission and mandate of our Publishing House." At times of particular urgency, her low pitched voice would crack and fluke up or down an octave. "What would become of our House motto *Traditional Excellence—A Legacy for All* were such an unmeritorious rascal be allowed to publish his verse under the auspices of this distinguished House? I demand that his name be removed from the shortlist." As she hit her stride more than a few cautious glances flew towards the semi-private conference. Cassie expressed herself in the only manner she knew—forcible and passionate. Her occasionally faltering, but nonetheless weighty tones usually held sway with more than a few notable figures among those who made up the executive. However, Rudy was not budging on this issue. He had personally polled the entire board and found Cassie to be the sole dissenting member with respect to the eligibility of the young man in question.

"You reservations have been duly noted, Cassie," Rudy said, certain that she would not be placated easily. "Rigid protocols have been observed throughout the entire selection process, and there is nothing more to be said. Misty was a most thoroughgoing inquisitor. The candidates have now been determined. All that remains is for us to shape the ultimate poetic maze through which all of our candidates will imaginatively meander, as the case may be, in order for one of them to secure the editorial green light and a unanimous motion of executive approval to become the ZG Ambassador. Now if you will please be seated, I'd like to call this meeting to order."

Against her better judgement, the widow Ellis shuffled back and resumed her seat. This was not over yet, she thought to herself. Maze indeed. She already smelled the rat. His name was Speller. Then, she immediately set about contemplating how she might convince the board to frame an assignment which Speller would inevitably find impossible to successfully complete. The board was wilful and often somewhat arbitrary, but pressure could be brought to bear.

Nor was she alone in her secretive plot to disestablish the legitimacy of this young lad who had made so strong an impression on the majority of the board members. Nathan Balfour and Anne Morris both favoured Trevor Upton over the other two candidates and were covertly attempting to frame an assignment favourable to him as the Poetic Ambassador. The other contender, Cynthia Davison, was the popular candidate of choice for Maureen and Donavan. Only Rod, Norma, and Rudy appeared to be entirely objective in their assessments of the candidates' relative strengths and weaknesses.

Objectivity is an underestimated quality that depends entirely upon who or what becomes the object of one's affections. At least that's the exact thought Donavan Blake had at the precise moment that he first became enamoured with the oddly eccentric shape of Maureen's pendant hoop earrings. Maureen not only knew that there was a fish in the text, she also knew exactly who he was, and as she toyed with her earrings she speculated as to how she might best continue playing that fish.

Ultimately, when it came to the more serious business of to-night's proceedings, Rudy's opinion was the most decisive. Voting was done openly by a show of hands. As CEO, Rudy exercised the right to cast two votes, along with the power to veto anyone's vote he might select. His authority was binding and after the veto, he cast the final votes. Fortunately for the applicants, whose future history had a lot riding on the outcome of the evening's proceedings, he was at this moment entirely non-partisan.

Bang! Bang! The sound of Rudy's gavel punctuated the board-room conversation, with its rifle shot echoes virtually shooting down whatever diverse dying vestiges of spoken thought yet lingered. "Ladies and gentlemen," Rudy began, "we are in closed session. Will the secretary please open the meeting?"

Stephanie Nolan cleared her throat and raised her customary, warm, Southern drawl: "Speakers will call for the Quill and limit themselves to two minutes for the first half hour." A low murmur began. It ended abruptly with Norma Paterson securing the Quill.

"'Formal considerations' have been determined as our first order of business and I would like to submit that each assignment contain no fewer than six sonnets, three Haiku, two experimental free verse poems, and one lampoon."

There was some preliminary informal discussion among the executive officers at this point before Cassie Ellis called for the Quill. "The reasoning behind the choice of a lampoon needs to be explained. I would personally prefer one ode and one villanelle."

An animated discussion followed during which it became evident to all but the most hidebound conservatives that lampooning had gained so favourable a following among the general populace, that it resembled a trend. It was fast becoming commonplace so as to be almost tradition. Cassie still considered it as practically subversive.

"At the very least," Donavan maintained, "it deserves to be considered as a traditional verse form and should be seriously discussed for inclusion in the assignment." Donavan Blake's ensuing short but persuasive speech held sway: "Members of the Executive, some have said the lampoon is nothing more than a leech on the soul of poetry. I would remind those who follow this logic of the oft-heard adage—Imitation is the sincerest form of flattery. To lampoon a song or a verse is to elevate its status. We must be quick to remember that in some circles, poetry is a dying art form. Include the lampoon in this assignment, because it revivifies poetry; include the lampoon since by nature it is an added poetic emolument that endears itself to all poets; but most of all, include the lampoon because any poet worth his salt should be capable of eliciting a good belly laugh."

There followed a short debate, punctuated by Maureen Staples' customarily vitriolic outburst. Her vociferous derogation of the lampoon subsided with her calling it a "paltry, insipid, emaciated little dried up piece of dead doggerel wood." The executive listened politely to her vituperative diatribe and proceeded to include the lampoon in the assignment. Maureen toyed with her earrings in absent-minded disgust, while Donavan looked on with unfeigned interest. The boardroom business continued to steadily revolve around selection with all the natural alacrity of an evolutionary process, as if the final portfolio assignment was some spiral nebulae, trapped in a perpetually looping galaxy far, far away.

After three quarters of an hour, the tally of formal verse requirements included seven sonnets, four Haiku, one each of experimental free verse, a lampoon, a general free verse poem, a basic rhyming poem, a ballad, a villanelle, and an ode. Cinquains and Concrete verse had, along with a series of other lesser verse forms, been discussed and voted against. Rudy knew they still had to consider the time limit for the assignment, but he had other things on his mind.

Eleven

OBJECTIVITY ON THE WANE

Boardroom politics was never quite as simple as one expected. Rudy's eyes strayed across the table to an aged and irksome problem. Still not satisfied with this selection process, Cassie Ellis stood up and called for the Quill. She had *making things difficult for a certain someone* in mind, and she spoke in favour of having each candidate submit a minimum sixty-line verse in rhymed Alexandrine couplets. "No tradition merits our attention more than this classical form. Nothing can compare with it in terms of solemn regal splendour. In it we see the grandeur that was Greece and the stateliness that was Rome. Anyone who has mastered the fine-honed skill of poetry should be able to craft finely-wrought Alexandrines—Alexandrines whose vigorous cadences epitomize eloquence seen in its greatest and highest form." Cassie's hyperbolic speech worked wonders with almost all of the elder statesmen and women of the executive council, of which there were a few. Still and all, even some of the others were swayed.

After much debate, they voted five to two in support of Cassie's Alexandrines. Maureen and Donavan alone remained unconvinced. But Rudy had not yet voted. He brought down the gavel declaratively. He ordered silence, and he spoke solemnly. "It is not in the best interest of ZG to impose overly stringent stipulations on our prospective Ambassadors. There is no denying the unique features of the Alexandrine, and Cassie has spoken rightly in recognizing its heritage. Yet the stipulation that the poet write a minimum of sixty lines in rhymed Alexandrine couplets, while undoubtedly a crowning achievement for any distinguished poet, is actually far too onerous. For that reason, I am vetoing Cassie's vote and placing my two votes in the dissenting category. The board room went silent and all eyes riveted onto Cassie. Her objective appeared to be vanishing from the horizon. At that moment, as she rose to raise her voice to object, a single thought crossed her mind: *I wonder. Just how discernible is Rudy's objectivity?*

Cassie's voice grew very careful. It took on a slight edge: that set, deliberate tone of someone bent on retribution. But to the untrained ear, she just sounded old and tired. "Since Mr. Sorensen has seen fit to squelch my vote, and deadlock our executive on this important formal issue, I would like at this time to remind the board of the ZG Right of Way clause. Stephanie, will you please read the clause."

Rudy shifted uncomfortably in his chair. His straining objectivity kept pulling him to the edge... the thin edge of the subjective wedge. "Now Cassie," he began, "there's no need to take this personal—"

"Rudy Sorensen," the widow Ellis suddenly spoke in an oddly (for the occasion, anyway) scolding tone, kind of like a mother punishing her petulant son. "Don't think for one minute I don't know what you're trying to do. *All* of these candidates deserve a fair shot at this position and I for one intend to see to it that they *all* get a fair chance. If that means setting up a high standard, then we as a board ought not to be afraid of doing just that. And I won't even dream of making it easy for you to make it easy for any *one* of these candidates. ZG has traditions and you should know very well that the Alexandrine happens to be one of them. If you're going to veto my vote, I have the right to put it to a Right of Way. Now as I was saying, Stephanie will you please read the clause."

Stephanie had taken the ZG Traditional Rules of Council Manual out and was looking up the Right of Way rule. "Just a minute," she said tentatively. "Okay, I have it: The Right of Way rule states that any executive member who has had a vote vetoed may in the event of a deadlock, reconstitute the issue to be decided and call for a revote. But the outcome of that revote shall be determinate."

Cassie looked at each member in turn, gauging their support from her experience of them and from the expressions on their faces. "You all know how I feel about this issue," she said, laying the groundwork carefully. "Should we defeat the Alexandrine, we may well shatter the one truly perfect mirror through which our Poetic Ambassador might reflect the world for beauty. That's right, I said beauty. Contrary to popular opinion it's not a product." She levelled a piercing stare at Maureen whose entrepreneurial status in the cosmetics segment of the consumer realm was renowned. Maureen simply parted her lips slightly, giving Cassie one of her trademark dazzler gat-tooth smiles. Cassie continued. "Should we defeat the Alexandrine, we may well destroy the one truly perfect crucible worthy of singling out our Poetic Ambassador. The question you must answer for yourselves then is, 'Should we defeat the Alexandrine?' I hereby call for a revote."

Anne Morris scrambled for the Quill. She pounced in a matter of moments; spearheading, or rather appearing to spearhead, a rather pedantic attack on Cassie's position. "Ms. Ellis's grand stand regaling the glories of those long dead civilizations is a tad misleading. Formally speaking, the Alexandrine isn't. It is not a form of poetry, I mean. Rather, it is a metrical form. And it dates back not to the grand old classical era at all; instead it hearkens back to the not-that-distant neo-classical era. Its most ardent adherents are found, not in the English, but in the French literature, most notably Baudelaire, to whom Cassie rather obliquely alluded a moment ago. In his poem *Beauty*, Baudelaire writes, 'I freeze the world in a perfect mirror.' That said, I have no qualms about setting four dozen Alexandrines as the criterion for the assignment. Remember dear," she directed this specifically to Cassie, "the Right of Way rule gives us the right to reconstitute the vote. We would however do well to recall what Alexander Pope said about this particular metrical form:

'A needless Alexandrine ends the song,
that like a wounded snake drags its slow length along.'

Cynical to be sure, but there is an essence of truth to his sentiment nonetheless." As Anne concluded, and as she passed the Quill down to Rod Albright, she directed a carefully placed, politic smile towards Cassie.

Rod was forthright. "Regardless of whether it is a poetic or a metrical form, it is nonetheless a form. It is the contemplation of formal considerations such as these that often allows us to discriminate between the brighter and the lesser lights. That is why I agree that the Alexandrine ought to be retained as a kind of a litmus test. But Anne's amendment doesn't go far enough in my estimation. I would like to see it dropped by *two* dozen lines: I propose we drop the length from Cassie's sixty down to thirty-six. After all, consider the sonnets they have to write. Most sonnets are written in iambic pentameter. That means they've already got roughly a hundred lines of iambic pentameter to write over the course of seven sonnets. We ought to remember the adage that less is more, because as our editors know quality counts for more than quantity. So while I, too, advocate the inclusion of the Alexandrine, I recommend we opt for a thirty-six line Alexandrine, and I propose we drop the stipulation that they be written in rhymed couplets.

"The Quill, please!" Norma Paterson's shrill voice carried a sense of urgency. "The Quill, please!" She repeated herself, this time with special emphasis on the second word. When she received the flamboyant feathery token, she waved it in the air with a flourish. "Fine words sometimes falter, and fall on deaf ears, like misplaced caesuras. Harping on the follies of outdated form is not a popular pastime. But there is some comfort, no matter how cold it may be, that comes from knowing one is right. *I* voted for the Alexandrine initially, but now I must change my mind. It is an archaic metrical form, far less capable of producing good poets than it is of prolixity. As Rod rightly reminded us, less is more. That is always true in the Arts you know, unless money is not an object—and that is only the case in the movies. Some men wish that the *less is more* principle applied when it came time to voting; others feel it would be better applied to issues of... endowment, you know..." Here she bowed her head melodramatically and stroked her temple with the Quill. Straightening again, she surveyed her colleagues and made one last impassioned plea: "If less is more, free us from Alexandrines all together. I urge you all to free us from arcane practices by defeating the Alexandrine. I will not sleep until you do." Smiling demurely, as if to suggest her last statement was not mere hyperbole, Norma gingerly passed the Quill down the table to where Stephanie Nolan sat silently, patiently waiting.

Stephanie prefaced her comments with a formal reminder that although she was given leave to speak, she did not, as secretary, have the power to vote. Then she continued in her soft, genteel accent, "Neither slow snakes nor perfect mirrors figure uppermost in my mind when it comes to the metrical form that goes by the name Alexandrine. It is symmetrical, it must be thus and so. Unless, as Norma has suggested, the caesura leaves it lop-sided, both sides are weighted evenly. The constraints of this verse lend themselves particularly well to a wedding of form and function, and my preference is to allow our potential Ambassadors to prove their mettle by showing us how they handle this difficult and admittedly archaic verse form. They ought to be able to do it in thirty-six lines... no more, no less. Thank you for your attention."

A lull followed Stephanie's soothing and somehow satisfying speech, and Rudy soon stepped into the silence. Flourishing the Quill in one hand and the Council rule book in the other, he levelled a long, steady look at Cassie and then turned his attention to the assembled Council and the fading muttering growl of his waning objectivity. "Members of the executive," he began. "There has been much discussion concerning this slow-moving little snake of a line known as the Alexandrine." He paused, set the book down and pounded on it a couple of times for good measure as he proceeded. "But, we must not lose sight of our mandate. We must not fail to remember that poetic excellence is our goal. I would also like to remind you that my role as Chief Executive Officer of this Board as stipulated on page seven of the manual"—here, Rudy opened the book and proceeded to read—"is to 'diligently enforce the highest of standards in all ZG business.' Noble motives and arguments have been clear in your speeches, and I want to be clear about one thing. I am not here to discount the Alexandrine as a metrical form, or to dispute its origins or the merits of its pliability as a means of testing poetic excellence."

"Well then," Cassie interrupted plaintively, rising slowly to her feet. "Pray tell, why did you veto my vote and deadlock us by casting both of your votes against it?"

Stephanie's soft but insistent voice rose to cut through the heavy silence that followed Cassie's outburst. "Ms. Ellis, you need not stand. And I'm afraid you're out of order."

"Well he can darn well answer me, Madam Secretary. I think he owes me that much for pilfering my vote like a common—." Cassie Ellis was uncharacteristically upset. It had become a rather long meeting for her, and support did not appear to be shifting to her side. Besides, she wasn't about to let Rudy forget how he'd wronged her. But despite all this, she sat heavily back down into the soft cushioned seat of her chair after Stephanie cut her off abruptly.

"Now, now, Ms. Ellis," Stephanie continued, in tones usually reserved for small children at bedtime, "you will get your Quill time, and Mr. Sorensen has a right to his." Stephanie's tone softened even more as she added, "Let's just hear him out, shall we."

Rudy leapt into a jackpot that he hoped had now been softened by his able and affable secretary to a marshmallow melee, to a pillow fight fray. Doing his part, he sent out a warm smile directed toward Cassie. "My decision to move us to deadlock was in the interests of doing my due diligence in finalizing an assignment that will result in the highest standards. As I started to say, my dispute is not with the Alexandrine. I advocate our use of this formal method as a compelling criterion. However, I felt it did not go far enough toward allowing us to determine the poetic suitability of our candidates." He paused deliberately. "This is why I propose that our candidates be required to write their Alexandrines not in rhymed couplets, but rather into a five stanza ottava rima.

Twelve

WHO VOTES FOR OTTO?

This sudden announcement met with mixed reactions. Anne Morris cried out for the Quill. Ms. Morris was a silver-haired retiree who had spent most of her life in the trenches as a high school English teacher. She had previously wasted several fruitless minutes advocating for the inclusion of concrete poems (contrary to what you may be thinking, she was not an entirely hard-headed woman), and she had other things on her mind, but Rudy's proposition temporarily intrigued her. "Byron made ottava rima the darling of the Romantic Age by dropping it down to a deca-syllabic line. Who's to say our age won't rave about an ottava rima in Alexandrines! Yet again, however, I think we don't go far enough length-wise. Is it even possible? Some think not!" (still others have a one-track mind, she thought, thereby convincing herself that she was not one of them). Here she threw a conspiratorial wink at Norma Paterson, while Rod and Nathan rolled their eyes heavenward. "Nevertheless," she continued, "If five, why not six stanzas?" As I have said before forty-eight lines should do it nicely."

Rod Albright had hold of the Quill. "What we don't want is a lengthy debate on length," he said uneasily. "I propose we keep five stanzas and take Cassie's revote."

Cassie was immediately, or very nearly immediately, on her feet demanding the Quill. She had come to some new conclusions about Rudy in the interim. "I'm not so sure I want to invoke my

Right of Way privilege at this time. I'm an old ottava rima fan from way back. Let's just proceed, shall we. We're sure to come to a vote by and by." And as she passed away the Quill, she carefully avoided throwing even a quick glance at Rudy.

Donavan Blake and Maureen Staples fought briefly over the Quill before the young man with the daunting name to live up to nobly deferred. Passing the torch with what some might call a tactful verbal pratfall, he blundered on: "One can never win an argument with the fairer sex, they never play to type. Madam." So saying he passed on the Quill along with his own unique brand of equivocation.

Maureen levelled a telling stare at her self-professed rival and then drew herself up for a voluble attack on the ottava rima. "Simply ridiculous," she started. "To think that this snivelling *would-be sonnet wanna-be* should be dusted off and trotted out as suitable fare for a poetic repast such as this. Well, it boggles the mind! What's next? An epic?"

Donavan had not taken his eyes off of Maureen since their initial exchange, and he continued to stare in wide-eyed mock horror long after Maureen had thrown the Quill in his general direction. The others—used to shenanigans between these two—waited patiently, enjoying the temporary side-show diversion.

Donavan plunged in zestfully. "My esteemed colleague appears to have little regard for... no, let me rephrase that... there is no love lost between her and this... this *verse form*." His scurrilous emphasis on these last two words brought titters to the table.

The whispers began at once. Down at the end of the table, Nathan received the innuendoes from both sides. Anne whispered first, "If I had been mangled as badly *by her* as poor old *ottava* has been..." Then Rod, "a bitchier butcher of those types of verses was never seen by man or..." Nathan barely restrained a belly laugh.

Meanwhile, Donavan was in mid-stride. "...we have already had our epic tonight, friends. A classic epic... in short-sightedness. Wood bees? Wannabes? Dear me, are they stinging? Are the wanna bees stinging worse? Oh the poor dear ottava rima... what will become of him? Would ya? Could ya? Do ya wanna know?"

Nathan could not contain himself any longer and his guffaws were no less audible than the laughter Stephanie and Cassie and the others were letting loose now.

Maureen had sat patiently enduring this mock-heroic outburst as long as she could bear it, but when she saw Stephanie laughing, she took a cue. "Madam Secretary, why must *you* also take delight in this infantile ridicule? Compose yourself, dear girl."

Donavan wasn't about to let up though. "Ah, yes, were it only that easy," he intoned majestically. "Just to be able to say to that little rhyme, *Compose Yourself,* and have it happen, just like that. No skill at all. Pure inspiration. A mere mouthing of words. An utterance of performative stature like no—"

Don—ah, Mr. Blake." Stephanie's soft yet strident interruption was like a mild slap in Donavan's face-off. "I think it best that we confine our remarks to the business at hand, don't you? Fairer sex, fairer play, and all. Hell hath no fury…"

"Of course. My apologies. Now let me see. A while back this became a debate about length. Then, perhaps to forestall the inevitable comment about length not mattering, we shifted back onto the debate about whether or not an ottava rima was the best form for the Alexandrine. Along the way it became clear that an Alexandrine is only a metrical form, and therefore it would appear to be a form in search of a genre. Our trusty leader, ever vigilant in his search for the best means of ascertaining artistic excellence, proposed we wed the two. So I say, let's throw old Alex a stag party! And why not stretch it from four stanzas to eight?

Rod began pounding the table; Nathan took it up next; and Anne and Cassie soon got carried up in it. Before long even Rudy and Stephanie had joined in. Maureen and Norma alone remained outside the circle of camaraderie that had spontaneously been created in this large boardroom. Norma's mouth was set in a firm line. But Maureen slowly stood to her feet and began to give Donavan a solitary standing ovation. The irony was not lost on him. He didn't quite know what to make of it until Maureen spoke.

"You all remember the Eagles? Well, I'm as impressed as the Eagles are high, big boy (and they always were high-flying birds): I salute the 'darling of the chic, flavour of the week,' and I'll be *waiting in the weeds.*" Curtseying coyly, she repositioned herself on her chair. Donavan raised himself to bow at her, more at her popular cultural allusion, but all the while smiling broadly, caught up in the rich pretense that he wasn't really as dazzled by her shapely earrings as he was delighted at having rallied the executive on the back of his overblown send-up of her poetic pretentions. Meanwhile the board continued to size things up.

Still puzzling over his misunderstanding that Maureen had made a comment about soaring with eagles and what that comment might mean, Rudy took the Quill and forcefully re-directed the dialogue towards the debate over the number of stanzas. Some pithy dialogue about expediency ensued, and in the end the general consensus was that Anne's suggestion in favour of six stanzas would be suitable. All that remained was to determine the time limitations for the submissions. Travel along this route was soon detoured before the exchange once again became heated.

Thirteen

DIAMONDS AND DURATION

After a short recess, the Executive resumed their meeting and Rudy took hold of the Quill, reminding everyone that the potentially divisive issue of a time limit for completion of the assignment was yet to be resolved.

However, Anne was of the mind to have a run at the whole concrete poetry thing again, (a choice that brings this narrator's previous parenthetical comment about how she was not a hard-headed woman into some doubt) this time from another angle. She spoke persuasively, and the executive listened patiently. "Like the Haiku, the Diamante is a formal verse which depends upon linguistic versatility for its livelihood. Like the Haiku, it is easy to attain a mediocrity of style and content; and consequently, like the Haiku, it is a form that makes it far, far more difficult for one to ascend the heights of artistic excellence. Since the executive has not in its wisdom seen fit to include a concrete poem, I would argue that we settle for a diamond in the rough—the Diamante. Whoever offers nineteen pieces of gold, and can also bring out the lustre in this little nineteen syllable gem, deserves to be the first ZG Poetic Ambassador. That is my stag present to Alex."

There was not a whisper at the table as Anne's poetic peroration pressed home her rhetorical point. Slowly, with a rising crescendo, the steady sound of hands pounding the table grew louder until the room filled once again with the din of affirmation. This time, even

Maureen and Norma were among the revellers. Anne's perseverance had paid off (proving she was exactly the type of hard-headed woman singer Cat Stevens wrote about 'looking for'—one who takes people at face value). The final tally for the ZG assignment stood at an even twenty poems. All that remained to be decided was the time limit.

Nathan Balfour was the first to call for the Quill after the sound of Rudy's gavel diminished the buzz of preliminary discussion. He started out with a story. "The first poem I ever published was written while I was on the railroad. I'd been assigned two weeks on, four days off. The poem was an ode about the great wide prairie. I'd started it on the last night before goin' out and my wife bet me $20 that I wouldn't be able to finish it before returnin' for my next four days off." Here Nathan paused and let loose with one of his hearty belly laughs. "She was mighty jealous of my muse, so I guess she had some incentive to havin' me done with that verse. Anyways, I finished it alright. That $20 was some incentive for me, too. Hell, it was twice as much money as I ended up bein' paid for that damned old ode." Rod Albright was already calling for the Quill, but Nathan held on for a minute or so longer. "Now I don't reckon these young writers keep to such one-track patterns as we used to follow, but the way I see it, keeping them motivated in the right way means we let 'em know that opportunity don't wait for no one. Any writer worth his salt oughta be able to submit all these poems within two weeks.

Murmurs of respect and approval circulated as freely as some talk of shorter or longer periods, while the Quill made its way over to where Rod Albright sat, perky as a pearl tie tack and twice as sharp. "Ladies and gentlemen, I need not remind you that we are considering the bestowal of an unquestionably prestigious honour upon an as-yet-unnamed recipient. There is no doubt that this is indeed a significant inducement. Be that as it may, such motivation is neither adequate nor sufficient in and of itself. It may be easy to suppose that our shortlisted applicants will move heaven and earth to meet whatever deadline we impose upon them. Two weeks is neither an adequate nor sufficient limitation to impose. Sirs and madams, our applicants are professional versifiers. As Nathan has already hinted, they are people of multiple intelligences, multi-faceted, driven to succeed where hundreds, nay thousands before them have failed. These are the types of people who thrive on a challenge, live for a deadline, yearn to push the limits of their capacity. Make them sweat for it; make them earn it; make them a deadline they can be proud of having successfully met. Make them do it in a single starving week!" Rod succeeded in rallying quite a chorus of supporters, but the debate had not yet ended, and already Stephanie Nolan was taking the Quill.

Soft-spoken and sensitive, Stephanie nevertheless talked forcefully against what she saw as Rod's somewhat overly restrictive regimen. "The poetic temperament rarely responds to assembly-line factory mentality constraints. It is just such a mentality we will be rewarding by setting deadlines as stringent as the one recommended by Rod. Flowers need days of sunshine and days of rain, plenty of both and plenty of tending if they are ever to grow and blossom. Any poem worth reading is like those flowers. Force feed them, and they'll perish on the vine. We need to seriously think about extending a goodly period of time to our prospective Ambassadors. Let's say at least a couple of days per poem. I suggest forty days, or perhaps even three fortnights."

The room got fairly quiet for a long while after Stephanie spoke. It almost looked like Rudy was about to put it to a vote, when suddenly Maureen Staples asked to be heard.

She smiled serenely and glanced over at Donavan before she spoke in even deliberate tones. "Nine months it took your dear mamma to carry you to her delivery date. Perfection takes time. Nine innings it takes, at least, until a ball game finds a winner. Winning takes time. *Nine and a Half Weeks*." Here Maureen laughed her delicate, high-pitched, little highbrow chuckle. "Well, bless me, what a movie! Sizzling erotica takes time. Keep this tradition alive, give them just a little more time. Remember we're all about tradition. Make them perform. Give them nine and a half weeks!"

The Poetic Ambassador

Maureen's motley assortment of proofs and padding brought out a mixed medley of responses. But the executive did seem eager to wrap this one up with a vote. Rudy didn't disappoint.

"Four choices are before the Executive," he said calmly. "Your choices are one week; two weeks; six weeks; or nine and a half weeks. It was evident from the start that the schools of thought subscribed to by the likes of Rod and Maureen were in the minority, and in the end the votes were four to three in favour of Nathan's proposal of two weeks. In a surprising volte-face, Rudy turned the tables, declining to use his veto, and casting his votes on the side of the minority vote for Stephanie's suggestion of three fortnights. Amid the general hubbub that followed the meeting, the loosely divided group came to some grudging consensus that the six week option would most likely turn out to be a more fitly formed time-frame. So it was finally agreed that three fortnights was to be the time frame for the portfolio.

As the Executive left the board room, with a flurry of familiar goodbyes and a few meaningful farewell glances, it was obvious to all that the die had been cast for a highly competitive Poetry Portfolio assignment. Old alliances had been reformed to catalyze a crucible of innovation that could well propel ZG to the forefront of worldwide literary excellence. Providing that is, that these allegiances held firm in the trial to come. Muttering under her breath, while nodding conspiratorially at Rudy and Stephanie on her way out the door, Cassie Ellis wondered half aloud who would have the most significant influence in this new world of Poetic Ambassadors at ZG. Moving with a kind of natural, but ungainly grace, uncharacteristic in one whose age might bring constraints and limitations, and altogether oblivious to who it was she was passing, the dowager widow brushed by Cynthia Davison as she was coming out of the elevator for her after-hours rendezvous with the genteel Ms. Stephanie Nolan. The wide-eyed Ms. Davison excused herself politely. The widow dowager smiled guardedly and cleared her throat to speak as Cynthia held the elevator door. "Thank you. My, what a courteous young lady," Cassie intoned without enthusiasm. "But what brings such an attractive young lady like you to the thirty-first floor so late, and on such a blustery night?" But before Cynthia could reply, Maureen and Donavan bustled down the hall calling for her to hold the elevator. They jostled by together and once inside, hit the Down Elevator button. The moment was lost.

Ms. Nolan would, as it turned out, be some time yet, as Rudy Sorensen needed to debrief her on protocols and other considerations pertaining to dissemination of the poetry portfolio assignment, and besides Cynthia would find Misty more than ready and willing to keep her occupied in the CEO's office.

Fourteen

HEAVY PETTING AND FIRM INCURSIONS

It had been a week now since the celebration at the Afterglow, and no word from Cynthia had breached Trevor's dark, black mahogany door—or his even darker psyche—not counting the fact that he'd all but sublimated her absence into a kind of free-floating discomfort. He'd cancelled the papers and stopped the mail to concentrate on his work. Emergency calls he'd allow, but aside from the rather irksome reminder of an upcoming doctor's appointment, nothing had come through. He thought sure he'd have heard from Cynthia. Maybe she wasn't as into him as he'd thought she'd been. Stop that thought. It was her, not him.

One whole long grinding week had crawled by since the celebration dinner. He'd already progressed about a third of the way through the portfolio assignment, and he sure didn't need any negative self-talk now. She was no doubt knee-deep in the portfolio. Either way, he'd best put her out of his mind.

But there she was again. Like some unobtrusive but incomparable paint pigment that finds its way into the background of a masterpiece to majestically dominate an artist's painting—irrevocably stealing the show from the subject—the most memorable features of her face reappeared, overruling all objections, as subtly as a pair of oddly comforting mixed metaphors taken from law and fine art. Even while he was relentlessly working, some unexpected visual image he'd created with words would conjure up the subtle way she arched her left eyebrow when she sensed something he'd said was amiss, or the way the skin around her eyes crinkled up when she laughed at one of his funny jokes; and of course there was her sweet form, as succinct and expressive as a Petrarchan sonnet (especially when she poured it soulfully into that tight-fitting leather dress she'd worn at the Afterglow).

Nuances like this haunted him with the audacious and irksome regularity of a trump card that turns up again and again... in an opponent's hand (that could not be, he thought, wondering what may have put that thought in his head). Or was it more likely that it turned up in the hand of a long-lost comrade conjured up within the landscape of his prefrontal cortex, reminding him of an inescapable past, like one of Atwood's famous short stories (was it *Death by Landscape*?). As he made a conscious effort to turn away from whatever inviting avatar among his images most diverted his attention—however transient the fit may be—he returned to his contemplation of the intricacies pertaining to one of the most difficult features of the assignment: the Alexandrine Ottova Rima. Here he determined his best course of action, and set about dividing the poem into segments, beginning with the ending and working his way up to a noteworthy climax at the beginning, just as his relationship with Cynthia had begun with an end in sight –her end, his sight! (And now she resurfaced again like a convoluted matrix comprised of a series of successive approximations.) Back to the task at hand. Layer upon layer of meaning and subtext later, just when he was getting set to write the climactic opening... the phone rang.

Normally—and he had thought about things for a second or two—nothing would sway him from striking out at the hot iron of poetic inspiration, and from hammering away until his invention coalesced into a complete poetic construct. But there was still this recurring matter of Cynthia. She embodied both poetry and passion. He answered in the instant his call display confirmed that it was in fact the object of his fixation.

A 'for instance' of the speed with which he answered would be the comparable alacrity with which arachnophobia makes one invariably react when brought face to face with a massive spider. Such was his ambivalence. Needless to say he felt things happening in an almost frightening slow motion, which was weird because it all took place so quickly. At least that was how he perceived it. "Upton," he wheezed into the receiver, forgetting to clear his throat at first, and then immediately wishing to the lover's star that he'd cleared it before he'd answered.

"Trevor? Are you alright?"

Sultry and magnificently rich in undertones, and terrifyingly Cynthia! The very voice he'd longed to hear. Trevor threw in the metaphorical towel, soaked it in gin, and wrung it dry down his parched throat. A second later he faced the music. "Hello Cynthia. How goes the mid-wife crisis?" he cried with all the reckless abandon of (shake it off he told himself) a riven character in some long-forgotten video game. Masking his nervousness with an incomparable nonchalance (and this mutually acknowledged groaner), Trevor cleared his throat yet again and foraged onwards, as unsure of the way ahead as he was absolutely certain that the as yet unwritten opening finale to his poem would be an ending to end all beginnings. But what if that ending... more of that later, he thought, now fully diverted from his portfolio.

One must let Time unfold. For as sure as she's fallen for bluff after bluff, she'll yet again fold, and yet again unfold. His ideas raced to catch up with his rapid-fire, freefalling mind, which doubled down on his visions and revisions, rushing like a roulette wheel towards some ever-receding pay day (and yet another mixed metaphor). Cynthia, the croupier, sent him spinning. He was in... all in (he just did not yet know how much of a wager he was really making).

"Your pregnant wit is born more of Laurel and Hardy than Thomas Hardy—unless you are referring to the impending birth of my portfolio. But I can't talk now. What about tomorrow?" Her husky voice sent amorous spies on an aural survey, penetrating into the dark caverns of Trevor's subconscious, taking no prisoners.

Trevor was slowly beginning to realize that he was defenceless against her beguiling wiles. His musical kingdom—possibly his most stalwart emotional support—was almost exclusively bounded by the unabridged works of the Eagles, but fortunately for the women in his life, an early-seventies machismo arising from that LA country-rock scene had made next to no impact upon his customary interactions with those women (no matter how much he had always idolized Glenn Frey). Emotional whiplash at the journey he had made from that last sequence of thoughts to Cynthia's request, brought Trevor about sharply, and he didn't quite recover in time. Instead, he said, "I wish I could see your lying eyes Cynthia."

"Trevor, darling, you know I'm too much of a witchy woman to know whether we can make it in the long run, aren't I now? Well, I must be going. Tell me, are you going to be home if I should happen to call tomorrow night?" Trevor always appreciated how much of an interest Cynthia had taken in his musical tastes (she had never told him that her mother played the Eagles all the time while she and Anika were growing up). Actually, he thought she must have come to appreciate his favourite group through her parents, because by his estimation they may well have come of age back in the late seventies, which made them ripe for picking by this popular country-rock group.

At any rate, she knew all the old Eagles songs well enough to cleverly insert key phrases from their lyrical lexicon into her conversation, and it gave him no end of amusement. Yet he thought he now sensed the slightest edge of anxiety in her voice—or was it the deceptive bends? He could not say for sure whether he had gotten in too deep, too fast. Such edgy subterfuge was not that unusual for some women he'd known, but completely out of character for calm, confident Cynthia. Still. He'd best be about it, then. Sleuth it out.

"You're sounding more like some kind of desperado waiting for a train of thought to carry her away than your run-of-the-mill witchy woman. But what's the rush?" And then, as an afterthought (only slightly less tenuous, but infinitely more probative, than an afterlife... less for some than others perhaps? But surely not for you, my impeccable reader), Upton added, "Are you busy with some pet project?" (But he was careful to express his question in tones that worked hard to make it seem almost more of an aside.)

"Nothing like that, pet. So you'll be in tomorrow then," and his heart clunked heavily with the light mechanical click she made as she hung up the receiver on the other end.

Trevor hung up, too. And turned his back on the phone, but the caller still held him on the line. Like Schrödinger's Cat with its claws into Freud's couch, he both was and he was not hung up. Cynthia certainly had him in a box. First, she had evaded his question about the pet project. Second, she'd seemed overly brusque, brushing him off in a matter of moments. Third, she'd used his diction verbatim, throwing the word 'pet' back at him in another—decidedly uncharacteristic—context. Not that he was overthinking things at all. No. Cynthia was always original to a fault, even to the point of using selective synonyms instead of repeating a phrase word for word. He had grown accustomed to her layered meanings over their short time together (it had been a little less than a month). He had learned to recognize her cute little speech patterns, link them up with images and ideas used by those closest to her, and make the appropriate conclusions.

When he'd asked her about a pet project, she'd called him 'pet'. This was somewhat novel for her, or at least quite rare. She had once told him that she lived by the adage of keeping your friends close, but your enemies closer. What is closer than a pet? A poem is closer. You cannot create a pet, but you can create a poem. A small voice from somewhere inside of Trevor told him he needed to rethink this. Especially in the light of a certain Beagle who had all but faded from his memory and who was now threatening to loom ubiquitously large again. After all, the voice went on urgently, you could actually—through conditioning and training—create a pet from what once was a perfectly independent person. Trevor had heard this voice before.

It was definitely not his voice of reason. Or so he thought. He liked to think of it as his voice of irony, because the implicit message might as well hit him up the side of the head with its heavy-handed invitation to ameliorate the pervasive media problems—endless condescension and sycophancy to name just two—that have begun again and over again to domesticate the citizens of our country at the expense of good government and free thought. There, that should silence his guilty conscience. Just who were the real pets, anyhow? The voice digressed, it seemed... and spouted conspiracy theories. *All politics aside*, Trevor's inner voice interrupted interrogatively, *why do you want to be the ZG Poetic Ambassador?*

Now that he had arrived at the ripe old age of 29, Trevor felt the need to question all forms of his own insecurity, and since he had already made his peace with the ZG decision, he determined to ignore the voice and move instead towards the climactic opening of the ottova rima he was working on. It had to be good. No pressure. But it had to be good. That kind of urgent optimism, he realized as he tried again to refocus his energies on the poem at hand, is what brought him and Cynthia together on their first chance meeting. They had both wanted it to be so good.

He'd stopped by the Koerner library at UBC one crisp autumn day early last month. Spectacular Fall colours were just beginning to enflame the trees lining the boulevard outside, and he was busily scanning Austin's *How to Do Things with Words* to remind himself of some of the distinctions between constative and performative utterances, when a woman appeared out of nowhere dressed simply in a peasant skirt and a coarse muslin blouse. Her plain-spoken clothing contrasted sharply with the ornate style with which she spoke of Austin. He was sure he must have seen her before. Perhaps in one of his classes. She had discounted this hunch immediately, dismissing it as a line, a come-on. Then she seemed to hit on him, saying if they had ever met before, she would surely have remembered so handsome a man. If she had not been so genuinely endearing, he'd have dismissed her coyness for a patent attempt to ingratiate herself to him. But instead he'd listened to her expatiate upon Derrida's view that Austin is reintroducing 'truth' into the performative when, he says, the speech act assimilates the constative into the performative utterance. They had argued differences and found common interests in the simulacra arising from the anxiety

The Poetic Ambassador

of influence. They had discussed the seminal poetry of, among others, Margaret Atwood, Carol Ann Duffy, Craig Raine, and Leonard Cohen. They had fallen for each other's sophisticated mind (first they took Manhattan) long before she allowed him to explore her exquisite frame (then they took Berlin, for the burlesque).

As these vague recollections of intimacy hovered inchoately over the vicinity of what served for Trevor's jaded old soul and fragmented psyche, (both pawned on the cheap for a quick fix of sensual ephemerality, like gaudy gems picked from the rear pocket of a pair of faded designer jeans) he spurred himself on to finish his ottava rima in the wake of his own minor epiphany.

He had the sudden realization that if romance is a line, and the subtext is fishing, then it is easy to imagine that there is a sea of meanings in which to let down nets (unbeknownst to Trevor who had forgotten the connection at the time, this awareness was in fact the by-product culminating from yet another of the old dog Belton's lecture series on semiotics and interpretation, and he sensed as much at some level, but discounted it almost at once, because why disillusion himself about his epiphanies, he almost thought, before immediately ignoring his inner voice again).

Like a wise man named Stanley Fish once asked, 'Is there a fish in this text?' Cuteness (or cheesiness) aside, the big question about romance is whether it is coerced or has meaning, and if so, is its meaning enmeshed in the nets (nets that seek to entrap if not to bind) of our world, or is it swimming in the high seas of personal liberty? So it seemed that Trevor's sudden realization—voice or no voice—pursued him, almost as if it were directing him towards the beginning of his poem's surprising end.

⋯⋯◉⋯⋯

It would also seem evident at this point that authorial issues of some complexity lay at the basis of the conundrum you will find at the heart of this text. Not far from ZG board member

Donavan's trite jibe about literature writing itself is the idea that characters within the pages of any novel are at least partially responsible for their representation. Should it be true that Mr. Chomsky merits our support for his theories of manufacturing consent, what might that mean for the people who populate our modern novels? A character's incipient wisdom lies fallow as a harbinger of future bumper crops only to the extent that he or she is acting autonomously because the proverbial seed must die to itself if it is to bear fruit. However, if I as the author am compelled to write as a kind of Dick Tatorhead, possessing each character in turn, in order to force his or her hand, so to speak, then what drastic steps will my purported omniscience lead me into when said character develops headstrong ways and maps out routes towards happiness and self-fulfillment (or tragedy) quite apart from my purported tyranny—or will public acclaim arising from this character having asserted self-acceptance and self-determination be a lasting part of an enduring legacy and a guarantor of "truth" or at least true potential? What if the character twies to make jokes at my expense, or at the expense of one of my narrators? What if public disdain is more forthcoming than public acclaim? Maybe an author should allow his narrators more of an opportunity to interact as characters and vice versa, as I have been encouraged to do (by them) in the present text. Or maybe I ought to walk gingerly among my characters, and carry a big stick. Then again, it is probably in our best interests to give them their head, letting them steam and stamp like stallions who have just been ridden hard, and let them get on with the story. Any way you look at it, the reign of the character as narrator certainly opens up more possibilities for everyone, and should be especially intriguing to you, the concerned reader, who likes it, or so the people in this text tell me, when characters develop greater complexity.

The Poetic Ambassador

Trevor slept most of the next day, and he was dreaming deeply and vividly when the phone rang late that afternoon, so he did not hear it ringing—at least not on anything but a strictly subliminal level. At 7:30 pm, after some work on his portfolio followed by a long hot shower, he shaved, dressed, blew dry and brushed his dark, dishevelled locks and popped a ready-made meal in the microwave. After a quick protein drink, he set the table and soon he was eating ravenously. Nothing quite like stuffing on Stouffers.

He would make it meaningful, he thought. Tonight was going to be a meaningful night. The voice said, only if you spell meaningful b-u-m-p-y. "Bolt it, Betty Davis!" he muttered, caught between half-gritted teeth and a half-baked theory that his 'voice' was nothing more than a disembodied manifestation of his father, kind of like being Luke Skywalker and having to contend with his own personal Darth Vader, out to conquer what was left of his galaxy (must watch the rest of the Star Wars saga someday, he thought, knowing he never would). The door chimes broke into their distinctive xylophonic melody, like a crystalline dream through the fantastic illusion of Trevor's Freudian trip down cinema lane with all of its Oedipus overtones. He knew immediately that it was Cynthia.

He pushed the intercom button, and asked his customary curt question. "May I inquire as to the exact nature of your business?" (Curt for most was prolix for Trevor). A pause in the preliminaries was punctuated by an exploding exhaust, as a passing car accelerated by the house, inadvertently censoring his guest's expletive-laden response. But, not to be outdone, Cynthia's familiar voice luxuriated across the speaker, with a quickly inserted term of endearment appended, to where Trevor stood anticipating her arrival.

"Trevor, darling. It's me, Cynthia. Break out the glasses, I've brought bubbly, because 'there's no telling what a man might do after the thrill is gone'." He was always amazed at how easily he let down his hanging garden, like some rustic Rapunzel, as she irrigated it with her best husky disco strangler whisper, upping the ante on the allusive thrills for good measure—not to mention just the right metaphorical mixture to enrich the parched soil. He was at the door letting her in just as he began to imagine that she had broken in on his fragmentary narrative fermentation by telling him how much her body needed him so. Or was it that irksome voice again, angling to deceive?

Suddenly she was in the room. "The thrill may have been gone temporarily, but she's back now." Trevor smiled at her as he took her into his arms. He held her in the soft, but strong crush of an ardent embrace, while his lovelorn lips lingered like rose petals fluttering to fall upon so warm a cheek, on so lovely a face. Then, as if they inhabited some dollar store romance kicked up several notches kind of like the operatic scoring of a long-anticipated aria arranged with tender feeling, her lips met his. Their tongues darted deliciously, teasing and caressing with all of the restless abandon of wild things only just released after long captivity, while the Troggalogue voice-over played for the tourists in the bus watching the action.

"I thought you were going to call," Trevor said, finally disentangling his tongue, but still content to hold her captivating body in thrall. "You've done your hair differently."

"Isn't this a call?" She teased slyly, tossing his long dark curls over his eyes in her playful way. "What kind of a call did you expect, you blind Milton. Isn't man a paltry thing, though? Had it done. Something different. Don't know if I like it."

"That's Yeats," he cried, pushing his hair back out of his eyes, "not Milton. Milton was all about 'justifying the ways of God to men', at least in *his* lost paradise, anyway. I liked it better the way it was."

"The paradise or my hair? Let me have my sin again or *your* paradise will be lost." Cynthia moistened her lips and smiled. She set about rearranging another entanglement of tongues. Romeo never knew what hit him.

They fastened their seatbelts, because it was going to be a bumpy night after all—and because father knows best (and because of a couple of other old film clichés the voice vaunted irrepressibly, ironically, and ineptly). But by the end of the evening, Trevor had arrived at the opinion that the less father knew about Cynthia, the better (oh, and he had also arrived at some other far cozier places in the process). In his amorous advances, he had pushed across the Rubicon (now he was beginning to feel the voice really was his father—or his mother... and suddenly he felt strangely nauseous), but lingering longer at the delta as they found the alpha and the omega again and again, meant that further incursions were met with firm resistance. They'd both agreed that the firmer the incursion, the better (and the more resistance, the stronger the electricity that hung in the air like a dynamo hum... apparently the narrative voice was a bit of an impresario, which begged the obvious question—was the Moon Unit conceived before or after the Dynamo Hum?).

More to the point, was Cynthia's stated reason for the fact that after about an hour of mutually satisfying bumpiness (or dynamo humming, depending upon your perspective) she had to leave Trevor at around nine. Apparently Saturday night was the only time she could meet Anika about some family business she needed to handle.

Trevor didn't mind.

He still had his playdate with good old ottova rima. She left him feeling sated, and he picked up where he had left off—only now he was both sated and elated, and in a prime condition to write (fortunately, their firm incursions had long since helped him forget about that other bumpy business with the Beagle, but there were rumours, unbeknownst to Trevor that the Uppals were in the market for a new dog, bigger and younger and more vicious!). Writing called for alertness. At last. He was ready for an end to his beginning, and a beginning for his end.

Fifteen

TEQUILA SHOTS AND MOBY DICK

So I got the call from Cynthia the other night. Fantastically, she found my phone number written down on that receipt for tequila shots from Mick's that she'd thrown in her change jar during our late night tryst last Saturday. Now here it is Thursday, and we're back doing tequila shots at Mick's. I laugh loudly when she turns her winsome face to mine and says, "I know I can trust you."

"Don't trust me unless you are prepared to follow me," I reply happily, taking a healthy swig of my beer.

"Following is easy, but trusting is hard," she says emphatically and in a tone that could pass for glib, but edges more towards earnest (if the earnestness was tinged with the rue of satire).

"Tell me, where did you get to be so jaded?" I reply, with emphasis.

"Don't you mean how did I get to be so jaded?"

"The location invariably prefigures the cause, just as time colours location. You give me the where and when and I'll happily supply the how." It's all in the numbers," I smile confidently, not quite sure of what she might say.

"Zack, an art connoisseur such as yourself surely knows by now that painting by numbers is perhaps the most banal definition of derivative art." Her tone, tinged with haughty disdain, mocks my sophistry.

"Ah, but the numbers do not lie!" I press on confidently, sensing an advantage where there seemed to be none, an opportunity where most would retreat. Another round of drinks has arrived, and we chase two more Tequila shots with beers.

A warm buzz of conversation envelops us, intensifying with the rush of the alcohol, and I feel myself letting go again. It's easy with Cynthia. Her infectious laughter pulls down my barriers. Hers too. Soon she is confiding intimate details, disclosing history in a torrent. About her family—her mother, aunt, father and grandmother. This was a lot more information than I'd ever expected. And when I get down to figuring out how it all adds up, there ends up being two or three times as many reasons as previously existed for me wanting to know her better. And fearing where it all may lead. Turns out both she and her mother have twin sisters. And that's where things start to get interesting. Cynthia's mother Melanie grew up with her twin sister Jill in a small city in the Interior called Kamloops. Her grandmother was a single parent, and the two Kamloops girls grew up never knowing, and always wondering who their father was.

While listening to Cynthia share about her family, I quickly come to appreciate how empathic she is and what a powerful force family is in her life. If there was a familial cause for Cynthia's jaded outlook, it seemed clear that Kamloops was the only place to start looking for it. Long before she was born, Cynthia's mother Melanie and her twin sister Jill lived with their mother Samantha. Switching perspectives like a seasoned raconteur, Cynthia gives a compelling seemingly firsthand account of her family background—*first from her Aunt Jill's perspective.* I find myself intrigued by her inauspicious origins. And by her compelling narrative:

Melanie and I are twins. We were born in 1961 to Samantha Damsella, a chambermaid at the David Thompson Hotel in Kamloops. We never knew who our father was for sure, but we had it on good report that he had a controlling interest in the hotel. If that was true, mama never let us put on airs. From the time we could walk, we worked. First it was washing and cleaning, like Mama Sam (our mother had for years become a kind of den mother to all hotel employees). Then, when we were older, it was waiting tables in the dining room, and eventually in the lounge. We learned to hustle and avoid being hustled in that niche of notoriety nestled slightly south-east of the Overlander Bridge. And we had other bridges to build.

Soon I spent most of my time serving cold beer in the DT Zoo. The Zoo was an awkwardly affectionate nickname for the David Thompson Pub. Located on the far end of the hotel, this shady establishment catered to a strictly working class clientele. Between it and the hotel disco sat the DT Lounge, an upper class lounge frequented by rich and sophisticated hotel patrons who preferred highballs to beer and the traditional elegance of a piano and lounge singer to the loud rock bands of the Zoo or the beat-driven synth-sounds of the disco. Melanie favoured the DT Lounge, but I preferred the rough-cut, in-your-face antics of the Zoo's snaggle-toothed denizens. When she asked me about it, I just said, with a melodramatic pause, that I loved... living dangerously.

We came of age in the 1970s. Disco was big, but we loved the Eagles. And the Eagles hated disco. We did betray Henley and Frey to find our way onto the disco dance floor sometime in 1979, and I'll never forget the look on Mama Sam's face when she saw me dancing with a certain someone that we'd known practically forever. It would not be the last time I'd ever see him again, although Mama Sam said that I might as well eat poison as look at him. I could tell from the look in her eyes that she meant business, and I knew right then that I'd been dancing with my daddy.

Melanie said we had to do something. That was how I knew the truth would come out. She always got what she wanted. Though I was always first into things, she would invariably be the one to find out how to get the best out of them. Melanie was the best at everything. She had more than just charm, it was a gift. No. It was a calling.

That's how I knew that she'd have something to say when she saw me dancing with Mr. Montaigne. Then I heard mom light into me about staying as far away from him as "time is from eternity" (that is exactly what she said). Seeing as how he was the General Manager of the DT, we were pretty sure that was not going to happen any time soon. Besides, if our suspicions were proven true, we'd want to get to know Montaigne better, rather than keep away from him.

We stayed up talking really late that night; in fact, we were still up when night lost yet another battle for supremacy with the dawn, whose fresh light brushed a warm glow over the rose-coloured walls of our hotel room. "It's him!" Melanie whispered triumphantly, as soon as the two of us were alone in the room. "But listen, Jill. We've still got to find out for sure."

"Mom will never tell; he'll probably never tell; and so, we can never know," I complained disappointedly.

"Go over in your mind all you know about him, describe him to me in rich detail, and we're sure to uncover some credible clues to his paternity," Melanie exhorted excitedly; and together we clamoured with eagerness, building the undergirding for the game-work we designed to gauge the pedigree of our elusive father figure. The more we talked, the more we built up our hopes about Mr. Montaigne's alleged fatherhood until they loomed as high on the horizon of our expectations as the dog star is above Tod Mountain (the local ski resort at the time).

He had our nose. Or rather, we had his. Our eyes were a blend of his azure blue and mom's emerald green. And clearly our straight teeth and dazzling smiles, hid behind our ever-so-slightly pouting lips were from him and mom as well. These were the outlines of a roughly fleshed portrait we painted that night. But there had to be more convincing details yet to come. We could not hope to get close to him ourselves without raising suspicions, and this is where the game-work got tricky: there had to be a way to corroborate his identity as our father, but attaining that dream might prove to be a more difficult process than we had imagined.

Here Cynthia, dams the flow of her narrative to pierce me with a look. It could have come straight from the ancient mariner himself. Then, she delivers an explosive verdict on my auditor's skills.

"Damn! I never took you for such a deep space cowboy. You're either completely bored or totally enthralled. And I can't quite tell which."

It is just after eight by this time, we had switched to coffee some time ago, and the staff must have been ordered to up the ante on ambience, because out of the ether comes one of my favourites dancing nimbly towards its plaintive opening vocal with a whimsical acoustic riff: It is Mad Season's *River of Deceit*. As I rise to the occasion of my response, I let the music pour itself like chains of liquid gold binding the completely unknown until it assembles together in a mutually-assured collective unconsciousness. It might be the tequila, I think, but to hell with the hive. Time to break free from chains of social conformity. I reach across the table and envelop Cynthia's hands in mine. "I've been content thus far to run marvelling with the current alongside your storyteller's stream. If it seems, now and then, to eddy in *coming of age* shallows, only to sweep one away down-river among deep treasures of the type of teenage wonder we all once shared—each in our own chosen way—it's because I've long been a student of how 'way leads on to way.' But what you so generously bring to the table tonight is a trip upriver to the familial headwaters. If you really want to take me there, along the road less-travelled, I'd love to share the journey." No sooner has 'journey' left my lips than what seems like an extra-loud part of the song punches through the white noise of the crowded pub—that part of the song where the line about how my pain is self-chosen cuts like W.S. Merwin's proverbial thread the colour of absence through the eye of the needle of self-awareness. This could well be a painful journey, I conclude. But I banish the thought upon the occasion of its appearance. Instead, as soon as the lyric ends I share with Cynthia the short Merwin poem that free association had brought my way. And we talk about the colour of absence. "Sometimes we choose the pain of absence because we think that separation is a means of protection. I am not saying your elusive grandfather did that, but I find your story fascinating, Cynthia. I'd like to find out more about why Samantha kept her secret so long."

Cynthia gives me a long look. She smiles shyly and speaks quietly. "You're sending out some pretty probative and erstwhile impressions, Mr. Zachary Speller."

"Well, Ms. Davison, since you put it that way, It would behoove me to ensure that only the good ones endure, and to that end, would you agree that your story, and my full critical response to it, would best be served by a more intimate venue?"

"If you're asking me whether or not I want to blow this Popsicle stand, then all I've got to say is that even Shelley's wild west wind has neither the breath nor the force of will to blow it with as much gusto as I have now marshalled to regale you with all my heretofore well-buried background in order that you may proclaim with vigor to echo and rival the intrepid Ahab, 'There she blows.'" So saying, she sipped her steaming black coffee.

Cynthia's theatrical flair is amusing—on so many levels. It propels her headlong into this little monologue, sketching out in outline form her personal etchings, and ending here with that old sea captain's declarative dream of one day being able to harpoon his nemesis of a white whale. "Well, call me Ishmael," I smile gravely, with only a nominal nod at her allusion to Melville's famous quest novel. "Just don't—"

"Call you *'late to dinner?'*" she interrupts in an amusingly tipsy tone that seems at once a mixture of disdain and lowbrow condescension, leaving me slightly at a loss.

"If you're going to put things in my mouth, make sure not to tar and feather me with bitter bits of banality," I tease, pinching her for emphasis. "I was going to sway a little, and tell you not to leave anything out."

She continues then, smiling as if to veil the barest hint of an admonition in an otherwise playful manner. "Regardless, better to be late for dinner, than that I should witness your premature arrival upon a scene that has not yet been set."

We realize our coffees are going cold, and now we decide to settle up with the waiter, so we can prepare for a bracing walk to the parking garage a few blocks away. The weather is windy and wild. And I'm no longer feeling the effects of the alcohol. So I help Cynthia with her coat and we step out into the cold rain. It is gusting now, making the walk to the car seem a little like a quest for that white whale we'd alluded to moments ago. As I mouth the words of this wee bit of a joke to Cynthia, she pulls me up short, steps up on her tiptoes, and presses her lips to mine in a firm embrace that seems to last just long enough for a saturation that is so full that it rivals Sting's big fat river in flood. I belong to the generation which would rather find other ways of talking about that concept customarily characterized by never having to say one is sorry, and up until now the only regret I'd had was not so much ever having worked at the Trope as having to say I worked there. 'What am I thinking?' I say to myself. 'Cynthia's kiss is still on my lips and all that's on my mind is work?'

I find myself provoking Cynthia with this old chestnut: "Romance is just another social construct designed to keep productivity at bay." She gives me her best come hither look as if to say "let's get unproductive, then," and twines her arms in mine as we shuffle on through the rain showers like Gene Kelly and Debbie Reynolds in slo-mo (without all of the singing). I ready my keys for the ferocious green-coloured Moby, whose pale, spectral form looms large in its spot somewhere around the block in the bowels of a parking garage. I could tell Cynthia was cogitating upon my latest one trick pony. I begin looking to see how many moves deep I could get before she sacrificed her next knight. Needless to say, this plan was obscured by the sudden appearance of a Leonard Cohen song on the horizon of my consciousness. I'd all but decided that he must have had Cynthia's firm, intelligent, humorously inviting kiss in mind when he wrote about getting in a thousand kisses deep because even only one of her kisses is the equivalent of Cohen's concept. So what if he probably only meant that the depth of a relationship can be measured by kisses. Gives a person something to look forward to, now, doesn't it?

Cynthia lets five minutes pass as they walked along together in the deepening deluge. Then she stops Zack once again and with the pretense of another kiss, she broaches her theses and raises a thorny question: "If Productivity must be kept at bay, it's because it is wild and dangerous. 'The means of production' is a Marxist concept. But if it is not the money, but the love of it that is the root of all evil, then the true source of evil today is those who control the means of production. What does productivity produce, besides capital? But if Romance really is a civilizing force, by whom is it designed? Is it just another one of productivity's means to the end designed by multinational corporations to satisfy the people's need for—"

Still waters certainly do run deep, I think to myself quietly, before I shatter Cynthia's sophisticated thought by finishing her sentence with the electrifying punchline of a favourite Sting song of mine, "—a big fat river in flood?" Then, bending down, I pick her up by the waist and spin her around. I am almost convinced for an instant that love really is stronger than justice and thicker than blood and all those other cute clichés, in all those other silly love songs, in all those other small town gin joint jukebox dreams I'd ever heard of over the years. I hug her close and then let her go. "Still waters..." I smile knowingly. She smiles back. I continue with some profundity of my own. "Romance is Schrödinger's cat writ large: It is and is not... a corporate product until you open Pandora's Box." We walk on towards the parking garage. "But to be a little less cryptic, capital determines one's significant relationships only to the extent which the corporate world's designs influence Romance. Relationships by design always involve money—and money makes many mad."

She is laughing immediately at my concluding line. I know what is coming before I insert the key and she shouts, "Thar she blows! Then, continuing the previous thread of thought, she concludes, "I might have to check your poetic licence, Zack. Context over content: The content of the diction seems to be determined or driven by (excessive) alliteration. Are you suggesting that without money there can be no romance? Or that romance breeds madness? We've nowhere to go but down, and it's a slippery slope."

I put the key in the ignition and turn over the engine. "Snakes and ladders," I laugh. "Down one way, and up another." We pull my green-gilled Moby out into a slow stream of traffic heading for the bridge. I hit the windshield wipers, and turn on the air to cut the steam from off of the windows. Then I give my response to her critique: "Context amplifies content. Repetition of the initial 'm'-sound in adjacent words can involve a comforting locution, connoting that something is 'good'... hence Romance is as good as money and involves madness. You have to be a little out of your mind to be in a big fat river in flood."

"They say storm-chasers are a little out of their mind. I dabbled with that for a while. And my mom grew up in a town that had a river running through it," Cynthia adds thoughtfully, "and when it flooded, there were a lot of basements under water. I guess that big fat river in flood involves getting a little wet... literally and subliminally speaking." She slides over next to me on the seat. "We already got a little wet tonight, right? How wet do you like it, captain?"

"Up periscope, gunner!"

As the street lights bleed greens and reds in blurred blobs of brightness against the sharp wet darkness of the road's shadows, I think of baptisms of fire and water, of wars not yet waged, and of songs yet unsung; and that Cynthia was making this ZG contest quite competitive. Then it's my turn to gun her, sweeping my Moby through a deep puddle and spraying the empty bus stop while speeding through the last yellow light before the Second Narrows Bridge. "That was nothing," I wink at her, smoothly. "Let's get waterlogged?" But she turns away to gaze at the night, while I drive the rest of the way home in serene contentment, happy with the occasional glance at her reverse reflection in the passenger window, accentuated by the passing street lights running in the raindrops in the wind.

Only when we're home, does she lean over to punctuate the silence. In the dark, she whispers "Too much water, no fire: One need have just enough wick to allow for the burning of a steady flame." She squeezes my arm, then relaxes her touch as I turn my Moby into my driveway. Inside the house, I ignite the gas fireplace,

The Poetic Ambassador

take out a five-year old Chablis and pour a couple of glasses. Soon we are curled up comfortably on the dark green leather couch.

"Ready to hear about Jill and Melanie's plans to ferret out the facts about their unknown father?" Cynthia asks as she sips her wine and studies my countenance for clues to character. I do my best to remain inscrutable, which is more difficult than one might imagine, considering the fact that I really am genuinely hooked on finding out whether old Montaigne would eventually be fitted with the suit of clothes Jill and Melanie were designing for him.

"We left off at the point where they were up late one night discussing Montaigne, didn't we?"

"Yes! *And I was almost finished giving you Jill's perspective. Here's the rest of her story:*"

The mirror ball glittered and glowed on the night I danced with Mr. Montaigne, but before long the morning sun was rising like the old song about a red rubber ball. And there was a bounce in our steps the next day, even though we hadn't slept at all. I remember we were studying *Hamlet* in my Twelfth Grade English class with Ms. Lodge. Melanie and I took this class together, and in our reading she was given Hamlet's part where he says, "To sleep, perchance to dream." I was blown away. She gave me this piercing, puzzling look. I hastily scribbled a note and passed it to her as soon as she had finished her reading. "Eternity and time are a blend of sleeping and waking dreams," it said. "That's a timeless truth."

Later that day, when we took our daily walk around MacArthur Park, she said, "You got there first again, didn't you? Rushing on ahead and stumbling into ecstasy! Remember when mom said you should stay as far away from Mr. Montaigne as time is from eternity? Well, I'm willing to bet that time is not far from eternity at all! It is as close to eternity as black holes are to anti-gravity. And if life is but a walking shadow, then eternity is a series of wakeful dreams. This is the proof we need to usher in Mr. Montaigne's inquisition." But it would be many years before I finally learned the truth about my father.

At this juncture, Cynthia rises and crosses the room like it is a catwalk, to where the Chablis stands compromised and sweating in the ice atop a marble counter pass-through affording a peek in at my French Kitchen. "You look like you know your way around a kitchen," she sighs more than says. Then she moves towards me with a confident deftness that would have made a sworn celibate take a vow of silence in exchange for the opportunity to ravish her in her own language.

"Some kitchens are more inviting than others," I reply coolly, trying not to notice the slightest physical undulation of her languorous hips, while at the same time impressed—considering the philosophical maturity in ones so young at the time—by the story of her mother and her aunt. The last time I'd met with such a heady combination of brains and beauty was when I'd been interviewed by Pamela at ZG (and although she had looked lithe and beautiful, too, she was clearly a lot older than Cynthia). This was turning into a colourful family saga, I knew that much for sure. She leans up and gives me a long kiss. How many deep was I now? I get the feeling that with Cynthia the one thousand mark would come faster than a good doctor finds a fake fettle.

She nestles in for a cozy cuddle and asks me if I've been in many 'wakeful dreams' lately. Choosing my words like skipping stones thrown in the rivers of time, I tease her luxurious red locks gently, and reply with a small amount of the measured reserve I had set aside for just such an occasion: "Were all such dreams comparable to the one I now hold in my arms, I could say I've had my share. But truth be told, these dreams are as precious as they are rare. I don't know how you feel, but I fear the hour is growing late—and you, my dear, have more, much more to relate."

"All I have to relate is that Time is relative." Cynthia sows this little gem with a definitive genuflection. The type where grace vies with carefree candor for an effect only slightly more meaningful than the improvisation of ballet stars. "But she never spends it with her poor relations. Ba, da, boop." And the comic turn is complete.

"Clinking glasses, thinking passes," I chirp awkwardly, like a parrot testing a rhyme. Then as if to counter the froth, I continue on a loftier level: "If to relate is both to communicate and to signify familial blood, and Time relates what it translates, foreign tongues speak forth from mud. For Time's grape harvest new wines suffuse; inhibitions melt like moments until there's nothing, but nothing to lose, and 'those who share the gift of gab are quick to grab the perfect prize that waits upon the shelf,'" I add, more like a rhyme testing a parrot this time.

"Okay, I'm pretty sure that last bit was from a 1970s America song," she says (passing the recognition test with flying colours). "What was it? *The Tin Man,* right? Something Jedi about that line 'Oz never did give nothing to the Tin Man that he didn't already have.' All we have to do is find our best abilities by searching inside of ourselves, or some such tripe. But Time certainly does translate, I'll give you that much. And the truth is as much within you as it is 'out there' like some bizarre X-Files serial. I have an idea about the type of 'perfect prize' you're looking for tonight, honey, but even if it does not turn out to be a shared prize, I bet you've got time for *the story about how my mom and dad met,* don't you? *I'm going to tell you this one from my mom, Melanie's perspective.*

I draw the curtains to give us a little more intimacy, soften the lights, and put on some mellow Vangelis. I make my own provocative sashay—nowhere near as attractively done as hers—over to the Chablis and top our glasses. We are ready to go back to Kamloops.

Sixteen

LIKE FALLING OFF A LOG – SUMMER 1979

Jill doesn't suspect that she's not always the first to get her feet wet. I know that sounds horribly cliché, but walking into the changing tide might be the best metaphor in this case. We were four years beyond high school graduation when I found out the truth about Mr. Montaigne. I couldn't tell Jill. You see, Jill's impetuous nature means she has no boundaries and no ability to hold back when she sees something that she wants. She is impulsive and headstrong. She's always been this way, and I've grown accustomed to protecting her from herself. And the truth is, Ernie Montaigne knew that as well. Turned out he'd been keeping his eye on us all of our lives. But I would need help finding that out.

I met Kristos Cervantes for the first time at Riverside Park in Kamloops in the middle of a long, hot summer during the year after living dangerously made Mel Gibson fall for Sigourney Weaver in the Peter Weir film vehicle for wee Linda Hunt. Kristos was on a hunt of his own. We were both walking the logs that divided the swimming area in the river from the rest of the Thompson River. He came up unexpectedly, out of nowhere, from behind me, and pushed me into the fast-moving current. I recovered, gasping for air, reached up to grab his ankle and give it a sharp yank. Suddenly he was pulling me under, and as we fought for oxygen, equilibrium and some small semblance of equal access, he was soon rending my entire world asunder. His dark curly hair was much longer then, and he had the sexiest handlebar moustache. We both giggled like school-girls at our futile attempts to right ourselves again on those slippery logs. Eventually, we gave up, found our towels on the beach, and lay there side by side, watching our chests rapidly rise and fall. When we finally caught our breath, he introduced himself as the Zorro of Zaragoza. He was working for Arnold Yardbird, a local history professor up the hill at the college, and he was part of an exchange program. They were returning to Mexico in September. Jill promised not to tell Mama Sam. When it came to boys, she acted like we were still in high school and in need of a chaperone. I set about discovering how to get Kristos on board for a little research of our own. I'm talking about Montaigne of course. What did you think I meant? Not all girls just want to have fun, no matter what Ms. Lauper tells you! (For some girls having fun is living dangerously.)

I promptly put Mama Sam off the trail by enrolling in a summer session at the college. The course was in dramatics. Something I'd had more than a little practice with already. Professor Daniel Eaton lectured for an hour three days a week on famous plays and playwrights. Things like *Oedipus Rex* and *The School for Scandal*. After class, Kris and I would take a corner of the cafeteria and discuss our schemes for "outing" Ernie Montaigne as our father. The first strategy in our master plan involved having Kristos approach him formally. He would adopt his professional persona of course, and enlist Montaigne's help with his research. Kris had to dig into all kinds of labour practices and record the relationships between employers and their staff. He got a charge out of adopting the pose of an articulate, artsy immigrant, keenly interested in posterity and "a piece of the provincial pie." At the time, I figured he probably meant the money. But with Kris, it was never just about the money. The more we conspired, the more passionate he became to help us solve the paternity puzzle that plagued us.

Kris's English was always as immaculate as his attire; he was so nuanced and well-spoken. Anyways, we put the plan into motion as soon as Mama Sam was out of town for the last week in July. She took off for Salmon Arm to spend some quality time with her sister, my Aunt Jocelyn, leaving Jill and I to our own devices—but by then I'd already decided to keep Jill out of the loop. All I could remember is what Mama Sam had said about staying as far away from Montaigne as time is from eternity. I knew her well enough to know she was serious, so I figured that the less Jill knew, the better. Plausible deniability.

Jill and I stayed away from each other more and more that summer, and I was actually glad for it, because it made it easier to be secretive about what Kris and I had come to call the M-Factor. She never suspected and I never let on. But you're probably eager to hear what our research project uncovered, right? Well, it turns out Montaigne had a lot to say. At any rate, that's a conversation better left for him to share. When I finally told Jill many years later, it nearly killed all the positive aspects of our 'sibling rivalry'.

My Antonio Banderas of Zaragoza was never really much of a Zorro, but he did turn out to be a real tiger; and his smooth-talking style, at once so solid and self-assured, disarmed me as effectively as it did Montaigne. Kris made getting around old Ernie Montaigne look as simple as making me fall off of a log at Riverside Park. And even though Kristos and I were both swept away together in the end, I never made it easy for my young Mexican to get around me.

Seventeen

VELOCIRAPTORS HAVE THE MOVES

"You likely have had him wrapped about your little finger for years now, haven't you?" I say teasingly as she concludes her story. "Daddy's little girl!"

"Papa Extra-Special K (PESK is the apt acronym) made me a lean, mean, fighting machine," she sighs and settles herself into a soothing, smouldering blanket of bliss all over me. She thinks about how much to share about Papa Kristos. She decides to go slow. "But it was always mind over matter with him," she adds quickly. "I made sure he didn't mind, then it didn't matter."

"He sure knew what he wanted. And he moved on your mom with the rapidity of a velociraptor." Then, in an effort to accentuate my meaning, I swoop Cynthia up in my arms and twirl around the room, giving her an impromptu tilt and whirl. And just as quickly drop her on the couch, hovering over her with a feinting, mock-plaintive plea, "Move your giggling lover's cross of a body on which I'd gladly die."

"Well it's no string of riverside logs," she says laughing. "No rushing current to fall into."

"Enough twirls and swirls, though, right?"

"I suppose. But no meaningful quest to bond over."

"No? You've not heard of the competition for ZG Poetic Ambassador?"

It was as if both the House and the Stage held their collective breath.

Cynthia speaks first, with probative precision. "Have you begun the ottova rima?"

"Done but for the final edit. You?"

"Mine is incomplete, like *Kublai Khan*—a work in progress. But it will be done long before the deadline. Must leave time for the fine-tooth comb."

Sensing that this is a topic best returned to at another time, Zachary gives Cynthia another friendly squeeze, and returns to the subject of her parents. He couldn't help but think of her story as a kind of initiation or trial run for a meet the parents evening. He had horrible visions of some worst-case Fokkersesque scenario. "I'm sure your ottova rima will put Coleridge to shame, and I want to talk more with you about it, but listen Cynthia: I'd like to know a bit more about your father—before I enjoy the privilege of meeting him in person, I mean."

"Of course," Cynthia replied. "I've got a few more family stories to share with you anyhow. Then maybe we can spend a little more time discussing the competition. This next story is in the shape of an interview. Before he was my dad, Kristos had a talk with Ernie Montaigne. Ernie's recollection of the encounter was transcribed during his dying days by his amanuensis, my grandmother, Samantha Damsella—who plays a small part in his narrative as well. So here is Ernie's view of that first memorable encounter with my father as a young lad in his twenties.

Eighteen

JUST WHO IS THIS CERVANTES? - SUMMER 1983

Big brown eyes have always spelled bullshit in my books. So when I say this, you'll understand my initial mistrust of this 'accent in a blonde camel-skin blazer' who strolls into my office apropos of nothing and tells me his name is Senor Cervantes. "You mean like the *Don Quixote* Cervantes?" I inquire, offering him an over-solicitous impression, because I'm sure of nothing short of the fact that I want to suss out this guy's true pedigree. I think it was the summer of 1983, but one year is as good as another (the year of my own birth notwithstanding), right? Anyway, my secretary has already introduced him, and like I say, his introduction smells smarmy. Besides, I've never been the type of guy to tilt at anyone's windmills, regardless of how well-connected they may appear to be—and I don't mean the windmills. I am all set to give him the old heave-ho, when he up and drops another name in the middle of his response to my opening gambit.

"Distant relatives don't concern me as much," he replies, and then goes on to say, "as more immediate connections. Like the one between you and your good friend, Dennis Scrimshaw. How long have you been managing his hotel?" His direct approach surprises me at first, I got to say. So I sets about sizing him up right away.

"Say Sancho," I snarl, leaning into him across my desk, "who let a bright star like you into my constellation?" I've been known to toss trouble down a few flights in my day, but I didn't suppose this wetback had tumbled on to my rep yet, so I settles for sending him a gruff glare with my ironic emolument. But he isn't biting. He tries to kill me with kindness, delicious fruit of the poisoned tree or some such bull.

He extends his hand, and reluctantly I gives him a firm shake. "Pardon my blunt question, sir. I'm working on some labour research for a book that Professor Arnold Yardbird is writing, and I was wondering if you could spare some time to help me with a few labour-related questions?" Just like that he ingratiates himself to me, makes it easy for me to put my guard down, and ushers me into a whole new era—the publishing era. Well, right then the phone rings, and wouldn't you know it: It's Scrimshaw. The first question he asks me is about the new manager of the disco, a guy by the name of Jersey Doll.

"Jersey's a wind-up doll," I quip 'hilariously', guffaws rolling off my tongue and out over the phone lines. I can be a card at times. "he won't go far without special attention," I add, padding my punch line for extra measure. Cervantes seems amused by the show. Scrimshaw on the other hand is intent upon disabusing me of my pretensions to comedy. In tones as bored as they are passive-aggressive, he lays his cards on the table.

"I know he's a Doll, Ernie; it's his name for crying out loud! But is he just another bean-counter, or can he fill the seats and keep them drinking all night long? He's been there for over a month now. What are the numbers telling you?"

If I know one thing about Scrimshaw it's that he's got a one-track mind. He'll go at a thing any number of ways until he achieves his goal. I could see Doll needed an ally or he'd be bearing the brunt of the boss's wrath. "Well he's not playing house, DS! It's too early to call, but you'll want to hedge your bets with Jersey," I suggest, my voice pitched like a canary in a coal mine—ringing cautionary bells. Dennis Scrimshaw's direct, no-nonsense style was just as much a part of his substantial character as a wandering eye was part of his tragic flaw. But every now and then, everyone is prone to a momentary lapse of reason. The conversation over, I hold the

The Poetic Ambassador

dead line and make believe I'm still listening, while studying this Cervantes character; and I slips into a reverie on slips I know Dennis has had. Jersey fades into the backdrop. Cervantes is taking it all in with an acuity every bit as sharp as his camel-skin blazer. He's probably thinking about how gently I will not go into that good night, because it sounds from the one side of my phone conversation he has heard that I might be playing jeopardy with my job. He picks up briskly from where we left off as I hangs up the phone.

"You're in control of the entire hotel, right? I'd like to ask you about your staff, okay?" This Cervantes certainly is direct, I thinks to myself again. I could use a guy like that in middle management. Kind of a go-between to take some of the flak, cushion the blows— the slings and arrows of outrageous fortune that hector and humble fall guys like me. Well, cut to the short hairs, I zero in and tells him everything he asks and more or less just the way it might have happened. He seems especially interested in the bartenders, waitresses, and chambermaids. Even gets a little close to home when he asks about the underground economy of a hotel like this one.

"Underground economy?" I ponder, playing it as innocent as a baby dove in a brothel. "The closest thing to an underground economy that a classy hotel like this one might have is a meter for the lower-level parking." He smiled at that one.

Suddenly, he's up on his feet, strolling around the office, complimenting me on my green thumb (I don't tell him that when you've got your secretary 'under your thumb', it don't need to be green for your plants to thrive), and gazing like a sunburnt mule at the pictures on the wall. Well, I'll be damned if he don't stop and lollygag in front of your picture. The one with you—the proud Mama Sam—and Melanie and Jill when they was all decked out in those graduation gowns. You, all bright and bonnie in your own dress, arrayed like royalty at a regatta. Remember the picture? Well he's all curious about who you are and so I've got no choice: I smiles and walks up beside him. Trading congeniality for an understated affability, I says to him, "You see these three women? These are three of our best employees. It takes a shining star like you to point out stellar quality like this." Then I mention you by name, Sam, and laud your work history. "Samantha here has been with us since the beginning. Her daughters, Jill and Melanie are two of our top waitresses. If all our employees were half as dedicated as these three, we would be guaranteed a five star ranking from now until eternity." That's right. I said *eternity.* He hesitates, as if uncertain for the first time of what to say next. Then he swings around and faces me squarely. The next question he asks me gives me pause.

There are moments in some conversations when time seems to contract a hit out on you. And down you go. This is one of those moments. "Do you really believe that all of one's many unremembered, nameless deeds impact eternity," he asks. And from behind the penetrating brown wells of wisdom that reflect truth within his eyes comes the tolling supernatural knell of the knowledge that I have been wildly wrong to suspect him of insincerity. Now that I know that the brown in them was not even close to being a sign of the bullshit I'd been expecting, I have to respond honestly. His earnest conduct impels an honest answer.

I turn to your picture. Stare intently into the brightness of your eyes. Out of the corner of my eye, at the razor's edge of my perceptions, I see him watching. He studies me. He seems to be memorizing my movements, my methodical emotional release. I am reluctant to say what comes next. But I do not falter. In clear, deep, measured tones I speak to him, but I address your image. "I am certain there are choices people may regret, but time brings opportunities for redemption, and with it comes choices they may make without regret. A great man once wrote of *Love's Labour's Lost,* but when a labour brings about love, the result can sometimes be a twin blessing. And this," I add, "is a timeless truth." Of course he asks me if he can quote me on that, for the book and everything (just when I was so sure he was sincere). What can I say? I've been kissed by the Blarney Stone, so once in a long while I kiss back.

Brings to mind a tune I like. Last year a band called Fleetwood Mac put out a song called *Gypsy* that touched me deeply right after Melanie played it for me for the first time. "Lightning strikes, maybe once, maybe twice." Striking while the iron is hot has always been a motto of mine, and I tell him that as well, leaving him to draw his own conclusions.

Cervantes turns to leave, but hesitates again, and asks his last question with his back turned. "If you ever hurt someone so deeply that you'd do anything in the world to make it up to them, how could you ever repay them for having offended them?" I am grateful he cannot see my eyes as I struggle for control.

You still stare at me from your picture on the wall, though. Or rather the image of your joy and proud accomplishments resonates, and it brings my answer. "I'm not a religious man. But I would give everything in my power to repay them. Ultimately, if it were possible, I would take upon myself the offense, and carry it forward until I could release them from its bondage forever." Hastily, I wipe my eyes before he can see the moisture and add, "These are but the ramblings of a sadder and a wiser man whose albatross has long weighed him down."

Slowly, deliberately, and with as grave and sincere an aspect as I have ever seen in my office, Cervantes turns, clasps my hand with judicious warmth, nods affirmatively and shows himself out of the room. A calm farewell in the eye of an emotional storm. I close the door behind him; I sits down at my desk; and I thank you, Sam, for recommending the still, sad music of D. H. Lawrence's *Piano*—a poem which has often helped me to see that it is neither unmanly to appreciate poetry, nor embarrassingly feminine of me to "weep like a child for the past." Because the past still remains, though we must leave it behind, as perhaps the most irregular and eccentric route to the future we have at our disposal. I don't know whether that Cervantes got me thinking along philosophical lines, but I do know that your influence predisposes me to recognize kindred spirits when I see them, and I concludes my interview with this observation (you'll see from this couplet that even crude louts like myself can toss off a decasyllabic line or two if need be): Many brave heart knights arrive and depart, but this Cervantes has the stoutest heart.

Nineteen

PATERNITY — SUMMER OF 1960

After Cynthia finishes, I sit in silence for a while, and then speak softly, "When labour brings about love? That's what he said, right? Your mom was the labourer, and good old Ernie was the lover, right? That's what it sounds like. And that Coleridge allusion: Unrequited fatherhood must have been quite the albatross, wouldn't you agree? But likely more 'unfulfilled' than unreturned love."

Cynthia and Zachary move onto the thick shag carpet in front of the fireplace. He leans forward for emphasis as he speaks. "Sounds like Ernie was devoted to your grandmother. Did you get the impression he was talking directly to her picture, even when answering your father's questions? And they shared a love of poetry!"

"He would appear to be the one, if all were as it appears. Mom and Aunt Jill only found out the truth about their father when they found the following pages in my grandma's journal." Cynthia smiles at Zachary's patience, and gives him an affectionate squeeze as she pulls the sheaf from her satchel. "You've been introduced to mom and dad, Ernie and Aunt Jill. Time to meet Samantha. We all get our poetic passion from her! She loved art and literature; she dabbled in short stories and poetry; but she read far more than she ever wrote, and wrote far more than most people ever read. Most of all, she lived. With an unfaltering vitality, she lived! In her retirement, she travelled all over Europe, took in the culture. Oh how I wished

I'd been there with her. Listen. You can hear my grandmother speak through the words of this pivotal journal entry of hers:

Like a robot, the clerk asked her name. "Samantha Damsella," Sam replied with an air of indifference.

"Occupation?" the clerk barked, autonomously.

"Chambermaid," came the curt reply.

"Full time or part time?" The question sounded like a decision, but it was not her decision.

"Part time," Sam admitted reluctantly, and on and on went the litany of bureaucratic questions and answers in what seemed like an endless cascade of callous disdain, until the appalling peroration brought down the dismal curtain on her welfare claim: "Claim denied."

Of course there were the babies to consider. Jill and Melanie were just six weeks old, and she hadn't even gotten her figure back. Where were they going to get the money for food, clothing, and shelter? Jocelyn and Ernie had helped when she was pregnant, but she would have to fend for herself now, and who would look after the little ones if she was going to go back to work full time at the hotel? How had she ever gotten pregnant in the first place? That's what Jocelyn had asked her, and who was the father? The truth was hard to tell. A burning question she could never quite bring herself to answer.

The summer of 1961 would soon be over, but her troubles had begun with the birth of that turbulent decade known simply as the Sixties. Jocelyn had warned her not to slip. "Don't let things slide on you. Like those literary standards. I mean, what is this world coming to when a book like *Lady Chatterley's Lover* is ruled as not obscene? Then you have a congressional committee looking into payola. And so it goes... I tell you sister, there is a growing corruption, lax moral standards, and an underground economy all around us." Jo claimed that vigilance was critical in the light of what she called 'backward tendencies'.

Well, her sister Jocelyn always was the snobbish prude in the family, thought Sam. Her husband, Tom Sneed the accountant, exerted an overly conservative influence upon her, and it did not help with their attitude that Sam volunteered for the local ladies' auxiliary, who promoted everything ranging from the newly available birth control pill to women's liberation. Sam wasn't trying to ruffle her sister's feathers, she just wanted to make her own choices. Now it looked as if those choices were bringing some unexpected consequences. So it was more than a little ironic that she had said goodbye to a big chunk of her personal freedom by giving birth to twins on that sunny morning in May of 1961.

It had been those lax moral standards Jo had been most concerned about—or so she had said, anyway—that had got Sam in the family way in the first place. But what had looked like a series of cloudy days had 'blossomed into a sea morning' with the arrival of those twin bundles of delight she named Gillian and Melanie. Still, what would she say when the girls grew old enough to ask the same question that was on everyone's lips? How could she tell them that she had been... put upon to put out? Every word sounded both false and simultaneously slutty. Would they want the sordid details? It was this context and these questions whirling about Sam's head whenever she thought back to that hot August night in 1960.

Ernie had always promised that all she had to do was entertain the guests. If she showed them a good time—a very good time— then she could live permanently in the hotel, all expenses paid. Ernie was always a man of his word, always a regular guy. The arrangement was gentlemanly at first, but before long some of the men told her that they had paid Ernie for something a little more. She knew they meant sexual favours. Sam was indignant and offended at first, but after Ernie made it clear that the hotel room lease that she wanted came at a price, and for the right 'disposition' she could expect a little something extra herself, she had decided, why not? Jo had always warned her to steer clear of Ernie's schemes. She had said that Sam's honey curves, her smouldering emerald green eyes, and her husky contralto voice would surely send the wrong message. "Men want one thing," she said. "Give it to them once,

The Poetic Ambassador

and they keep coming back for more." Jo never said "I told you so" after the pregnancy. At least not in those exact words. But she did say it in so many other ways that Sam finally shut her out. For many years, anyways. Anyhow, back in August, 1960, it turned out that Jo was the least of her worries.

The owner of the hotel, Dennis Scrimshaw, had noticed her. He had begun to pay her some attention, complimenting her on how well the guests were enjoying their rooms, and swinging by with a colourful bouquet of marigolds and zinnia now and then just to show his appreciation for all her hard work and special attention to the guests. It didn't take Sam long to figure out that those bouquets—merely floral tokens of affection, she thought at first—meant he was looking for a little special attention for himself as well. Scrimshaw was a big, brutal man with fierce blue eyes and a rock solid jawline. He more than filled out a formidable six and a half foot frame. A little on the beefy side, but muscular and fairly hard—on the employees. He had been athletic in schools back east, a football quarterback. But when he had tried out for the Toronto Argonauts after graduation in 1937, he failed to make the team. Meniere's disease meant recurring episodes of vertigo, eventually leading to hearing loss. A couple of years later, he would be exempted from military service because of it. His bitterness at not having gone pro intensified when he realized he'd never fight for his country in the war either, and taken together this had left him with a cruel streak that he barely masked with extreme shows of generosity and affectations of benevolence. He out-gave every businessman in town at Christmas time. His loss of hearing meant he had ears everywhere and always 'listened' with an ever-greater acuteness to those 'ears', as if he must 'experience' everything he could to make up for all he felt he must be missing.

Of course this type of over-compensation meant that he had gotten wind of Ernie's little sideline, and although Sam wasn't the only hustle in the game, her full-figured shape had already taken on quite an allure for him. He'd caught wind of the promises Ernie had made to Sam; and although he was a man of limitless means with a fairly firm control over his libido, he'd come to appreciate enough of her hidden charms to find himself powerfully drawn to her. His fiancé was out of town. They were planning to be married at the end of the month, and they had decided to honeymoon in Hawaii, celebrating its recent status as the 50th U.S. State. One last fling would be just the thing. But he had thought of another way to celebrate in his own way this upcoming special day.

Sam had just drawn a long bath. It was her birthday, August 18. A quarter of a century, and where had it gone? Suds and lavender saturated the water. It had been a long, tiring shift, and nothing disturbed the even tranquility of her time in the tub, not even the solitary ribbiting of a bullfrog lost and alone upon the strand of beach somewhere out near Riverside Park. A lingering lassitude made her tarry as she sprinkled the warm water in rivulets of moisture along her upper arms and up her neck, baptising every part of her body in a fine liquidity. All was silence and golden slumbers again. Sam found peace, and slipped into a customary reverie on exotic ports of call she would someday like to visit.

Athens. Paris. London. Crete. Crete? Even as her mind wanders about her world of dreams in search of cultural highlights, a misfit appears to mar the reverie. She starts again with artists whose works she would love to see: Picasso. Van Gogh. Renoir. Magritte. Magritte? Alas. *The Treachery of Images.* When is a pipe not a pipe? When it has a dream attached to it?

Sam stares with somber intensity out at the full moon, turning her musings to literary giants she has read. Shakespeare. Keats. Hemingway. Dante. Dante? Hell is an ardent flame who attracts the rebel heart, but soon fizzles and fades in the chill dark dawn of despair. Sam's mind wanders to that old Hemingway story she'd learned in school. What was the name? *Hills Like White Elephants.* What was it Jo had said after reading it? "Jig never had a choice. She was railroaded into submission." Half a decade later, in the summer of 65, Sam would hear a new Motown song: *The Tracks of My Tears.* This song prompted her to cry while she was teaching her children to read subtext for the first time, because she remembered how she had, while she was still a young girl, cried for the hills running into the distance off to one side of Hemingway's railroad tracks, for the anguish of an unexpected pregnancy—Jig's, not her own. Not yet.

By the summer of 1960, Sam has not even heard of concepts such as the Big Bang theory of the creation of the universe or the discovery of new celestial bodies known as blue galaxies. But her world is about to be irrevocably transformed in ways no less profound than either of these concepts involving space, time and other dark matter. The soft summer breeze plays through her bathroom drapes, gently soothing her as she steps dripping from the tub. The water has cooled, but her spirits are warming to the easy, gracious, homespun melody of an old radio tune, lilting down through the twilight air. She has been favoured with a two-bedroom suite with a rather large kitchenette. It is located at the far end of the third floor. It's the top floor, and the view looks out northwest towards the river. She could hear if someone came up the stairs from the second-floor landing, especially when the person had a heavy step. Sometimes, she recognizes a man by his steps. Ernie has a quick, concentrated gait. His step is easy to recognize.

By nine, she pours a glass of wine. Her smooth, slender fingers—strong from years of folding hospital corners—flutter gently about her open nightdress, then casually caress the rim of the wine glass. The heat from the day had not yet fully worn away. She sips the dry liquid slowly, savoring its delicate bouquet. Five minutes pass. Ten. As time crawls to well beyond a quarter past the hour, she finds herself thinking back to 1949. A giddy time for thirteen-year-olds. Soldiers would still don their regalia on August 14th to commemorate VJ Day, the official end to the Second World War. It had been four years since Japan had surrendered to mark its official end, but victorious memories were still fresh in many men's minds. He had been a corporal. It was the VJ day celebrations—Victory over Japan day. His uniform was freshly pressed. She wouldn't say his name. Best to forget painful memories. Who marries a thirteen-year-old anyways? "Lots of men," Jo had said. Sam is reminiscing about that day—streamers, parade floats and kissing booths. She drifts off in comfort, pushing thoughts of those old days from her mind, when she hears the knock on her door. Afterwards, she'd remember having recognized the heavy step on the stair, but that was a memory she never had. The mind plays tricks. Time slows down, but details get blurred because it speeds up again as it 'lifts a hand to wave goodbye' (an anachronism from a 1978 song reaches back in the moment that it takes to see her granddaughter in her unborn daughter's eyes). Best to forget...

Sam remembers her muffled shouts, the broken wine glass and a spilled red stain on her cream-coloured carpet that silently screams 'rape' even when she mutely chokes back the tears, because by then he is on her, with his hand on a towel that has somehow worked its way over her mouth. In an instant he is inside her, penetrating her again and again. His weight? It was like a dead weight that lay heavier than hate upon her. With his hot, hulking, sweaty body on top of her, it seems like he cannot sate his sudden lust, and then he is as suddenly spent as he was violently aroused. She does not even hear Ernie enter the room just as Scrimshaw is finally finishing with her, and releasing his suffocating grip that had muted her screaming mouth. Sam remembered afterwards that she'd heard Ernie's quick, concentrated step on the stairs. But that too was a memory she never had... or at least for a long while to come.

It is difficult for her to say whether Ernie had been waiting until he knew Scrimshaw would have finished, but because of his timing, Sam always had her suspicions. Scrimshaw seemed disoriented, like he was standing in a room that had spun out of control. If he hadn't let go of her, he might have choked her to death. Maybe that's what he intended. A way to put a permanent end to what he had done, put the vile act away forever (only years later would she sense what she had finally come to know as the 'defensive projection' inherent in that logic). The ultimate denial of a crime of passion. Could either he or Ernie be blamed? Had she asked for it? She feels a new weight now—the weight of social pressure and prejudice. Shock. Disgust.

The Poetic Ambassador

Horror. Disbelief. Disbelief? Suddenly Ernie was there in the room, hauling Scrimshaw off, and wringing out his remorse like a eulogy wrings tears from mourners at a funeral. At first she thinks they are crocodile tears, but Ernie makes Scrimshaw swear that he'll always do right by her if he doesn't want his fiancé will find out about his 'indiscretion'. He swears.

Just over nine months later, a pair of beautiful twins are born. Two new blue galaxies swimming into view, and the world will never be the same. Now how could she tell them who their father was? Wasn't her silence part of the bargain?

———))(((———

Zack lets out a long, low whistle. "To think that such beauty arose from such an act of brutality. So it would seem that good old Ernie was not much more than a father *figure* after all. I'm also guessing you got *your* figure through the maternal line." As he plays musical fingers, tracing the contours of her shapely hips, she squirms seductively, tantalizing him coyly, and pulls away until, finally, his bad timing dawns on him.

"Anything else stand out?" Cynthia gazes expectantly at Zachary.

"Your grandmother must have been ahead of her peers by decades. I'd have loved to have met her. The things we might have discussed. I mean, she appears to have an element of... how should I say it? Refined cosmopolitan artistic and literary tastes. You inherited that from her as well." Zachary takes Cynthia in his arms once again, but she continues to hold back. Then he caps off his comment by adding, "While it might be nice to meet the grand dame, I'd much rather mate the granddaughter." Standing swiftly, she bends to slap him playfully, but he catches her wrist in a sudden 'catch and release' movement; and in an instant they're both standing. Zack laughs uncomfortably. The pause lengthens.

"We're not playing chess, but I've a feeling you're trying to rook me," Cynthia finally says sullenly. Without trying to lighten the mood, she turns towards the wine. "Enough for two I think." You want a top up? By the way, I've still got one knight left."

"I'd love a top... and a bottom, if you've one to loan me." Zack seems to have tunnel vision. "And leave off on the Phil Collins, please; one more night may prove too much for me. Oh, I'm sore from the floor—this pile is not as thick as it was wont to be."

"Oh, you pile it on pretty thick yourself, my friend. Now and then, when then is now again (you know like at the reunions), we may, though we applaud the ends, mock the merits of mercenary means." Cynthia waits for a moment for her wit to sink in. But it seems Zack is deliberately being obtuse.

"By all means. But are you feeling the spirit, sister?"

"Can I get a witness? No really, Zack. Let's consider an anachronism." Cynthia is not about to let it go. "If Ernie had told Samantha in 1961, just after her twin birth, that 'thunder strikes maybe once, maybe twice,' it would have been anachronistic. But if some outmoded racist or sexist idea from the past miraculously reappears in the present, what do we call that?"

"An inverse anachronism?"

"I call it bullshit!" Cynthia punctuates her pronouncement with a long loud sip of her wine. "Grandma Sam worked within the system to find her own freedom, and—."

"Are you sure Ernie wasn't your grandfather?"

Cynthia nearly spits out her wine, and gives Zachary a frosty look. "I'm as positive as a double negative," she says. But then she rejoins Zachary, melding back into his comfortable dark green leather couch. She is not entirely satisfied that she's made strides for the fine art of negation as a means of compromise, but she wants to appear willing to give a little more than she is getting.

"I guess it's a twin thing with the doubles." Zachary shrugs, oozing nonchalance like honeybees ooze nectar. This is the point at which he decides to pour on the sweetness. "But listen, Cynthia, the circumstances surrounding your mother's conception were not exactly normal. Just when did your mother find out the truth about Scrimshaw? And when did they tell you?" He can't tell by her expression whether or not there are even more skeletons in the family closet, but it's kind of nice to know her grandmother Sam seemed to have had a pretty good handle on the whole ugly situation. Hell she even had the relative objectivity to pen the entire episode in an impersonal narrative. He says as much to Cynthia.

"Maybe more than we might think," she replies enigmatically. "Ernie died just before the turn of the century. That's when they found out. Mom wrote it all out in this transcript of a telephone call she shared with her sister on the occasion of their 40th birthday. It was 2001, and I had just turned 16 that year. So listen with your soul, because it's a heartache for the mind—oh and, you may still meet Grandma Sam someday. She's still a feisty feminist at the ripe young age of 75":

Twenty

ETERNITY AND TIME – 2001

Melanie and Jill hadn't spoken to each other in years, but turning forty has a way of helping to put things in perspective. Ernie Montaigne had passed on two years ago, and Dennis Scrimshaw had preceded him by a year. Secrets gone to the grave. A strange fidelity paired with a loyalty bred by the basest of betrayals. Letters from Montaigne to each of them had finally related the truth about the man who really was their father.

Jill spoke first. "Hello Melanie. I decided that knowing who our father was is the same as having no father, because even if he was our father, he had never really been our father. And he never will be our father. The farther along that beach I walked in the changing tide the surer I was that this was one paternity paradox I could finally fathom. Hey, it's the first year of the new century, maybe it's time we changed some attitudes. But not about him.

Guess what, sis? Mama Sam found a quarter of a million dollars in her bank account, deposited by an anonymous donor. Her retirement is secure. Europe beckons her. She'll be living la Vida Loca!"

There was a long silence on the line. Both sisters had a well-earned disdain for fatherhood in all its forms, and suddenly they found it strange to be fighting back thoughts about the pecuniary advantages which had mysteriously arisen out of the unexpected twin blessings Mama Sam had always said that they were.

Choked with emotion, Melanie found no words. She reflected on the cryptic script that had been inscribed upon Ernie Montaigne's tombstone: *Labour Delivers Love.* Kris had told her that Ernie once suggested the result of this aphorism was sometimes a twin blessing. Then she found the words she knew Jill would most appreciate. "Do you remember the note you scribbled that day way back in 1979 in Ms. Lodge's English class?

Now it was Jill's turn to reflect in silence. She did not fail to grasp the irony. "What note? That was twenty-two years back! High school was a life-time ago, Melanie. It all seems like a dream that time once conjured into reality. Don't tell me you remember. You don't, do you?"

"If you could see me right now, you'd be dazzled by my smile, sister dear," Melanie exclaimed enthusiastically. "I saved your note, and without knowing it, you almost repeated it just now, verbatim! It is a timeless truth. That's what you said when you wrote these words: *'Eternity and time are a blend of sleeping and waking dreams.'* Jill, Ernie knew we all live with regrets. But remember what he told Kris about how 'time brings opportunities for redemption.'? If we dare to dream eternity awake in time, it will surely have a positive effect upon our eternal redemption."

Jill thought for a second and replied, "Melanie, how long have you been this dizzy? Do you ever get vertigo? Because I do. And my hearing is not what it used to be lately, either. I distinctly thought I heard you say something about eternal redemption. If there is a heaven, then whoever gave Mama Sam all that money probably made the list, but I'd hate to love him. Love to Kris and your own twin blessings: Anika and Cynthia must be in grade 10 this year, right? Sweet sixteen! Let them get away with a little bit now and then. Remember what a sergeant-major Mama Sam was. Don't wait as long as she did to mellow out. Those kids need lax discipline so they can have a few happy accidents of their own and avoid making all the mistakes we did, you know? Like testing the boundaries. Love you, Melanie. Happy Birthday."

"We don't need any more happy accidents! But, yeah, I think Ernie got religion before he died. Listen, the only definite thing about the next life is that it sure as hell is not going to be like this life, because you really can get too much of a good thing now, can't you? And if change is as good as a holiday, you had better find someone to make it for you, because there is only one constant currency in this world and that is relative change. So, love you too, Jill. And before you go and change your mind, sister, give Mama Sam a kiss and a hug for me. She'll be 66 this year, and I agree that a retirement trip would do her a world of good. Kris sends hugs and kisses, too."

In unison, as if they'd never allowed acrimony into their tight relationship, the twins recited Eliot's final framing device from *The Wasteland:* "Good night ladies, good night, sweet ladies, good night, good night."

<hr>

Cynthia stared coolly at Zachary as she put down the transcript. "Ah, yes, the endgame of "A Game of Chess." He said, wizening his imaginary beard. "Logic would seem to be against the existence of miracles, and yet there, in your grandmother's bank account, is the money, vaunting itself right into the vault. It is almost enough to make a man believe in eternal redemption. I might even be persuaded to give it a try—it if it wasn't such an interminable read. But that business about it being a series of waking dreams, now that sounds vaguely compelling." Then, in what might pass for a non sequitur, he added, "Besides, who needs music when the conversation is so bracing."

"Well I wouldn't say eternity precludes music, but yes, I will follow suit with Time in taking the most direct way, Zack. It has stolen up on us, hasn't it? It must be nearly one in the morning. I am eager to hear more about what you have to say regarding my family and there remains that portfolio business to discuss, but my light headedness from the wine is being sublimated by an overweening weariness. Next comes the fever and the fret unless I get some sleep. I know you have your bottom line, but tonight is more a night for a guest room, if you don't mind."

Cynthia stifles a yawn calculated to corroborate her story, and Zack gently nods, conjuring up a quip about her having used 'sublimated' as a malapropism for 'submerged', but deciding instead to acquiesce easily. "Hey, if wasn't the twenty-first century, I'd never let you get away with a ruse like that. But since it is, follow me. Your bedroom awaits, madam." He relieves her of her wine glass, sliding it onto the counter, and switches off the fireplace and the living room lights. First, he pauses at the first door on the right, to lean in and show her his king-size waterbed-dominated master bedroom. "This is where you can join me in case you get lonesome," He whispers invitingly. Then, after He shows her the washroom, they proceed down the hall to the third door. "The guest room has a nice queen. You two should get along admirably."

Zachary gives her a short kiss on the cheek, and wishes her good night, before leaving her on her own.

Finally he disappears into his own room, and she completes her toiletries, something that makes her grateful for having listened while her mother had taught her to carry along a bag with personal effects wherever she went. But back in the blue room, under the original Georgia O'Keeffe, lit from below with a light suffused through an obsidian lens with an opaque topaz camphor glow, Cynthia gazed up at the central image—an ebullient monument to ostentatious wealth—the Radiator Building on a rainy night. The painting resolves into quadrants: A flash of red off to the center left, a smoky swoosh of white to the center right, while darkness vies with office-window fluorescence straight up the centre to an imposing apex that stares down atop the building with a monolithic menace seemingly out to exact compliance, conformity, and so many more complex concepts than she ever thought could belong to one weary queen. And it is this last self-contained, self-satisfied phallic symbol of an image which sends her off to dreamland.

Somehow one last vestige of a straggling night terror makes its way into the depths of her subconscious mind: *I'm being raped by the painting in the blue room.*

A few minutes later, Cynthia rolls over, and if one were sharp of hearing, the following mumbling fragment could be discerned: "...better to be raped by a painting than painted into a corner by a rapist..." Moments later, she is fast asleep.

Twenty-One

THREAD OF SEPARATION

Morning never came early enough for Zachary Speller. His regular regimen includes a protein drink, 200 push-ups, 100 sit-ups and a half hour on the stationary-bike. Weekends or workdays, the routine never varies—but there was always room for enrichment and improvisation. Zachary's heart quickens, but not from the exercise: He suddenly remembers Cynthia chose Georgia O'Keeffe over him last night. She sleeps late. Maybe she'd like a run. More likely a breakfast snack. Fruit salad; bran muffin; tapioca or yogurt. Better furnish the nook counter, slide out the rosewood chairs. Set out the stoneware plates, but don't forget the soft brown woven placemats, the brightly shining silverware and the green napkins, soft, rich, and fresh from the laundry. Cynthia's family could do a lot worse than wanting to meet a guy like Zachary Speller, he thinks oozing self-congratulatory confidence. What is he talking about? Zachary Speller! You deserve that girl; just like you deserve to be poetic ambassador. But what if you can't have them both? Who or what would you choose? Well, what if she won? The next best thing to being, might be to have and to hold the poetic ambassador. Best not to get ahead of himself. (The only thing worse than the 'L' word was the 'M' word—there are worlds in those words).

Sometimes it is better to be able to select from among a wide array instead of only two options. So Zachary glances through his massive assortment of CDs and settles on some old Al Stewart. Just as he puts it on, Cynthia ambles blearily down the hall towards him. Giving comfortable hugs is something at which she is particularly good. "Getting used to that is now officially on my list," he proclaims, hoping that it comes off sounding less obsessed than he thought it did.

"Does that mean my kiss was on your list? Because that would just be corny, and a teensy weensy bit desperate." Cynthia is less somnolent than she appears. *He doesn't really think I'm buying his domestic bliss bullshit, does he?* Cynthia graciously accepts the chair Zachary slides out for her, and they sit down to an opening gambit.

"I don't really have a list." There was something about direct honesty. It was not only refreshing in what some were beginning to call the post-truth era, but it also cut through a lot of the subterfuge. Zachary dishes out the fruit in two bowls and gets a selection of yogurt from the fridge. "That was just something I said, for effect; like in the movies. But I meant the sentiment behind the grandiose claim." He stops before he goes too far. He hopes.

"Good strawberries," she says, smacking her lips at the succulent juice. "I'll have some kiwi and banana yogurt, because Kiwis have the best bananas." She is still licking her lips as he hands her the yogurt, and their fingers momentarily lock around the small white container. He pulls his away first, then picks up a large red strawberry and teasingly holds it in front of her slightly open mouth. She coaxes it dextrously from his outstretched fingers with her tongue and teeth. *What is this? Some Henry Fielding Tom Jones fantasy food fetishism.* Cynthia smiles as she opens her yogurt, and asks for some orange juice. "Listen Zachary, you've had the chance to meet my folks—figuratively speaking. Before we talk about that ZG business, why don't you tell me a bit about your background?

The Year of the Cat plays softly in the background, and he thinks about what it means to follow 'til your sense of which direction completely disappears. Was he falling for this woman? True, all the formal requirements were there, and they shared more than merely

The Poetic Ambassador

a passion for poetry it would seem. But still. Was there insufficient information to adequately assess the situation? He decided he had to put her to a test of mettle. He would tell her his Heartaches' story. Then he would see what she does with the defining issue. "Okay, Cynthia, come with me to Chicago. Come back with me to an earlier time when I was a rock and roll singer in a band called the Heartaches."

Again with the fetishism—this time rock and roll—does this guy ever grow up? I wonder if I am a part of his rock and roll fantasy. Cynthia reaches over and strokes Zack's arm, assuring him she'd love to hear his story. She is intentionally going against character by placating him condescendingly. But then again, it seems high time to get further into his head and put him off his poetry.

Aphrodite! He thinks. Save me from the maneuvers of a wily woman. "Cynthia, you know that I left my home in Windsor, Ontario for the Windy City straight out of high school and never looked back. Dad worked part-time construction, but he never made much of himself; mom was a hairdresser; and when the two of them came together it was like dada on speed—it could be art, hell it could be a relationship... if it only stopped moving long enough to finish a sentence. I'd decided early on that my sentence was already over long ago, and the sooner I ended it the better off I would be. When I saw my chance to put a full stop on it for good, my exclamation point of departure was the westbound train from Detroit to Chicago. I traded a fractious family life for a feast of friends; dead-end jobs for a rock group and a guitar; and I gave up Lake Erie for Lake Michigan. There would be no regrets on the first two counts, and as far as the lakes go they're both supposed to be great, but that could just as well signify the irony that they both have equally vast amounts of pollution. Which just goes to show, the more decrepit the chassis, the more bodywork that is needed."

"Did you just compare a stunning natural body of water to a run-down jalopy?"

"That wasn't really the purpose of my analogous juxtaposition."

"What was the point?"

"Entropy."

"Entropy what?"

"Things fall apart, and what appears to be order devolves into disorder."

"Didn't you leave a family in apparent disorder to embrace a new order?"

"Now you've got it! One must take a proactive stance towards entropy. Remember old Merwin. I'm just stitching with the thread of separation, and its colour is the colour of absence. They're sure to miss me enough to want to change, don't you think?" Zachary is clearing the table now, shuffling all the plates and silverware away into the dishwasher.

I love the way he pulls poetry into real life and makes it seem so relevant. Cynthia! Fraternizing with the enemy can only lead you to one conclusion: he's going down, stitching or no stitching. She helps him wipe the table. Al Stewart is crooning about theatre footlights now, and about having seen familiar faces there from ancient times.

Zachary shuts down the music, and they revisit the living room again, resuming their comfortable conversation. "You know the problem with numbers, don't you?" He crinkles his face, puffing out his cheeks at the same time, so he looks like a slightly ridiculous porky pig wannabe.

Cynthia shakes her head coyly. *Enough with the riddles, already.*

"They're too predictable. They always conform to a logical pattern or follow each other so stoically in a linear sequential procession from one to forever." He adopts his cleverer-than-thou pose, assuming that she finds this side of him attractive.

"See, now you've disproven your thesis. By rights, four should come before the number five, but here it precedes 'ever.' I've even seen it precede 'play' and in some rare cases 'sight' or 'shadowing.' But more of that to come, yet, right?"

Laughing partly at her silly cum stellar wit and partly to tease her, he urges her to stop; pleading with her to be more careful about not putting the mule in formulaic, and then he takes a moment to introduce the band, and his stage name. "My real name did not exactly typify rock and roll, so I adopted the stage name of Jules Desmond. 'Meet J. D. and the Heartaches?'" he says waving his hand to conjure them with an elaborate gesture. But instead, Zack pulls out the short story he has written about this phase of his life, and he begins to read in tones that carry all the emphasis of drama but with an understated ferocity that never fails to edge closer towards intense, especially when the action escalates. Somehow he senses that if he is to impress this 'belle dame sans merci', he must remain more subdued than is his wont. He doesn't always succeed.

"And it's a holiday. And we're having a party!"

Twenty-Two

MR. RELIABLE

For The Heartaches and their friends, Independence Day 1999 meant it was not just another party at Gina's house on Delaplaine Road in Chicago. It had been an annual extravaganza for three years in a row, but by party time on this particular year, the band would never remain quite the same. People are always changing of course, but it all-too-often happens that their destiny is largely determined by other people's choices. J. D. and the Heartaches were no exception to this rule.

Gina Venice and Cyndi Sneed were mature for twenty, having both lost their parents in tragic accidents at a young age, and subsequently having become poster children for catastrophic causes. The girls each turned away from what they called a 'vapid lifestyle' and embraced music to fill the void.

So far, so clichéd. Cynthia continues to express an interest though her thoughts carry her in an entirely different direction from the one he hopes his story will take her. *Does Zack really think I'm buying this 'feast of friends' malarkey? Realism must come naturally. Still, he's proven himself to be a good listener, even if his wit and behaviour sometimes appears as contrived as last dance efforts for would-be Lotharios on cruise control. But I'll give him the benefit of the doubt, and constrain my more caustic criticisms.*

Gina played keyboards like Tori Amos, and some said she looked a little like her as well, with eyes of sapphire flecked with hints of light grey; meanwhile, Cyndi was another Suzanne Ciani on the synthesizer, and she had dark green eyes that threatened to drown anyone who looked too deeply into them. Cyndi and Gina also sang backup, rounding out the group's vocals with an astounding depth and range. These attractive young red-heads both had a twisted sense of humour, and the young man they especially liked to tease was twenty-one-year-old Dean Stimpson, who played a mean bass guitar.

Dean was never quite sure how he'd gotten to be what both Gina and Cyndi characterized as 'reliable'. He had never thought of himself as one of those kind of guys. True, they could be putting him on. They'd done that many times before. But it was also true that he had always been relatively conscientious, and even somewhat sincere, on the odd occasion. Mostly he was what some people call 'taciturn', but he was also level-headed and sensible. Didn't the girls also frequently tell him he was responsible, selfless, and 'downright debonair?' Yes they did. But Dean had never thought that reliability was a compliment. More of a death knell, really. He saw it as an abstraction, and a final irrevocable step down to becoming a guy he called 'the doormat'.

Doormats were dependable, you could always count on them, they seldom if ever took risks, and they didn't deviate from the crowd; but, this didn't matter at all in Dean's opinion, because the one thing they could invariably guarantee is that they would be constantly stepped on and overlooked. It went without saying that Dean suffered from a persecution complex, which simply meant he spent a goodly amount of time getting defensive for no real reason. Dean balked at being labelled reliable. There had to be another layer of meaning. But he couldn't quite get it. He wasn't stupid, he was just drawn that way. Like a progressive variation on one of his more memorable bass lines, he travelled only as far afield as the rhythms of the music allowed. And he was speaking of music here only in the strictest, most instrumental sense one could possibly perceive. Namely, as a metaphor for social conventions. Dean consistently held a steady, punchy groove on all The Heartaches' hits. There were no substitutes. No stand-ins. No matter how much the girls kidded him about being Mr. Reliable, they knew his eccentricities were tame by comparison with the other members of the band.

Gina had spent all afternoon primping for her party, and she skyped Cyndi just a little after four. "It's about Dean. Can you pick him up? He said he'd be ready by eight. So predictable. Mr. Reliable all over again?" The two women shared a laugh about their private pet joke. "You could set a metronome by him. He always says what he's going to do, and then he does it." More laughter. *Not like a certain someone who went by the initials J. D.*, Gina thought to herself obliquely.

Cyndi put on her mock serious look and fitted her voice to the image. "He certainly is all that and a fine piece of coloratura, in the bargain, Gina! It's all about that bass—no treble." Gina laughed and told her that would make a catchy song. Cyndi rolled her eyes, and said, "too trite, and the play on words is weak. But what's say I shake up Dean a little. I'll pick him up, not at eight, but at eight thirty. That is sure to throw him off his game."

Gina's vivacious musical laughter floated down through her spacious living room, with its half dozen patent brown leather couches, each flanked by a pair of Areca Palms. "Don't be surprised if he's already taken a cab by then, Dee. He prides himself on his good timing, and I've already told him that Jules and the others are going to be here by nine. Hunk or not, you know that he can't stand to be late, because he's—". Just then the doorbell chimed, prematurely ending the conversation.

Cyndi knew what Gina was about to say anyways. She took no small amount of pleasure from being able to correctly finish her friend's sentences. "Because he's such a gigolo," Cyndi said raising her hands to the blank screen that stared back from where her friend's face had recently laughed.

Then she switched off her computer and went on with her daily rifle through her wardrobe. She took her time, finally settling on a gypsy theme, and narrowing down the blouses, coloured skirts and petticoats until she selected a nice bright yellow blouse with a dark green skirt combination. Candled artistic designs in leather made up the skirt's fringe, and she knew that her new LV purse would set it off perfectly! She also knew she had just the right pair of large golden hoops, and a pure white petticoat to undergird the whole affair. It was good that she'd gotten her hair done earlier. If her gorgeous red curls were any wilder or wavier, she'd have to apply for a mermaid position with Old Triton himself.

This train of thought led her to recollect Keats' nightingale "on the foam of perilous seas, in fairy lands forlorn." Jules had turned them on to the Romantics and as she laid out her eveningwear, she mused over the themes of freedom and independence. Maybe it was the holiday or something, but she found herself comparing Dean and Jules on these issues. Trading the safety of a cage for the precariousness of liberty so that one may sing freely always sounds like an overture at first, but it often ends up like a cacophonous deluge with some honest doubt about whether or not you'll be able to live to play another day. At least the cage is personal. Even if it is only an emblem of personal constraints.

Still, she wondered. What if liberty were only found in the midst of the cataclysm? Dean would know, she said to herself. And laughed aloud at the irony. But Jules *would* know and act on that knowledge, without hesitation. Turning this thought over in her mind as if she was flipping to the other side of a favorite vinyl album, Cyndi concluded that he who hesitates is more fun! With that, she went to work finishing her playlist for the drive across town to pick up Dean. She spent another half an hour or so wondering what he was going to say when saw her new red Mustang convertible. She decided that getting used to the new vehicle was a good excuse for being late. Not late for Dean, but for Gina. Cyndi pulled out of her driveway at 7:30 rocking out to *Everything Will Be Alright,* an anachronistic single from the *Hot Fuss* album by The Killers. Cyndi always was ahead of her time.

Twenty-Three

CYNTHIA'S SMILE

Cynthia smiles a coy unkempt smile. It is sloppy in the same sense that betrayal is unseemly in children. Zachary knows coyness when he sees it, but wilfully mistakes it for the essence of intrigue, because face it, he says to himself, she's out of your league. Therefore to prevent that situation wherein she must be "described as a warm friend cooling" he thinks that one must prevail upon her heart to the very chambers in order that it remain fervid and unfocused on all but the hot pursuit of *his* truth. They work at cross-purposes without either of them really fully knowing what the other is trying so hard to prevent, apart from getting at the truth about one another.

"Your friends have fertile imaginations." Cynthia's smile slides off into a veiled snicker as she stifles a yawn. "Do you find it warm in here?"

Zachary rises, deflated, switches off the fireplace, and crosses back to the couch with an idea that upstages him en route: "Which of my friends do you like least so far?" He wasn't expecting the rapid-fire satire.

"J. D."

"Technically, an alter ego could classify as an imaginary friend."

"What do those initials really stand for? Juno Domini? Judas Deist? Earth to Zachary. Roger that, we're clear to go, Houston. Lift off in 3-2-1. No really, I can, of course, relate to your appreciation of the best among the Romantics (what a sizzling little Keats ode that was!) and who couldn't completely fail to find fault with The Killers. It seems that Cyndi and I might be soul sisters. From your initial description, it would appear that Dean has all the right stuff that Cyndi might need to reach the outer limits... of her skill set."

"There is the question of whether or not personal freedom should ever be constrained. I have always felt that Cyndi was on the verge of writing that theme into a Grammy winner. She came close to nailing it on our last album. Maybe there was less there than met my eye, but what I saw seemed sound. And it was more real than most of our music turned out to be."

"If I was your girlfriend," and Cynthia's smile seems to be vying with the hot curves of Zachary's vintage green 1969 Porsche 911 as she says this, "I would slow dance a long waltz off with a short peer."

"Who might that peer be? Why does he have to be short?"

"It would appear that I've rankled you?"

"Still harping on appearances, woman! "Let be be finale of seem. The only emperor is the emperor of ice-cream."

"Wallace Stevens makes such delicious flavours, though, doesn't he? Sometimes—"

"Spread that around on rockier soil, we're still enjoying our screaming ice here in the loam."

"No. Seriously," Cynthia said smiling. And her smile was an epiphany trying hard not to be a symphony whose deconstruction was orchestrated by literary critics. "I've always pondered the extent to which Lennon and McCartney's charmingly understated "Let it be" was an homage to the very Wallace Stevens poem you just quoted a moment ago. After all, they shared a love for Picasso. Remember Paul McCartney's tribute to Pablo Picasso on the Band on the Run album. Wallace Stevens own tribute was of course *The Man with the Blue Guitar.*:

"You are basing this, these on one tenuous link: Picasso."

"Don't forget the parallels in syntax."

"Oh yes, of course: identical constructs except for the sudden insertion of an indefinite pronoun—the glaring, "it!" At once so amorphous in its reference as to be almost entirely generic. The Beatles rubber stamp of the status quo. And don't get me started on their *Revolution* that is so non-revolting it is revolting."

Cynthia poised herself on the edge of her seat, smiling with all the patience of one of Job's daughters, and then with one of her bewitchingly captivating twinkles that creased two tiny teasing dimples out of each of her otherwise smooth cheeks. "Okay, so it looks like you might need some help with the Beatles."

"*Help* was one movie that needed more help." But we've gotten off track. Pop music, regardless of how refined, cannot compare with the scientific detachment of a competent published poet like Stephens. Don't forget it. When he starts off with a simple word like "Let..." he is setting his text up against one of the most profound biblical passages ever written: *Let there be light.* So in that context, with that legacy of logos, the next few words are critical. "Let be be..." Here his construction echoes another highly allusive Shakespearian pair of *be's*: "To be or not to be." Now we've contextualized it even more, with these two resonant passages, one from the Bard one from the Bible."

"Something borrowed." Cynthia's smile was wistful and watery as a blue Laguna sunset. She was applying lip gloss. She stood and walked to the balcony, facing the glass doors, back to the room, looking out over the sleeping city, into the shadows of her own reflection, and further back into deeper lights and darker shadows within the room to where Zachary sat somewhat pensively, brooding over his own private thoughts.

"'Let be be the finale...'" he said after a lengthy pause. "What does that last word mean to you?"

Cynthia smiles her tolerant smile, the one that holds the promise of sarcasm but at the moment, without the heart to strike. "Ah, the elusive finale. Is this the famous final scene?"

"Exactly! And the presence of this type of theatricality, combined with the associated ideas of Shakespeare's metaphor about all the world being a stage, suggests that all 'performances' should be played as if they are one's last."

"And if there are mistakes, there will be room for redemption," Cynthia slides back next to Zachary and lobs it back to him with a simple, "right?"

"Yes, a nice solution to the problem of mistaking illusion for reality before finally coming to terms with it makes for a compelling reading of the poem, wouldn't you say? "Let be be the finale of seem" could mean that existence is reality, and reality exists; this reality should be the ultimate truth underlying all illusory appearances, and to which all such appearances lead."

Cynthia hides her patronizing smile with a conspiratorial wink. "I have my doubts. Couldn't it also mean that appearances are the ultimate test of reality and that these two must always be juxtaposed to facilitate that test?"

It was Zachary's smile now, broad and beguiling, that completely disarmed his interlocutor. "You have proven my point. Unlike most pop music lyrics, allusive poetry such as this resists simple interpretations. Are you up for going back to my feast of friends?'"

"The more the scarier," said Cynthia, giving her best 'white knuckle ride' smile, and settling herself in for what dreams may yet come and what seams may or may not thread themselves into this highly stylized version of reality Zack had chosen to present from his illustrious past.

Twenty-Four

GLADIOLAS FOR A GLADIATOR

Tony stood waiting at Gina's door, virtually hidden behind the huge bouquet of gladiolas he was holding. He thought he could hear Gina's light step coming down the hall, but he couldn't be sure—maybe it was the wind chimes. He leant in and pushed the doorbell again. In a moment the door opened, and Gina peered out at his colourful camouflage. Pressing his face through the petals and blossoms, Tony did his best Arte Johnson imitation: "Very interesting; but also very stupid."

Gina laughed cheerily. "Oh, Tony. You may have been born too late for *Laugh In*, but your humour is always vogue. Now what's with all the gladiolas, darling?"

"Well I hate to say it, but they're Andy's favorite. You know tonight is the anniversary of our first official date. If you could put them in a vase and keep them in the sunroom, I'll collect them later this evening." Tony passed the bouquet to Gina, giving her hand an appreciative little squeeze.

"Sure thing, Tony. Gladiolas for a gladiator, right? Don't you worry, we'll make sure the arena is full for tonight's skirmish between the lions and the Christians." Gina exited into the house on cue, leaving Tony to scowl in solitude. Though he never did like them, those Romanesque allusions never got stale. Originally, it had been Jules who had associated The Heartaches with the lions, playing on the similar sounding word 'lines.' Within a couple of years, their fan base had grown exponentially, and the group became gladiators, devouring their lines, and inhabiting the music like the crowd inhabits an arena, standing against any weather.

Andy Milner played a mean lead guitar. He was classically trained, so he seldom used a pick, preferring fast finger action, like Lyndsey Buckingham. And Tony Franco was the Mick Fleetwood of The Heartaches, a dynamo hummer of a drummer, with the whole killer kit and caboodle to keep the beat going on and on, time and time again.

Now, as he turned back towards his Jeep Grand Cherokee parked in the driveway, Tony was feeling famished for a man of the cloth— a man of the loin cloth. Tony jumped into his truck, turned the key in the ignition, and cruised back down Gina's poplar-lined driveway, thinking of togas, tequila, and strip-tease. If Cyndi were speaking, he knew what she might say: 'Tonight monsieur and mademoiselle, will be the stuff of dreams." Cyndi could keep her convoluted elocutions, Tony thought. His hobby was haiku and he loved to make them up on the spot. So as he opened his sunroof, he shouted at the Chicago skyline, "Viva la vida! Tonight we make memories!" Home was a life sentence away, but he'd gotten time off for good behaviour. He'd stop at *Spurs* for shots and stars, and he'd be home with Andy by six, with plenty of time to spare. "Heartaches forever!"

Meanwhile, Gina was already on the phone with Andy. She knew he hated surprises. In fact, she knew his reactions to surprises could be fearsome. But she also knew just how to render those gladiolas a negligible risk to offend. Tony need not know she'd intervened. Andy had just emerged from the shower when he heard the phone ringing. Still dripping, he cinched up his rich magenta bathrobe, tightened it snugly around his burly six foot, four inch frame and took the call, immediately putting it on speaker.

"Hello. Andy Milner," he said, hopefully. He was really in the mood to talk with Arnie Frey about the holiday surprise he was planning for Tony for the last week in July. Although he hated surprises himself, he had come to appreciate the transformative effect they had on his partner. Since Andy was expecting Arnie, he was surprised to hear Gina's husky voice on the other end of the call. He was even more surprised when she suddenly asked him whether or not he knew any male strip tease artists. She told him that their Independence Day party was just a pretext for the real celebration.

"We're throwing Jules a stag, because as you know he's planning an August wedding." Gina's announcement was meant to be equal parts melodrama and misdirection.

"Why a male stripper?" Andy immediately asked. "Has Jules joined our team?"

"Not as far as I know," came Gina's overly chirpy reply. "But stranger things have happened, you know. At any rate, I've already got a voluptuous young ingénue for him. No the male stripper is for Stacey. I'm throwing this surprise stag for both of them. Simultaneously!" She practically sang every single six syllables of that last solitary adverb as if she were achieving multiple orgasms, one per passing second, and by virtue of the sheer emotional intensity, she promptly fell into an endless loop of giddy bubbly giggles, until Andy cut her short.

"Gina!" cried Andy, interrupting her evanescent fettle with the bracing idea that "stags were not meant to be celebrated in tandem by the impending couple," and then going on to regale her with his perception that "Jules and Stacey are actually having relationship difficulties anyways, and something like this might easily make matters worse."

True, Jules had told the band that a summer wedding seemed likely. Nevertheless, Andy hesitated with good reason. He remembered the irritatingly intrusive call he'd gotten from Jules just the other night. Then, inexplicably, he capitulated to Gina's little scheme. Later, Gina and Andy would wonder whether their party plans precipitated the bad end, but at the time they only knew that they were scheduling singing stripper Arnie Frey to perform for Stacey, as J. D. and The Heartaches looked on. The gladiolas were sure to pale in comparison with the excitement of the evening's activities. They would end up being far less of a surprise than Tony originally imagined. Which was good, because Andy hated surprises.

Twenty-Five

HOW TO SOLVE A RIDDLE NAMED STACEY

Before they moved into the penthouse suite in the Upton Building, with its spectacular views of the city and the park, Tony and Andy had been together about a year. But they'd known each other ever since The Heartaches formed two years ago. Three days before Independence Day they were excited by the prospect of fireworks in Lincoln Park on Saturday, the Fourth of July. They both agreed that everything—from the view to the immense living room with the stained-glass double doors opening onto their large penthouse balcony—was perfect. The first album Andy played that evening was Diana Ross's *All the Greatest Hits.* When her *Endless Love* duet with Lionel came on, they danced on the balcony in the starlight under a full moon. The mood was also perfect, but that wasn't all that was memorable about that night. Fifteen minutes into the pre-show, the phone rang, interrupting what would surely have been a passionate half hour of foreplay. Andy let it go to the answering machine, but they couldn't ignore Jules' imploring tone.

"Pick up. It's imperative that you pick up." Tony reluctantly disentangled himself from his lover's not-so-tender embrace, walked back into the apartment and grabbed the cordless receiver, ready to verbally assault the source of this rude disruption. The voice at the other end of the telephone line sounded depressing, like it was barely reaching up from a well's dank bottom. It was Jules Desmond alright, lead singer and rhythm guitar player for The Heartaches. Jules seemed to be drowning in a deep pool of water. His cry was a desperate last-ditch appeal. Tony resigned himself to having his sexual drive put on hold, and handed Andy the phone. He and Jules had more history together, and Andy was a much better listener than Tony anyways.

"Andy, they're not listening. We don't speak the same language. We're from different planets. Andy, it's much more than just critical now. It's…" and then came that word again: "imperative. It's imperative that our paths wind up together, intersecting in infinite patterns. Andy, what can I do?"

Jules always spoke in clichés when he was near the end. He had been near the end before, and Andy knew he must be fairly desperate. Now that he seemed to be in his philosophical phase, there was no telling what he might do.

Tony cozied up again, distractingly. Andy pulled away from Tony, extending his palm toward his partner with a stop sign severity, and focused exclusively on Jules. J. D.'s histrionics were legendary, and his girlfriend—a nubile young girl named Stacey, not quite out of her teens, but often out of her jeans—did not fully grasp just how precarious and integral to his sensitive nature his psyche really was. "I just want to give you a head's up, Jules," Andy cautioned, "because if you're being frivolous in this desperate bid for attention, you're already breaking through the thin ice of our friendship! Things were just about to get really busy here, if you know what I mean." This was more for Tony's benefit than for Jules'. There had better be a good reason for anyone—Jules or no Jules—to go about breaking apart their lovemaking. He knew that Tony needed to understand the situation as well, and that was the entire rationale for Andy's explicitness.

"Listen Andy," Jules started again. "I wouldn't bother you if I thought there was anybody else." Jules' voice fluked up an octave, making him sound like he was soft-selling a romantic song in some kind of "Stay Awhile" styling. Kind of ironic, because what he said was "I think I'm going to lose it for a while."

The Poetic Ambassador

What Andy sussed out was that the damage had been done, it was just a matter of time before the casualties accumulated. What he said was, "I can't quite hear you, Jules. Tony just put on Frey. He's singing *Somebody's Gonna Hurt Someone Before the Night is Through*," and Andy motioned for his lover to drop the volume. "Jules, you've got to get specific," Andy said sternly. "Who are you talking about?" He had tempered his earnestness of the moment before with his most soothing, calming voice, which Tony took as a sign that the conversation was going to take a little longer than they'd originally expected; so he headed for the kitchen to try a different tack at solving his problem. But first he put on Dylan's *Tangled Up in Blue*, hoping Andy would get the message and curtail the counseling session.

Out of all Jules' sobs, angry outbursts, and random sequences of disconnected thoughts, Andy managed to piece together the essence of what might be portrayed most grippingly, if it were ever filmed (Andy liked to see himself as a film connoisseur), as a chronic, pernicious malaise in the visibly wizening form of a young otherwise vigorous man; and, although he meant the aforementioned characterization metaphorically, he also liked to keep his options open. Not so open to having their daughter marry so young were Stacey's parents. As the big picture came into focus, Jules turned the prism of his friend Andy's camera lens so he might heat the paper-thin pretensions to which he clung in mercurial desperation. Stacey had finally agreed—after much pressure from her parents—that it would be in her best interests to put distance between Jules and herself by enrolling in Vassar. She was to leave for Poughkeepsie on the first of August. "Aren't you almost over this one anyways, Jules?" Andy could hear the Sheena Easton irony in his voice the moment he mouthed the allusive lines of this crass comment, and he soon realized he had probably provoked Jules' ensuing outburst.

"Almost over oxygen. Almost over light. Almost over water. Almost over food. Almost over sleep. Deprive me of these and it has the same freaking FX as being without Stacey. You know damn well that I'm never going to be over her. Almost over Funk. Almost over Soul, for crying out loud. What are we going to do, Andy? I need your help." If Jules previously sounded histrionic in a subdued kind of way, now his cloyingly tortured plea practically plumbed the depths of the melodramatic.

Andy thought for a second, and then in a hushed stage whisper, he broached his plan: "Can you get Stacey out to our next practice, Jules?"

"She doesn't leave until the first of August. That's a month away. We're scheduled to practice again next week. So sure, I guess she'd come. Why? What's a practice got to do with anything?" Jules mood seemed to pick up, he was alertly on the scent, looking for Andy's specific plan of action: "Listen Andy, just tell me what you've got in mind."

Andy decided that he had to give him just enough to set his mind at ease. He continued with a heightened confidence—almost his stage persona really—and let his certainty carry them away. "By the time we get done with her, she'll have a new purpose and a new reason to stay. Leave it all to me, Jules." He wasn't about to hang up before he'd convinced himself that he'd convinced Jules that they'd be able to convince Stacey not to go. He told him he wasn't merely telling him what he wanted to hear, or feeding him some kind of a line (like a gladiator).

"Andy, you're always so reliable," Jules said "I feel as if a weight has been lifted off my sagging shoulders. Thanks for being such a true friend. You do know that the best lines are felines, don't you? Jules quipped, attempting to rally back to his good old joking self.

"And I thought it was Dean who was so reliable," Andy said laughing good naturedly at what they both knew was Cyndi's and Gina's running gag with their bass player. "So, okay, I'll bite. Why is a feline the best line?

"Because it's a line you get paid for—a 'fee line.'" Although he could hear Andy groaning at his grade school humour, Jules laughed for the first time, and then got quickly serious again, in a crazy kind of a way, adding "Much better than a malign, because too much character defamation makes for a premature deadline." This seemed to be rendered in a stark deadpan delivery, incongruously contrasting with his humour of a moment ago. But Andy didn't stop to think much about this erratic behavior. Tony was waiting. Erotic trumps erratic every time.

"Well this is my byline, Jules," responded Andy, not wanting to prolong this random and seemingly somewhat insane kind of wordplay. Then he hung up the phone, turned to Tony who was just coming back into the room with a bowl of whipped cream, and said: "Damn, Tony! You know I hate surprises. You better have some blueberry pie to go with that whipped cream.

"You'll do, cutie-pie."

Andy suggested this was just another tired old line. Tony tried to say he'd been fed the line, but that it definitely has a tasty hook. They picked up where they'd left off prior to Jules having called. Things got a whole lot sweeter, and before long the planets aligned once again. And for once since his conversation with Jules, Andy stopped over-thinking things. For a little while anyway.

About three in the morning, Andy awoke with a start. He lay awake wondering whether or not he was taking Tony for granted. If Tony left would he have moaned in the same way that Jules was mooning over Stacey, all manic with malaise, all distraught and dangerous in despair? After laying there for twenty minutes or so, he threw off the sheets, pulled on his robe, and made his way out to the patio to study the stars over Lincoln Park. He was still thinking when twilight heralded the pre-dawn hush. She might like becoming president of their fan club, but only time would tell whether or not that would be enough to change Stacey's mind about Vassar.

Twenty-Six

GAME OF KNOWLEDGE

"It seems that your temperament for handling rejection is as erratic as your friends' taste in music. Frey I can understand. According to mom, he was the original heartbreak kid; but Diana Ross and Bob Dylan are strange bedfellows, aren't they?" An alert observer could have detected an ever so slightly understated satisfaction in Cynthia's smile. Almost as if, having felt a twinge on her line, she now moved to set the hook.

"That was eons ago. I'm sure they are more selective," Zack parried.

"And you? Are you more selective?"

"Probably still less selective than you are discerning. But we can always work that out," he said, immediately regretting that he'd made it sound clingy, or like some kind of muscle stiffness easily cured with exercise.

"You are giving my discernment quite the little work out already, I can tell you that much. Who is the more tragic figure—Gina or Cyndi? Now as to Andy: is he a classic codependent or merely a really good listener? And the Tony for most self-absorbed goes to—"

"Ladies and Gentlemen, I'd like to thank the green-eyed beauty next to me for her pointed critique of my performance. She has always stood by her penmanship, but she'd probably fall just short of my calumny if she were not so fettered with social conventionalities." Zachary levelled his best mock-serious gaze at Cynthia, aware that he was coming off as far too heady an intellectual.

"And to think, I came so far with reciprocities: hosting dinner parties, planning birthdays and weddings in exchange for banal pleasantries." Cynthia's smile was augmented with precision, and a few other select adjectives, any one of which the astute reader can easily imagine.

Zachary had begun noticing Cynthia's smile. It had the unsettling effect that da Vinci had somehow worked into his *Mona Lisa.* He could not help noticing that Cynthia's smile had been getting much more pointed, and seemingly somehow more knowing. "Society has its privileges. Sacrifices must be made," he said, aware that he was becoming somewhat depressed. It was just that the next part of his story about Chicago days always left him downcast. But it was all a catalyst for healthy change, he thought to himself. Must remember that.

"True. Civility is a game with wins and losses, and it requires commitment, like any other game."

"What game are you committed to, Cynthia?" Zachary's direct approach signalled to Cynthia that he had come to a decision.

"The game of knowledge," she offered indulgently if a tad misleadingly, and with all the specificity of a sententious proverb, "...is its own reward."

"Knowledge is a vain pursuit unless employed virtuously," he replied evincing the amusing misdirection of a sanctimonious air (at least he thought it was amusing).

"Unless vanity employs knowledge successfully, virtue is misapplied."

"Aphorisms are merely the attenuated limbs of logic." Zachary shifted the weight of the conversation. "You suggested that Gina might be more tragic than Cyndi?" His smile was linear, terse as a proverb and twice as sententious as her opening gambit had been.

"Hack those limbs—give me more aphorisms! I'm actually more interested in Stacey. Did she ever get to Vassar?"

"You might say that things came to a crisis on Independence Day."

"Just as long as the rest of the story is not a big sleep." Her frozen smile melted none of his remaining reservations. Punishing humour was, or so it seemed, one of her specialties. Perhaps no joke escaped with impunity, unless it were rescued with a punch line corollary.

"Well it's definitely not as much of a snore as this final paragraph might seem to some. You might even find it bracing or jarring at times. I know I did when I lived it." His good natured laugh barely mitigated its barb, and in the next instant he squared himself off with Cynthia. "In all my life, I never imagined that a stripper could be a confidante." With that enigmatic tease, he put her patience to the test once more and read her towards the brink of one of his life's most momentous crises.

Twenty-Seven

OFF THE BALCONY

Arnie Frey left his fifth floor apartment after an early dinner just as Jules stepped out onto his fourth floor balcony with jumping on his mind. They lived in the same building. It was half past four on Saturday, July 4 and Jules had been home alone for the entire day. He was building a case for despondency out of the festering resentments he'd begun to agglomerate into a ticking time bomb of self-doubt and recrimination. He decided to jump.

By the time Jules hit the ground, he had just about done a full somersault. He'd landed on his back in the hedges just as Arnie stepped out onto the sidewalk in front of the apartment. Arnie was on his cellphone in an instant, dialing 911. His amateur efforts at CPR managed to get Jules breathing again, and within minutes the ambulance had arrived, sirens going and lights blazing, with two sturdy paramedics ready at their stretcher, taking both Jules and Arnie to the hospital. It turned out Arnie had a passing acquaintanceship with the victim, so he was needed for identification and other particulars.

Multiple contusions, scratches and bruises, and a few broken bones later, Jules arrived at the hospital in a lot of pain, and after the doctors finished with him, he came to in his room just in time to see Arnie wiping his brow with his handkerchief.

"You got anybody you want me to call?" Arnie asked in what he hoped might be his most soothing tone.

"You know any good hit men could finish the job?" Jules cracked through gritted teeth.

"Didn't anybody tell you? Four stories are not enough to do anything more than maim your sorry ass?" Arnie responded. Having decided against killing Jules with kindness, he took another tack. "I bet the topic never came up. Right? Besides it was probably those shrubs and gardenias that cushioned your fall," Arnie commiserated, cursing Jules' rotten luck. "If you hadn't have been so lazy, you'd have climbed to the roof, lined yourself up with the parking lot, and finished what you started for good."

"Damn straight," Jules smiled painfully. "You seem to know a lot about it. Only I didn't start it—she did."

"Oh I see, Arnie said, blindly searching for inspiration. "Some squeeze-box trying to put you in the corner, telling you she wants you to make her feel like she's the only girl in the world?" He lit up a cigarette and passed it over to Jules.

Jules took a long drag, glanced sideways at Arnie, and gritted his teeth again. It was a pain as concentrated as it was pervasive. With a deliberate effort he continued: "Nah. Neither she nor I buy into any of that Rhianna shit. My girl's got a healthy disposition. It's her parents I can't stand. Especially when they try to keep us apart, saying I'm no good for their precious daughter."

"What do they know from shit?" Arnie smiled agreeably. They probably want her to get an education instead of slumming with you and The Heartaches, am I right?"

"Whatever! The Heartaches don't owe me anything," Jules shot back angrily. "We're square."

"Sensing he'd hit a nerve, Arnie played out his hand with brash assurance—a response that walked a fine line between deft and daft. "You outgrew that group a long time ago. I knew it. They knew it. We all knew it."

An edgy pause lingered, prevailed and practically grew nine months pregnant before giving birth to another angry expletive.

"Damn straight." Jules agreed weakly, finally breaking the rapidly growing tension with the feeble affirmation of someone who'd

The Poetic Ambassador

been through too much of an ordeal—and breaking it as decisively as if it had been one of his bones breaking again. But this pale show of fire was a bit much, even for him, and in the end he had to give in to his fragile condition, so he tried to relax himself back down in the bed, bit down on his pain and anger, and then breathed a little heavier.

At that moment, a nurse with a brusque demeanor (not as rare as one might imagine) breezed in, carrying water and painkillers on a tray. "Well Mr. Desmond. How are we feeling? I'm afraid visiting hours are nearly over for now. You've got some rest and recovery ahead of you, so your friend is going to have to leave you in a few minutes to let you enjoy what's left of your Independence Day, right? Just take these pills and you'll feel fine in no time."

So saying, Nurse Tammy picked up the pills, put them in Jules' hand, gently moved it to his parted lips, and gave him a glass of water to chase it down. "There, there. Now you just set back and let this sedative work. Please sir," she said firmly, turning suddenly to Arnie. "You'll have to leave your friend, Mr. Desmond alone for a few hours. If you like, you can come back after 7pm.

Nodding, with growing confidence, Arnie smiled at Jules and abruptly left.

Jules began to experience a mild light-headedness, along with a sort of numbing feeling that seemed to spread throughout his body until the pain gradually subsided, faded away almost entirely, and was replaced with this pervading sense of well-being. Whatever it was, this medication seemed to work quickly. He remembered that stuff Arnie had said about his girl being the only girl in the world, and he realized that he'd been behaving like she was. He'd let her get inside his head. Her *and* the Heartaches. It was hard to say which had been the bigger heartache.

What was that old saying about near death experiences giving one a new lease on life? He'd be better off without them all. Clearly this guy Arnie knew more than he let on. His perspective seemed solid. As solid as the truism that time steals youth. If Stacey was heading East without him, he would fly to the West without her and the band. It was time he went solo anyways. The solution gave him a kind of awkward comfort, like the shrubs that had rushed up to break his downward fall. He would have to cut away from all old ties. *Today is Independence Day,* he thought. New century around the corner. Time for a change. That was the last thought he remembered before he faded away into the oblivion of a drug-induced, much needed sleep.

If he had fallen asleep in a sort of buzz-town bliss from the effects of the pain-killers, agony returned upon his awakening. Jules gritted his teeth against the pain of his injuries, and fought back the tears. It had been a relatively peaceful night in the hospital, but broken bones took time to heal and although he could still walk, both of his arms were in slings, and he would need full time care while he convalesced.

T here were times of tension within the months of rehabilitation and recovery that followed, especially after Jules made everyone aware of his imminent departure. The Heartaches were not willing to let him go without a struggle. Stacey quickly manipulated her parents into letting her come back to him in his hour of need. She made a big show of standing by him through his convalescence. They all waged war, both individually and collectively, against his newfound independence. No one really believed he would leave the band. Gradually, as to block the warm sun of a summer's day comes a single cloud, whose shadow dances down over a field of golden grain, he moved—despite his doubts, and maybe even because of them—ever more surely toward complete self-reliance. And he became the sun, and the cloud, the shadow, and the wind through the grain. Deliberately, and with definite resolve, his own certainty refined itself, purified itself, and coalesced in a newfound need to discover all subterfuge and every veneer of fidelity, accentuated his quest for independence by subordinating experience, memory and desire to truth, clarity and authenticity. From now on he would be so up front with people, he would never need to hide behind a false front again, and he made a firm resolve never to be another front man, regardless of who may be displeased by his decision.

Twenty-Eight

A MATTER OF PERSPECTIVE

Cynthia had listened with interest, stifling only a dozen or so yawns in her concerted effort—as carefully disguised as Jules' true motive for leaping from his balcony—to appear only casually interested by Zack's account of his former life. At times she vacillated between a decision to lead her critique with style or substance; at times she pondered a deconstruction of the role of Arnie the stripper as an unreliable confidante or the role of Jules as an unreliable narrator; and at other times she would settle her head upon Zack's shoulder and close her eyes as if to sleep away peacefully her wild animal dreams. Now that this ambivalence had passed, she found herself refreshingly ready to take an altogether different tack.

"Stacey seems nice in your history," she smiled knowingly. "I wonder what she's overcompensating for though. It would seem that there is something more behind her manipulation, something your narrative omits. And I'm not merely referring to how she coerced her parents into letting her come back to you—and by 'you' I mean the hospitalized Jules of course—but also before that when she played with your heart by running back to mommy and daddy in the first place. Because her parents don't seem to do much of anything if she doesn't want them to do it, do they? Or was somebody else pulling the strings?"

Zack decided it was his turn to smile, and she could tell his took effort as it was, she knew he hoped, even more deprecatingly savvy than hers had been. His smile was in fact so savvy that it almost slid completely off his face. "Unfortunately, the young ingénue was brought up to privilege. She simply could not fathom rejection of any type. I think she sensed that I was pulling away from her. That's why she pulled away from me. If only I'd known the effect on her that her choice to pursue an education apart from our relationship would have, I might not have acted so rashly that day."

"Yes she seems to have been brought up to privilege, alright—to privilege the prestige that comes from a rock and roll lifestyle. But I have a question for you, Zack." Cynthia had pulled herself away from him now, and was sitting quite still and erect at the far edge of the couch. "When a narrator does not really know himself, is it fair to say that he is an unreliable narrator?"

"If you mean Arnie, he's not really the nar—"

"Actually, I was referring to you as Jules," she said smoothly.

"It's more a coming-of-age account, wouldn't you say? An excursion into self-awareness that dawns as a result of a personal crisis. Kind of like the personal crisis of growing up with a burning desire to find out who your father really was."

"That would be more of a quest. But for the sake of argument, we can call that a journey of self-discovery too, if it will facilitate our own journey." It was a compromise Cynthia was prepared to make in the interest of disclosure. She sailed ahead into the coming storm, luffing expertly as she appeared to leave Zack in the wake, where she secretly hoped he might flounder. She had about rigged his sloop to tow astern her cutter, when she realized he had been trying all the while to keep an even keel without having to jettison too much of his own sordid baggage.

"Yes we are all on our own quest," he said with an exasperated tone, "so let's not quibble about semantics, shall we? Motives are always suspect, no matter who you turn to for counseling, and if I'd made Arnie the narrator of my story, he'd probably be classed as unreliable. Since I am the master of my destiny, flaws and all, I've not got the luxury of second-guessing my choices, in spite of how suspicious my motives might appear to have been when I jumped off that balcony. Does that make me an unreliable narrator? Only if, to my own detriment, my vanity transcended my virtue—and for the sake of my pride, I still maintain that it was not the case. As I have already mentioned, that is the litmus test, and it works for self-knowledge as well as its other forms." Zack stood after making this declaration, walked over to the cupboard, and took out a couple of tall glasses. He put a few cubes of ice from the ice-maker into each glass and poured a couple of cool glasses of lemonade from the fridge. He returned to the couch and set one glass down on the waiting coaster upon the coffee table in front of Cynthia before settling his own on the opposite end of the table where another coaster sat ready for his use. They both sipped their lemonade reflectively. Zack let the aftertaste linger. Cynthia had another sip immediately, luxuriating almost as much in the lemony intensity as she did in her own thoughts.

"So who or whatever induced you to make the sudden leap from full-time rocker to professional poet?"

"Wouldst thou pluck out the heart of my mystery, fair wench?" Zack eased mirthfully back into his role as raconteur, ready, he hoped, for all, come what may.

"Not I, milord. Nor would I dare," she said in that playful jesting tone that had endeared her to Pamela on their first encounter—a tone that masked all malice—"to affront you about your choice never to be a front man again, but if you succeed in becoming the poetic ambassador, doesn't that mean you'll be fronting for ZG?"

"Vive la difference, mademoiselle!" Zack gave an ebullient laugh. "Eternity and time are a blend of sleeping and waking dreams. Isn't that what your mother told you? My dreams of poetry touch both time and eternity so in them, my "eternal summer shall not fade." Rock rolls on, it is true; but each poem has a beat all its own. Now that is where my debts accrue; and like a bird, it takes flight when it is known." Zack sipped his lemonade quietly, letting his thoughts assemble around the fair, petite, shapely form of his companion.

"The heart of darkness flows within, none has known where it

The Poetic Ambassador

begins. Freely flies the captive bird, by false bravado long deterred." All in a moment, with a pretty pucker, Cynthia punctuated her musing profundity by downing the rest of her lemonade, and returning the empty glass to its coaster.

Zack grinned. "Since when does captivity lend liberty to those it holds within its clammy cells? You do know how to sell a contradiction, though." He paused, looking at her empty glass. "You could do with another one to enjoy while we take a little trip back to Chicago." As he headed toward the fridge to refill the glasses, he paused in mid-stride and turned back towards Cynthia. Then, leveling his most piercingly direct gaze, he said,

"If night swallows all fowls, no light for a landing
will beckon the white owls of great understanding."

"I see you've been working on your Alexandrines," she said. "But since when do owls need light to land?"

"Only those with great understanding in the community of owls can most readily benefit from moonlight or starlight, while the others are wont to fly all night in the howling storm, like the invisible worm that ended up in Mr. Blake's sick rose."

"And whose destruction does their 'dark, secret love' presage, pray tell?"

"One night several years ago on a riverboat tour in Chicago, I knew an answer to that question. Now, just over a decade later, I am suspicious of anyone claiming to speak with certainty about such questions. He returned her replenished glass to the coaster. "Perhaps your reader's response to that heartache may point us towards some mutually satisfying answer, but I have my doubts." So saying, he took up the story where he'd left off.

Twenty-Nine

THE ORIGINAL ARCHITECTURE TOUR

Halloween happened to be the date The Heartaches set for what critics had begun to call their R & R Concert: not for Rock 'n' Roll, but for Rehab and Recovery. It was a well-kept secret that it would be Jules' last night as their front man. Aside from J.D. and the Heartaches, only one other person knew: His replacement—the singing stripper who had once saved his life. The venue for this concert was a trippy old mausoleum of a hall named after the most famous of all long dead presidents—Lincoln. The concert was billed as a masquerade ball. Jules decided to go on stage as the cowardly lion. He had been preparing for his adrenaline-pounding super-set ever since his doctor had given him the green light six months ago. He wanted to go out on top. The entire group had been practicing their fresh material for months as well. Jules had exited rehab by early May, and the summer had been highly productive. Now that the crisp, cool Fall days of Autumn rolled themselves out one after another like a wad of fresh hundred dollar bills, restored health and a fledgling sobriety had brought with them renewed inspiration. Jules had written several new songs, both alone and with The Heartaches. His old self seemed to have returned. Not only had collaboration with the band been productive, they all felt like Jules was re-entering the human race. If he was not genuinely engaged, it was one of the most convincing cons ever perpetrated.

Speaking of engagement, Stacey had seemed eager to set a

new date for their upcoming wedding. Never were her bright emerald-green eyes so ravishingly religiously radiant. For if Jules was himself her famous cult, then she was his most fervent convert. The thought of recanting never crossed her mind. Not until one night, late in October. They were on one of the famous Wendella ferries, walking about the deck during the Original Architecture Tour. It was a clear, windless Chicago night and the blackening starry mantle above formed a rich sparkling counterpoint to, and was reflected in, the dark swirling current of the river below. Leaning out against the railing, they stopped for a moment to reflect upon the passing tide of time. Jules held Stacey close and felt the warmth of her youthful body; he immersed himself in her sweetness, her innocence, and the apparent depth of her commitment. All these qualities, and the tenderness with which her love had been offered up to him, cried out to him, leaving him conflicted, but ultimately decisive. He'd ask her one last question for confirmation, and then... would it be a fitful farewell? She swept back her long luxuriant golden-brown hair, and then she locked her hands in his. She would never be as inviting, he thought. She would never be so ambivalently mine and not mine with as involved and invested a fervor—and so remote an otherness—as she was in this magic moment.

They talked of an end to knowledge, as though it had an end. But she was at her best when she talked of innocence as if it were just another sense—oblivious to the possibility that one could perhaps lose it altogether as well then... as if it really were just another sense. Jules laughed with her, and said "innocence is the state of oblivion, the state of being in no sense." Stacey replied that this was utter nonsense. Then they both laughed again—as Jules later said, purely for the sensation—and in conversing further, agreed that innocence was probably a senseless or insensate state of being. Finally, Jules concluded that "the more innocent people are, the more senseless or insensible they must be."

When the tour ended, they disembarked, but they left what was left of their innocence behind, along with any vestige of commitment to each other, because before they had departed off of the deck of that riverboat, Jules had asked her the one question against which even her purported innocence could not prevail—he asked her whether she could love him if he was no longer fronting for The Heartaches. He had correctly predicted her answer, but it still rankled, and left him feeling like he'd just walked through some strange mirage. In this illusory oasis of her love he had long stood basking; as it now turned out to be in the sunshine of his own self-delusion. And now he was increasingly alienated from all those who had once supported him.

———— ·《◉》· ————

E arly the next afternoon, Andy was working on his lead guitar solo for Jules' new song *Artful Inelegance* when Jules himself stopped by the apartment. Tony answered the door smiling. "Good to see you, J.D." How are you feeling today?"

"Feeling a little bereft... with just the slightest tinge of artful inelegance," Jules replied, sombrely. He'd heard the guitar and recognized his melody in Andy's riff. "How's it going with you guys?"

"Oh, you know: rough and ready as ever! You look like you need a coffee—or something stronger?"

"Coffee is fine, thanks. I'm just going to interrupt Andy." Jules walked past Tony into the living room, taking in the stunning view across Lincoln Park before he turned towards Andy.

"Hey J.D., what brings you over? Andy asked, unplugging his guitar.

"Your idea to get Stacey on board sure worked," said Jules ironically. "Did you really think she would settle for being made president of the fan club?"

"I think you handled that one all by yourself," offered Andy, relaxing his grip on his axe, but not on his aloof disdain.

"Well, regardless, it's all coming to an end, just like in the song," Jules added cryptically. He walked over to the black leather couch and sat down.

The Poetic Ambassador

"Oh, you mean that line from *Artful Inelegance* about the ship having sailed into the setting sun? I always thought that was a little cliché. Don't you agree?" Andy grimaced a little as he spoke the word 'cliché' and remained standing imposingly, his Fender slung over his shoulder.

"It's the context that makes it original, Andy," replied Jules. "Surely you can't be oblivious to the context.

My ship, bereft, sails into the setting sun
because of all it has left... undone,
because of the race not yet run.

You can't just rip the line out of context like that, Andy."

"You are a like a line ripped out of context yourself, aren't you, J.D.?" Months of pent-up hostility was seeping out into Andy's gruff demeanor now. "Nothing we've said all these past few months since you tumbled off that balcony has made much of a difference to you has it? Dean, Cyndi, Gina, Tony and I could speak with the tongues of angels, and you'd still be determined to battle your demons alone, wouldn't you? How's that for artful inelegance?" Andy spit out these words with recriminatory bravado. Up until recently, he would never have dreamed to confront their lead singer with so provocative a tone and so disrespectful an attitude. His insolence was like a slap in the face to Jules, who had always received nothing but support from his lead guitarist.

"I had hoped *you* of all people would understand, Andy," Jules shot back testily. Just then Tony came in with the coffee. But Jules coolly declined his offer, saying, "Thanks anyways, Tony. I have a race to run." And with that terse farewell, he got up quickly and left to pick up his lion costume.

Thirty

THE RAPIER'S THRUST

"It would seem that the owls are not yet out of the woods," Cynthia said pursuing her storyteller's previous poetic digression. She pursed her lips in a taut, reserved smile as she added a mildly caustic turn of phrase, "regardless of how your peers and your fans try to lionize you." Sliding over on the couch to physically shrink the distance between them and mitigate the severity of her deflating remark, she extended her arm and rested her hand upon his, where he had placed it on his lap, holding his manuscript with the other. A small, but meaningful gesture, a white owl of understanding landing, however momentarily. And, indeed, it had no sooner alighted, than she withdrew it quickly. A removal as unexpected and as sudden as a sting of unwanted recognition. The glimmer of an offer rescinded? Time would tell, and it might have been a dream forgotten, but for the barest hint of an imprint of pressure on the back of Zack's hand.

His hazel eyes met her radiant green ones. A concentration. A beat. Another. He broke the gaze, and its attendant short silence, with a compliment and a slant rhyme Alexandrine.

"Few have grasped that hidden message implicit in my costume choice, Cynthia.

Fame finds little comfort in fortune with false friends,
still less with a consort whose love is but pretense."

The Poetic Ambassador

Zack's couplet impregnated another pause. And in the moment that it took for that moment to grow large with meaning, Cynthia delivered a compliment of her own. "Nothing compares to a finely crafted slant rhyme, but not all the pretense of friends, nor consorts for that matter, need be false." Then she cleared her throat and, in perfect pitch, offered her own slanting rhyme in the form of a sing-song limerick:

"Not all friends or lovers
are false one discovers;
though some must burn,
others are worn,
like swords or thrusting rapiers."

Then, she capped it off with an almost flippant afterthought that cut sharply into Zack's half-submerged psyche, threatening to sink it totally. Her trenchant addition, "...or our fears," left her with the dim surmise that her own unsheathed rapier was slicing through the armour of his fears, so she graciously turned away, focusing upon the painting on the living room wall, which she pretended to have just noticed for the first time now. "I must say that I found the O'Keeffe in the guest room a little imposing last night. But this has a much more calming effect, I think. The stiff folds of the guitarist's white outfit afford a striking contrast to the black mask and the bright patterns on the wall in the background. And I especially like the angular parallel lines created by the hat and the neck of the guitar. Is it not a Severini?"

"One of his later works," said Zack, "marking his break from Futurism and Cubism. He captures the Neo-Classical spirit well in this famous painting of *Pierrot the Musician*." Zack had held his gaze on Cynthia, while talking. He couldn't help but admire the way the curly tendrils at the ends of her straightened red hair waved ever so slightly about the fringes just at the point where her patterned collar adorned her long white neck. "It is a print, of course. The original was painted in 1924." As she became aware of how he was looking at her, she turned her head away from the painting and found that he had quickly averted his eyes back onto his manuscript.

"We should talk painting sometime," she ventured, wondering whether her passing mention of thrusting rapiers had done its work. She could not know how well. That is to say, she could not let on how well she knew the poetic sagacity of her talent. "Did you always feel you were hiding your true self when you adopted that rock and roll persona for performance purposes, Zack?"

"Ah... you who would dissemble, must of course above all else know dissemblers... like Pierrot with his commedia dell'arte costume, one must disguise one's true self in a masquerade of feeling wherein reason abandons the mind for the sake of the show. This Severini reminds me that it was really no sacrifice to leave the life I once held so dear, but rather a culmination of sorts or maybe it was as much a sorting of culminations. And that my life of poetry gives me a chance to cast off all masks and pretensions in order to free myself of those constraints once and for all."

Cynthia toyed with the idea of suggesting to Zack that poetry itself may be the most consummate of masks, and that Stacey had been far too young to realize what she had in him anyway—that her own masks meant that she could probably never merit his true affection—but she somehow sensed that he already knew that. Besides, after her earlier coolness, he would surely consider such suggestions as purely placatory—maybe even obligatory—consolations, and therefore dismiss them as ingratiating. Besides, such niceties were really not her style. On the other hand, she was confident that his ego would continue to respond favourably to her verse, and she was not above giving him a shove towards the edge of what she liked to call the cliff notes version of criticism, if it meant seeing him tumble over himself in an effort to slant his rhymes at some imaginary windmills on the way down to a second- or third-place finish in this ZG competition. Nor was she above resorting to ad hoc invention. "Sylvia Plath style confessionals won't wash with ZG, you know. So your chequered past might as well be off limits. Do finish the story, though. Now, your love of painting is another matter, and I think you might find some fine subjects for your poetry in the world of contemporary or even neo-classical art."

"Do you really think ZG would be impressed by that type of an approach to this competition?" Zack's solicitous, if somewhat condescending query was tempered with a wariness he did well to hide, so he tried to keep his incredulity out of his voice. His having just taken a long slurping drink from the glass of tart lemonade did wonders to make him appear like a guileless bumpkin, although he knew she knew he was neither. But he was not above enhancing that foil of an impression. "Your opinion is valuable to me, so I'd appreciate the candor."

"ZG is interested in poetic excellence. I cannot help... but think that a blend of art and poetry might move ZG to a favourable decision. I'm thinking of the possibilities myself, but that shouldn't stop you."

"Don't worry. I wouldn't dream of asking for your help with the portfolio. Nevertheless, I welcome your honest opinion; I appreciate your astute objectivity; and I esteem your professional expertise—they are valuable, on all counts. I also know that you won't go down without a good reason, and I plan to be the voice of that reason! So what do you say? Do you feel like a little music? Because the last chapter starts with a dance."

"Maybe something classical," she said, testing his range.

Zack rifled deliberately through his vinyl collection and found what he was looking for. He put the record on the turntable, dropped the diamond tipped needle, and handed the sleeve to Cynthia. She was immediately impressed with his discerning taste. It was a classic 1974 cover of six Mozart sonatas by Jean-Pierre Rampal. "I admire your selection," she said. "Now let's hear about that dance, shall we?"

Thirty-One

MRS. RELIABLE AND THE HEARTACHES

Gina's moves taught elegance itself to sway with the slightest hint of an understatement tenderly transformed into the whispering hush of a soft embrace. *Me and Mrs. Jones* was being played on the phonograph, with all the warm-sounding precision that only pure vinyl and a sapphire tipped needle can muster. In mere moments, seduction spilled from that soulful ballad and began to suffuse the barely touching bodies of everyone on the dance floor in Gina's big game room. Cyndi was working her momentary magic with her latest beau. Tony and Andy steamed up the room with their own delicious brand of gay abandon. Meanwhile, Dean held Stacey's hand consolingly. Arnie's strip-tease performance was cancelled, but he already had his eye on bigger game. Dean had just taken the place that Arnie had recently vacated next to Stacey, and if it had been a few decades earlier, he might have echoed George Harrison, saying there was something in the way she moved. Had Jules seen it all unfold from his hospital bed, he might have put his tongue into his cheek and called Stacey Mrs. Reliable. But neither Harrison, nor his latter-day apple scruff Jules (yes, of course there were male scruffs), was in attendance that night.

Speaking purely in terms of influence, it was always the most spiritual Beatle who had meant the most to Jules. It was even rumoured that his mother had played Cloud Nine's *Got My Mind Set On You* while she was giving birth to him. Whatever ridiculous apocryphal or anachronistic half-truths or unbelievable birthing rhythms haunt the tattered fringes of Jules' legend, there was certainly never any doubt that he would one day take his rightful place as one of the many distinctive singers in Chicago's illustrious history (and that includes the likes of Peter Cetera, Nat King Cole, Sam Cooke and of course the amazingly soulful Eddie Vedder). With Jules at the helm, The Heartaches created an eccentric, perhaps timeless, blend of lithe harmony, memorable lyricism, and irrepressible musicality. But there could be little dispute regarding the fractious legacy Jules bequeathed his group on that Independence Day back in 1999.

At Gina's party that night, all anybody could talk about was Jules' suicide attempt. His reigning spirit was ubiquitous, and he had insisted they not cancel the much-anticipated affair. Each of The Heartaches had gone up to the hospital prior to the party. Cyndi and Gina went together of course. The girls tried to keep things light, but ended up cajoling him into promising that he'd never do it again, and then commiserating with him, in agonizing detail after detail, over Stacey's parents' rejection of him as a suitable match for their daughter. They offered consolations on her behalf, telling him she had wanted to come but could not. There was also a good deal of harmonic caterwauling, amid talk, mostly about how they could never hope to get by without Jules.

After the girls left, Tony and Andy arrived with Dean. They took turns reinforcing the view that heartache was the only true thing you could rely upon to give you an authentic sense of humanity. Tony had drummed that thought into their minds prior to their arrival at the hospital. He used an impromptu haiku to drive the point home: *Heartaches are the pains / Purpose and Identity / of Life's True Meaning.* They shared that with him and took time to give him examples of difficulties they'd experienced on their own or together, trying to point up the individual life lessons to be taken from each separate situation. Jules, who was really in no condition to listen, still could not help but wonder whether such a templated solution-based approach was all that helpful. But their well-intentioned reminders of all the songs they'd written and recorded endeared them to him once more, so he thanked them for their loyalty and promised he'd cherish those memories forever. Then he reluctantly told them of his firm decision to leave the group, and affirmed his desire—upon recovery—to record one last album prior to his departure. Understandably, they were heavy-hearted at this news of his choice to leave. Despite their misgivings, they reluctantly agreed that they would respect his decision. They still could not believe Jules would really leave the Heartaches behind.

Jules had his eyes closed when Arnie came in. He asked whether Jules' nosedive off the balcony had been a precipitous strategy. As his eyes fluttered for an instant before coming fully open, Jules levelled a long, penetrating stare at the stripper who had saved him, and whose own eye—unbeknownst to Jules—was now singularly fixed on the position he had decided to abandon. Arnie wanted to become the new frontman for the Heartaches. His cynical inquiries would later be clearly seen by Jules for the ambitious designs they had so carefully masked. But for the moment, Jules was oblivious to this true intent.

"Isn't that some kind of oxymoron—the phrase precipitous strategy, I mean?" Jules asked finally, stretching himself painfully on his bed, and yawning with feigned nonchalance.

"More of a paradox, actually," replied Arnie, stroking his forehead meaningfully.

"You mean to say that I acted only after lengthy and impetuous consideration," Jules replied with the emphatic force of a declarative utterance, "and that after careful deliberation, I suddenly jumped to certain death." Jules paused as if to point up the ridiculousness of such a motivation. Then he continued, restating his ideas in terms that made Arnie's proposition seem all that much more ludicrous. "That after making up my mind, I acted with rash abandon. Such an action might well be characterized as an elaborately staged act performed by a trained professional. Were that true—and I'm not admitting that it is, mind you—what do you suppose might be the pretext of such a performance?" Jules subsided with this question, exhausted by the potency of his strident rhetorical flourish.

"Perhaps only the actor can accurately answer that question," Arnie speculated, feigning his most benign smile. He added an equally disarming if not superlatively trite closing comment, couched in equally pompous and melodramatic terms, on his way out: "Perhaps at long last, only time will tell."

⸺⸺✦⸺⸺

Some historians say that history repeats itself. Others maintain that history is the biography of time itself running out of time itself running out of time... Perhaps time and history are both redundancies created by the need for a comprehensive philosophy that will wed both concepts to the nascent ideology known as "latentativity" (such an ideology must by definition concentrate on the speculative potential of both overarching disciplines along with the imminence of lag time with respect to the outworking of each—and whoever fails to see that time is as much a discipline as history has never been late). Narrative digressions aside, however, it must be said that J.D. and The Heartaches made themselves widely felt through their recordings, performances and their onstage antics before *their time ran out.* If Jules Desmond tried to run out of time prematurely, his intention was somehow subverted, but if he tried to fail to try, his intention was somehow successful. So for him, in this case at least, his claim of inadvertency was the only clear route to a satisfying conclusion. The Heartaches were of this place, this time. When Arnie's CPR brought Jules back in time, he gave himself a new book: 'Reinvention' was its self-titled cover, and Independence was its subtext—the opportunity to reinvent himself beyond this time, this place; kind of like Fitzgerald's Jay Gatsby.

The foundation for betrayal was being laid that very night at Gina's party. The entire building would be completed over a year later on that Wendella riverboat, when Stacey made it clear that she loved loving the leading frontman part in a Heartache role more than she loved Jules—the man who had decided to abandon his lead role in that band.

Is it foolish to make a woman into a grail? Jules dreamily decided it depended on the woman. He smiled, shifted in his hospital bed, and thought of turning another page in his new book. Self-determination would do nicely for his new heading. He'd decided he'd had enough of having to live by other people's choices. Of what was this day made, anyways? An answer came to him from the last line of his favourite classic movie—John Huston's *Maltese Falcon*: "The stuff that dreams are made of." He knew that Stacey was a dream he'd awakened from. He also knew he could depend upon her not being there when he opened his eyes—Heartaches or not, she was definitely Mrs. Reliable.

Thirty-Two

CONFESSION

The Mozart had long ago faded away. Zack's story was done. Cynthia stood. The balcony beckoned. He opened the sliding door. They found themselves looking out on a sunny afternoon view of Stanley Park, its dark forests—mysteriously green—were pierced through with a narrow cut on which a road full of commuters crawled along towards, or away from, Lion's Gate Bridge and its engineered grace under pressure. Beneath that bridge floated one of those magnificent ocean-going hotels, a cruise ship departing for Alaska, or perhaps for more southern climes. For a long while, they both just took in the fresh air; for a long while, they reflected upon things like how the geography of a place determined the manner in which it was settled; and for an even longer while, they pondered whether things like pretexts could be made to appear so plausible as to convince almost anybody that their prime causes invariably command performative effects. Zack was the first to break the silence.

"Objectivity might be the most subjective of all subjects, wouldn't you agree?"

"Perhaps," replied Cynthia, considering her words carefully. "Provided one avoids constative terms... and keeps things in perspective."

"Are you suggesting that my choice to jump was irrational?"

"Reason often keeps little company with impulse—or mental health issues."

"And impulsive people lack self-control, is that it?" Zack turned his back on the view—and upon her subtext, almost sure she was having fun at his expense, throwing his sanity in question. He gazed back through the glass into the living room at Pierrot's mask. "It is, of course, true that the rock and roll lifestyle to which I had become accustomed put me at some risk for wild behaviour; it is also true that such behaviour intensified as I became involved with Stacey and the 'advantages' she possessed; but what you do not know— what lay completely buried beneath the text of my manuscript—is that Arnie and I had just ended our intense, but short-lived clandestine relationship. He was not really coming out of *his* apartment on the day I jumped, but in fact he had just left *mine,* after giving me an ultimatum: I was to come out, by going public with our affair, or we were done."

Now it was Cynthia who turned away from the view to fully take in the depths of this not-entirely-surprising perspective which she had already discerned as a submerged feature of his story, and watch Zack lift off the layers of his mask. She found herself questioning how guileful this new development might be, but she ended up cautioning herself about overthinking things. She wore her own duplicity so well that it was like a second skin. Therefore she was always alert for the tell-tale signs in others. Experience compelled her to ask about the true role Stacey had played in his tumultuous relationship with Arnie. Long a student of triangulation, she could not help but wonder about such things. But she worried whether he would continue to be as forthcoming about Stacey as he seemed to have been about Arnie. She turned her gaze back to the cruise ship, fading now on the western horizon, following the cooling sun as it graciously conceded one more race across the azure sky. Her eyes were averted as much out of her sense of propriety— borne out of her awareness of Zack's need for personal space—as it was for respect of his need to have some semblance of privacy in this moment of frank disclosure. She softly added nothing more than a simple, "no easy read ever does justice to complexities like this, and you my friend are no easy read." For a moment, he pondered whether or not to challenge her on which of the two meanings inherent within that statement she had intended, but just as quickly decided to leave it alone, when for the second time that day, she reached out and placed her hand over his, as it lay resting on the railing. This time she left hers to rest upon his until he spoke again. Surely she must be massaging his ego, he thought.

Zack disclosed that he had never told anybody but Cynthia about the affair with Arnie. Sorting and processing his feelings about that moment in time had taken years. He had moved all the way across an entire continent—and from one nation to another neighbouring nation—as a means of escape, only to find himself forced to face the memories of his old struggle. The unseen ghosts of his old relationships had resurfaced again and again, until he had found that by writing his story and by doing with his characters what linguists do with the elision of sounds in order to change the sense, he could rewrite that story if not history itself, and establish within his mind the significance of former relationships in a manner he found truer than truth. At least truer to his own perception of self. This is what he thought. This rationalization is what he had convinced himself... before Cynthia came into his life. Prior to her arrival, he had deceived himself into thinking that there was such a thing as true knowledge—even true knowledge of self. Such knowledge implied honesty and integrity, or so it seemed. But could it be that all knowledge was at best partial, fragmentary. Now here he was, baring his soul. Did he still dream that true knowledge might be attained? Could he be getting too close to an adversary? Could such proximity prove perilous for his professionalism... or his portfolio? Her hand had remained on his hand longer this time. What might that connote? Best not to read too much more than a mental massage into such things, he concluded.

He sighed, and cleared his throat. "'There are things in heaven and earth that are not dreamt of in your philosophy', Cynthia," he said. And if we stand on the backs of giants, we sometimes fall into the arms of angels—other times, we merely tumble into low lying hedges. Any way you look at it, we all too frequently 'depend upon the kindness of strangers' to see us well enough so that we may eventually come to see ourselves as we really are, and know the place... (thank you Mr. Eliot) for the first time." And it is a good thing, he thought ironically, that I am not troubled by the anxiety of influence.

The afternoon had tumbled down quickly upon them. As they both watched the sunset, picking out the early stars twinkling with robust regularity over the wan, wearisome headlights on the bridge, an unaccustomed camaraderie came over Cynthia. She seldom questioned her mercenary motives, but nothing could compare to the intimacy of the moment that had passed between them, and she found herself becoming not altogether unfavourably disposed towards this enigmatic young man. It was neither the scenic vista, nor the aural vestiges of the flautist's superb Mozart, but it may have been something to do with the way all of this combined with Zack's heroic personal revelation of the unexpected motive behind the histrionics that had landed him in the hospital all those years ago, and that they had not really, as it seemed, arisen entirely out of a misplaced affection for a girl. Then again, it may just as well have been heartburn—or gnawing hunger. Was there a meal in her future?

Surely this man had not won her heart. No. Such nonsense was not even an issue. She stood strong proof against it. She was as sure as Carson McCullers might once have been that her lonely hunter of a heart had not yet found itself a worthy adversarial range of harmonics to play and replay. Yet there was that little thing they call verisimilitude, and Zack's works and ways certainly held a wide array of tones—both over- and under- whatever bridges Cynthia might be inclined to burn. Was it the autumn breeze in the air that prompted her to accept the possibility of some kind of true knowledge in the face of his stark confession, or was she just con-soling herself with the reminder that her acquiescence was merely feigned? Of what had he been guilty? Misdirection? She had done the same. Not coming to terms with his sexuality? Who hasn't? Infidelity? Did it even apply apart from marriage? (She knew from personal experience that it did not!) Perhaps he was guilty of all of these. Perhaps none. All hinged on his take away lessons. But the worst of these lay behind him. Was he not wilfully self-deceived?

"When you deceive yourself," Cynthia said, in a hesitant tone she hoped would reflect his so-called nascent ideology of latentativity, "you play the fool, strutting and fretting your hour—"

"Upon the stage, like Lear's shadow." Zack pre-emptively completed her thought, shifting gears in the bargain. "He who would be master of his own play must live by what he proposes to say. And there's no tool like an old fool." He grasped her hand again in his, and slid the other one around her waist, continuing his thread of thought while he held her close enough for him to see the feral animal spirit in her eyes. "Now that proposition might make or mar the man who would arise like the morning star. But lo and behold, the brightest light may be obscured by a cloudy night. Then when dawn's true knowledge comes, a settled peace calms, and soothes the troubled breast within whose heart rests the seat of Taste."

Cynthia let a long pause gather the weight of his words, and then she fled from his philosophical foray, and as she moved away, placing her hand on his shoulder, her restless gaze flashed back and forth between the darkening skies and Zack's increasingly cloudy countenance. "Looks can sometimes talk, and Taste can counterfeit a walk. For one night, a guest is welcome company, and I've enjoyed our repartee, but we've both vast worlds of verse to create, so you'd best begin to expiate for sins of omission long left behind, and I'll be leaving, if you don't mind." Cynthia's banal conclusion more than made up for her skewering reference to Zack's need for personal atonement concerning his revisionist account of Arnie (and maybe even Stacey—she still felt there must be much more there to discuss, or else why take such drastic action?).

But Zack was not as troubled by her stylistic faux pas as she had expected he would be, and instead of scorning her doggerel, he leapt all over her for suggesting he ought to be making some kind of amends for his selective rendering of the "truth". This was better than she had hoped for, because she could tell his obsessive nature would render him a slave to both the never-ending process of rationalization and self-recrimination and their highly constrictive corollary, a vicious cycle of that peculiar type of cognitive dissonance that her mother used to call having an 'itchy brain'.

Zack seemed untouched. He continued with simple prosaic elegance as if in corollary: "If the picture is done, what need have I for more paint? It is but to embellish that I stand daubing on, when, in truth, art beheld holds a realism both unnatural and contrived for those who look only to see their own self or some other false image. Beyond this lies true knowledge, all else is lost in shallows. Though you cannot—without the pretension of what may have been—perceive my self-portrait of that period of my life and friends for what it once was—and now has become through my embellishment—you may be forgiven for projecting your misperception of who I must become upon who I really am. For me there is little distinction between the two. It is all revealed over time. It is purely latentative." Cynthia had moved inside while Zack spoke, following her, and they were now both standing back in the living room, in front of the colourful Severini.

"Don't you mean to say I did not perceive 'the *projection* of what may have been' and that I 'may be forgiven for *pretending* to misperceive who you really are'?" This subtle innuendo that he was so riddled with guilt that he must be not only be obfuscating but also injecting into his logic random malapropisms that sublimate his own defensive mechanisms, this was Cynthia's coup de grâce. She had pounced with the alacrity of a sidewinder, and now she savoured her victory, smiling at the painting with barely concealed disdain as her eyes seemed exclusively bent on following the satiny folds of Pierrot's costume, all the while scrutinizing Zack with her peripheral vision, and carefully crafting a fitting famous final scene.

If Zack seemed not quite taken aback, he was nevertheless a little unnerved, as much by her precise elocution as by the fact that she was clearly playing him. Struggling to maintain his composure as he determined his best course of dialogue, he followed her gaze and also reflected upon Pierrot. But he saw a far different portrait than Cynthia was busily constructing. When he finally spoke, it was in a hushed contemplative tone: "Some deliberately misconstrue meaning in order to arrive at altogether different themes. Others do this inadvertently. Either way, the result is the same—a sorrowful disregard for artistic intent and composition. One may look the player and see the comic; another may look at the comic and see the player; but both are there and both parts must be integrated into the whole. Just as the blue flowers have both green and white leaves with rust-coloured stems. It is the integration of this repetitive pattern that forms the optical illusion of depth. Cynthia, I hope you don't wade in the shallows too long, and I hope even more that you don't let some misguided notion about an inchoate sense of my nostalgic yearning for days of yore prevent you from tearing off that mask once in a while, so you can let the 'still, sad music of humanity' haunt your ghost of a soul into discovering true knowledge of yourself and those around you."

Cynthia wavered. Or rather, she appeared to waver. Then with what she called a knee-the-jerk-in-the-stomach reaction, she blurted out her best mock-heroic caricature of this true knowledge Zack seemed so intent upon catalyzing. "Could it be that my ambition has led to this misjudgement?" She laughed to augment the comic effect, but they both knew it was as hollow a laugh as the guitar on Pierrot's lap. Her legs were as rubbery as the painted hands in the Severini appear to the probative eye of the art critic. She glanced at the couch. Took a deep breath. Exhaled. Then, she smiled stoically at her competitor. She'd luffed, but there was no wind. Becalmed, she drifted towards the guest room to collect her things. Zack busied himself in the kitchen. Cynthia returned, carrying her satchel, with her jacket on her arm, a haughty look on her face, and her overnight bag hanging off her shoulder. "I still trust you," she said plainly. "But I cannot follow you. Especially your choplogic. The only true knowledge is that the knowledge of truth is a language humanity will never learn." Then, with something closely resembling a child-like innocence that could be as artful as it was endearing, she batted those dark green eyes at him and said simply, "Bygones?"

"You are plenty well versed in choplogic yourself, but please don't tell me that this is the stuff dreams are made of, sweetheart, because I'd hate for you to go away angry and disillusioned."

"You should have thought of that before you skewered me with that rapier wit, Bogie. Do you really think personal placebos are a panacea for regret? As Craig Raine once said, they leave one with an abstract portrait done by Picasso. But I have no illusions about the utility of anger or verities like the untruth of truth. And my dreams are definitely not stuffy." Cynthia was busily distancing herself from her failed attempt to bind his spirit in obligation, as was evident from her dense, heady poetic bricolage, and her defensive tone. Interestingly enough she seemed also to be suggesting that insofar as her relationships go, Martian poets alone need only apply.

But Zack was having none of her games. "She giveth with one hand and taketh liberties away with the other," he said with matter-of-fact Elizabethan complacency.

"Are you going to drive me home, or do I have to call a cab?"

"Well, if you're not going to stay one more night and brave the wild seas of my waterbed in hot pursuit of the white whale, I guess I'll have to pull out Moby for the scenic tour."

"I think we're still talking about your Porsche? Directness is evidently undervalued, in both your prose and your poetry."

"She may be a Dick, but she's *my* Dick."

"And they say men don't overcompensate for anything with their cars! Thanks anyways, for that indirect direction."

"Sometimes a car is just a car... unless it's a Porsche 911."

"Right Magritte."

Zack had been turning out all the lights, leaving only the halogens that shone down over his paintings, and in a moment, he and Cynthia descended the winding stair. "Let me alarm my homily of a hacienda, and I'll drive you home directly," he said with just a hint of disappointment in his voice. Cynthia smiled knowingly as they entered his garage. She was more than a little amused at the polyglot pretention inherent in his phraseology. How much Spanish did he really know? But she didn't deliberate upon his deliberate diction that long, because in the next instant, they were ensconced within the belly of the White Whale, bound for glory and the upper levels highway, with the dolorous melody of *Artful Inelegance* quietening down the mood and curtailing conversation.

Cynthia got the groaner of a message: She should listen to the Heartaches. He must be tired, she thought. I hope he writes with as much panache. But, deep down she knew as soon as she felt the acceleration pull her back into her cushy seat that the race for the position of poetic ambassador was to be even more competitive than she'd suspected earlier on. They had both already hit the road running. Although she still felt somewhat becalmed after having had the wind taken out of her sails by the clenching way he had critiqued her in their earlier conversation, she sensed that the freshly acquired knowledge she had gained of this worthy adversary piloting her home so smoothly would not only buoy her spirits as she pressed on towards her second wind in pursuit of the perfect poetic portfolio, but it would also go a long way towards her ancillary goal of pitting Trevor against Zack.

The male ego could always be relied upon. She took no small satisfaction from knowing that both of these men were attracted to her. Green-eyed jealousy could sideline them both, but one must be wary they grow not weary of her world-view. Alluringly, and with just the right touch of sarcasm she spoke. But not before she had moved her left hand over in the darkness to where his lay resting upon the stick shift, thereby completing her trifecta of tepid affectation. "This ghost of a soul wants to be haunted by your 'leaf-fringed legend'—whether being or becoming. But if your morning star should fail to rise when on the mountain in Darien with wild surmise your realms of fool's gold leave you cold, then glut your sorrow (here she withdrew her hand) on a mourning pose and ply your poetry in allusive prose." Glancing over at him, she saw that his jaw muscles had begun to work. She turned her eyes to look out through her passenger side window at the streetlights racing by in the darkness, and she smiled reflectively.

Gunning it into the wide turn that emptied down out of the

cut, he revved the engine, and shifted into high gear as they sped onto the second narrows bridge deck. Traffic was light and he wove through it easily, acutely aware that she had turned his previous caustic critique of her ghost of a character against him while simultaneously suffusing her comments with the unmistakable sensory aura of one of his favourite Romantic poets. The only way to fight Keats was with the soundtrack to one of the best punk movies of all time—*Sid and Nancy.* Unwittingly, she had triggered his memory of one of the songs on this movie's soundtrack. Zack quickly thumbed through his CD collection, and soon he was shout-singing along with the relentlessly raw energy of The Pogues wanting to be haunted by the ghost of precious love.

Bemused by the force of the frenzied fettle she imagined that she'd catalyzed, and more than a little taken aback by its sheer volume, along with its hard-hitting heft, she let herself go a little, and began to enjoy the ride. This seemed over the top, even for Zack. Did he really want to be haunted by the ghost of her precious love? Obviously this was meant to be taken with irony, and he was toying with her once again, suggesting that he wanted to leave her behind, like a spirit leaves its body. Besides, a ghost is a mere pale reflection. What did this say about his view of her as a lover? Cynthia found herself wondering about the song. She scoured the CD cover for clues.

Sensing his advantage, Zack powered down his Porsche as he headed east towards Cynthia's Burnaby Mountain apartment. He was still savouring the song, but vestiges of her grandmother's story hit hard at the jagged little edges of his heart, and he found himself thinking like Alanis Morissette once implied, of what a bitter pill it was to swallow. "Don't let your grandmother's words come back to haunt you, my little moonchild. I would not want your poetic aspirations to be a 'pipe with a dream attached'."

"Sometimes a pipe is just a pipe, Magritte," she said self-assuredly, "and sometimes, the stuff dreams are made of, and sometimes a dream..."—and at that moment her voice seemed to falter ever so slightly, though Zack did not suspect she had dissembled for effect—"…never amounts to anything more than a dream… a dream of a pipe!"

"Ha! Pip, pip. Sweet dreams, darling! Here we are at UniverCity. Where did the time go?"

"'Past the near meadows, over the still stream, up the hill-side; and now 'tis buried deep in the next valley-glades.'"

"You're awake still, but you need sleep for your dreams, dear moonchild." In an instant he was opening her door, bidding her adieu, and gently kissing her upturned cheek. Alas, he thought as he sped away, 'the fancy cannot cheat so well as she was famed to do.' Like the self-possessed young lady in the famed Saki short story *The Open Window*, romance at short notice was also his speciality. The truth was, he now felt confident enough to consciously acknowledge, that Cynthia certainly had more than merely a passing penchant for such a brand of romance herself. But as he pondered this he found himself wondering whether her brand of romance was that peculiar kind which readily makes something out of nothing. But oh, he thought, in the same vein, if it were, what a difference it might make for me. One difference was that she did not realize the extent to which he could see that her ulterior motives were more readily discernible to him than one might initially assume them to be for most. Which is not so much to say that he completely saw through her psycho-sexual mind games. Only that he saw himself as she seemed to want to see him for the one-eyed jack she longed to play—a jack he himself knew would only be satisfied by one day becoming king. But for now, he'd settle for becoming a lowly ambassador.

Zack took one detour upon his return journey, stopping to gaze into the deep, dark waters of Burrard Inlet. He found himself wondering how close to the flames this particular moonchild might dance before catching the fires of desire once again. He did not usually speculate long about emotional issues, or not so much that he would readily admit, but he had decided just as recently as yesterday that he would have to put a little more skin in the game if he wanted to win this one. Cynthia was proving to be much more complex a read than Trevor represented himself to be. He was not surprised that she had already sunk her teeth into that one too, but he was determined not to let her have the upper hand there. He knew a thing or two about triple plays. No matter how fast they may run or how smoothly they slide, as long as you keep your eye on the runner, you may be able to throw your opponents out singly, and you might even be able to ultimately have all three thrown out, providing you have team-mates working in synchronicity. He briefly wondered how far Rudy Sorensen's political clout would go with the board and his editorial team. But he didn't dwell on it long. He was anticipating another call from Sorensen. It had been over three weeks since he'd gotten the unexpected call from the CEO (prior to his having gotten official word that he had been selected as a contender) telling him he'd been shortlisted and that he could expect support from only one or two of the other board members. With luck and a kind of a ZG team on his side, he'd yet ensure that his other two adversaries were 'thrown out' of the running. Unfortunately, the only problem with sports metaphors, he thought, as he pulled into his driveway and hit the remote to open his garage door, is that the vehicle doesn't always carry the weight of the tenor. Baseball may be a fine vehicle, but this particular tenor is pitched beyond the normal range, and therefore impossible to carry off for all but the most vintage vehicles. Zack always knew he really needed sleep when he began to mix his metaphors.

Not only that, but he was beginning to wonder whether he should also have been cautious enough not to mix his professional business of poetry with his personal brand of pleasure. Ah well, he thought. That was a lesson he could perhaps learn another day. Right now he concentrated on unwinding after a long session with a wary adversary. He hit the pillow listening to a favourite recording—Ani DiFranco's casual cover of the old Bob Dylan tune *Most of the Time*—and then he finally drifted off to sleep, perchance to dream... of electric sheep—like all aspiring latentative androids.

It seemed—and then again, maybe it was—only a matter of minutes before those carefully counted sheep short-circuited the electric fence they were jumping, and Zack found himself rudely awakened by the insistent buzzing of his doorbell. He threw on his robe and shuffled into his slippers, hit his night lights, and padded down the hall. Wiping the sleep out of his eyes, he entered his living room, and glanced out of his front window, down at the driveway. A strangely familiar red Hummer sat in front of his garage, glinting in the bright glow of the streetlight, and striking a stark contrast to the shadowy dark green of Zack's pyramidal cedars.

Thirty-Three

WHO IS PLAYING WHOM?

Zack's telephone rang just as he turned away from the front window view of that red Hummer in his driveway. He decided Upton could wait. He picked up the receiver, "Speller here, make it quick and make it clear." The doorbell rang again. Trevor seemed as impetuous as a night owl is predatory, or maybe it was that he seemed as predatory as a night owl is patient. Either way, he was definitely eager to speak with Zack, who now found himself engrossed in this unexpected telephone call from Cynthia. Her bracing but tepidly teasing tone suggested that something big was in the offing, and Zack found himself wondering why she had not previously disclosed what she was now slowly unveiling in language as measured as it was laconically taunting.

"Ready yourself, Speller. You might want to dust off that old lion costume."

"Cynthia, please. Come to the point! I'm tired, and I have someone waiting at the door." Indulging his sense that a show of impatience may not only disarm the coyness of his adversary, but also go a good long way toward deceiving her into thinking that she had nettled him, Zack punctuated his excuse for curtailing their conversation with an uncustomary demand: "No more sly, snide reminiscent references tonight! What are you talking about?"

"One of your lengthier portfolio pieces will be required for performance at a gala 'All Hallows Eve' presentation on the 31st of October."

"What do you mean gala?" Zack was suddenly all ears. Meanwhile, outside, pounding on the door now, Trevor was all white knuckles.

"Why, you must prepare yourself for the ZG Halloween Gala, of course!" Cynthia seemed to take delight in her imperative disclosure, relishing the fact that she knew more than he did about their impending portfolio presentation just as much as she was enjoying Zack's evident shock and chagrin at not having had this knowledge brought to him through the proper channels. She could not know how her phone call had catalyzed Zack to question the extent to which he could now fully rely upon his 'inside' contacts at ZG, but she sensed her advantage from his abrupt reaction.

With an oath of imprecation that he hoped would lead her to misjudge the hold her machinations might have on him, Zack hung up the phone and headed for the door just as Trevor rapped the knocker once again for the third time.

Sweeping the door wide open with a flourish, Zack smiled at his nemesis, and invoked Tony Orlando: "Knock three times on the ceiling if you want me, Upton. What could you possibly—"

"Cut the crappy allusions Speller." Trevor's testy provocation ran against a type to which he had long ago found it useful to ply his extensive verbal skill set. He was, to put it simply, exasperated and exhausted, particularly after being obsessed with Cynthia for days, not to mention being hounded and haunted by the ghost of the Uppal's dead Beagle by night. "I won't circumnavigate the issue. I've come over to talk directly."

"Well then, Upton, we should talk, directly; but, since you've come all the way up town, we'd best brace ourselves for what schemes may come. Let's talk over a glass of Scotch, shall we?" Zack closed the door behind his weary foe and led him up the stairs to the Living Room.

"Just two fingers for me, thanks." Trevor took in Zack's spacious, open living quarters, and finally positioned himself in front of the large window that fronted the modern split level house.

Zack returned with two squat glasses, half-filled with whiskey. He passed one glass off to Trevor, and as he did so, he clinked it with his own, the briefest of salutes.

"Now what was so urgent that you had to drive across town to see me?"

Trevor took a short sip of his drink, then levelled a cool stare at Zack. "I think we're being played."

Speller returned his visitor's intent gaze, and with an offhand flippancy, he tossed off a glib response. "Immaterial. Anyone with hands gets played sooner or later. Besides, I don't know about you Upton, but I play to win!"

"Winning at all costs, I suppose. But it's not how you play, but who you play that tips the scales in your favour, isn't it, Speller?"

"Is this what you mean by not circumnavigating? I suppose you will come to the point, directly?" Zack took another sip of his whiskey, savouring it almost as much as his irony.

"Alright, then." Trevor downed his Scotch in one gulp, and slammed the glass down on the coffee table. Then he took a step towards Zack and punctuated his terse question by jabbing an angry index finger into his chest. "You've been meeting on your own with my girlfriend! And either she's out to work us up against one another, or you're trying to pit her and I against one another in this rivalry for the poetic ambassadorship."

"Now hold on a minute!" Zack stepped back, surprised as much by Trevor's apparent lack of emotional control as by his evident naïve ignorance of Cynthia's sensual appetites (although truth be told, he was probably more surprised by Trevor's lack of awareness of the latter). He decided rather quickly that although experience had taught him to hate fostering illusions, Trevor's truculence led him to conclude that it would not be in his best interest to disabuse the young lad of his underdeveloped perspectives about his girlfriend's sexual proclivities or his limited imagination concerning any possible promiscuity on her part. "Hold on just one minute! Professional consultation about the Portfolio is encouraged for one and for all.

You have a decided advantage over me in that your personal relationship with Cynthia pre-dates our *amicable* three-way rivalry. If anything, it is I who should be worried that you two might collaborate with a greater degree of... shall I say efficacy, thus winning an advantage over my contribution, no matter how singularly successful it may prove to be. Now why don't you just take a seat and we'll have a frank discussion about it."

Trevor backed up. He stood for a minute just studying Zack. Then he grudgingly slid into the Settee opposite the couch where Zack had made himself comfortable. "Just so we are clear about terms," he said taking care to adopt a more affable composure, one which he assumed as easily as the furniture on which he now reposed conformed form-fittingly to his body, "I mean that to consult or collaborate does not mean to copulate."

"Naturally," replied Zack, after the slightest hesitation but without missing a beat. "It grieves me to think you would suspect collaboration would not mean anything less."

"More or less, it means the same to me. And I think your equivocation speaks volumes."

"Circumnavigating those volumes might lead us to the same direct conclusion, and neither the journey nor the destination would be entirely... direct—or far from your own experience, wouldn't you say, Upton?"

"Does it not follow by indirect direction?"

"Perhaps that depends upon who is doing the following, and upon whether the lead is buried as the foundation is laid."

"Perhaps Speller. Then again, it depends as much as upon what kind of an edifice the enemy is planning to erect, wouldn't you say?" Trevor found himself beginning to discern what he perceived as Zack's intent. He paused, and then, before Zack could formulate a response, he posed another, more probative question. "Do you believe in sleeping with the enemy?"

Zack hesitated, as much as for inspiration as for emphasis, and then pressed onward. "Were I you, I might well answer in the affirmative. But we are adversaries; not necessarily enemies. As to the pith and marrow of your question, it is not as easily answered as an ethical issue of right or wrong might be, so under the advice of wise counsel I ground my answer in refusal, a refusal to accept the initial premise that I have enemies. For what is an enemy, but a friend who has not yet been converted to such a position of responsibility."

"So, you will sleep with anyone, then!"

Zack smiled drily, and extended his open palm. Then he added, "Admittedly, Taste involves certain restrictions, but such mundane barriers mean one can really afford very few options but to let Taste dictate to the senses what taste will dictate to the senses. Take that in whatever sense you wish."

Trevor balked. Then delivered his best knuckle ball. He brought his knuckles down in a crisp rap upon the coffee table in front of him. "Damn it, Speller! Your equivocal banter may work on some people, but I'll be a mangled metaphor if I'll let it work on me. I'll wring a confession out of you as surely as if Cynthia were Lady Lazarus herself!"

"And who, my friend," here Zack flung an arm casually across the back of his couch and relaxed even further into its comfy recesses, happy to have inspired so profound a display of emotion from his wary adversary, "who is to say she is not?"

Trevor stood and turned again to the view of the street, looking out the window into the darkness which was punctuated here and there by a few street lamps. Then he returned once again to face Zack, and resumed his seat. "How long?" he asked calmly.

Zack finished his whiskey, got to his feet, and walked back to the bar where the decanter stood waiting. He poured himself another drink, motioning the bottle towards Trevor.

Upton hesitated. Then he shook his head, elaborating upon his previous bi-syllabic inquiry: "How long has this—this 'collaboration' been going on?"

Speller walked over to where Trevor stood, clenching and unclenching his fists.

Upton got a hold of himself. He relaxed, almost as if the whiskey were still thrilling through him, and he made what might for some seem a surprising gambit. He put out his hand to lay hold upon Zack's shoulder. "She's more than I can hold," was all he said.

Zack faced Trevor. Their eyes locked. For an instant they seemed to share a single thought. Then Zack spoke. "She is like a mustang: some have an untameable spirit, and they can never be broken. But for us? For this time: She is like the hardware— the doorknob and the hinge—to a door. I am the door and you are the doorjamb. She is the hinge, attached both to the door and to the doorjamb, and she either keeps us apart or brings us together."

Trevor smiled. He graciously removed his hand from Zack's shoulder and smiled again. Then he extended his right hand, taking Zack's in his and shook it effusively. "You're right, of course," he replied, "and ZG is testing the door, the jamb, and the hinge. It cannot keep all three, so it wants to see whether it will keep the door, the doorjamb, or the hardware." Then as Trevor turned to go, he paused. Speaking cryptically as if to the Severini, he went on for a few seconds like this before he turned slowly to punctuate his apogee: "Then again, is she not more like the nucleus of an atom around which protons and electrons are held in a valence of conflicting emotions." Here Upton let his metaphor hang for a moment, evidently still overcome by his feelings, before punctuating it with a final paradox: "Some are held at the outermost point for so long they may begin to feel positively negated."

At this point, Zack reached out with his right hand and squeezed Trevor's arm, extending his left hand for a warm handshake. An uncomfortable second passed, and then Zack pulled his overwrought adversary in for a close and genuine embrace. They hugged for a moment, and then breaking away, Zack took a second to change gears.

"Cynthia tells me we've got a spoken word performance to make in a couple of weeks."

"Yes, the Halloween thing." Trevor seemed to be still distracted, and spoke woodenly as though it were an irritating memory.

But Zack was working out the angles, wondering about logistics.

He asked, "When did you find out about this 'Halloween thing'?

"A few days ago," Trevor responded, disingenuously, warming up to Zack's piqued curiosity.

"Exactly how many days?" Zack was not about to let this go.

"Let's see now." Trevor moderated his response, working slowly from another tentative gambit towards his deliberate but definitive conclusion: "Maybe a few hours before you and Cynthia hooked up at Mick's last Saturday night."

The unexpected hook hit Zack as hard as Trevor had intended.

"Hold on there. You said at the outset that 'we were being played', but now it seems like you're the one who's doing the playing! I mean, who told you about—"

"About the Halloween thing? Or about you and Cynthia drinking together at Mick's? Because Cynthia is the common denominator in both cases, my friend!" Upton now decided he'd best appear to be coming clean. "You see, Paul Schultz—my bosom buddy to whom I had previously introduced Cynthia, and who sent his regrets and could not attend our Afterglow celebration due to a sudden visit from his uncle Karl which meant you never met him—works weekends at Mick's, and he is what I like to call a 'reliable narrator'. He told me that he kept a low profile last Saturday night, so Cynthia never noticed him, since she would certainly have recognized him if she had seen him. But he nevertheless kept close watch on you two."

Zack let loose a low whistle. "So you've been playing the spy, 'Upton, Trevor Upton'? Have we been a pair of lovers lost in a web of wanton lust? Have we been pandering to your dark desires for some literary ménage à trois? Should I be checking my *house* for listening devices?"

"I assure you, Speller, the only devices I use are for literary purposes, not listening purposes. It was quite by accident that Schultzie just happened to be working last Saturday, on the same night that Cynthia just happened to visit me a short time prior to meeting you at Mick's. She just happened to tell me that night about the upcoming spoken word presentation. Did she not tell you about it on that night also?"

The Poetic Ambassador

"She did not! She mentioned it for the first time on the telephone a few minutes ago, just before I let you in. Where did she get this information?"

Trevor hesitated, and then decided to hedge. "She tells me she has sources in ZG that prefer to remain anonymous."

"Hedges have always been my friends and saviors. Whether from a fifty-foot free fall or from the mouth of a fickle adversary, I recognize them when I see them. Come clean Upton. She obviously trusts you more than she trusts me. Tell me what you know. Unless *you* prefer to try and win this thing using less than fair-minded methods."

"Honestly, I know only what she's said about it. And who are you to call me fickle! But I'll tell you that all she disclosed is this: 'The truth about ZG is as misty as a lost lagoon; only by swimming in the lost lagoon can one discern this misty truth'. And I'm quoting her verbatim."

"Intriguing. I remember something she once said about her Aunt Jill being addicted to ambiguity. Maybe the niece and her aunt are more alike than one can imagine. Regardless, I have a feeling there is more to this little allusion than meets the ear. Perhaps we had both best meditate on this misty matter. At any rate, such cogitations will keep. The hour is late, and we have much more to create, but sleep comes first, so we must part and soon rehearse our well-wrought art. I bid you now adieu, and thank you for your candor. What verse of yours may yet accrue, I promise not to slight or slander. And if you will extend to me the self-same courtesy and grace, I vow to leave our hinge unoiled, as door to doorjamb gives some space." So saying, Zack bowed the low bow of an illustrious host, and extended his hand towards the stair.

Not wanting to be outdone by unrehearsed verse, but neither wishing to seem the unmannered guest, Trevor simply smiled and exclaimed, with succinct precision: "The door may come unhinged! But what means that to the innocent jamb? To who knows whom, with darkness tinged, the knob may yield, like the little lamb. Tigers in the night forests cannot compare! Yet when the door swings double wide, the hinge must then beware. Let's not forget that there is a matching set to this 'hardware.' Her name is Anika" and more may *hinge* on her fair... mind than we may find in one so kind.

"Well played, sir knight, we're at an impasse. Were we to remain, we would do well to raise a glass... to that peerless pair. But for now we must say our fare thee wells, and rest our care on a pillow where sleep may cast her spells. Thank you for showing me how *we* are being played. Come again when you can linger longer, but right now I've a solitary gig with my bed that should not be delayed"

So saying, Zack ushered Upton silently out into the 'passionate embrace' of his bright red Hummer, whereupon Speller himself headed back to his bedroom, where his own 'misty dreams'— regardless of how soothing an accompaniment the plaintive strains of Ani DiFranco's version of Dylan's classic 'Most of the Time' proved to be to them—could not dispel the unsettling sense that he had about how Anika was now 'at bat' and may get a single to bring Trevor safely to second, while Cynthia could easily slide smoothly into third. So much for that triple-play, he thought to himself as he turned the pillow to the cool side.

Thirty-Four

ZG HALLOWEEN GALA

The Red Robinson Show Theatre wore its Halloween regalia like a militant drag queen copping an attitude as much for kicks as to be seen getting those kicks. All around the stage, spun like silk in red and black twirlers, hung contrasting spiralling streamers interlaced with white and garish golden trimmed bow-tie bows, while beneath the proscenium in four foot high bright purple letters ran around in a tightening spiral the words 2010 ZG HALLOWEEN GALA. As if to contradict the garish tone, or perhaps more to augment it, a baker's dozen show stopper farmer's market award-winning and huge, lavishly carved hideously smiling pumpkins perched like overweight ogres precarious as 'griffins carved in granite' all along the front edge of the stage, each one receiving its own tight circle of a different coloured spot light; some red, some yellow, some green, some blue, some indigo, some violet, but none orange. The bright orange spot was reserved for the lectern, soon to be inhabited by entertainers. There were comics aplenty interspersed amid the dozen or more honorary poets selected from among those several would-be-contenders who had applied to become poetic ambassador, but were not shortlisted. Each of these also-rans had however been commissioned to present a short piece and receive the mocking tribute of the comics assigned to satirize his or her work. Then, of course, there were Zachary Speller, Cynthia Davison and Trevor Upton, whose lengthier poems were interwoven as main attraction showcases within the 'fabric' of the evening. Their evening wear was much more than an accessory after the fact; in fact, it figured prominently in the heavily aromatic scene of this delicious crime-of-the-century gala.

Zachary Speller, elegantly dressed as Gomez Adams in a white shirt finished off with a loud purple crushed velvet and black dress vest augmented by accompanying MC Hammer pants sporting a single purple stripe down each leg to match, thought he could discern among the less conservatively dressed attendees a range of the more familiar—if only because more conventional—monsters taken from the marquees of a by-gone era. And if he were asked to surmise their true identity, he felt confident he could guess that they were members of the ZG board of executives. Nodding in the general direction of where the Creature from the Black Lagoon sat whispering and gesturing wildly in the vicinity of the ravishingly spectral Bride of Frankenstein's ear, Zack said as much to his own consort of the evening—the devilishly delightful Morticia Adams aka Anika Cervantes. She smiled and asked, "How do you know the board members?"

"Don't you mean to ask how I know that wet about the edges Creature and the bored Bride he's accosting are board members?" Zack countered inscrutably while absentmindedly fingering the large bright red poppy-shaped button he had pinned to his purple cravat with his left hand, as with the other he affectionately brushed up and down the length of Anika's long satin gloves, as much in character as the debonair Gomez as the Creature he seemed to be scrutinizing from afar appeared to be uncharacteristically land-bound, an odd fish strangely out of water.

Anika leaned in towards his ear, shaking her equally long black tresses to one side as if their conversation needed to be covered over like her own blonde locks had been by the special wig she had chosen for the night's festivities, and whispering conspiratorially, as though his interest needed more piquing, she laughingly replied, "I imagine you know as you are known for knowing, no more and certainly no less of a soulful Gomez for all that, Zack."

The Poetic Ambassador

Playing his left hand over the carved gold cufflink on his white right sleeve, Zack glanced back at where the Wolf Man sat trying to inspire a haughty Cruella De Ville around the table from where the Gill Man was cupping his webbed wet-suited fingers around a dry martini. "Who knew such silver screen matinee idols could elicit so many belly laughs," he said. "This is the stuff legends are made of."

"Dreams," Anika replied. "Don't you mean to say that 'this is the stuff dreams are made of'?"

Just then Cynthia Davison sat down beside them. A couple of the snakes in her elaborate frizzy coiffure were oddly akimbo, leaving her Gorgon effect ever-so-slightly off-balance but perhaps fittingly so, as this proved to be a feature which only enhanced this Medusa's appeal for all that slithered, and was not gold. The room was getting full now, and the buzz of conversation made it hard to hear over the eerie music the band was playing for background ambiance. But Cynthia had caught her sister's last words, and she knew her part by heart, although it was yet to be improvised and definitely not rote. "Yes, Nika. Zack knows all about dreams. Especially the thwarted kind. Or should I say, he's like a cat who has nine lives and knows when to sacrifice one of those lives in pursuit of a better dream. Never mind who gets lost with that offered up life."

Zack could not let this dig go by without responding. He parried with a thrusting jab. "At least this cat still has skin in the game! And besides, I know when a dream of a pipe is just a pipe," Tossing this off almost peevishly, he seemed more irked to have Davison pre-empting his tête-à-tête with her ravishingly pale-complexioned twin sister Anika than Cynthia supposed he might have been at her cryptic allusion to his veiled motive for his choice to *jump* all those years ago.

Nevertheless, she sensed and was contented in the knowledge that she had left him the worse for wear than when she'd arrived. So, Ms. Davison simply smiled at her sibling and said, "More's the better for the rivalry, Nika. I'm off to see if I can win some friends and influence a few animés." She winked at her sister, signalling mutual mirth at her inside joke at Sailor Moon's expense, and then smoothing her serpentine sheath, she 'slithered' away into the crowd that had begun to move passionately in time with a soundtrack that increasingly felt like a Badalamenti score. Soon she was 'writhing' around to where the Bride was fending off the Creature before he could snatch away one of her skeletal earrings.

"Marvelous costumes in display at this table, and yours is one of the most 'grisly' gowns at the gala, but how was the Tenth Annual Business Excellence Awards Gala, Ms. Staples? I understand it was held here in this very theatre on the night before last. How many awards did you receive?" Cynthia's sources were as impeccable as she was ingratiating, and she was like a good lawyer in that she always knew the answer to every question she asked before it was ever vocalized.

"Why Ms. Davison. Is my make-up slipping?" Maureen Staples laughed. "I'd have sworn this little disguise would have kept them guessing all night. Yes in fact I received an award the other night. I cannot recollect exactly for what it was bestowed, perhaps something like 'most becoming' business or 'most promising' business or—and this if memory serves is what it actually was—'most lucrative' business. It is just nice to be acknowledged in some manner or other, wouldn't you say?"

Cynthia laughed her most charming laugh, the one that sounded almost identical to a tinkling spoon being gently tapped against a carved crystal wine glass, and then she deliberately but softly grasped her favorite board member's shoulder, carefully nudging her ever-so-deftly in the general direction of the table she had just left. "Do you notice there where the heads of the Adams family are in attendance? Señor Gomez is looking dreadfully pale tonight, wouldn't you agree? I don't know, but what the music (or the pressure) is getting to him. Perhaps this is his swan song! Or his 'last resort!'"

"Lamentable how humans inevitably destroy the places they find beautiful," Maureen intoned, as if Henley and Frey were on her speed dial. But as for 'Gomez' there, he might just have *another* tango left in *him*. Though I'm sure you'll have something to say about that. Yes, I'm certain that you've got a few new moves to show us all, once you braid your way toward the podium." Ms. Staples then smiled demurely and took Cynthia's offered hand. "Hearts or legs. Break them all, Ms. Davison. Break them all."

Shaking her favorite board member's hand, Cynthia Davison turned, and working her way back through the crowd, she soon found herself humming along to the strains of the opening melody of the *Twin Peaks* instrumental being masterfully played by the orchestra. Though they were situated at the farthest outer periphery of the stage, well behind where the presenters would be delivering their performances, they managed to perform as unobtrusively as if they had been playing from the outer lobby. She knew she had recognized Badalamenti! A more movingly moody rendition could scarcely be imagined. Looking around her, Cynthia realized that there were many more people here than she had thought she had expected to find, but then she quickly recognized another well-intentioned costume by the voluptuous proportions of the woman who inhabited it. Distinctively feline. She was coughing. The Cat Woman seemed to have a fur ball, but maybe the drink had just gone down the wrong way. Cynthia patted her gently on the back, and asked politely, "Misty? Is that you?"

"Why Cynthia, I'm turning to stone just looking at you! You make a girl want to slither along to the music with the snakes in the playground."

"Where is the playground, Misty? So far I've found only one of my adversaries, one board member, and now one interviewer. You are my third strike! I was hoping for a CEO, but I've no idea who he might be dressed up as. Maybe the wizard?"

Ms. Traviss laughed her delicate, high pitched laugh, followed by a distinctively un-feline snort. She said, "Cynthia your instincts are a little off tonight. Wizards are a bit like absent-minded professors. Although she's playing against type tonight, our Stephanie Nolan has become the WOZ figure for the gala. She's all decked out as a white-haired bespectacled mage in a black pointed cap and a black lab coat with silver and gold stars and moons all over it. That will be our Southern lady of the ballroom. Don't tell her I sent you." She laughed again, and lifted her left paw to her freckled, furry cheeks, parted her whiskered lips and lifted her right paw up and took a small sip of her Tequila Sunrise. "I'm not entirely sure who Rudy has done himself up as, but I understand he's wearing one mask over another in some kind of dualistic Jekyll and Hyde affair. Nolan and he are never far apart, though. Good luck sussing that one out, dear." Then Misty sashayed off with the languid luxurious stealth that only a big cat has—after first delivering one of her deliciously snarling tiger cat meows.

Off to see the magus and her apparently schizoid boss, Cynthia departed for parts unknown, but not before stopping to adjust her form-fitting sheath, and the majestic wings that extended from where they sat snugly strapped to her shoulders. Then she abruptly stopped. Who was this with the body of Adonis? In a full tightly fitted gold body suit! Leaving nothing to the imagination. Accessorized with only a single sword and donned with a winged Greek helmet. Had Medusa met her match? It seemed to be Perseus. Cynthia strode straight up to her nemesis and grasped him by the shoulders. The crush of people around them seemed to fade away in the distance. Then, she kissed him full on the lips. The band was halfway through that old song "Spooky" when she broke off her embrace. As if in reaction, he half-turned put his arm about the waist of a woman she scarcely recognized. With gentle pressure he prompted his date to move forward until she stood side by side with Cynthia, and he revealed his stunning Chinese Vampirella with white makeup muting the yellow tones of her skin, and contrasting blood red stains issuing from her black lipstick. Her long dark hair was not a wig; it hung in luxuriant curls around her attractive face, and it cascaded around her body to extend over halfway down her back.

"You remember Miranda?" Trevor smiled, raising his sword as if in mocking defiance.

"It is a pleasure to see you again, Miranda," Cynthia said calmly and unconvincingly. "But you look like you've been a bit sloppy with your make-up—either that or you two are doing way too much necking!"

"I see you've been prowling with the Cat Woman," Monica replied casually, ignoring the lame pun. "Her qualities kind of rub off on you like static on fur, wouldn't you say?"

"Don't take it the wrong way, but cutting a classical figure kind of clashes with the cultish pre-pubescent fantasy world now, doesn't it?" Cynthia's cold smile was designed to pierce Trevor to the quick. She looked wonderfully hideous with her writhing hair harridancing like loose ends on her head and her dark purple lipstick smudged by the 'imagined' kiss of death she had planted on her adversary's lips.

"Careful Medusa, this sword cuts both ways. But tell us: Which stone faced consort did you conscript to be *your date*?" Trevor inquired evenly.

"I'm being chaperoned by mom and dad tonight. They're at the table. She gestured offhandedly toward one of the premier tables a few feet off, before stage left, in front of a particularly ginormous leering pumpkin whose lurid features were swathed in a bluish spotlight. A beaming Kristos dressed as Zeus waved his lightning bolt back at her, having spotted her indicating them, and then resumed an animated conversation he was having with his heavily bosomed wife Melanie in the robes and golden sash of Hera whose luxuriant golden braids were bound as tightly upon her head as her daughter Cynthia's Medusa tangle of serpents seemed bent with writhingly unkempt fervor upon escaping her scalp.

"What? No date?" Trevor's caustic insinuation was clear. Then he pounced for the debilitating blow: "Isn't that Eddie Patterson over there at your table, all done up to resemble the Wolverine?"

"Well if you must know," Cynthia retorted shortly, "Eddie Patterson is also at our table because he is presenting a poem tonight." Then, as if prompted for clarification, she offered what she hoped would be a plausible rationalization: "He asked if he could join us at the last minute, as his intended date Heidi Egan—who was unfortunately not selected to share poetry—had an unexpected costume ball to attend. Sadly, he seems to have glommed on to my mother and father and he is attempting to insinuate himself into the conversation whenever possible. As I previously suggested, the classical world clashes with the contemporary cultish world. It is a stain on our feast. Especially since reader response is all Eddie seems to think about."

"More the pity," Miranda replied curtly. She was well aware of the sting of such a revelation, and she thought it not proper form to pour vinegar upon a fresh wound.

Trevor simply added, "Your mother's considerable experience with counseling will stand her in good stead. She may soon guide him to another table entirely." He was attempting to be gracious, but he could not help adding, "That is, if your father doesn't electrocute him first with that lightning bolt!"

"My father may work for the IBEW, but he's no electrician. His experience is in union organizing. He's more liable to unionize the poets here long before he ever short circuits Patterson. But I'll leave you two to your plotting." Cynthia had spotted a likely lead. "I see someone whose mask is slipping, and I think he's wearing another beneath it. Don't fall on your sword, Upton. And beware the fangs of the fallen. B-movie villainesses seldom make the A-list."

So saying, Cynthia seemed to slink away, but she was not fully out of earshot when Miranda found her voice again, mangling Paul Simon's titular song, "Still catty after all these years!"

Pretending she had not head the groaner of a comeback, Cynthia drifted off toward another clutch group of classic movie characters. She noticed several of William Castle's 13 Ghosts seemed to be hanging on every word of one of his more memorably eponymous characters. Yes, it *was* two masks he wore. One on a kind of hinge that seemed to slide on and off the leering grimace of... it *was:* Mr. Sardonicus. And there was the white haired mage herself at his right hand. How fitting that Mr. Sorensen should be accompanied by a bespectacled Ms. Stephanie Nolan in her pointy hat and sable robes adorned with so many golden suns and so many silver moons. But wasn't that spectacular rictus of a leer superb? Rivaling with ease the horrid pumpkin faces atop the stage it seemed to stretch from chin to nose, and from ear to shining ear. The cameramen were eating it up, competing, in a controlled frenzy—elaborately orchestrated with the utmost care and delicacy—for the best footage and still shots. Cynthia slid into place with deliberately deft precision. Her pale make up contrasting with her purple mascara and purple lipstick (which she had just touched up), all vividly juxtaposed with the gold and green snakes that went into a mane seemingly intent upon making a vigorously animated escape from the haughty mien of her head.

She edged herself brashly to within close proximity of the tight group, wondering at whom they each may be. She thought she recognized the Bound Woman as that elderly spinster she had seen while Cynthia herself was coming out of the elevator on the night she had met with Stephanie Nolan (Was *she* the Cassie Ellis she had heard about? Undoubtedly!), and the others were surely board members as well. All the ghosts were represented. There was the Angry Princess: possibly Anne Morris? The Torn Prince could be Rod Albright. The Withered Lover was likely Norma Paterson. And The Jackal or The Hammer would have to be Nathan Balfour. Cynthia looked at each of the ghosts then scanned the names and faces in her mind of the board member roster she had committed to memory weeks ago, but all the while she listened intently to Ms. Nolan and Mr. Sorensen, waiting for an opportunity to break into the conversation. At the next lull, she seized her chance.

"Yesss!" she hissed sibilantly, "there is an audible assembly of awe-inspiring characters on display here tonight. Wouldn't you agree Ms. Nolan? ZG has certainly put on an admirable gala!"

"Ah, Ms. Davison, I presume? My dear! You *are* sporting a fine front tonight! Macabre and malevolent; maudlin and morose; pithy and repugnantly luscious in eloquence and irrepressible pursuit of poetic excellence, all in one inspirational go. Look at our front-runner, Mr. Sorensen. She has all the earmarks of a real contender, has she not? A tangled Gordian knotted mass of snakes atop her well drawn visage. A veritable feast for the eyes! And what, pray tell, is the nugget you will share with us tonight, child? Do tell us more about—"

Mr. Sardonicus interrupted at once, unveiling his mask to reveal his true self, his shocking, tightly stretched hideous grimace, a most alarming leer. Cynthia was quite taken aback to feel the force of his ardent stare so close at hand. It really was a marvel of a mask. His chilling gaze seemed to speak volumes, but Sorensen's own paternal voice broke in, jarringly cordial by contrast to the superbly constructed mask of horror: "Now Stephanie, we must not spoil the show. Don't encourage the young lady to divulge all of her secrets. She'd be better off not disappointing us by even so much as hinting at the nature of her poem, until her hour has finally come. But indeed, we are pleased to welcome you, *and* your family to the festivities, my dear. How has the portfolio been going? I trust that you have found it challenging enough?"

"Immeasurably rewarding. Unaccustomedly bracing. I'm forging new fields in the interim now. Restorative, but taxing. Inexpressibly enticing. I'm extolling the virtues of standing at the prow of the poems I've written for our portfolio that lead us to show from here to wherever we have yet to go for the sake of ZG to whom we say, simply, 'Bravo!'."

The Bound Woman smiled and raised her cane toward the ceiling. "Well said, young lady. Well said. We are sure you will surpass expectations!"

"Thank you Ms. Ellis." Cynthia replied, smiling cryptically and with seemingly unfeigned humility.

The Angry Princess, refusing to break character, snapped out a reply that matched terse with terser. "Prowess speaks volumes, though words be few. We look through what you say to see what you do."

The Jackal smiled with rue, and shared of *his* mind, "When you are on track, the freight is delivered, along with the train of your thought. It has been a rough ride thus far, 'tis averred; much of it is perhaps best forgot! But the station is in sight. Do not disappoint us tonight!

"I will do my best to live up to your expectations, Mr. Balfour."

"Call me Nathan," smiled The Jackal, aware that, for a moment, he had lapsed out of his own colluding character. Or had he? Cynthia could not be sure, but she sensed from his overly-familiar overture that his support for her was unvarnished no matter how tenuous a hold he appeared to have on the notion of her stability.

Only the Hammer, the Torn Prince and the Withered Lover stood in stony silence while the others exchanged stage whispers about Medusa's formidable appearance and her imposing comportment. Finally, as if to hasten her departure, the Withered Lover turned to the Hammer and said "Pound Alexandrines into the dust they came from, / though her eyes be clear, game they seek is zero sum. / Foes to frieze in panes stained glass depict malaise / yet still may rise to withstand she who has no grace." The Hammer replied to the Withered Lover, "Playing one against the other is risky game / when she discovers there's no bar to fickle fame / and when they both find out that they are being played / not one but two foes set the stage to be waylaid."

Cynthia seemed transfixed, as if she had turned herself to stone by viewing her reflection in a mirror. The crowd, even the music seemed mute.

She was taken aback at this forthright poetic evaluation, but she nonetheless strove to remain unfazed. She simply smiled, and replied to the general group, "Your costumes are all superb. It looks like a William Castle convention here tonight. Enjoy the entertainment. I look forward to talking with you after the show." So saying, she took her cue and resumed sitting in the only vacant chair at her table, with the other seven guests (there were several tables each with eight to ten guests), all of whom had of course by this time assumed their own seats. Dining hour had long passed, and the meet and mingle moments were drawing to a hasty conclusion.

The head tables, two at front and center—equidistant from the main podium—were reserved for the Executive and the Editorial Staff, who would be mainly responsible for adjudicating the portfolios and recommending the successful ambassador. Ranged around to the right and to the left, and down at back of these head tables were the tables for each of the short-listed contenders and their guests. Other tables contained friends and families and patrons of the arts, and authors, poets and writers whose works had been published by ZG. There were also numerous seats in the balcony that had been paid for by donation to the literacy charity ZG funded with such bequests. The Red Robinson Show Theatre was full to capacity and with the dinner dishes cleared away now, and the mixing done with, it was fast approaching the 8pm start time. The Mistress of Ceremonies was making her way in and around the tables, offering a few preliminary asides and gleaning what remained to be gleaned in preparation for her opening monologue.

Trevor was talking with his sister Kate whose domed R2-D2 costume incongruously topped by dreadlocks seemed to be a companion (were it not for his classical Greek helmet and the sword) to what might have passed for a golden C-3PO body suit. "Any other Star Wars costumes tonight, sis?"

"I've seen two Princess Leia suits and four Darth Vader suits, including dad's fierce finery. The Force is definitely with us!" Kate laughed happily.

"Oh, go back to Alderaan, why don't you." Trevor punched her playfully in the arm.

"Careful, Trevor." Celeste spoke out from across the table. "She's liable to enlist you in the Resistance!" Celeste was as dazzling in her Wonder Woman costume as her twin sister was in her Vampirella gown.

"Kate could definitely do that," Ginny laughed good naturedly from the other side of her daughter. "As you know she's got lots of practice, Trev. Mostly of the passive-aggressive kind. She'll guilt you into the Resistance if nothing else!" Ginny was dressed as the colourful Ahsoka Tano, with a blue and white two-horned headpiece surrounding her orange and white mask, which contrasted nicely with her bright blue eyes. She fit in perfectly with the rest of the family; except for the athletic Perseus look Trevor was attempting. His six-pack girdle went a long way to helping him carry it off.

The rest of the table included several of Trevor's friends from the Afterglow celebration, a few of whom were also sporting vampire costumes, along with a Thor and an Ironman; and Schultzie had even managed an unexpected night off from Mick's to make an appearance tonight, choosing to don the Batman mask, cape and tights. The judges for best costumes, male and female categories would have their work cut out for them.

Zack and Anika were engrossed with talk of Winterfest celebrations at her school, only six weeks ahead. Anika was preparing to sing a song at the event. There was a teacher's band called the Cold. They sounded better than the name suggested, Anika assured him.

"Cute name. Plays on a reversal of expectations, right? After all, since nobody wants to catch the Cold, and it's de rigueur not to want to be a 'somebody,' being a "complete unknown" in Dylan's terms is equivalent to being a 'nobody'. Hence, everyone wants to be a 'nobody'!" Zack was miles away with his pretzel logic. "Don't you see? Everybody wants to be the 'nobody' who wants to catch the Cold! He smiled enigmatically, congratulating himself on having successfully sublimated his impending perfor—oh no, there he was again, walking up to the podium in his mind's eye. If he could see this far in advance, he'd take all the spontaneity out of his presentation, despite how much he had already rehearsed it again and again until it was almost a peon to artful inelegance. He concentrated instead on Morticia Adams who sat as tantalizingly authentic as a latentative human tarantula in front of him.

"You're looking at me like you're thinking I might bite you," Anika murmured pulling up her long black gloves and smoothing down her long black gown, with its raised braille-like webs woven as assiduously as if they were designed by some fat dimpled spider, itself intent on capturing its prey with a diabolical precision that was even worked into her tiara, shining with rich green finery that its web-like silver weave stitched so seamlessly as to cast a wanton spell over all who might become ensnared in its nettings.

"Would you? Please!"

Just then Cat Woman appeared at their side, purring mellifluously.

"I couldn't help but overhear. Anika is it?" Misty's soft, but probing voice spilled out her own special brand of liquid honey once again. "Aren't you Cynthia's twin sister?" As Anika nodded dreamily, Misty poured forth again. "Well, child. What song will you be singing at this year's Winterfest?" she prompted with genuine interest.

"I'll be singing with two of my colleagues. We will be covering the February 21, 2010 La Diva rendition of "Angels Brought Me Here". YouTube has this performance, and we'll be attempting to channel it." Anika was clearly shy about sharing her upcoming song, and because she did not want to take any of the spotlight away from her sister, she turned so red that her face burned a pink hue that even shone through the heavy white makeup that covered it. "But please don't mention it to anyone," she insisted.

Nevertheless, Cat Woman affirmed her intention to share this juicy bit of catnip with everyone else, once the time was right.

Anika seemed visibly shaken by this prospect. She followed Cat Woman's progress from table to table, and quickly realized this woman was none other than the Mistress of Ceremonies. Once she was struck with this realization, Morticia practically begged her Gomez to do something. "Zack, you've got to stop her! I would hate to come between Cynthia and her limelight or in this case pumpkinlight."

"Nonsense, Anika. This is an evening of sharing, or a sharing of evening. It will all even out in the end. Besides, I have not yet expounded on my theory of latentativity."

But despite how carefully he elaborated upon how her 'latent' talent could only be fully realized if her fear of the 'tentative' were allowed to run its course and culminate in a pervasive renewal of self-confidence, like a river of dreams leading inexorably to an oceanic awakening, Cynthia's adamant twin was not persuaded, and she sat pensively, a photographic negative image of that ocean swallowed in sunlight, anthropomorphically dreading the pending outcome of her imminent exposure, and certain there could be no positive developments in her fated unfortunate future, tragically caught in woven webs, infinitely more intricate and ornate than those aforementioned embellishments enriching her own costume,

The Poetic Ambassador

but ultimately ensrared by her own flawed design. Her talent was certain, yet her fear of uncertainty blocked her progress towards practicing latentativity. Yes, she was her own worst enemy.

Zack did his best to forestall the inevitable. He teased and cajoled her, and he even tried to tango with her when the music seemed appropriate to such a dance. Nothing would work, and her dark mood deepened into a lingering morbidity strangely consonant with her costume and pale visage. She ceased being Anika and retreated into a consummate portrayal of her 'role' as Morticia Adams.

At last, just before Zack had decided he must call upon Kristos and Melanie to elevate her feelings, Cat Woman pounced up onto the podium with an audacious snarl. Her vivacious caterwauling was infectious. She must have had help from the sound technicians. The roaring was larger than life, and the decked out denizens of the 2010 ZG HALLOWEEN GALA that had assembled to be entertained in the Red Robinson Show Theatre cheered, whistled and shout-screamed for the full-bodied, full-throated Mistress of Ceremonies. And for what had finally come at last, the much-anticipated opening of this Halloween extravaganza! Cat Woman did not disappoint. Her flawless delivery came out in a clearly articulated stream of consciousness that began by invoking one of Beat poetry's most ardent representations.

Thirty-Five

ZG HALLOWEEN GALA II

"Ginsberg's 'Howl' inflicted a catalogue of calumny upon a world," purred Cat Woman. "A world that would be forever changing and rearranging the notions of ignominy and greatness, of inertia and indifference, of dispassionate pathos culled from the antitheses of the nearest reaches of infamy and the furthest shores of heroism, culled from the ghosts of the least loved beat poet to the inverse equational divider of the greatest ghost of a close encounter with a godless, mindless, soulless philosophical see-no-evil, hear-no-evil, speak-nothing-*but*-evil, so help me we have been flawed," she paused for a breath and continued in an even more eloquent vein, "Flawed ever since the mined raw product is neither consumed nor moved out from the bowels of the Bestial constellations humankind charts in order to progress beyond our expectations of something more than enough for satisfaction, something approaching mutual contentment, something contemporary society lauds as ZG!"

The roar, the whistling, the hooting and applause was deafening. Everywhere within the room, a loud hullabaloo went up, down and around. It was a din heard beyond the walls, and it resonated with the sentiment being shared, but perhaps more persistently due to the occasion of the event, and the diversity of costumed citizenry assembled within those same walls. Gradually after a minute or more of sustained frenzied fettle, silence descended once again on the room, and Cat Woman rose once again to the occasion.

The Poetic Ambassador

"We've got a caustic tribe of satirists, mock poets and toasty roasters in the House, so hold your applause until I've named and blamed them all!! Give it up for 'Shiny' Robert Robertson, he'll put you up and put you on, to pull you down to size you up on a pedestall-tactical manoeuver from which you won't soon escape! No, no. Hold your applause until the end, please. Then there's the Rogue Superstar Henrietta "etta boy" James, famous for haranguing around with all the wrong poets! Now we are going to hear from some of those also-ran poets tonight. They were interviewed for the position of poetic ambassador, but they never made the short-list. Nevertheless, they merited an honourable mention because their poems were selected for inclusion tonight. The evening's festivities will get underway momentarily, and you will be seeing several poems presented for the very first time under the ZG brand. Interspersed with these presentations will be our comic talent, in many cases satirizing and lampooning our poetry in a kind of circuitous comic feedback loop. So let's hear it for our first 'also-ran', Eddie Patterson, who will be presenting "Ode to a Run-On Sentience." Give it up for Eddy!"

The applause dwindled significantly from the gusto of the opening salvo, but it was still enough to make most people a little hard of hearing. Eddy was waiting in the wings and he strode confidently out to his optimistic audience, many of whom leant in to cock an ear, if not exactly lending him all of their ears. Truth be told there were other conversations going on at this point of the ceremony. But kudos to Eddy. He soldiered on through all 36 of his not always captivating lines. Perhaps his best pair of couplets were the last lingering lines of the poem, recited in solemn clipped monotone rhythms, mostly intoned as spondees:

"If I dye my hair before I wake, I say, 'my word has become fake!'
and if I wake before I lie, then 'what wonder!' would I cry,
and should my mind lose sight of place, how, then how could I save face
at all the towns and cities gone, beyond the pale of Alderaan,
and on, and on, and on we run, a sentience sapient, puissant, homespun."

Naturally, this got a mixed response. Some like Melanie counseled restraint, quick to find the good and thought-provoking in what others who hooted and jeered dismissed as down and dirty doggerel. These same intellectual infidels laughed and applauded at the satirical jibes offered by Shiny Ar Ar as Cat Woman jokingly referred to Robert Robertson: Shiny's take on those same lines was the crowd's first taste of the ways that lampooning 'returns' poetry into a comical send up of the human condition that comics decided to take, each in their own inimitable turn-taking style:

"If we all spike our 'air before we slake our thirst, won't our mothers think we are the worst? And if we tear our eyes out in the storm, won't we all decide it's just the norm? And would a keystroke more or less, make my mind erase itself like Porgy or his blessed Bess, a poor black man who knows his place is anywhere love dwells in this whole human race."

With its egalitarian spin, and comical irony, Shiny RR showed that comedy can be bracing and not nearly as self-involved as some of the honourable mentionable presenters. The crowd loved Shiny and his applause was audibly louder and arguably more genuine than the voluble praise garnered by Eddy. Cynthia sat at their table silently fuming as her mother tried to suggest that Eddy's poem had been more ideologically and structurally consistent than Shiny RR's. She secretly despised Eddy for what she saw as drivel that brought the entire level of the evening down. After all, if the comedian who lampooned his verse could bring in more acclaim than the poet whose work is being ridiculed, then what kind of a precedent would that set for future presentations?

Cat Woman was already at the podium, exciting the crowd by telling them to get ready for two more also-ran poets and two more comics to come before the first big prospective Poetic Ambassador hopeful would appear: "He is Perseus the Medusa-slayer!! Trevorrrr Upton is in the House! Don't worry, Medusa herself is also a contender, and she'll be up later this evening, so you can judge for yourselves what hope if any our Medusa-slayer really has!! But now our ZG Publishing House is pleased to present for your entertainment, Heidi Egan!"

Cynthia looked over at Eddy, but he seemed as shocked as she was at this surprising turn of affairs. She doubted the veracity of his word more than ever now. He was a sham poet, and probably a bigger liar than she imagined. After all, there Heidi was on the stage in complete contradiction to his having informed them that she had been passed over for this honour and would not be in attendance tonight.

Heidi stood tiptoe at the podium sporting her navy blue Alice in Wonderland dress with the white apron and the white ribbon in her golden hair and her striped red and white stockings descending down to where her tiny feet fit like buttons into her shiny black shoes—and the room seemed to telescope around Cynthia as she shuddered with rage sending her snaky tendrils spiralling outward, while she imagined them picking up roots, transforming to menacing crows and descending in a murder towards Heidi with a malevolent melange of myopic mind-numbing malice. "Mm-mm-mm," she thought sweetly. "Wouldn't that be nice?"

Over where the Adams sat, Anika kicked Zack under the table. All she said was, "That woman is asking for trouble." She knew her sister better than her sister knew herself. Zack seemed disinterested, though he perked up when he noticed that Cynthia's hair seemed to have taken on a life of its own, and was vibrating visibly. He gave a low whistle, and said, "I see what you mean, Anika."

Meanwhile, Vampirella was letting loose with a deep throaty chuckle. She, too, saw the quivering snakes trying to flee from Cynthia's variegated coif, and she sensed her rival for Trevor's affection was becoming more than a little bit agitated. "Your adversary appears to have a slight problem with our girl's unexpected appearance here, Trev. Could it be that she's suffering from a smidgeon of performance anxiety, or do you suppose it might have more to do with her anxiety at having to follow Heidi?"

"Cynthia creates rivalries like poetry, out of nothing at all. Her rich fantasy life is unparalleled, vying with itself to construct that rarest of all pleasure domes whose churning walls can at once deconstruct themselves only to find that they have been reconstituted at a whim on a hope rooted in a prayer at her exclusive sacred altar of self-discovery. And woe to anyone who may get in the way of that process. She'll double down on a double-dare, and in an instant leave you unaware of where you found that sunny day, because alas! It's gone away! She's not like you, Miranda dear! Your love is true. And when you say you'll stay near, your truth is truer than your word, I need not fear some strange fate awaits me from another man, to whom you also told your truth, or some strange suit you choose for me, to dress me up and make me see a side of you that you have hid, or some unkind lie by which I'm chid. With you I have more than gold or fame, and I know that you love the game, but I know that you will not play me, and that you will not try to tame me. So let's not talk of Davison. She's always game when her game is on, she's always playing, always winning, from her end at the beginning." Trevor ran his fingers through his pale love's dark hair, teased a fanged smile out of her, and returned it with a genuine smile of his own. Then they turned their attention to where Heidi was putting the finishing touches on a fine 40-line Alexandrine.

Heidi's voice was smooth, languid and pitched in richly cadenced, sophisticated tones, a delivery that stood in stark contrast with her poised petite figure. She had begun in trenchant prose, introducing her theme of beaches and bounty; pillage, rape, and marred beauty; enduring love versus transient pleasure. She elaborated in eloquent terms of how specious endearing words could be if not tempered and tried in the fires of lasting commitment. The audience was held rapt by her narrative and after she wrapped it all up in the final six Alexandrines, you could have heard the proverbial pin plunge to the floor outdoing a cannonball's roar with its deafening silence. After a pregnant pause, the cannonball did roar, though. The applause strove to surpass the initial outpouring of emotion and Cynthia saw what it was to receive the word-applause Ms. Duffy had alluded to in her concise tripartite 'Talent'!

Neither Zack, nor either Trevor or Cynthia would forget those final thirteen poignant Alexandrines, nor the simple, though profound manner in which Heidi so vividly and painstakingly presented them to her gala audience:

Years passed, time's banner stood. Echoing sacrifice
among the weeping lost. Audible defiance,
Sheltering her heartache, pulled like snow-slowing steps,
as homeward she did trudge. Visible compliance
tempted her yet to yield: Enduring paradise,
dressed to look like a hell of low glowing depths.

And into this muted plain her stoic smile gleams
as she raises her banner, high atop a hillside,
hope springs, rusted, shuttered, a trophy of malaise,
reminds her of the manor, a doorstop suicide.
'Into every life must fall' a little praise.
Love is not the sum of a heroic child's dreams,
And yet not all we see is as it sometimes seems.

Now Cynthia had her resounding rejoinder to Eddy's banal banter, and none of the comics would dare to lampoon this one, she thought. Or wouldn't they? This anguished lovelorn tripe was ripe for the picking, wasn't it? Cynthia found herself getting her hopes up, and she waited pensively as Cat Woman reappeared at Heidi's side during the crescendo of applause that did not seem to want to abate.

"Our own Heidi Egan!" Cat Woman was positively beaming. "Would you like to thank anyone or cite any influences that contributed to your excellent Ottova Rima in Sextets, dear?"

"I would like to thank each of the three contenders who are vying for the position of poetic ambassador for believing in me, encouraging me, and special thanks go to Trevor Upton for suggesting the Ottova Rima as an appropriate form for this showcase. My formal influences include the poetry of Ms. Margaret Atwood and thanks to Cynthia Davison for suggesting that I study the poetry of Carol Anne Duffy. And a big thank you of course to ZG for their pursuit of traditional excellence in contemporary poetry. It is a tremendous opportunity to publish with a House who holds such values. Finally, thank you to the audience without whom we would not even be talking about these issues." Heidi blushed, smoothed her dress, and looked for all the world like she was about to join the Mad Hatter for a tea party.

"Well, you've certainly raised the bar tonight, Ms. Egan. Now for something completely different! Here's that Rogue Superstar, Henrietta, "etta boy" James to provide some comic relief!!" Cat Woman relinquished the stage to ettaboy, who came out with a stand up routine/roast that centered upon the multiplying villainies of William Castle.

"It seems we've a Castle crowd in the theatre tonight. Which begs the question: Who is the King of the Castle? Some say it is not a king but a queen we should be looking for, though. But by switching genders, we've only a princess, it would appear. No queen! No queen!? Alice is better off with this situation anyway, isn't she? No more 'Off with her head!' She gets to keep her noggin safely on her shoulders. I shouldn't think lopping her head off would be all that popular anyway, would you? Not after that tour de force of a poetry reading!! Let's have another round of applause for 'Alice'!"

This was happy occasion, and Cynthia smiled ironically just thinking of it. To revisit the glories of yesteryear no matter that the audience had just about overdosed on accolades for the 'tiny tot from Wonderland.' They nevertheless took great delight in clapping themselves silly again. "Must be something in the tea," Cynthia opined to Melanie, while she was in the middle of a cloudy cogitation about how terrible this comic was.

But I don't think the Angry Princess would make a suitable monarch to crown as the Castle regent, do you? Far too petulant to wield the sceptre. No there is only one true royal that must merit the throne that Castle built. That is of course the eponymous Mr. Sardonicus himself. True, he is a bit of a schizoid, but monarchs must get used to seeing things from more than one perspective! And they have to keep things close to their chest—hopefully their treasure chest! Mr. Sardonicus wears at least two masks—his normal face and his menacing face. This is perfect for the king of a Castle as

The Poetic Ambassador

he must be fierce to fend off his enemies, and he must be mild to placate his people. So who is the king of the Castle? I give you Mr. Sardonicus! Besides, I have it on good account that his real identity is none other than Rudy Sorensen the ZG Chief Executive Officer. And he has the broad shoulders and physique of an athlete, a man born to lead. That's l-e-a-d, lead as in lead foot Rudy. You'd have to be the king of a William Castle empire to pay for all the speeding tickets old lead foot Rudy has gotten over the years, am I right? But seriously folks, Rudy is a born leader of poets. Why just a few weeks ago when they say he was leading the debate about the length of one of the poems our presenters are sharing tonight, the discussion turned to size. Now Rudy is over six feet tall, so it is pretty easy to see that size matters a lot for him. Now let's give Mr. Sorensen a round of applause for being such a good sport. But seriously folks, it is not only a matter of the size of a poem, but content as well. We ladies know that if you are content with the size, it doesn't matter either. When it comes to a poem, if it is good, it doesn't matter how short it is. And that is also true of other matters as well, I think. So for that matter, it might be just as well to revisit the issue of who should be king of the Castle. If size doesn't really matter, then why don't we consider replacing Mr. Sardonicus with oh, let's say The Bound Woman from William Castle's 13 Ghosts. After all if she's 'bound,' she's also probably 'determined' and that is always a good combination. Besides that we don't know what she's 'bound for' but I have my hunch, knowing that it is Ms. Cassie Ellis who is disguised as this woman that she is bound for greatness! Unless she is bound and determined to fail!! In that case, the Castle Empire is bound to fall! Oh well, that's show business. Up one day and down the next. Let's give it up for Ms. Ellis, another good sport. So Cat Woman? Who's up now?"

With an alacrity that put the pry in spry Cat Woman upstaged Henrietta James by saying she should have spoken with a Scottish accent so she could say she put the Rogue in Brogue. Knowing that the line would fall flat, she had decided to try it anyway just to hear the 'badabump' and 'crash' of the drummer's symbols, as he had been adding that ad-lib roll on and off throughout Ms. James' routine, thereby helping the laughter considerably. Well one poet had escaped comic calumny. That was two down, eleven to go, with the three poetic ambassador hopefuls still to come. Misty clapped her hands signalling the next poet would be taking the podium. She welcomed Blaise A. Trayle (not his real name) to the stage, and asked him to introduce his poem.

Blaise had donned the weeds of the scarecrow from the Wizard of Oz, with hay superannuating his homegrown raggedy Andy style coveralls and sticking out everywhere. Oh how he must have itched! Regardless of his appearance, and of the bright red oversized heart that he had safety-pinned to his lapel, he certainly upped the ante considerably by telling the audience he would be reciting his ballad of cannabis culture.

Blaise proceeded to give an account of the enticements of weed, the feeling state associated with a 'rolling stone' approach to life (which he immediately explained consisted simply in never coming down from a marijuana high), the ongoing development of the deleterious effects of the drug, the difficulties one faces when attempting to quit, the stigma of chronic use, and finally the ultimate release that comes from getting off of, rather than off on Mary Jane. His narrative account of the cycles inherent in marijuana use yielded a mixed bag of responses, generally favourable.

Cynthia's mother Melanie and her father Kristos were both highly supportive, and their applause was perhaps more enthusiastic than most of the other tables on the floor space. The rafters held a motley collection of poetry fans, and there was considerably more support from that contingent. The Castle crew, as a whole, were less than enamoured with the content, but they clapped tepidly for the ballad structure, the clever use of rhyme, and the frequent enjambment that tied one quatrain to the next with finesse. What with Donavan Blake clapping his webbed hands at the oddest places, and Maureen Staples applauding raucously when the goodbye to Mary Jane broke the cycle of abuse, it was undoubtedly a success for all that.

The Poetic Ambassador

At the end of the presentation, Cat Woman again asked whether Blaise wished to express gratitude. He did so proudly, thanking Melanie Cervantes for her counseling guidance, and his 12 Step Recovery Group for their support in his struggle. He also expressed appreciation to ZG for their endorsement of his poetic talent. One of the more memorable excerpts from his ballad was this eight-quatrain segment, punctuated after his shout-out of gratitude was ended by Blaise saying, "The Wizard tells me I've had this heart all along. If I'd only known":

Rolling stoned leaves me with smoking pipe dreams!
I feel a fantastic freedom within
budding forth like neological memes,
as finery flippantly fingers sin!

A wasted not want not metrical slant
keeps me alive to the possible road.
Far ahead lies closer to homegrown plant.
Hydro costs more than I'm willing to load.

But my talent like smoke goes up from flames.
My mind on trivial things, uninspired
flits like bubbles; can't remember the names
of concepts after which I'd inquired,

of details, of old familiar faces,
of chords I once played, of songs I once sang,
of chess moves I once put through their paces,
of all of these and more of Auld Lang Syne,

And still more, not yet known who long for my
spark, for my once vital spirit to fly
like an ark upon the seas of the sky
where Love is waiting for MJ to die.

And then one fine day it happens again.
And again, and again, and then, once, when
control of my body arose like the sun,
parting the clouds like a powerful Zen!

And I'm back! in the land of the living!
Consisting of days filled sometimes with dregs,
but others of wonder, joyous giving,
and at last, at long last, I've got my legs!

Freedom, I thought, was inhaling the weed!
But what I caught was impaling my need
for some other seed, for some other creed,
upon the cross, on which Jesus did bleed!

Misty got all misty-eyed, so she had to wait awhile, take a deep breath, after they had repeated this moving section of the ballad, and then voila! Presto! Cat Woman leaped back into action. "And now we have Ellie Camino! Come on out here, Ellie."

Ellie wore a bright red polka dot dress, in the vein of Little Lotta and she was squeezed into it tighter than an extra ratchet snug up on that backstage drum kit. But her humour was looser than Charlie Chaplin's baggy pants. She started off with a cruise control ride over some of the similar ground that had been covered by Blaise, and she did not fail to fathom that the laugh track for his name would likely run off on automatic pilot with just the slightest bit of her prodding.

"Well what about that last poet? He sure was true to his name, wasn't he? He be blazin' trails all right. Trails of glory! All the way on the path to Acapulco Gold! There's for sure Gold in them there hills. Blaise A. Trayle to the munchies, my friend! But the truth of the matter is that he made a change. It's a sure thing he wouldn't be making no change, if'n he kept on paying for the killer weed, cause that costs you a lot of dough. Just imagine if the government ever legalized it! You'd be paying practically double, that's for sure. But he got religion, and that's good too, cause the church for sure don't pay no taxes, and that's why they can afford to run all those good programs! Scare people straight, they do!! That's for sure. Now listen, there's some good people here tonight, and I won't make fun of them one bit, that's for sure. Take that woman sitting right down there next to Zeus! That's his wife, I'm sure. If he's Zeus, she's for sure Hera! Now

The Poetic Ambassador

Blaise gave her a shout out, saying she was doing some fancy guidance counseling for him! I say that's one hero of a Hera!! That's for sure. Now Zeus! If you are gonna shock Hera with that lightning bolt, you just shock her good; I mean give her a good shock, if you know what I mean! Cause we women don't mind a good jolt now and then, if you know what I mean! That's for sure. And you there, with the gold body suit and the Greek helmet. You're Perseus aren't you? That's right! You. Sitting there beside little miss curvy-Q Vampirella! If you really are Perseus what do you mean by giving that old Medusa such a fright? She be shaking like to death, her hair it's up and gonna leave her scalp for all the quivering it's doing. You're stalking her with your costume is what you're doing! That's for sure. Missy M. you don't pay him no mind, he ain't gonna decapitate you on our watch, no ma'am! That's for sure. That's it for me, folks. And remember high times ain't always good times. Don't forget what Mr. Blaise A. Trayle taught us all about that! It's the truth, and that's for sure. I ain't sure about much, but that's for sure.

On the trail like a cat on Cat Nip, Misty once again assumed her alter-ego personality as the Mistress of Ceremonies, thanking Ellie Camino for her mutually assured detour down the road of certain certainties. Her roast of Blaise's road to recovery had been short and sweet, and she'd highlighted some of the foibles of certain costumes at the expense of a couple of would-be ambassadors. All that remained was for Cat Woman to call in the first contender to the position of poetic ambassador. She did this with the dignity and aplomb commensurate upon the first premiere featured poet of the evening, and built up his pedigree without sacrificing his pretension to the prestigious post of ambassador to the ZG House. While she was regaling the room with these particulars, Trevor made his way to the wings, where he stood waiting confidently for Misty to signal that it was time for him to perform his Ottova Rima.

"And now direct from the underworld, Perseus, uh, I mean to say Trevorrr Upton, the first of three who would become ZG Poetic Ambassador with an Ottova Rima he crafted specially for this occasion.

Trevor stepped up to the podium, and began his opening remarks. "Many among you tonight may feel that love poetry is kind of like Sir Paul McCartney's little ditty about silly love songs: "some people want to fill the world" with them. I agree with Sir Paul's verdict. "What's wrong with that? ... Well here I go again". This is my Ottova Rima about the intricacies, nuances and foibles of love. I dedicate it to the ZG staff and executive, and to my adversaries in what has been a highly memorable and challenging competition thus far. I wish you much success and may the best man or woman win!"

He let silence envelope him, and then slowly and with deliberate emphasis and even pacing, Trevor began to read his poem:

The Dance

She loves being in love, but she doesn't love 'love'.
I love her erudite wit, waylaid to adorn.
She wore her smile—well-read, lipstick glossed, hair blown
in windswept nettings out of which her bird had flown—
in case there might just be a witness to suborn
or seduce, because seduction fits hand in glove
with her charming countenance, and her gaiety,
fulsome as wanton wind, though scarcely as carefree.

They held to their world view that involved saving space
by living on the edge. Recycling jobs paid bills
neither one acknowledged, but still they made their peace
with outward shows of grace and a long-term short lease
on a life without regrets or other mean wiles
an average day contains and saves but to deface
or flout, like winning hands in the bridge game of life's
little journey, cherished until the end arrives.

We met one day when Time stood—still along the way—
a pair of star-crossed wayward souls at a concert
in L.A., where people seldom take Time to think
(and she likes it that way). We stopped off for a drink.

The Poetic Ambassador

Her manic friend was there, so wide-eyed and alert
you knew he really cared. He said he could not stay,
I asked him for the time; he said I don't take Time
to drink (and she likes it that way). He was sublime.

As he left, she told me just how mellow he was—
as intensely mellow as Pearl Jam's *Difference*.
But she pronounced the song with a slight French accent
(as if Derrida would show at any moment).
Oh, but she raved on him... as if in a love trance,
certain that her pert cachet would stop and give me pause.
Guess I kind of liked her; she grew to like me too,
Here we are, years later, and interest has accrued.

We said we'd never marry. Time enough for that.
But Time would not tarry, or dally with her throes,
she was not always good to us, her pitch was off,
and when her coloratura became too rough,
she'd leave us to improvise within our own woes,
while she'd drag herself homeward as late as our cat.
Over time the mellow man and my carefree bird
created quite a stir; you might have even heard.

If the music fits the memory, and the cadence
cheats so well that the sense of what's been said and done
casts a magic spell on the reader of the rhymes
printed down upon the page, then the rest, betimes,
may seem a little strange. Relationships are fun
if the fettle fits the course, providing the dance
is held without remorse—like a pirouette spinning
around from the next deep bend to the beginning.

As with Heidi Egan's poem, there was an initial surmise, a hesitancy at the close of Trevor's poem, a hush, the audience grown gravid. There had hardly been even a cough during his entire presentation. Now, after the delayed response, came a sudden gust of gratitude, an ardent outpouring of raw emotion. His audience loved it. They cheered, they shouted hurrahs and bravos with dogged determination. The verse was delivered and it was paying handsome dividends. The executive were on their feet, and soon the entire audience had followed suit. Everyone except Kate—and a handful of other wheelchair-bound people—were standing. And Trevor soaked it all in with joy. This was his moment. No matter what happened from here on in, he would always cherish his victorious reading and his audience's ringing endorsement!

Other lesser poets followed in succession, punctuated by still more comics, some raucous and ribald others cerebral and sedate. None of the works of other poets that came before Cynthia were as noteworthy as those excerpts of the admittedly dimmer lights already recounted herein, and before long Cynthia's turn to shine arrived. Misty turned on her considerable charm as the Cat Woman. She invited Cynthia to share her brief biography and asked her to mention notable influences as she had done with previous presenters, and the petite seductress who had channelled Medusa so convincingly, not to mention having surreptitiously seduced both of her adversaries in the quest for poetic ambassadorship found that the only words of appreciation she had to share—aside from the obligatory thanks she attributed to the audience, her university professors and the ZG Publishing House for making all this possible—were for her mother and her Aunt Jill, to whom she attributed her formative influences and support—and without whom, she said, she would be lost.

Then, without waiting any longer than the momentary lapse it took for silence to descend upon the impassive face of the crowd, she launched her formidable poetic assault on all who had come before her, taking a mere moment to preface her poetry with a telltale aside that pitted her front of carefree abandon against her inner voice of calm reasoned self-reliance and an irrepressible spirit of individualist thought:

"I've set this untitled sonnet down against convention and the

The Poetic Ambassador

trite truisms that often arise when outmoded desires cloud the world as it is and turn so many inward toward the world as it is not. You may enjoy it for what it is or spurn it for what it is not, but it stands alone as a prelude to my longer piece:

Belief suspends its objects of desire
for as long as time withholds final proof.
Though ardent be an artist's palette's fire,
its framed impression is not good enough.
For beyond the edges of the canvass
reality comes singing like a bird,
to dream forever into life's expanse.
It's the sweetest music we've ever heard
among those who suffer, sad and alone;
and others, too—both wealthy and absurd—
who live apart to play a role long gone
upon a time that disbelief suspends,
when desire gains interest from misspent ends.

With only the hush of expectancy to act as the chiasmus betwixt the preface and her Ottova Rima, Cynthia breathlessly intoned her title, and pressed onward with a reading that was voluble for its tact and surgical precision, pausing only for the following preamble: "We were subjected to the jibes and roasts of a 'court jester' of sorts who sent us in search of a monarch earlier on this evening. My longer poem is on fame, and while the vision of Queen Fame high on a throne—replete with her diadem—may now seem archaic and elitist to some, then if an image well-bred sets her quite apart from all of the hoi polloi and hooting rabble, you might do well to take heart at her status of royalty. Without further fanfare, I give you my Ottova Rima":

On Fame

Arcane to some, well-suited Fame—saintly, flawed,
known only by name—heads out for the coast on a
summertime train of thoughtful regard and heedless

disdain, pertaining to privacies; and needless
to say, she never explains her taste in bona
fide drama. Seldom at a loss for an abode
that matches her carpets and drapes, she neither gives
without taking pay, nor sits and sups with knaves.

All walks of life, regardless of stature, have felt
the sway of her mien. Little is known of her birth,
yet few can deny she's a queen. Caught unawares
by her chequered past and by her shady affairs,
many sing praise of this grand old lass whose mirth
and alacrity share the stage, sans signs of guilt.
Playful and responsive to the needs of fickle
fate, Madam Fame winnows her fields with a twinkle

in her eye and a spring in her step. Imagine
those with whom she deals, whose crass notorious chaff
she blows away. Rewarding skillful acumen
with widespread reports—new and varied—no omen
good or best could but portend. No pretense dare laugh
to scorn those callow few whose obscure horizon
quite fails to forfend their fates, presenting only
reductive views in song or verse or homily.

Lesbian, Gay, Bisexual, Transgender, Straight:
The worldwide web is wealthier than you might think,
and all of humankind acknowledges that Fame's
a fleeting thing once you're in. She mars, she maims;
her songs she sings; and then the spin: you rise, you sink,
you're wrong, you're right; hesitate to wait at the gate
at your peril. Keepers signal her arrival.
Are you here for her audience? Or her trial?

Here are the buskers, giddy and trim as icons
of track and of stage. There are the players so sleek
and so buff, out to impress Queen Fame on the page.
Inerrant performers belie the old adage—

The Poetic Ambassador

a quarter an hour a shot: Give me a week
or a month or a year; let bygones be bygones;
Fame soon appears. But if she is partisan, would
she step down, afraid to lose touch with common good?

Fair damsel, royal dame, on a throne sits the Queen.
If her image seems archaic to some, think for a minute
from where we've come: sexism rampant cuts both ways.
Ageism, racism—we've got them in spades. Days
like these, mama said there would be. Fame helps spin it
so we can win it for all who know what we mean
when we say that elitism no longer flies
in a world where Fame her own privilege decries.

In the moment that it took for the last word to leave her lips, Cynthia's auditors were on their feet applauding. She too heard the bravos and hurrahs, the whole giddy hullabaloo. But her din deigned to build its intensity and lasted much longer than any of the previous and her audience carried on for well over a minute, before the crescendo wall of sound gradually began to dwindle and hush, and then came individual and eventually collective shouts of "encore," "encore!"

Cynthia had prepared for such an eventuality. She shuffled her papers confidently, and cleared her throat for the next go-round. She knew where her greatest threat lay, and it would be him to whom she would direct her opening salvo. Firing it across his bow, she cleared her throat again, and took a sip of the water that had been set out below the dais. She found her voice, raised it like the glass she now held aloft before her:

"I raise my voice like this glass to toast my most beguiling adversary, whose poetry you may like more or less than mine, though you've yet to hear it. But this little untitled sonnet is all mine though it is dedicated to him! To Zachary Speller, a man who never hesitates to jump right in to any new venture with both feet!"

Last week we were one, subsequent pages.
Our book bound to take us on a wild read.

261

Plotted to twist, an end for the ages.
Rising action kept on feeding our need.
Where is the sequel? God from the machine?
Who next arrives to cross all of your tease?
What is the subtext? What does it all mean?
When will my honey lure his let-it-bees?
Your agent's calling. Advance sales are great.
The market will bear whatever you write.
Does your leading lady spurn death? Cheat fate?
Mix motives like metaphors out of spite?
  Rewrite your sequel. Fix your destiny.
  My character now craves complexity.

"Go on without him, now, lass! He's not in your league." The deep British voice boomed from the back of the room. Laughter mingled with applause as more general shouts of derision directed towards Zack filled the hall. Shouts from the women in the audience went something like "Honey if your let it bees won't lure him he's not worth your trouble!" and "You could mix your motives in a mix-master and you'd still be the better poet, sister!" or "Your character is plenty complex as it is!" Cynthia took all this in with a grain of salt. She well knew the fickle nature of the crowd, and how a pleaser tonight might be a plotter tomorrow. Besides, Zack still had plenty of lines left to play to win back the approval of the audience here tonight. Still she savoured her triumph for the moment, and stole a sly glance at Anika, congratulating herself on how she had managed the situation so well.

Into the flotsam and jetsam of partisan disdain she had left in her wake, Cat Woman waterskied ably behind Cynthia's power boat of poetic brinksmanship. She quickly called up Tony (the tiger) Inagroin who at once found more than enough material in Cynthia's encore sonnet.

"Sooo, last week two of our potential ambassadors were "subsequent pages" in a "book bound" on a "wild read," eh? Can you spell bondage, Speller? What kinds of twists were in that plot? And was it a grave plot? Are we talking necrophilia? Will Zachary

Speller's poetry 'kill' Cynthia Davison's or will there be a sequel? I mean really! If the drama keeps building that god from the machine there's no telling what proportions it will take! Can you spell 'deus ex machina' Speller? I know the goddess named Cynthia aka Medusa has expertly oiled her well-tuned machine, and baby it's humming! I mean really humming! And isn't that Cynthia's sister sitting beside you as Morticia Adams? Is she the next arrival to "cross all of your tease?" Or is that too much complexity for you? Maybe you're too busy mixing your motives or your metaphors! I mean really!"

Since the evening was going overly long, and recent developments had set the executive table buzzing, Rudy gave Misty the signal to wrap it up with Zachary Speller's performance, so she decided to let Tony Inagroin's send up be the introduction to that presentation. She cued him up by saying, "And in this corner, taking on all contenders, Zacharyyyy Spellerrrrr." Zack barely had time to compose himself, but he was used to improvisation from his Rock and Roll days. He bounced up onto the stage like a prize fighter ready to box!

All the while, amid ongoing discussions among the editorial staff and the board of executives outlining formative evaluations of each of the candidates vying for the position of poetic ambassador, conversations over—and thwarted expectations with—Cynthia, mingled with unexpected surmise at the considerable contributions and talents of a couple of those not short-listed, yielded some surprising conclusions about those who had been and those who had not. There was high talk about Cynthia having flagrantly flouted convention by exceeding the bounds of her allotted time regardless of how much the crowd had incited her behaviour. That behaviour was ostensibly unbecoming for prospective ambassadors who would be bound by duty and the rigors of diplomacy to follow the edicts laid down for them by the very board of executives with the authority to ultimately determine what role they might play in that position.

There were several executive directors who wondered aloud whether so evidently promiscuous, so openly antagonistic an adversary could even hold so necessarily diplomatic an office as that for which she now contended. Had Ms. Traviss not vetted specifically for qualities such as circumspection and a complete lack of salaciousness? Rudy as always hoped that cooler heads might prevail, but he himself had questions. Trevor would have to be given an equal opportunity to showcase one or two of his sonnets, at the minimum. Then there was the wild card, Zachary Speller. How consistent with the bounds of decorum and good grace could his contribution hope to be, given the provocative prefatory remarks Ms. Davison had given him in her sonnet?

The board of executives continued to hold deliberations in their impromptu 'closed' board session, clustered like a reunion of Castle characters bent upon determining the fate of their future poetic diplomat, while the editorial staff sat huddled at *their* table, pouring over the gala poems that they had gathered prior to the start of the showcase presentations, in an effort to garner professional probity and ascertain public appeal and approbation in an effort to better assess who might be best suited to the job.

Meanwhile, into this world of scrutiny, all abuzz with portent, yet wholly oblivious to its possible effects for him or his adversaries, Zack bobbed and weaved, readying himself—for his response to Cynthia's poetic send up of Queen Fame, her incendiary sonnet, and the soulful love saga Upton had unleashed—with his own unique brand of energy and commitment. "Thanks to everyone here for listening to my verse, and special thanks of course to the executive and staff at ZG. I would first of all like to read my own sonnet dedicated to that most sincere among women to ever flout Fame in one sweetly exhaled breath all the while courting it with another even sweeter than honey luring let-it-bees to a pollinated fate worse than the death her leading lady spurns and the fate she cheats, though she would never cheat, right Trev? Anyway, I dedicate this sonnet to Cynthia Davison, one of the most complex characters I have had the good pleasure with whom to have had a wild read!" So saying he shuffled his papers, cleared his throat, and plunged in feet-first:

The more secret the tryst, the less one knows:
Secrecy betrays sceptres of power.
Like lovers who conspire in purple prose
so as to desecrate and devour,
subconscious desire fights for its own,
taking no prisoners in the battle.
Sharpest the knife that cuts straight to the bone,
muting pain with a wound that proves fatal.
Seek not when you search for the victory
someone whose conscience is clear as blue skies,
for the one with flawless delivery,
is the one who wears cool death in her eyes.
If immortal morals fail to please you,
console yourself with white lilies and rue.

The crowd listened quietly immersed in his verse, busily making connections between the object of its derision and Ms. Davison, and Speller knew he'd hit a nerve, because no one leapt up to deride *his* lament. He'd set a solemn tone and now it was time for him to turn the page to where she'd dog-eared his chances at a reversal of fortune. Abruptly switching gears, he raised his voice, and quipped, "So much for the drama. Let's get on with the long verse, and let the poetry speak for itself, shall we?" His preamble ranged from formal requirements of an Ottova Rima in alexandrines, to contextual cues: "This is a poetic digression on the nature of art versus literary and musical play," he said at last:

Art versus Play

Fresh off a wild tangent, Jackson came to the point,
calmed his distorted mood with a fifth of rare Scotch
sustained by Suzi Quattro, because bass is quaint.
Since the need for loud rock is an itch one must scratch,
abstract is to art as poetry is to paint,
and a "couplet" of Pollock is a fitting wrench
to tighten up those loosening lines of reverse
discrimination that are the bolts of free verse.

Splattered spray in seeming echoes of disarray
crescendo into crevices on the canvass
as Jackson pirouettes in his discerning way
to the periphery of centrifugal mass.
If sound could from art come alive and have its say,
then 'see' would still be 'saw', and 'is' would still be 'was',
in a grammar where tense is a matter of sense,
and future perfect keeps the reader in suspense.

If 'will have been' is anticlimactic plotting,
as the curtain climbs up on the opening scene,
the Pollock hanging fire over the setting
shouts out forever as if it's yesterday's dream.
When hues of primary reds, greens and yellows fling
themselves in bright, explosive pigments to tag-team
eternal bliss with abstraction's wettest French kiss,
then smooth is the music you drink from her challis—

the challis of Chopin, Sade, Scheherazade
laced with a purple starlight aphrodisiac
scented with rosehip, and flavored with Marmalade.
The heroine is a confirmed insomniac.
Joan spends her late nights reading the Marquis de Sade;
meanwhile, by day, she is a nymphomaniac
who moonlights as a singer in a cabaret,
with fishnet stockings, and a silk lace tourniquet.

Just when the audience appears moved by her art
a misplaced coma comes to suspend disbelief.
Credulity and the tourniquet strain apart
as Joan's rich dulcet tones whet the edge of her grief.
This still life before us, this body à la carte,
this languid Lethe, listless as a severed leaf,
drinks in the Pollock, loses its venous colour,
and bleeds out on cue, in a scene hued with horror.

The Poetic Ambassador

Conjugate 'resuscitate' like a magic spell,
to stir the lifeless form whose spirit may have flown.
Perchance abstract art will 'witch' formal verse's well,
and free the frame or form, of fame or mere renown;
apart from tradition, the art of play lies pale,
but from abstractions pure, the concrete life is drawn.
If art can conjure life, Joan's metaphysics may,
like verse, breathe life to art, since art is verse's play.

It was as if, while one sat eating a pear at a sitting for a portrait, the artist's sudden motion prompted an abrupt stillness, and the painting itself was transformed by the transfixed subject. Though they could not know for sure why they loved this exquisite rendition, they knew that the parts transcended the whole to establish a rare and masterful piece. They also knew that a greater deal hung like their bated breath in the balance between Ms. Davison's work and Mr. Speller's. Finally, they realized that ZG had saved the best for last (or so they thought). As good as Cynthia Davison's work was, this Speller creation had surpassed it, transcended the narrow field of inquiry, broadened its scope until its unfettered canvass had resisted narrower definition and taken its rightful place, to stand completely on its own merit as an independent work of art about art, for art's sake in the greater context against the literary and philosophical world of play in play for play's sake (at least that is what the consensus among the editorial staff had been). As they sat spellbound, most people realized that there were bigger issues at play.

This is why the audience sat in silence, with only a smattering of applause here and there, dying down as quickly as it had started. Many were ready to file out of the building, and the Cat Woman had almost slunk away from her podium in the reverent silence, usually reserved for, say Remembrance Day, or for the passing of a loved one like an Atticus Finch, or in this case, for a special poem that merits a thoughtful approach, rather than vigorous hand-clapping. There was much finger-snapping.

Nevertheless, the executives, acting in concert with the editorial staff, had other ideas about how to end the evening. Rudy called Misty over and holding his hand up, uttered a hushed but imperative whisper in her Cat Woman's ear. She took a deep breath, and headed straight for the stage. Most of the audience waited in anticipation. "Mr. Trevorrrrr Upton. Resume your place at the podium with one or two of your sonnets. You have been called up for a reprise performance. Ladies and Gentlemen, the executive and the editorial staff wish you to know that this is an equal opportunity showcase of talent, and that the evening will be extended by at most a half an hour. Please remain seated and prepare yourselves for what yet may come."

As the audience settled themselves back into their seats, Trevor—who was somewhat taken aback—slid out the sheaf of his portfolio papers, taking a moment or two to collect himself. Then he headed back up to the podium and turning towards Zack, said simply "This one is dedicated to Zachary Speller":

> *It seems my lover dwells upon your bed,*
> *true though it is, you've long since set her free.*
> *It seems we share a love that now has fled,*
> *true though it is, she gave you o'er for me.*
> *Perhaps my mood of haste too rash has been.*
> *Perhaps too soon I spoke against your charms.*
> *If you would turn your ear to reason keen,*
> *If you would calm those heartfelt tempest storms,*
> *If spite and jealousy you now abate,*
> *If petty paltry malice turn to peace,*
> *If unto grace you run instead of hate,*
> *Imagine how our rancour would decrease.*
> > *We made a rocky start, I know 'tis true,*
> > *But we have much in common, me and you.*

Trevor ended perfunctorily and then proceeded with another, less terse, introduction: "Now if occasion permits me once more to reach from my heart here into the breach, and my aim does not falter, though its target move like wind, my next verse might yet hit the fair maiden known as Cynthia whose lines on Queen Fame most resemble who's to blame for her ambitious grasp that yet exceeds its reach. And as my diplomatic poem for Zack was meant to find a home within the hearts and minds of those who strive to win in verse and prose, so too this short and pithy poem will still return though far it roam. I dedicate this sonnet to Cynthia Davison."

A hundred thousand iffy qualms of love
raining down on ten calm placid lake-laps
would not melt or make the glaciers move
one iota from frigid hunting traps
your polar denizens depend upon.
And so, there is no skepticism sure
as love—your cynic's sacrificial pawn,
and apathy's retrenched, jaded inure.
Lest legalese inchoate hem you in,
and jargon like a jade, reprove your faith,
remember love is just another sin,
then repent, just like the Good Book saith.
Like sin and glaciers, your love moves slow,
since it's elixir of rapacious flow.

Trevor had articulated this sonnet solemnly, and with the just ever-so-slight curl of a contemptuous lip making it clear that repenting of love was something Cynthia was well-versed at, and that her version of the word 'love' was like an auto wreck that occurred in slow motion, or some slow acting hallucinogen that gave its subjects a trip that got progressively worse. His audience seemed mesmerised by this confessional poem, and not unlike with Zack's sonnet, the truth about Cynthia's illustrious love life left them a little shocked. Applause was spotty but robust. They might not like what they heard, but they respected the poetic sagacity of the man who had shared it. They were not the only ones who had been shocked—the executive and the editorial staff could not believe its ears.

They were revising their estimations of all contributions and they had reached a shocking decision of their own. Rudy caught

Misty's eye, and the Cat Woman crept hesitantly down to his table again. He spoke a few words into her ear. At first she seemed not to have heard him, then she double checked to make sure she had heard him correctly. Finally, returning to the podium, she covered the mike, and took a second or two to compose herself. Then she gave each of the short-listed candidates a meaningful glare, before uncovering the mike and proceeding in even, measured tones. "Our final performances tonight will be short poems from the two latest short-listed competitors for the diplomatic position of ZG Poetic Ambassador. I am inviting Heidi Egan and Blaise A. Trayle to each bring a new piece of poetry to the stage to share with our audience.

When they arrived on stage, Cat Woman spoke these words privately and rather dispassionately: "Your portfolio quest will begin tomorrow, and the completed list of selections must be submitted no later than December 15, 2010. The same expectations as were stipulated to our first three candidates—some of which seem to have gone by the wayside—will apply to you and you will receive them in writing tomorrow." Then she turned back to the mike and made the following announcement: "After due deliberation the board of executives and the editorial staff will make their selections over this year's Christmas Break and the winner of this contest will be awarded his or her diplomatic position as ZG poetic ambassador in early January, 2011. The executive directors and the editorial staff would like to cordially thank all in the audience who participated in this process. Vetting diplomats is never easy, and it became apparent during the proceedings tonight that a broader base of participants would be in the best interests of the ZG Publishing House. Please remain seated until the final two participants share their poems. Thank you!"

In the interim, while Cat Woman spoke with the audience, Ms. Heidi Egan and Mr. Blaise A. Trayle made preparations to share their two poems. Misty appeared visibly shaken by this unexpected turn of events, and she slunk off into the wings of the theatre without stating who should precede whom. Mr. Trayle offered to let the lady go first, but she insisted on him starting things off. So he grasped

The Poetic Ambassador

the mike and smiled the dazzled smile of a man who has just been handed a great honour, but one for which he feels ill-prepared and more than a little overwhelmed. He said as much, and introduced his poem as free verse and stated its title as "Graphic Sites" careful to emphasize that it was not S-i-g-h-t-s, 'sights', but S-i-t-e-s, 'sites' that the poem was citing and that he hoped it might yield many insights.

Seldom so
heavily committed
as a stark command
delivered by a
hard return

this arson of the mind,
avid artistry,
sends up all
in lucid flaming blue,

an objectifying scene
screaming out
in profane shorthand,

far-reaching in
its all-too-close-for-comfort
implications

the 'in' site
stood for nothing
clean cut as it
clear-cut a million
hits a day

commuting joy
to jadedness
with jaundice

and Jesus wept

271

A polite and well-mannered, 'arms-length' applause followed Mr. Trayle's poem, the only free verse poem of the night thus far, and a verse which many interpreted as a kind of caustic cautionary commentary on the other three would-be ambassadors' revelatory sonnets. Although judging by the crowd's tepid response, Ms. Cassie Ellis at least concluded that everyone seemed too cautious to "cast the first stone."

Heidi Egan thanked the ZG Executive and the Editorial Staff for bestowing the unexpected honour upon her, and she quickly read her rhymed verse, simply called "In Group We Trust"

"In group we trust,
haute couture,
consensus or bust,
mind meld to cure.

Muddled middle class malaise
edges violence up a notch,
with camera angles aimed
squarely at the model's crotch.

Prurience hypotheses increase the sample size;
control group scandals take the major share;
dogs of war aggregate the wealth and lionize;
politicos pose, then dole agit prop and welfare.

Band wagon chic is vogue as sports teams vie for various prizes;
fans pull when the push is on, going for the gear and
memorabilia;
when times are tough no one expects the GM to advocate
downsizes;
the bottom line has telescoped so often that we have mass
myopia.

Prescience experiments involve subliminals;
movie trailers offer up the cutting edge,
and the edgier the focus on hard core criminals,
the greater the angle of the thin edge of the wedge.

*Huddled masses congregate to watch
as their idols preen upon the screen,
never thinking twice about the catch,
or what the movie's plot might really mean.*

*Mind meld to cure,
consensus or bust,
hot couture,
in group we trust.*

Heidi's conscience-raising rhyme garnered her an enthusiastic fanfare. Once again, the audience sensed the reactionary tone. Heidi headed to the Executive table with Blaise to inquire as to when and where their Portfolio Package could be picked up. The crowd began gathering up its paraphernalia and exiting the theatre after a long and eventful night.

Speller thought he understood what his own silent applause had meant, as much as he understood what he imagined the reasons for the broadening of the short list might mean. He was more enamoured of his 'understanding' of the former than of the latter, and was initially piqued at this unexpected 'slap in the face'. But, it was well after midnight, and so he said his good night to Anika—who seemed anxious to head to her car—and then he retrieved his coat. Turning his collar up to ward off the cold and the damp, he made his way through the downpour to where his own green Moby Dick of a Porsche 911 lay in wait.

There was a Canucks game tomorrow, and he was taking Cynthia; they had arranged to meet his Uncle Roger. Maybe a few good hockey fights would bring her down to earth, away from all the vicissitudes of that fleeting and fickle majesty of Queen Fame. He vaguely remembered how there once was a TV show called *Queen for a Day.* These days we were never guaranteed anything more than our fifteen minutes. That has to sting—kind of like the lure of let-it-bees or some other type of transient whispered words of wisdom in times of trouble from a rock super group comprised of four fabulous superstars who parlayed that quarter of an hour into well over a quarter of a century, and then—by virtue of the strangle-hold corporatism had on capitalism—so convincingly captured the popular imagination that they guaranteed themselves as potent a market share of the next century as the music industry would allow. Zack just blew his mind out in his Porsche. That was what came of dating twins, he thought. Your mind races faster than your car can go, and you end up on a trip you never intended to have.

Or maybe it was on account of that inexplicable silent treatment he'd gotten back at the theatre. Spectral happenings all arising out of 'my elusive dreams.' "That about does it!" he said shortly, rifling through his music for his La Diva recording of "Angels Brought Me Here" to stem the tide of 'country music' that threatened to engulf him. As he drove the rest of the way home, he set about imagining Anika singing those memorable lyrics to him, and when he finally arrived at his hospitable hacienda, it was as if those angels really had brought him here after all. His rich reverie was broken only by the recorded message waiting on his answering machine. It re-solved itself into the form of a sonnet, and Zack could recognize Cynthia's voice:

The wind blows your sight rhymes out of your mind.
But true rhymes, like slants, are harder to find.
Have you forgotten our ties that do bind?
Or that cruel cuts are not all that unkind?
What if our games, a mirage, disappear?
Where then is an oasis for your soul?
What if our tryst, a billow, holds a mirror?
What buttress awaits to buoy a fool?
What sea change is here, your billow a tear?
Where are the days when our games filled our souls?
Is my reflection opaque and unclear?
If the play is the thing, let's reverse roles.
  You play the harlot; I'll be your mark.
  The setting will be the drop of the puck.

Thirty-Six

CLEARLY A DAY FOR A CHANGE

Ms. Stephanie Nolan was watering her flamboyant fern when Cynthia Davison arrived—head held high as the fern was ebullient—in Rudy Sorensen's outer office at 9:30 am on the morning after the gala.

"Hello Ms. Davison. It is a clear day for a change," the receptionist said.

"If the ambiguity in that congenial 'front' implies that you would like me to alter my course, you can come straight out with it; because, I can assure you, I've no intention of changing. Not for you, nor for anyone," Cynthia began.

"No need to get defensive. I implied nothing other than that it is nice weather for a change, however Mr. Sorensen may choose to stress things differently," Ms. Nolan said with a frosty cordiality. "He is ready for you. If you like, you can go right in.

Not one to delay the inevitable any longer than absolutely necessary, Cynthia glanced through the office window long enough to notice that Cassie Ellis and Maureen Staples were also seated in Sorensen's spacious office. She strode over to the door, grasped the knob, and hesitated ever so slightly before entering.

"Good morning Ms. Davison," Rudy greeted her warmly, but without approbation. "Thank you for coming in on such short notice. I'll come straight to the point. As you are no doubt aware we at ZG stipulate that our Poetic Ambassador is to be full of circumspection and wholly without salaciousness. During last night's performance, it became apparent that your 'fraternization' with Mr. Speller and Mr. Upton has, shall we say, transcended the bounds of professional behaviour."

"Who are *you* to question my personal life?" Cynthia demanded.

"Young lady," the widow Ellis spoke up in the intervening silence. "I am afraid you opened up this avenue of inquiry by making your personal sonnets public at last night's festivities. By publically airing your dirty laundry, you gave us no choice but to rescind our offer of this position."

"But both Trevor and Zachary—"

"Yes," Maureen picked up the torch and carried it. "Each of them will also be losing his opportunity to compete for the position of poetic ambassador. It is likely that Heidi Egan will assume that position, pending her successful completion of the portfolio assignment."

"Our decision will be made by January, 2011," Rudy concluded, standing. "We regret your having made the decision to openly broadcast your trysts with Upton and Speller in so public a forum as our gala, and hope that you might learn from this unfortunate situation, lessons about exactly what form of discretion and prudence and diplomacy the position of any type of ambassador must necessarily require. Thank you for coming in this morning." Rudy motioned his open palm toward the door.

"Heidi Egan? Can you be serious? That sanctimonious prissy chameleon is not worthy to carry my portfolio. Did you hear her self-righteous condemnation of haute couture last night? How can you think such smug sanctimonious moralizing will win you the readership your publishing house pedigree should garner?"

"Please, Ms. Davison," Maureen said in her most ardently soothing tones. "Our executive has chosen this path as the least obtrusive. Reporters have already been snooping about."

"Oh, and you're out to avoid scandal? Is that it? Well Mr. Sorensen, you and your board of laxecutives can expect a public scene over this decision! I'll be getting busy about that, Mr. CEO.

You have just guaranteed you can expect an ample share of negative publicity. Check your NDAs, my friend, because," and here Cynthia rose from her seat and opened the door, "any whiff of impropriety at ZG is about to be made more public than you'd care to imagine!" Having vented her spleen, she turned on her heel, and abruptly exited the room leaving the door open wide behind her; she swept by the shocked fern and made a beeline for the elevator.

"Well that went well," Maureen smiled tersely.

"About as smooth as an interview with a Typhoon," agreed Cassie.

"She'll simmer down," was all Rudy would venture.

"It is clearly a front," said Stephanie Nolan, appearing momentarily at the open door. "Whether it changes or not remains to be seen."

"More affrontive, than anything else, I would say." Rudy sat back down and consulted his files.

It was verging on 10 am and Trevor Upton was coming out of the elevator, having just missed seeing Cynthia as she was on the way down in another elevator.

Trevor arrived to much the same greeting as Cynthia had found herself facing: The same effervescent fern and the same agreeable comment about the day being clearly a welcome change. He hesitantly agreed with Ms. Nolan, thinking that she must have welcomed the normalcy of conventional attire as a relief from the costumes of the night before. Then he inquired as to whether Mr. Sorensen was ready to see him. When he was asked if he would mind waiting a minute or two while 'they' readied themselves for him, he wondered about who else might be in on this morning's meeting, but he averred that he was more than happy to wait, as his new faith in Christ had left him feeling more than a modicum of patience. How could he know that he would need more than a little patience and a little Christianity for the meeting he was about to have?

After five minutes of small talk punctuated by uncomfortable silences, Ms. Nolan's telephone light came on and she picked up the receiver. "Mr. Sorensen will see you now, Mr. Upton," she said.

"Good morning, Mr. Upton," Rudy said evenly. "This is Ms. Staples, and this is Ms. Ellis. They represent the Board of Executives."

"I am not prepared to make a present—"

"No, we've had ample experience with your presentations last night, I assure you." Rudy tried hard to keep the disdain from creeping into his voice, and then he turned to Ms. Staples.

She smiled ingratiatingly, hoping to avoid an unpleasant scene like the one they'd just had with Ms. Davison. "I wish to remind you of your sonnet. The one you shared last night." Here Maureen read the first four lines of Trevor's first sonnet."

It seems my lover dwells upon your bed,
true though it is, you've long since set her free.
It seems we share a love that now has fled,
true though it is, she gave you o'er for me.

You addressed this to Zachery Speller if memory serves. Did you not? Would you care to admit the identity of this 'lover' to whom you refer?

Trevor found himself turning red.

Never mind. We can see from your embarrassment who it was. And then if there was any doubt, you erased it when you dedicated your last sonnet to Ms. Davison. You remember? The one that ended with this couplet:

Like sin and glaciers, your love moves slow,
since it's elixir of rapacious flow.

Maureen Staples ended her carefully enunciated, tentative yet somewhat desultory reading with somewhat of an inexplicable sigh. It was not altogether dismissive. Almost endorsing, really.

Cassie Ellis looked at her sharply, and picked up the torch from where she had sloppily left it, and carried it to the slow-burning bonfire of Trevor Upton's elusive quest for position of poetic ambassador that now blazed bitterly before him. "You must understand Mr. Upton that our poetic ambassador's character requires the utmost circumspection and a complete lack of salaciousness? How could you jeopardize your prospects by involving yourself in a physical relationship with Ms. Davison?"

Trevor objected strenuously. "But I became involved with Ms. Davison long before I was short-listed! We met at UBC while I was in the middle of studies on my Master's Degree."

"Nevertheless," Rudy intervened. "You ought never to have made your relationship into as public an affair as you did last night. And by bringing Mr. Speller into this affair, by dedicating your sonnet to him, you tainted the official impartiality of our entire contest. We have no choice but to rescind our offer. You are hereby excused from further involvement in our portfolio competition. You and Mr. Speller and Ms. Davison have been removed from the contest. Your services are no longer required. Thank you, and good day."

Trevor stood. He opened his mouth to speak. Thought better of it. Then he turned and just as he seemed about to exit the room, reminded of his newfound faith and the need to stand up for his beliefs, he turned back again. "There are few words I could find to characterize so archaic an idealized view of life as you have used to vilify our values. Nevertheless, your vision of virtue finds itself a peak from which to vaunt itself, some seat of sanctimony sere from which to preen so pure. No form of understanding, no fairness fit or hale. No trial but to revile, to caper and cavil at morals less than sacrosanct from we mere mortals who your so-called standards dismiss as vile. I feel nothing but contempt for your ill-conceived gauntlet of pristine puritanism, and I am truly sorry for the purblind milquetoast whomsoever she may be that you select to represent the ghost of a house that ZG has now become. This is indeed a sad day for poetry."

With that pithy summation, Upton swung himself around and left the room. The door, once again, as it had with Ms. Davison's exit, stood wide open. And once again the shocked fern assumed its blank stare. Equalled or surpassed for blankness were the faces of the executive board members. Rudy shut the door quickly. He and the other two sat huddled in the office, regrouping for the final meeting of the day.

Trevor Upton ran into Zachary Speller as he was coming out of the elevator on the 31st Floor. The two men exchanged warm greetings. Thanking him for the impeccable sonnet last night, Zack was surprised to see his adversary in so murky a mood.

"I never knew how poetic my "rocky start" salutations would prove to be, my friend. Or just how much we really have in common. And you are about to find out. Just don't hold it against her. She's not to blame."

"What are you talking about," Zack prompted.

But Trevor just pulled a long face, ran his fingers through his dark hair, and headed onto the down elevator. "You'll find out soon enough," were his oblique parting words.

Zack walked slowly down the hall toward the door where Rudy Sorensen's name stood etched onto his golden nameplate. He paused. He was about to enter, when he got an odd premonition. Upton never acted so strangely before, he thought. Something is not quite right here. Then he retraced his steps to the elevators and pushed the Down button. He was back in the First Floor lobby when he saw Trevor standing in front of the revolving doors.

"That was fast," Upton remarked.

"What happened up there," Zack replied.

"Didn't you find out?"

"No. I never went in for the meeting. What happened in your meeting?"

"You sure you want to know?" Trevor gave him a sombre, studious glance.

"Let me guess. They revoked our privileges. They no longer require our services. They don't want us in their club any more. Probably something about personal indiscretions. Pamela, er, uh, I mean Ms. Traviss told me during my interview something about how an ambassador must be above reproach, "full of circumspection and wholly without salaciousness," I think those were her exact words. Did they lay a big guilt trip on you and make you feel like you had screwed the pooch or some such tripe?" Zack spoke

The Poetic Ambassador

with emphasis and more than a modicum of emotion, but he did not seem nearly as worked up about this as Trevor had been in Sorensen's office. If truth be known, he kind of appeared to Trevor as somewhat relieved.

"Best to let sleeping dogs lie? Is that what you think, Speller? What happened to all the skin you have in the game?" Trevor spoke in exasperated tones that veiled his secret abhorrence of all subjects canine.

"Actually my skin is thicker than all that, Trevor. Game or no game. I've just realized that there is more to this contest than ZG. And if they want to take all the cards and go home, they might find when they think they are home free, that they have been 'outranked' by someone else's deck."

"What in blue blazes are you getting at, Speller?"

"Just that Rank Publishing always has ample amounts of money to throw at projects which call into question the integrity of their rivals. What if we three disgraced would-be ambassadors, each having been short-listed and then unceremoniously dumped, were to co-author a tell-all exposé about ZG?" Zack spoke in a hushed whisper, but his smile vied with malfeasance itself to see who would first be ruled out of order by the curious passers-by.

"You sly dog," Trevor said, "grimacing even as he said it. "Do you have connections with Rank?"

Zack smiled again. The smile of a poker aficionado who is attempting to appear he is bluffing against an inside straight, when in fact he holds a Royal Flush. "You could say that."

"That... would be *ridiculous*, my friend!"

"No. What would be ridiculous is if we were to find out the truth about what happens behind the scenes at ZG." Zack stroked his imaginary beard. What we need is another 'Lear's Shadow' to topple the king and his entire court! And I think I know where we can get one.

"That *would* be better," Trevor intoned as they both walked towards the revolving doors at the front of the building. "Better than an eidetic fly on the wall of an Executive Board meeting."

Soon they spun round in the whirling doorway to exit the Office Tower, and Zack smiled with a crisp detachment not unlike the kind of crisp detachment commonly associated with the hostile take-over of a corporate merger. *"More intimate* than such an eidetic fly," he said dispassionately. "Much more intimate."

Thirty-Seven

A MILLION REASONS

Making conversation proved as easy for Cynthia as making time go limp as a soft watch had proven to be for Dali in his *Persistence of Memory*. Which is to say not that easy at all. Small talk can be as difficult as art. Especially when you've other things on your mind. Like she had once told Zack, 'it was all a matter of perspective'. "The traffic seems light for this time of night," she smiled with all the frigidity of a cold beer. Cynthia tipped the waitress heavily, took the handle of a hefty jug of lager and poured a pair of stout pints, with just the right heft of head on them, for Zack and his uncle Roger. They were sitting in a leather upholstered booth before a dark wooden table in the crowded sports bar that went by the name of the Shark Club.

Roger quaffed his beer, feinted away from her icy foray, and parried. "It seems pretty crowded in here, to tell you the truth. Just like I hear last night's gala was."

"I know not seems," Zack countered, wiping the froth of ale from his mouth, and not at all eager to discuss the previous night.

"You're nothing but a hound dog. A Great Dane to be exact," smiled Cynthia in a manner more strained than a colander might be. She was leading the pack as far as drinking goes, nearly done her beer and ready to pour another glass.

Rolling his eyes and his r's, Roger trotted out his best Scottish brogue and dismissively upbraided them both. "I'd deign to say that neither one of you two reckless renegades nor the Great Dane himself, for that matter, could ever do justice to the Bard's Scottish play or even Patrick Lane's best poem on words. Lane said 'only words can fly for you like birds on the wall of the sun. A bird is a poem that talks of the end of cages.' And that's the truth as only he can bring it."

"Ah, the Owls of Understanding alone could grasp that logic," Cynthia said, stealing a solemn glance at Zack as she took another healthy swig of her beer.

Zack was sitting beside Roger in the booth, and ignoring her pointed dig, he clapped him on the back, happy to see his uncle was representing the poetic side of the family. Meanwhile Cynthia had made headway into her second pint of beer. She searched her memory banks and quickly made a withdrawal. She offered up her glass to toast the optimistic Mr. Lane, and added her own spin: "The wall of the sun must be an oasis of sorts. Maybe it's a wonder wall, an imaginary friend who is there to save you."

"Save you from yourself, you mean?" Zack added in as jovial a tone as it was wildly humorous.

"Perhaps from your own illusions—or delusions of grandeur." Cynthia countered, provocatively, with an incendiary flare of her own. She offered her glass up for a toast again, but had no takers. The rowdy jostling crowd was a din in their ears, and it was all they could do to pry a word in edgewise here and there. Several of the screens were replaying highlights from the Canucks game against New Jersey they had just attended (The Knuckleheads won 3-0), and now there was a blue line face off from the first period being telecast.

"Wait! I think this is the fight," Roger said. And sure enough there was Tanner Glass squaring off against Brad Mills.

"What good is a game without a good fight," Zack gushed enthusiastically. "Look at those two exchanging heavy blows."

"Yeah for sure," Roger exclaimed without emphasis. "And down he goes. Who do you suppose won that one?"

"Tan yer Ass clearly won that one, just like I said before in the arena." Cynthia shouted over the din. She was in no mood to mince words when it came to hockey, or much else for that matter.

Nor was Roger above eliciting the sullen but crass Glass response from his nephew's outspoken rival. He had remembered her initial response when the fight first broke out during the first period. He figured she'd have the same burning reserve in the club as she had in the arena. And he was right. She was a hellion alright. Tame as a banshee in heat. A regular minx.

Roger decided it was time he did a little reconnoitering with his nephew, a trip down memory lane of sorts. He'd digress about Chicago, make Zack wonder why, then reel Cynthia in and see what her real intentions were toward his nephew. "You remember back in the windy city, when Grandpa Desmond gave you that ultimatum: Give up your music and enroll in the University of Chicago or lose your million dollar inheritance?

Suddenly the table went quiet, the hush of a silent trio amid a hubbub of chaotic chatter. Zack seemed to be wondering whether his glass was half empty or half full, but his mind was at home attending to his Severini. He quickly chose to enact both parts of his famed commedia dell'arte print—comic and player—and spoke in what he dearly hoped would come off sounding like a playfully amused tone. "You mean the day I decided to *hedge* my bets and go for *broke*?"

Cynthia cracked up immediately. She laughed a little too hysterically at his broken down hedge joke, lame as it was. And she saw through the humour. She too was thinking of the Severini, and she sensed Pierrot's mask was off-kilter, betraying his true identity, at last.

Roger raised his glass. Zack clinked it and quaffed the rest of his pint. He was not about to come to this woman hat in hand, explaining yet another revision of his account of that fateful day. But he was wondering whether he should revise his list of favorites among his father's siblings. He'd always been closer to his Uncle Roger than either Aunt Diane or Aunt Michelle, maybe even closer than he was with his own father, but now his uncle was skewering him in front of one of his most ardent adversaries. What was he to make of this unusual turn of events?

As if to twist the knife further, Roger paused dramatically and added his own special version of Zack's paternity cause: "Your chosen profession as 'poet extraordinaire' was born under the same 'auspicious' star as you were, because (I don't know whether anyone ever told you, but) you were even conceived under extraordinary circumstances, Zack."

Not aware in the slightest of what was about to come, but sensing that it would not be something Cynthia would benefit from hearing, Zack began to raise a protest, crying out that "such family matters might best be disclosed in a more intimate setting, Uncle Roger."

But Roger pressed on, seemingly oblivious to his nephew's protestations. "But did you not say that Cynthia was as discrete as a banker? Or was that a bank teller? I cannot quite recall now. At any rate, your family secrets are the stuff of legends, and legends rely upon popular appeal; therefore, we should share your secrets with the world."

Calling for another jug, the resources of which he hoped might drown his sorrows, Zack glanced over at Cynthia. He was sure she was enjoying this frank disclosure better than she had his tale of Heartaches.

"Well, Cynthia," Roger continued. "My brother Jeffrey, Zack's dad, is six years older than me, and in July, 1976 he was 23 when he went to Chicago to attend a Grateful Dead concert. The girl who just happened to sit next to him at that concert was another Deadhead named Pamela Desmond. They took a liking to each other instantly, fell in love at first sight, and spent one fateful night together. Zack was the happy result, and he was born eight months after Pamela married Jeffrey, within nine months of that highly treasured first night encounter.

Grandpa Thomas Desmond, Pamela's father, was a stock market millionaire who always had a soft spot for Zack—his first, and as it would turn out, his only grandchild. But it was a love-hate relationship. Naturally, he loved his grandson. But ever since that

Grateful Dead concert 'corrupted' his only daughter, he hated rock music! Consequently, that's the main reason for the ultimatum that he gave you, Zack, to either forsake the Heartaches or forgo your fortune. I bet you did not know that!"

It was Cynthia's turn to give a long, low whistle. "*I* had no idea! But I *am* infinitely grateful to you for having let the cat out of the bag, so to speak. It certainly puts things in perspective. A love child born to Deadheads who becomes the publically acclaimed lead singer for a rock band called the Heartaches only to throw it all away to enroll in the University of Chicago in order to please his rich grandfather. An unlikely story until you factor in the million dollar payday attached like the rider of a concert contract. A rider that stipulates the show can only go on if the Heartaches play solo, without the family Jules, so to speak! So Desmond was your mother's maiden name, Zack. Didn't Grandpa Thomas have some serious doubts about your musical aspirations right from the start of your career as a rocker, or at the very least about your choice to use *Jules Desmond* as your stage name? And why did you leave this pertinent information out of that oh-so-studied explanation of the dilemma you faced having to choose among the Heartaches, Stacey and Arnie?"

"Cynthia, I don't think you can say you have a full picture of our relationship from the scant few moments Uncle Roger has taken to drop his little bombshell. My grandfather taught me everything I know about playing the stock market, and his *support* took me a good way towards the emphasis on poetry and communication which has resulted in my success in these fields. I would not even be competing with you for this position as poetic ambassador for ZG Publishing were it not for the encouragement he gave me over the years prior to his death. The Heartaches was a group that came along early in my life, and when we were making music together I had not yet fully formed my values, my beliefs, my priorities and my desire for a profession apart from their energies and commitments. My grandfather Thomas Desmond helped me to articulate these important aspects of my life."

As Uncle Roger sat sipping his beer, amused at the fervid fettle his feckless trip down memory lane had wrought, Cynthia downed the final dregs of her pint, stood up and delivered a solemn and affronted indictment.

"I'm sure there were a *million* reasons for your choice to articulate those important aspects of your life, and at least as many reasons for you to omit this mercenary motivation from your original story about why you jumped off the balcony on that balmy Chicago day. But I'm not 'balmy' enough to believe even one of them. And if you think last night was a 'wild ride' you can bet the next few weeks are going to be even wilder. To put it in terms you'll understand, I'll leave you to your 'artful inelegance', so get used to taking the *white whale* home alone from now on; as for me, it was nice making your acquaintance, Roger, and I hope you have a fine evening. I'll be heading home in a taxicab."

Zack tried unsuccessfully to take her hand. "Cynthia! There is no need to leave in a huff."

"Oh I'm not leaving in a '*huff*'! I said I'd be taking a *taxi*, and either way there is really nothing *you* could say or do at this point to dissuade me from leaving. Good bye!" So saying, Cynthia spun on her heel and picked her way carefully through the crushing crowd that had assembled in the Shark Club for fun, froth and suds. Once out on West Georgia Street, she had no trouble hailing a cab, and before long she found herself being whisked away down the viaduct towards Burnaby Mountain off in the distance far beyond the neon lights of Vancouver's downtown core and the cozy klatch of Speller's hypocrisy.

Meanwhile back in the Shark Club at the Speller table for two a monolithic silence had replaced the killing frost heave of a dialogue which had precipitated the icy rain of Cynthia's departure. Zack's pause outlasted Roger's who felt he had to break the awkward tension with some humour: "Well that's one less shark we have to worry about tonight, right?"

"Make. That. Two." Zack spoke mirthlessly. And with that terse trifecta, he got up, threw down a fifty dollar bill, and stood;

The Poetic Ambassador

seemingly intent on leaving.

"Hold on, there son. You can at least thank me for letting the cat out of the bag."

Zack sat back down, glaring at his uncle. "You certainly did that, but I don't see why I should be thanking you for divulging family secrets. You saw her reaction, didn't you?"

"What I mean to say, is that whereas before you weren't sure whether little miss smarty-pants was a gold-digger or not, now we know for certain that she cares about as much for your fortune as Tanner Glass cares for losing a fight."

Zack stood again. "That," he said slipping his coat on over his shoulders, "is just what she wants you to believe. But actually the leopard metaphor is more apt than the cat in the bag: After all, Cynthia is one feline who can't change her spots. But don't worry about it at all Uncle Roger. It's probably best that she's on the prowl once again. Let Trevor deal with her if he dares. Besides, I'm sure I know what is rankling her even more than some old story about the family Jules. And what's more, I'm in the mood for a Kilkenny cat fight tonight.

Listen, the hockey game was good, but the highlight of the evening was the fight. And Cynthia's histrionic fit. Say hello to Aunt Helen for me, and next time do me a favour and give me a heads up before you go making my grandfather's ultimatums a pretext for one of your trial-and-error parlour games. But listen, as you well know there is more than one way to skin a cat. Especially when she's on the hunt. The trick is to focus that aggression!" So saying, Zack followed his grim smile out of the room into his Porsche 911 and across town to where UniverCity sat perched high on Burnaby Mountain.

Thirty-Eight

THE BURNING BRIDGE

"You're not listening to me, Cynthia. I have a way that we can make this work. Just let me in and we can discuss things, like civilized human beings, over a nice cool glass of Chardonnay." Zack stood outside of Cynthia's apartment at UniverCity on Burnaby Mountain. He'd rung her suite for a couple of minutes before she'd answered. But now he was waiting again.

The intercom was silent for the space of about a full half a minute. Zack almost despaired. Like when water is almost ice, and you could easily mistake it for ice, but are reluctant to walk on it. So he remained quiet, afraid to take the plunge, and consoled himself with that most fragile of all qualities, the thing without feathers—hope.

Then she buzzed him up, and the ice broke. He did a single fist pump, and bounded up the three flights of stairs, into the hall, down to the end where he was about to rap on 315 when the door swung open. Cynthia held it, and stared at him. She wore her leopard-skin robe and the brown bunny slippers. Along with a pout that she almost tripped on. "Zack, they rescinded our rights to submit the portfolio. Do you know what that means?" Her green eyes were moist from tears.

"Wasted days and wasted nights?"

"Come on. Freddy Fender is so passé. Besides, even you have got to be serious about this," Cynthia punched him hard in the arm.

"Ouch! You're supposed to punch me playfully," Zack smiled

with mock levity.

"I'll punch playfully when you start to take this seriously!" Cynthia motioned him into the room, then locked the door behind him. Excuse the mess. I'm not in the mood to clean. But the hockey game was a welcome relief, so thanks for that. Even if your uncle is a pill."

"Ouch! A pill, eh? What if I told you so is your Aunt Jill."

"I'd say the rhyme is forced. But what is that you were saying about wanting to make this work? Because it seems like you're more interested in being a jerk."

"Now who's forcing the rhyme? But listen, babe, let's knot wrangle!"

"I'm not wrangling." She motioned for him to relax on the couch.

"No I mean let's get together," he sat on the white couch, while she took a seat in the charcoal lounge chair. "Let's get together, and wrangle a knot that ZG cannot untie."

"Oh I see! Well then, you must know that knot wrangling is one of my favourite pastimes," Cynthia said smiling one of the most genuine smiles she had flashed in the past twenty-four hours.

Zack proceeded to fill her in about how eager his contacts at Rank Publishing would be to deal in dirt about their rival ZG. The biggest scandal would be their own stories—those stories of his and Trevor's and Cynthia's abrupt termination in the middle of their portfolio contest—but, and here he paused with a dramatic flourish, "wasn't there more scandal that could be uncovered? There were rumors of interns who had been paid hush money. What if someone who knew where the 'bodies were buried' so to speak could be persuaded to help them in this cause? Especially if she were persuaded that it was all being used merely for the sake of accumulating a little leverage, so that they might be reinstated as hopeful contenders in the ZG competition for poetic ambassador?"

Cynthia paused, smiling slyly. "Let's see about that Chardonnay, shall we." She moved languidly over to the fridge, took out a brand new bottle of wine, uncorked it expertly, grabbed a couple of wine glasses from the cupboard, and made her way back to the couch.

She placed the glasses on the coffee table, and poured the wine. They took a long look at each other, and raised their glasses.

"To knot wrangling," Zack said calmly.

"To not wrangling," Cynthia replied, crossing her fingers out of habit like bears cross a burning bridge—quickly and carefully. "Now who do you imagine our insider might be?" She took a long sip of her wine.

"There's only one Pamela suitable for this job, my dear."

Cynthia slowly exhaled. "What makes you think she can be seduced?" She observed their reflection in the patio door, ignoring the darkness beyond.

"Are you saying she cannot be?"

"Perhaps 'seduction' is the wrong term here."

"You are right of course," Zack replied as cautiously and hastily as those bears on the burning bridge. "Perhaps it would be more accurate to say she needs to be coerced or convinced to support our efforts."

"Such support might be difficult to achieve. However, I have reason to believe," she paused dramatically for another drink and then continued, looking distantly into the reflection of the patio doors—like the bears might look at the water far below the chasm spanned by the bridge—"that with the right inducement, she might well find herself favourably disposed to doing what she can toward remedying our unfortunate situation."

"I am truly pleased that you think so," Zack said, finishing his glass just in time to find their lips meeting in a self-congratulatory kiss, to 'seal the deal' amid a million little charred remains of a day gone bad, but all the while 'getting so much better all the time.'

Thirty-Nine

WHO IS THE BEST DROID?

Kate turned her head, as her brother Trevor adjusted the sling to better accommodate her seat and pressed the down arrow on the control button of the lift to lower her into place. "How does that feel?" He asked conscientiously.

"I need to be back a bit in the seat," Kate said.

Trevor unfastened the eyelets from the hooks on the lift, and then he pulled them loose along the sides of the wheelchair, as his sister tilted the chair back. After he had pulled the sling out from under her, and the chair was fully tilted, he slipped his hands under his sister's armpits and carefully pulled her back up into the chair.

"Is that better, Toots?" he inquired solicitously.

"Like a nested pair of spoons!" She replied, smiling. Her head turned again, this time towards the front door which her mother, Ginny, was just entering.

"Mom!" Kate exclaimed excitedly. She had once thought of hiding or somehow muting the good pleasure she felt at seeing her mother come through the front door, but had long ago dismissed that idea as the addled second-hand thoughts of an 'emotionally frigid' handicapper who in no way resembled the emancipated woman named Katherine whom she one day longed to become. Besides, she still felt a thrill at seeing her mother and believed in expressing herself unreservedly. "We had dinner an hour ago. Were you working late tonight?"

"Didn't Trevor mention that I had parent-teacher interviews to-night, Toots?" Ginny shuffled off her coat, slipped out of her heels, and ran her fingers through her strawberry blonde shoulder length curls. She glanced over at Trev who had taken a seat in the burgun-dy leather recliner, and then at her daughter who was maneuvering the joystick of her wheelchair to bring the seat down to the level position again. "Never mind. It was relatively uneventful aside from a few students who claimed they'd had epiphanies and promised never to misbehave in class again and turn in all their work on time, while their parents looked on with mild amusement after no doubt having heard about the same sudden realization for the umpteenth time. Oh there was also the customary assortment of 'A' students who wanted to know what they could do to improve their percent-age. You know, the 'usual suspects' who aspire to a 4.0 GPA on their transcript regardless of how pedestrian their prose proves to be. Or how 'inspired' their poetry proves not to be. Ah, *To be or not to be*, that is always the question, is it not?"

Kate smiled tolerantly. "Yours is truly a noble pursuit, mother dearest. Regardless of whether it is nobler to bear the *slangs* and *narrow passes* of outrageous fortune or by shirking warm glanc-es, to avoid the mall, we know not." She laughingly mimicked her mother as she exercised her own poetic licence and mangled her favorite dramatic lines.

"I see you've gobbled up my favorite Danish again!" Ginny laughed good-heartedly. She was happy just to see her daughter in so good a mood for a change. "But you're right about one thing: as mantras for my students go, the real contender might as well be 'We know not'."

"It might be nobler to have them avoid the *mall*," Trevor quipped.

Kate laughed, good-naturedly. "'Bite me!' they'd say."

"Katherine, you've gone from Bill Shakespeare to Bart Simpson in 60 seconds flat! I'll thank you not to juxtapose genius with the low end of the gene pool in so cavalier a manner." Ginny smiled as if to undercut the seriousness of her tone, although Kate's and

The Poetic Ambassador

Trevor's mutual knowing glances revealed their own subtext.

"Bite to remind the bitten, bigger / Mouth repaying tenfold wide" Trev tossed off this lyric insolently, knowing his sister would finish the chorus.

She didn't disappoint. "I'm above," Kate intoned mirthlessly in a flawless Layne Staley imitation. "Over you I'm standing above. Claiming unconditional love. Above."

Ginny's smile had coalesced in a tight line and she began to move her head back and forth like one of those immobile doggies whose head bobs in its stationary socket, back and forth with the motion of the car as it accelerates or decelerates at the whim of the driver. Now that she thought about it, Kate realized that her mother's head-shaking had reminded her of one of her father's favorite songs. "How much is that doggie in the window... Tell me is that doggie for sale." And then she realized that her dad must be working late too. Weren't they supposed to be having a family meeting tonight? They had better be getting at it or it would be past midnight before they finished up. She turned to her brother. "Maybe daddy bought the doggie in the window, Trev. You know the one?"

Smiling at her, and delighted to see their minds were on the same track, Trevor added, "I hope he bought the one with the waggly tail." He stood and walked over to where Kate had moved her chair near their mother's recliner. He punched her affectionately in the arm. "You deserve the best doggie money can buy, Toots. Even if it's not for sale."

"Oh don't go getting her hopes up," Ginny said, looking up from her advance copy of Craig Raine's *How Snow Falls.*

"Your pessimism suggests that you've been unduly influenced by that Brit's morbid fascination with death, mother," Trev replied. "Kate is here and she is real. She needs us now. She needs to be set free. She needs us here and now. Do you hear me now?" He spoke so simply, and his language was so uncharacteristically epigrammatic that Kate wondered whether he was talking to their mother in childlike terms to make her grasp the simplicity and the urgency of the moment. Kate knew something big was about to happen.

She had been aware for some time that her brother seemed more agitated since the Halloween gala.

But what did Trev mean by saying she needed to be set free? And what was this talk of death? Kate remembered a metaphor her brother had used recently about how a seed must die in order to bear much fruit. He had said that seed represented the life of the true believer who must lose it in order to find the true life involving self-sacrifice and service for others. Kate remained puzzled. What could he mean about true life? And wasn't this always what she had wanted—emancipation as the woman named Katherine she longed to become. Not just the Katherine her mother called her when she was being short with her for some foolish indiscretion, either. But how could she help others when she was so physically challenged herself? Kate turned her face up toward her brother. "Trev?" she asked reflectively, "How can you set me free when I cannot even walk anymore?"

"You see," Ginny cried defensively, "You're getting her hopes up with your unwarranted optimism. Where are you getting these ideas, lately?"

"Mom!" Kate shrilled, her voice raising hackles, like the brakes of a car squealing urgently behind her mother's vintage vehicle.

Ginny hit the gas, swerving to avoid the collision. "Now dear, I'm sure Trevor means well, but you must understand how much added stress he's been under lately. In just over a week, he needs to submit his portfolio in the competition for the ambassadorship of the ZG Publishing House. The competition is very fierce. And he's—

"Yes, mother. I am well aware of Trev's competitive spirit. He has shut himself up in his own house even more these past few weeks than if it were a federal election and he were back writing speeches for the Conservative Party. Tonight is the first night he has visited us since the Halloween gala. But last week he and I had a very serious heart-to-heart, as you know. He shared several things during that discussion that made me realize he was undergoing some profound changes in his outlook on life. Don't you remember what I shared with you about our talk, mom?"

"Now dear. Trevor has been under tremendous strain. He cannot be held to account for any of the unusual ideas he may have expressed to you about Christianity or spending his life in your service. You would not want to be responsible for any rash decision he may make to abandon his ambitions by taking care of you on a permanent basis, would you, dear?"

Kate wondered where this conversation might lead. She felt kind of like an upended turtle in the middle of the road, like some Blanche DuBois always depending on the kindness of strangers.

"Mom, after having dinner with my neighbours the Uppals the other night, I was struck with just how much Christian love could move a person. I killed their dog you know! And although Paul Uppal was at first ready to tear me apart for my carelessness, the other night over dinner he expressed genuine remorse for his rash behaviour and even asked me to forgive him. I could not believe the true Christian love shown by that man, despite all I had done to his Beagle. I don't know why, but I found myself wanting to have that type of selfless love. They led me to know Christ, mom. And I assure you that is neither an 'unusual idea' nor a 'rash decision.'

There was surely more to what Trev was saying than her mother was willing to let on, Kate thought. Not that it would matter when her father arrived, because—

No sooner had she mentally imagined the overbearing presence of William Upton than he materialized before them, striding confidently through the door as if on cue.

The barrister's booming voice filled the room, eclipsed only by his boisterous presence. "Ciao, mio bello amico! What is the argomento?"

Trevor turned to his father and said simply, "The topic of our conversation tonight is Kate's health care, father. And it is an occasion that requires a little less Italian bravado than you appear to be bringing to the table. I know you can afford to pay for her attendants, but I am also aware of the fact that she wrangles with them, and they are often overly brusque with her, offering scant little or less in the way of what I would call meaningful contact and quality personal assistance."

William Upton had by now kissed his wife and patted his daughter affectionately. He was hanging up his coat and rolling up his sleeves. He appeared not to be listening to his son. But the sleeves were a 'tell' that Trevor knew from experience had always alerted wary legal adversaries who faced him in court that he was impregnating a pause that invariably preceded a formidable attack. He crossed to his easy chair and sat with an air of what may to less discerning eyes have passed for indifference but which only disguised his deeper concerns and heartfelt passions.

"Variety," he began after clearing his throat, "is a course best savored, regardless of whether some dishes are neither delectable nor even digestible. The dignity of the diner is seldom harmed by a choice to digest the meal, regardless of whether it is served by an ape or an ambulatory toad! I am sure Kate will thrive in any eventuality, as she has accustomed herself to the *variety* endemic to her situation."

Glancing over to where Kate had assumed the attitude of serene stoicism she usually reserved for such occasions, and one which he found as aggravating as his father's 'stiff upper British lip service' to her real needs, Trevor made an abrupt decision. "Not that smattering of Italian you flourish so gregariously, nor your oh so readily trotted out British veneer of *Duty* is enough to placate my indignation tonight, father. Kate has to put up with far too much as it is to warrant her suffering on needlessly at the hands of care aides that are as impenitent as they are incompetent. And she is not a toad!"

Ginny added her placating commentary in tones she hoped would be soothing to her son's frayed nerves. "None of the nurses we've had have been perfect, Trevor. But it is equally true that they've all been both competent and willing to learn. And what is the position of care aide if not that of a student: a student of character and of methodology. Take Brianna, the current nurse, for example. She wasn't aware of how the sling sometimes sheers the skin until Kate cried out and asked her to be gentler when pulling it out from where she'd tucked it under her leg. And now—"

The Poetic Ambassador

"It is the ways we compensate for these small 'indignities' that determines our character, son!" William liked to finish his wife's sentences regardless of whether or not the mood of his conclusion fit with her intended sentiment. He had heard somewhere that old married couples liked to finish each other's sentences, so he always did his best to accommodate himself to that archaic adage.

"And *that*," Trevor snapped, with surly disregard for his father's attempts at consensus, "is cold comfort indeed. It is when we attempt to over-compensate for the inexcusable that we set our character on a course for ruin. Sublimating our feelings with defense mechanisms which—"

"Freudian psycho-babble! Say what you mean without the mumbo-jumbo, son!" William slapped his armchair haughtily. There was no love lost between him and his own therapist and he wasn't keen on having Trevor find out about exactly how much sublimated denial he tended to project onto his wife, his children... and his narrative style. "For what exactly are *you* over-compensating?" For an awkward moment William almost forgot the cardinal rule lawyer's lived by: Always be sure you know the answer for any question you ask of a witness! But then, thinking quickly, and guided by his better lights, he added this quick query: "I mean to say, do you have an overdeveloped sense of responsibility for which you are attempting to overcompensate?"

"I think," Trevor continued, after taking a moment to get over his father's barely eluded faux pas, "that our defense mechanisms cover up the facts of Kate's inadequate care, and our denial is one of those mechanisms. Your attempt to justify the status quo and dignify her stoic acceptance of unacceptable situations, to tolerate the intolerable, is just one more way that you force her to endure what is to both of us unacceptable."

Neither Ginny nor William spoke.

In the lengthening silence that ensued, Katherine found her voice. It was not that she rarely contributed to these family discussions so much as that she contributed significantly less than the others. Therefore, when she did speak her words carried far more weight. There was also her disability, which shouldn't have factored into the equation, but which nevertheless lent her voice a greater authenticity. Before speaking, she moved her wheelchair to a point in the room where she could face her family, and there she stopped in a position equidistant from each of them. "MS does not define me, unless my care is less than adequate. Then it limits me. Trevor means well. You all mean well. But a well is a deep hole in the ground into which we all may fall, all the while meaning well. Nurses also mean well. And their care is neither unacceptable, nor unendurable to me, Trevor. But who can tell why nurses come to help, and that is what a brother was born for—for help in times of adversity." She turned her attention to her parents. "Trevor means to help me, and I've half a mind to let him. We have always been closer than most siblings, and he'd probably take much better care of me than most nurses who are more mercenary than they'd care to admit. Since I was diagnosed at 16, I've had to quit UBC before graduating due to the progression of the disease. Then, as the symptoms of the disease got worse, I've had to go from being fairly independent to being in a wheelchair and having nurses man a lift to get me out of bed in the morning, and back into bed at night. These are just a few of the 'indignities' I've come to endure, father. There is no doubt but that Trevor would, in most cases, make these easier to bear. But I would never want to become a burden to you Trevor." She ended her speech by looking her brother in the eye. Then she added, "Or make you feel like you are 'Above... claiming unconditional love'."

"If ever, it would only be for a mad season, Toots!" Trevor smiled at his sister, walked over and hugged her affectionately, enjoying their private joke nearly as much as their mutual respect.

Kate smiled back at him, and went on. "Still and all, I think it best that we maintain the status quo, rather than have you give up all you've worked so hard to attain. After all, there are many issues pertaining to my health care that you know next to nothing about, and I am not speaking exclusively of feminine hygiene matters. Truth be told though, Trevor, I would rather you not have to clean up after my toiletries or help me when my time of the month comes around. So let's just let sleeping dogs lie, shall we."

Trevor seemed visibly shaken at her conclusion—she could not have imagined how the mishap with his neighbour's dog would affect his response to such metaphors—but Kate thought he was only reacting to the idea of having to help her with her tampon or something mundane like that.

Ginny spoke first after the silence that followed the 'sleeping dogs' remark. "Yes, son. We would be advised to respect your sister's need for privacy and that means maintaining an appropriate distance between her and her private nurse, wouldn't you agree? Besides," she turned back to her husband and continued, "Trevor has more than enough on his plate right now without interjecting himself into the role of maintaining Katherine's personal care, isn't that right father?" Ginny nodded expectantly at William.

"What?" Upton Sr. seemed to have been lost in thought. "Oh, yes. Certainly. We have done our utmost to see to it that Kate is receiving first class, top-notch care. You need not doubt that it is anything less than the best care money can buy, son. You're better off leaving things to the professionals. You need not concern yourself with your sister's nurses. They know best how to care for her needs. Just set your sights on becoming the next ZG Poetic Ambassador if you want to make us all proud.

After a slight pause, during which Trevor almost considered coming clean with his parents about recent ZG developments then thought better of it, he re-focused his own attention back to the matter at hand and replied with a crisp, "Yes sir!" Then he continued, "And I'm sorry if I came off sounding a little strident earlier on. I think we all want to advocate as energetically as possible on Kate's behalf. You know how close we all are, and I'm just not always completely certain that she's been getting the care she needs." He had moved over to where his sister sat, and put his arm around her shoulder.

"That's alright, Trev," she said, looking up at him with love in her eyes. "I'm well taken care of, and if it were anything less, I would be the first to let you all know."

"Well, good," Trevor replied. "Now the time is getting late, and I've got a little more writing to do tonight. So I had best be getting home. Thanks again for supporting me at the Halloween Gala. That meant a lot to me. And by the way dad, dressing the family in the Star Wars theme costumes was a very nice touch. I received several compliments from friends, ZG board members, and from my competitors, as well.

"Luke, I am your father!" William intoned in his deepest bass.

"You need not remind me, dad. Some of my more satiric friends wondered how much 'type-casting' was involved there. But doing Kate up as R2-D2 in dreadlocks, that was a stroke of genius."

"The best droid is a dread-droid, I always say," laughed Kate. "Besides, who says an android cannot be a Rastafarian?"

This brought out a few belly laughs from everyone, and hugs all around. The family meeting was ending on a high note, just as the phone rang. Ginny picked up. She listened quietly for a moment, then the colour drained from her face. "Trevor," she said suddenly. "It's Miranda. She says you're no longer in the contest. Is that true?"

Trevor struggled with his disambiguation and decided to mingle his genuine hope with just the slightest bit of disingenuous over-confidence. "Not necessarily, mother. Zack and Cynthia are planning a work around so that we can continue with our contest. ZG just needs to be persuaded. You need not worry yourselves about it though. Honestly, I don't know where Mira gets her information. I did not want to trouble you with the details tonight. We will persevere, in any case. Our poetry will prevail."

There seemed to be nothing one could say to contradict that logic, or so at least that was what Trevor's family concluded (although William had his doubts about what he felt must surely be obfuscation on Trevor's part). After first hopefully placating them all with assurances that it would not be in ZG's best interest for them to allow the board to abandon their shortlisted contenders upon some obscure pretext, and then wilfully obscuring the most incriminatory key details of his most recent meeting with Sorensen et al., Trevor said his goodbyes and headed for home, giving Mira a rather heated call on the way. He was far happier with the way the family meeting had gone than he was with his on-again girlfriend. Regardless, he would have to depend upon his ex-girlfriend Cynthia if his poetry were really going to prevail. Much like Kate with her wheelchair and lift, Ms. Davison was a form of support that one did not 'love' so much as 'tolerate'.

Forty

OWLS OF UNDERSTANDING

Entrapment never felt quite so delicious, but then again this beverage wasn't bad either! Ms. Felicity Traviss aka Pamela aka Misty aka Cat Woman reminded herself of that fact as she was enjoying a Frappuccino while busily examining the finer points of her ZG contract. She had recently come to understand that her responsibility to shortlist the candidates who were selected to compete for the position of ZG poetic ambassador was accompanied by certain rights, as well. Ah yes, she thought, reflecting back on the evening which the board had spent half the night deciding exactly which types of poems and how many of them would comprise the portfolio assignment: She remembered having considered how 'freedom came through trials, and a close examination of one's mistakes led one to learn greater self-awareness.' This trial and error approach to liberation and education meant that entrapment invariably cut both ways—mainly due to the sticking points in her cleverly negotiated contract. That is what Misty found herself thinking one morning a week after the Halloween gala while she sat in the Starbucks lounge finishing her Frappuccino awaiting the appearance of Cynthia Davison.

"Are those original Manitoba Mukluks?" The inquiring voice was pitched in a husky contralto.

Misty looked up expectantly, her face cloaking her pleasure. "Why yes. This is the snowy owl grain. Clever of you to have noticed, Cynthia."

The Poetic Ambassador

"I'm an ardent fan of the Owls of Understanding," Cynthia said rummaging through her vintage leather handbag—and looking comfortable in her Lululemon turtleneck sweater—as she slung herself into the low-backed chair opposite Misty. "You are almost done your drink. Can I get you another?" She sprang to her feet. "I'm having one. Won't you join me?"

"Thanks, I'd love another! But who are these owls of understanding?"

"They fly by night, and they always know exactly where to land; unlike myself: I land by night, and never know when to fly." This brought a flurried flutter of lips from Misty, who waved her away with a brusque turn of hand.

A minute later, Cynthia was back with two Frappuccino drinks and she settled herself in for conversation with the auburn-haired beauty whose bright yellow floral print maxi dress barely concealed the fine lines of her lithesome body.

"Nice dress. My goddess! You really nailed the Mistress of Ceremonies gig at the gala the other night, Misty!"

"You don't think I was too catty?"

"If I said 'yes' you'd probably say I was too 'snaky' for a Medusa, so no! You were just exactly catty enough!" Cynthia smiled her most feline smile, and her green eyes twinkled like emeralds (no one but Misty could tell they were contacts!). "But what was up with the board opening up the competition to the honourable mention set, anyway?"

"Rudy Sorensen wouldn't say why; just that they'd decided to cast a broader net." Misty was non-committal. Except for the way she moved in that dress (it fit to a "T" putting the 'tease' in commitment!).

"That's not what he told me. It seems they've decided to eliminate Trevor, Zack and myself from the competition altogether. Some prurient bilge about propriety and decorum. Surely you know something about that?"

Misty sipped her Frappuccino and said nothing.

Cynthia continued as though her question had already been

answered. "Since when is the winner of a poetry contest determined willy-nilly, and not exclusively by the caliber of the poetry?" Cynthia was exasperated. But she sipped her Frappuccino demurely, doing her best not to appear unduly ruffled.

Misty toyed with her straw. Then she arched her back and sat straight up in her chair, offered her best impression of a fixed figure, and crossed her legs with flamboyant finesse, for flair. "Circumspection, child. And a character wholly without salaciousness. These are the rigid protocols that all prospective poetic ambassadors must follow."

Cynthia snorted into her Frappuccino. "Balls to the protocols! You know my poetry speaks for itself. Can't you do something about it, Misty?" After a pause in which it appeared there was no conciliatory offering from Misty on the horizon, Cynthia turned on the charm and made a direct appeal couched in an allusion to the mutually admired *Talent* of Ms. Carol Ann Duffy: "I know there is no visible word-net to catch our indiscretions, but won't you cross that word-tightrope on our behalf?"

Misty hesitated. She set her drink down. Then her dark eyes intently searched Cynthia's green eyes, as if looking for a sign. "If I were in a position to do something about it, Cynthia. What would your owls of understanding be prepared to do? Would they take flight or drop down for a landing?"

Cynthia smiled with a warm lack of reserve, and held Misty's gaze, steadily. "Whatever flight they take might go against your snowy owl grain. Could your ruffled feathers live with that kind of word-applause?"

The auburn-haired beauty gazed back fixedly, then smiled. "There is no luck like that of a mukluk with a snowy owl grain, darling, and I'm not talking about the footwear either." Misty reached across and tenderly rubbed Cynthia's shoulder. "Lululemon has such fine fabric."

Then Misty stood, indicating the meeting was at an end. She collected her green leather satchel, once again arose to her full statuesque height, and extended her hand in a formal seal of approval for whatever business had been transacted, pulled Cynthia in close after she had taken her offered hand, and spoke her famous final words. "And, since we're not discussing apparel any longer, you might as well know that my contract with ZG stipulates that all contestants nominated from my short-list must be given the benefit of the doubt when it comes to things like 'circumspection and salaciousness,' so you three can get back to work on your portfolios, because as long as I'm employed by ZG, one of you is going to walk away with that position as poetic ambassador or..." and here she drew her mouth close to Cynthia's ear and whispered her final statement: "my name is not Cat Woman!"

Cynthia's smile was a warm affirmation, a reader-response criticism— both long and drawn out—pertaining to a memorable Misty moment. It added an ambience not quite seen so much as felt, like languid purple prose hanging aromatically in the air so as to envelope the invisible essence of Misty's perfumed presence still felt long after her absence has been left palpably behind, after her very vital being disappeared having stolen itself away, along with her shapely body, in the bright yellow floral print maxi dress, leaving Cynthia alone in a crowded room, bereft of all but a rich sense of Misty's rare soul. Thinking upon their brief encounter, and on the delicious irony of having so efficacious an ally as Misty in their ZG contest, Cynthia found that she had 'come to' (back to her senses that is). And it was then that she arrived at a most resounding conclusion: 'Entrapment never felt quite so delicious, but then again this beverage wasn't bad either!' And she was not talking about the Frappuccino as much as the snowy owl taste which Misty had left her savoring.

Forty-One

PILLOW TALK

When the second year of the decade started off with the ZG declaration of an unexpected poetic ambassador, it was not the only surprising 2011 New Year's celebratory occasion. Donavan Blake finally secured Maureen Staples' consent to allow him the opportunity of stripping off her earrings and a few other... shall we say, 'inhibitions.' Winning her discrete acquiescence at their year's end executive board party prefigured a memorable evening, and now they were imbibing in the intimate medium of pillow talk.

"I thought Norma and Rod might see the light," Maureen whispered, smiling. "Cassie had come around. She already favoured Cynthia and was willing to overlook her considerable indiscretions for the sake of her even more considerable talent."

Donavan propped himself up on an elbow and with his left hand, he teased at Maureen's red curls. "I know. I'd have thought we'd have swayed them and won the vote. After first allowing Misty to exercise contractual rights to have her shortlist vie for the position, I thought Rudy was making an official reversal of his position against unbecoming conduct and an ipso facto endorsement of their candidacy."

"...and not really just buying time for his hidden agenda, you mean?"

"Yes. But also saving face to forestall negative publicity from

The Poetic Ambassador

Speller's camp."

"You mean Rank Publishing."

"Sure. By appearing to allow open competition, Sorensen was keeping public criticism at bay, while at the same time opening up the field of competitors to a more 'suitable' candidate—his candidate."

"Yes. That's why I was so sure we'd win over Norma and Rod in securing Cynthia as our new poetic ambassador."

"Objectivity is an underestimated quality," Donavan mused, fingering the lobes where Maureen's earrings had moments ago dangled. "It depends upon exactly who is the object of one's affections."

Pushing away from him, Maureen bridled slightly. "Misty is one person Rudy should never have underestimated, and her objective seems to be settling with ZG for a six figure severance package. She knows her shortlist and the portfolios they prepared are far superior to anything else that landed on our editors' desks, and she's not about to let some upstart English student walk away with the distinction of becoming our poetic ambassador without a fight. It's enshrined in that contract of hers."

Gently pulling back her hair, and then kissing the nape of her neck softly, Donavan brought his face close to hers and said, "You women! Always fighting. But I'd be surprised if the latest edition of *Outranked* magazine doesn't have the new poetic ambassador on its cover. I've a feeling it is going to profile the three disgruntled poets, former adversaries for the ambassador position who are, I am sure, bound to unite for the right to be heard dishing dirt about ZG."

She arched her back and moved ever so meaningfully into his embrace. "What I would really like to know is how Heidi Egan managed to ingratiate herself so fully to Rudy Sorensen that he would maneuver her into the position of becoming our first poetic ambassador."

As Donavan shut her "wild, wild eyes with kisses four" they bent their energies to the task at hand. But not before he found himself once again musing that objectivity depends entirely upon who or what becomes the object of one's affections. And he broke out of their firm embrace long enough to suggest that "Jonathan Holland might yet have something to say about that choice."

As she moved languorously, sensuously, then energetically upon him, she suddenly stopped short. "Yes, I would agree. Especially since Rudy was so willing to overlook a considerable lack of talent for the sake of Heidi Egan's even more considerable indiscretions, wouldn't you agree?"

Donavan's rich laughter filled the air.

"You mean, considering the fact that you did just that with me?" was all he said laughingly before triggering a resumption of their improvised efforts at making the beast with two backs.

Both of them found themselves thinking it was ironic how the boardroom had ended up being foreplay for the bedroom, and how bedroom pillow talk came to focus so assiduously upon boardroom politics. The fish in the text was proving to be especially slippery—a beast that would appear all the more elusive considering the vast array of numerous nets deployed daily to acquire the distinction of having initiated its dazzling photo-finish.

Then again, Donavan could not help but think of how he himself had been landed long ago—dazzled by the lure of a pair of dangling hoop earrings. Romance at short notice is after all, just a line, and the subtext is fishing. If you catch my meaning, you may already be caught... up in that magic moment known as the afterglow, where we'll leave Maureen and Donavan and their pillow talk about the poetic ambassador to muse on what might have been a strategy as unorthodox as an interview, long ago...

Roger Wayne Eberle is a connoisseur of prose and poetry. His prose has been noted for its originality, creativity and exuberance. His poetry has been described as image-driven, innovative traditionalism and is published in the Eclectic Muse, Breath & Shadow, and Shared Voices, among others. He was educated at Cariboo College (1985); UBC (1991); and SFU (2011). This is his first novel.